TURNING THE TIED

Turning the Tied
Edited by Jean Rabe & Robert Greenberger

IAMTW President Jonathan Maberry, Executive Vice President D. J. Stevenson

"Building Bridges" © 2021 by Rigel Ailur
"A Study in Crimson" © 2021 by Derek Tyler Attico
Introduction © 2021 by Raymond Benson
"Kit Carson/Allan Quatermain: Inappropriate Allies" © 2021 by David Boop
"The Truth About the Cats of Ulthar" © 2021 by Jennifer Brozek
"The Adventure of Leonardo's Smile" © 2021 by Max Allan Collins & Matthew V. Clemens
"Formerly, Miss Mina Murray" © 2021 by Greg Cox
"In Earth and Sky and Sea Strange Things There Be" © 2021 by Keith R.A. DeCandido
"What Men Ruin, We Shall Raise" © 2021 by Kelli Fitzpatrick
"Legacy" © 2021 by Robert Greenberger
"Catfather" © 2021 by Nancy Holder
"Cyrano De Bergerac and Baron Munchausen Go to Mars" © 2021 by Steven Paul Leiva
"The Death Song of Dwar Guntha" © 2021 by Jonathan Maberry Productions LLC
"Behind the Tonto Rim" © 2021 by Jeff Mariotte
"The Trials of Baldur" © 2021 by Will McDermott
"Paraíso" © 2021 by Yvonne Navarro
"The Magic of Nadia" © 2021 by Weston Ochse
"In the Time of the Martians" © 2021 by Scott Pearson
"Let Nothing You Dismay" © 2021 by Jean Rabe
"A Prisoner Freed in Oz" © 2021 by Marsheila Rockwell
"Loose Threads" © 2021 by Ben H. Rome
"A Model Sailor" © 2021 by Aaron Rosenberg
"Blood of Dracula" © 2021 by Stephen D. Sullivan
"The Comet Cannon of Planet X" © 2021 by Robert Vardeman
"Children of the Wild" © 2021 by Tim Waggoner

Publication design by D. J. Stevenson
Cover design and art by Kathleen Hardy

ISBN: 978-1-7362524-1-3

All rights reserved. No part of this book may be used or reproduced in any manner whatsoever without prior written permission except in the case of brief quotations embodied in critical articles and reviews. For information: www.iamtw.org

First edition

TURNING THE TIED

Table of Contents

Introduction 1
    Raymond Benson

Formerly, Miss Mina Murray 7
    Greg Cox

The Adventure of Leonardo's Smile 17
    Max Allan Collins & Matthew V. Clemens

Inappropriate Allies 37
    David Boop

In Earth and Sky and Sea Strange Things There Be 73
    Keith R.A. DeCandido

The Death Song of Dwar Guntha 83
    Jonathan Maberry

Building Bridges 101
    Rigel Ailur

Paraíso 117
    Yvonne Navarro

A Model Sailor 125
    Aaron Rosenberg

The Trials of Baldur 141
    Will McDermott

Behind the Tonto Rim 167
    Jeff Mariotte

In the Time of the Martians 189
    Scott Pearson

A Prisoner Freed in Oz 213
    Marsheila Rockwell

The Comet Cannon of Planet X 223
    Robert E. Vardeman

The Magic of Nadia 241
    Weston Ochse

Table of Contents

The Truth About the Cats of Ulthar 253
   Jennifer Brozek

Children of the Wild..265
   Tim Waggoner

Blood of Dracula 287
   Stephen D. Sullivan

A Study in Crimson...309
   Derek Tyler Attico

Legacy..329
   Robert Greenberger

Loose Threads...345
   Ben H. Rome

Cyrano De Bergerac and Baron Munchausen Go to Mars 369
   Steven Paul Leiva

What Men Ruin, We Shall Raise..389
   Kelli Fitzpatrick

Let Nothing You Dismay 411
   Jean Rabe

Catfather...421
   Nancy Holder

A Word from the President 435
   Jonathan Maberry

For A Good Cause 439
   D. J. Stevenson

Founding the IAMTW..441
   Max Allan Collins

Introduction

Raymond Benson

Raymond Benson has published more than forty titles, but his footnote in history is that he was commissioned by the Ian Fleming Estate to be the first American to write official new James Bond novels (six originals and three film novelizations). Other tie-ins include two *New York Times* bestsellers in the *Tom Clancy's Splinter Cell* franchise (written as "David Michaels"), two adaptations of the *Metal Gear Solid* videogames, and more. He is also the author of many original works such as the acclaimed five books in *The Black Stiletto* serial, and more recently, *Hotel Destiny—a Ghost Noir*, *Blues in the Dark*, and *The Secrets on Chicory Lane*. www.raymondbenson.com

Introduction

The International Association of Media Tie-In Writers (IAMTW) is an unorthodox, rowdy, and fun-loving group of people. I know, because I've been a member since its humble beginnings in 2005. ("I don't want to belong to any club that would have me as a member!" Groucho Marx famously said. In this case, though, I'm happy to be one.)

Founded by Max Allan Collins and Lee Goldberg, both tie-in authors extraordinaire, the IAMTW is that *other* writers' organization that shares members with such respectable outfits as Mystery Writers of America, International Thriller Writers, Romance Writers of America, and who knows what else. What sets IAMTW apart from those more well-known societies is that we're all writers who publish stuff by piggybacking on the coattails of intellectual properties we didn't create.

That sounds a lot sleazier than it really is. In truth, "media tie-in writers," as we dub ourselves, perform an *essential service*! Let's say you're addicted to a particular movie or TV franchise, or a videogame series, and you want *more more more*. Well, we're the ones who provide your fix.

In short, then, a tie-in writer pens novelizations, continuation novels, graphic novels, and other fiction, including short stories, that are licensed by the estates or companies that own the rights to a specific character or fictional universe.

3

The IAMTW is full of these kinds of authors. That's what we do. In fact, we hand out annual awards for our work. They're called the Scribes. There are several categories, such as "General—Original" (a tie-in set in a franchise's special world but is an original story) or "General—Adapted" (a tie-in that is a direct adaptation of an existing work such as a film or a television series). We also have "Speculative" categories to handle the extensive science fiction and fantasy genres that are so prevalent in tie-ins.

My colleagues and I in the wonderful IAMTW look at tie-in work as welcome bread-and-butter income that supplements what might be our "real" writing jobs of penning original novels or whatever. Some of us are better known for the latter. Max Allan Collins, for example, is the author of so many books that you must click the "Next" button a zillion times when perusing the pages of an online catalog displaying his titles. Others might be more celebrated for their tie-ins. Despite having published a bucketful of original creations, my footnote in history will likely state that I was commissioned by the Ian Fleming Estate to be the first American author to write official new James Bond novels.

I am often asked if anyone can just sit down and write and publish a *Star Wars* or James Bond novel. No, you must be commissioned by the licensor. Well, you can *write* it, but you might experience some legal difficulties if you attempt to publish it. But wait! What about characters and series now in the public domain?

That segue smoothly snaps the spotlight on this bubbly concoction of tales. Edited by the inimitable Jean Rabe, IAMTW's winner of the 2020 Faust Award (our "lifetime achievement" honor), and Robert Greenberger, of DC and Marvel Comics fame, *Turning the Tied* presents a host of tie-in short stories featuring characters in the U.S. public domain. To clarify, an author's work usually goes into public domain seventy years after his or her death (it's ninety-five years for corporate authorship). Thus, we have within a tale starring Sherlock Holmes by none other than Max Allan Collins. Current IAMTW president Jonathan Maberry delivers a gem starring John Carter of Mars. Nancy Holder brings us a story featuring Frankenstein's creature. Kelli Fitzpatrick takes us *20,000 Leagues Under the Sea*.

I don't know about you, but I can't *wait* to dive into this anthology (at the time of this writing, I have not seen any of the stories).

The International Association of Media Tie-In Writers

So, settle back and allow yourself to drift back in time. The characters in these stories originated in another era, but they are still beloved and marketed today. Some of them may be familiar to you, others not so much. Our authors would like to show you how this tie-in thing is done, for this collection represents some of the best and brightest of our members and their talents.

Don't just take my word for it. Come and play! We're going to have some good, rowdy fun.

Raymond Benson
December 2020

Formerly, Miss Mina Murray

Greg Cox

Mina Harker was introduced to the world as a protagonist in Bram Stoker's 1897 Gothic horror novel *Dracula*. She has been seen in most stage, film, and television adaptations of the seminal work.

Greg Cox is *The New York Times* bestselling author of numerous novels and short stories, including the official movie novelizations of *War for the Planet of the Apes, Godzilla, Man of Steel, The Dark Knight Rises, Ghost Rider, Daredevil, Death Defying Acts*, and the first three *Underworld* movies. He has also written books and stories based on such popular series as *Alias, Buffy the Vampire Slayer, CSI: Crime Scene Investigation, Farscape, The 4400, Leverage, The Librarians, Riese: Kingdom Falling, Roswell, Star Trek, Terminator, Warehouse 13, The X-Files*, and *Xena: Warrior Princess*. In addition, he is a Consulting Editor for Tor Books. Visit him at: www.gregcox-author.com

Formerly, Miss Mina Murray

"Quincey, will you get the door, dear?"

"Yes, Mother!"

Mrs. Wilhelmina Harker, a handsome woman of a certain age, checked her appearance in the large, gilt-framed mirror adorning the piano room. She frowned briefly at her head of gray; once, many years ago, there had been flaxen curls there, along with a younger, smoother face. The frown faded, however, as Mina heard her daughter come running enthusiastically down the stairs into the adjoining entry hall.

"Wait, Quincey, wait!" Lucy Harker called, blonde and beautiful. "Let me get it, please!" She hurriedly joined her older brother at the front door. "It has to be Peter!"

Mina brushed a stray hair back into place and hastened to the foyer. She was eager to meet the young man who had so impressed her daughter. Lucy was now twenty, after all; it was high time she became engaged to some suitable gentleman, perhaps even this "Peter."

Lucy was opening the door even as her mother approached from behind. Mina saw a tall, thin figure on the porch, standing in the shadows of a cloudy April night.

"May I come in?" he asked. His voice was impeccably upper class. *Promising,* Mina thought.

"Why, of course you can come in, you silly goose! Did you think we were going to leave you out on the porch all evening?" Lucy laughed gaily. "Mother, Quincey, this is Peter Carlyle, the boy I was telling you about."

"Yes," Mina acknowledged. "The one you met at the opera last week."

"We were introduced by Miss Claire Stapledon, a mutual acquaintance." He stepped out of the night and into the comfortable London residence of the Harkers. Gaslight dispelled the darkness obscuring him before.

Peter Carlyle was unquestionably a fine-looking young man, Mina noted. He was slim and well-groomed, with dark brown hair, blue eyes, and pale skin. Almost too pale, if truth be told. His unblemished complexion was pearly-white.

Did her suspicions begin with that observation? Perhaps.

Nevertheless she welcomed the handsome young caller to their home.

"I'm grateful for the invitation," he replied, lightly shaking her proffered hand.

His flesh was cold to the touch.

Mina succeeded in repressing a shudder. Do not forget, she told herself, he has only just been outdoors, away from fire and furnace. Then again, it was almost summer. The night couldn't be that chill, could it?

She had not felt hands so cool for a long time. Thirty-five years, to be precise.

Ancient memories, never very far away, intruded into the present:

Cool skin. Red eyes. Sharp teeth.

Suppose, just suppose, this boy was one of—

"Mother?"

"Hmm," Mina murmured, pulled from her reverie by her daughter's voice. "What is it?"

Lucy eyed her mother curiously. "I'm going to escort Peter into the parlor now, if that's all right?"

"Oh, certainly. I'll be right with you," Mina said. "Forgive me, Mister Carlyle. My mind was wandering, I fear. It happens more frequently as one approaches my advanced age."

"No need to apologize," he said courteously. "I understand, although you appear quite undiminished to my eyes. And please call me Peter."

Lucy led him away, followed closely by her brother. Mina lingered in the hall, hoping to order her unruly thoughts.

"Calm yourself, old woman," she muttered. This was the present, in the year nineteen hundred twenty-five, not those darksome days of long ago. Oh, why couldn't she forget those times? Jonathan seemed to have done so. He never mentioned the old battles, although his deadly kukri knife still occupied a position of honor on the wall of his study.

Jonathan. Yes, there was something she could do now, something far more constructive than all this foolish fantasizing. Mina climbed the stairs to the second floor and came at last to the sturdy wooden door of the master bedroom. She eased the door open and peered in.

His Honor, Judge Jonathan Harker, was asleep sitting up in the bed. A pair of thick spectacles dangled at the tip of his nose, threatening to fall onto the heavy lawbooks in the sleeping man's lap. His breathing was hoarse and labored.

Again the present collided with the past in Mina's mind. This was her Jonathan these days. He worked, he slept, and he slowly, inevitably decayed. Occasionally they still found time and vitality enough to laugh and enjoy each other's company, but not often, particularly now that his health was failing. She decided to let him sleep, while she tended to their visitor herself.

But how, exactly?

She chided herself for asking that question, for even entertaining such dire fancies. It was no use, however. Her doubts, her suspicions, followed her down the stairs. Despite herself, she tried to remember how Peter had looked standing outside in the shadows. Had she truly glimpsed two tiny pinpricks of scarlet burning like fire in his eyes—or was her memory simply playing tricks on her?

And he had waited outside, hadn't he? Until he was invited to enter the house. That was what *they* were required to do.

It was also simple courtesy, she realized.

Smiling, her face deftly concealing her unease, she entered the parlor. Quincey, Lucy, and Peter were already seated around the drawing room table. Quincey rose and fetched a chair for his mother. "Will Father be joining us?"

"Alas, Jonathan sends his regrets. He's feeling somewhat under the weather."

"What a pity," their guest said amiably. "Still, I'm delighted you can join us, Mrs. Harker. Quincey was just telling me of the fine dinner you enjoyed earlier this the evening. I must apologize again for arriving so late. I assure you, it was quite unavoidable."

Yes, Mina thought. *You had to avoid both the dinner and the daylight.*

Lucy smiled at Carlyle, forgiving him his tardiness, and Mina felt a sudden chill. This could not go on! She had to learn the truth, one way or another.

Think, she told herself. Test him. Use that "scientific method" they speak of so highly these days.

"Would you care for a glass of wine, Peter?" she asked.

"No thank you. I appreciate your hospitality, madam, but I choose to refrain from spirits."

"How admirable." Mina tried not to frown. That was no good! Abstinence could hardly be taken as evidence of undeath. She needed another test. A better one.

What would Van Helsing have tried?

Lucy chattered away to her guest about some popular novel she had recently read. Quincey and Peter listened attentively, sometimes commenting about this or that, while Mina searched her memories for tidbits of esoteric lore she had not had occasion to call upon for decades.

Garlic? No, that was ridiculous. One could hardly offer a visitor a handful of odorous vegetables. There had to be something else, that could resolve her doubts once and for all.

Inspiration struck.

"Do you like music, Mister Carlyle?" She smiled graciously and corrected herself. "Peter, I mean."

"I adore music, Mrs. Harker," he answered. "No truly civilized soul can say otherwise."

"Well then," she said, playing the doting parent as casually as she could, "perhaps you would care to hear Lucy play one or two of her favorite pieces. She really is an accomplished musician, you see. And there's a fine piano in the next room."

Not to mention a large, revealing mirror.

Peter fell easily into her trap, swiftly overcoming Lucy's half-hearted protests. "Please guide the way, Mrs. Harker," he said as Mina led the young people from the parlor. Carlyle walked alongside Lucy.

"Do you know," the slim young woman said to Quincey, "that Peter has spent the past year traveling the world?"

"Oh, hardly the whole world!" Peter said with a laugh. His pale complexion continued to unnerve Mina; wherever he had traveled he not gotten much sun. "Just a small portion of the globe, really."

"You don't say. Where exactly did you visit?" Quincey asked. The group paused in the hallway for a moment, just outside the piano room.

"Europe," Peter replied. "Mostly Eastern Europe."

Mina's heart skipped a beat. The bleak gray peaks of the Carpathian Mountains surfaced in her memories, rising up from the past. She resisted the temptation to mention a certain "land beyond the forest," better known as Transylvania.

More than ever, she needed to get Peter Carlyle in front of that mirror.

"Come along, please." She pushed aside a pair of sliding pocket doors. "The piano is waiting."

"No more so than I," Peter said. "After you."

Mina entered the chamber and took her customary place at a chair opposite the ornate mirror. She waited, with all the patience she could muster, until Quincey and Peter seated themselves on a plush, richly upholstered couch nearby. Lucy glided straight to the piano and began to sort through a stack of sheet music and songbooks.

Mina turned her eyes to the mirror, hoping to see the entire room reflected back at her, including the entire company.

She saw nothing. The mirror's surface was obscured, fogged. Countless tiny beads of moisture dewed the mirror, like condensation clinging to a cold glass on a hot day. She turned and gazed at Peter Carlyle, who appeared entirely intent on the young lady at the piano. Mina smiled knowingly, despite the failure of her ruse. Her uncertainty was fading.

Very clever, she thought, but not good enough. *He* could summon fog, too.

Mina settled back in her chair. The music of Mozart filled the chamber. She was almost sure now.

There was just one more test.

13

Calmly, casually, she removed a hairpin from her coiffure. She glanced at Peter and Quincey to confirm that they were both concentrating on Lucy's playing. Neither was watching her.

Perfect.

Without hesitation, she stuck the pin into the tip of her right index finger and drew it out.

"Oh dear!" she exclaimed, drawing the attention of the two men on the couch. "I seem to have pricked myself!"

She held up the finger for all to see. Her eyes never left Carlyle's face as a red pearl of blood blossomed on her fingertip.

And there it was! On Peter's face: the look she'd been watching for. It appeared for an instant, then vanished completely, but in that fractional sliver of time, Mina had seen enough. She had seen that pale face flush with excitement, the thin lips peel back to expose the jagged canines. She had seen the lust, the hunger, in the young man's eyes.

And she'd recognized that look.

~

Later that night, after their guest had departed and all the household had retired to bed, Mina Harker stood silently outside her daughter's door.

The memories came flooding back, as they did every night. Once again, she saw that small, dark room in Dr. Seward's sanitorium. She saw herself as she was then, young and trembling, her blood surging through her veins. The moonlight came again through the window, and the mist and the swirling motes of lights. Then he was there. The Count. Red eyes. Cool hands. A hungry mouth filled with unquenchable desire . . . .

Some memories were simply too exquisite to abandon to the years. Instead they grew ever more intense and irresistible as time went on and one fully grasped what had been lost so long ago. Mina fingered her gray hair ruefully. She had come so close to immortality, to an eternity of dark secrets and delights.

She softly eased open the bedroom door. The gentle murmur of rhythmic breathing came from within. Lucy was sound asleep, doubtless dreaming of her handsome, ever-so-charming suitor.

Mina moved quietly across the room. She had to make sure the window was open.

First, however, she bestowed a look of motherly love upon her slumbering daughter.

"Don't forget, dear," she whispered. "Come back for your brother."

The Adventure of Leonardo's Smile

Max Allan Collins
&
Matthew V. Clemens

Sir Arthur Conan Doyle was a successful writer when he gave the world the consulting detective, Sherlock Holmes. Across fifty-six short stories and four novels, Holmes captivated first England and then the rest of the world. Doyle could never have conceived of the enduring appeal of Holmes and Watson or their influence on an entire genre of publishing.

Max Allan Collins is an MWA Grand Master. He is the author of the Shamus-winning Nathan Heller historical thrillers (*Do No Harm*) and the graphic novel *Road to Perdition*, basis of the Academy Award-winning film. His innovative '70s series, Quarry, revived by Hard Case Crime (*Quarry's Climax*), became a Cinemax TV series. He has completed thirteen posthumous Mickey Spillane novels (*Masquerade for Murder*) and is the co-author (with his wife Barbara Collins) of the Trash 'n' Treasures mystery series (*Antiques Carry On*).

Matthew Clemens is a long-time co-conspirator with Max Allan Collins. They have collaborated on twenty-six novels, more than twenty short stories, several comic books, four graphic novels, a computer game, and a dozen mystery jigsaw puzzles. Their latest Wolfpack thriller *Live Fast, Spy Hard* will be published in early 2021.

<u>Note from Max Allan Collins:</u>

For seven years, beginning in the first season of *CSI: Crime Scene Investigation*, Matt Clemens and I were the primary licensing writers for that popular TV series. In addition to eight *CSI* and two *CSI: Miami* tie-ins, we wrote graphic novels, video game scripts, and jigsaw puzzles. The latter involved writing short stories to accompany clue-laden images. In addition to writing *CSI* and *CSI: New York* stories, we were enlisted to do the same with *NCIS*, *NCIS: LA* and *The Mentalist*. Finally, Matt and I were asked to write a pair of Sherlock Holmes puzzles, but the company that had put out all of these stopped doing so, and the Holmes stories were never issued. We share one of these tales with you now—an adventure in which, in true game fashion...

The Adventure of Leonardo's Smile

YOU ARE DOCTOR WATSON, AND YOU HAVE BEEN INVITED TO accompany Sherlock Holmes to Paris. The great consulting detective has received a letter from young French forensics scientist Edmond Locard, who is attempting to track and capture a multiple murderer in the City of Light. The French police have little experience with this sort of crime, while Holmes is well known among European police for his behind-the-scenes investigation of the Jack the Ripper murders in Whitechapel.

When you arrive at the Hotel Ritz, where you and Holmes will reside during your stay in Paris, a young man in a black suit awaits you near the front entry as the Hansom drops you off. Holmes having wired your plans to his correspondent, you are primed to be greeted in this fashion, although you are not expecting Locard to be in the presence of an older, barrel-chested man.

The younger man, tall and wearing a bowler, has a long, thin face with a nose that looks as if it has been broken at least once. Beneath that, a smoothly combed black mustache flares up toward his high cheekbones. Above the bent beak of a nose, the man's eyes are lively, with an intensity of gaze reminiscent of Holmes himself.

The older man stands to one side, as if unsure that he wants to even partake in this welcome. His gray suit, fashioned of a more expensive material than his companion's, is as immaculate as that of the younger man. Both are fastidious, although the older man outweighs the younger by more than half, his own mustache longer, more luxuriant and waxed to fine curly points. He is balding, holds his hat in his hands, and somehow gives off the air of a man who thinks all of this business is beneath him.

As you near, the younger one steps forward, hand extended. "Monsieur Holmes? I am Edmond Locard."

His accent is thick, but his English is precise.

Holmes shakes the hand of the young man whose letter had summoned the two of you. Then, without any introduction, Holmes turns to the older man. "Lacassagne! How pleasant to see you."

The men shake hands perfunctorily. "I wish I could say the same, Holmes. But the circumstances prevent as much."

"Allow me to introduce my colleague—Dr. Watson."

You shake hands with both men.

"It is a pleasure to meet you, Monsieur Lacassagne," you say with an impressed nod. "I have read several of your monographs."

"Do tell," Lacassagne says, gruffly pleased.

"Your paper on biological disposition towards deviant behavior was of especial interest."

"Really?" Lacassagne asks, puffing up a little.

"You took Lombroso to task," you say.

Holmes says, "Don't be overly flattered by my associate's praise, Lacassagne. Lombroso is a short-sighted fool."

Cesare Lombroso is an Italian criminologist who theorizes that criminality is inherited, suggesting criminals can be identified by bloodline or physical defects.

Lacassagne, like Holmes, believes that criminality is more influenced by environment—that, under the proper circumstances, any man can be driven to commit a crime.

Holmes says, "Perhaps we could freshen up before dinner."

"Seems a sound suggestion," the older man says. "Since you are staying here at the Ritz, shall we eat in the hotel's dining room?"

"Splendid idea," Holmes says, clapping you on the shoulder. "Tonight, Doctor, we shall partake of the haute cuisine of none other than Auguste Escoffier."

A smile plays at the corners of Lacassagne's mouth. "You know Monsieur Escoffier?"

Nodding, Holmes says, "From his time at the Savoy in London. Gentlemen, might you give us half an hour before dinner? Then you may fill us in on the details you have accumulated in this case, without spoiling anyone's supper."

Locard looks eagerly at his mentor, obviously hoping that he might be allowed to join in a meal at a renowned hotel where he would never be able to afford one on his modest income.

"An excellent suggestion," Lacassagne says.

The Ritz, named for its owner, Swiss hotelier Cesar Ritz, opened earlier in the summer, June, 1898. Thanks to its opulence, the Ritz has quickly become the destination of many well-heeled travelers. Its elegance extends to a dining room replete with ornate decorations, huge mirrors, and tall archways.

Your group occupies a table in a far corner, away from the kitchen and the other diners, out of courtesy for the subject matter of the dinner conversation.

Despite wearing relatively new attire, you still feel underdressed among the ladies and gentlemen in their evening finery. The group has garnered more than one disapproving glance, but as usual, Holmes seems not even to notice. The room is filled with the aroma of the savory dishes Monsieur Escoffier creates for his wealthy diners. Having placed their order of duck cassoulet, Holmes seems prepared to get down to business.

Looking toward Locard, Holmes asks, "So—how many victims, thus far? You did not specify in your letter."

"Four," Locard says.

"All in the area around Paris?"

Lacassagne answers for his friend. "Yes, but in different parts of the city."

Holmes nods. "Those are the only four?"

"*Oui*," Locard says.

"Over how long a period of time?"

"Just over a month."

"Could there be more slayings of which you are not aware?"

Locard shakes his head. "The fiend wants them to be found. He practically *displays* them."

"Displays them?" you ask. "How so?"

Locard says, "They have all been left in very public places."

Holmes asks, "Which public places?"

"A virtual tourist's tour of Paris—outside the Louvre, at the Arc de Triomphe, the Palais Garnier, and the Eiffel Tower."

"Were these women murdered at these locations, or transported for effect?"

Taking over, Lacassagne says, "There was little blood. None with the first two victims, who were strangled. Each homicide has become more violent, however, the killer using a ligature now. The latest victim was quite bloody, almost decapitated."

"Good lord," you say.

Lacassagne continues: "But they have all been found in a state of rigor mortis. It would seem the victims were murdered elsewhere before they were, as Locard says, 'displayed.' That is the only way to explain the rigor."

"And the level of violence is escalating?" Holmes asks.

Locard says, "To my way of thinking, that is definitely so. As Monsieur Lacassagne says, each one has shown a greater degree of anger."

Nodding, Lacassagne says, "I am afraid our young friend is correct—Edmond misses little. The viciousness of the killings is absolutely increasing, and I am afraid we will approach the level of your Ripper killings before very long."

"So," Holmes says, his slender fingers tented, "what do we know about the victims?"

Locard says, "Four women, all employed at the Moulin Rouge, either as actresses or dancers."

"Then we have a starting point," Holmes says, lifting an eyebrow. "What have you learned from their employer and the other workers?"

With a weary shrug, Lacassagne says, "They do not, I fear, have much to say to the police."

"Perhaps that is where we come in," Holmes says. "Since we are not the police, they may be more forthcoming."

Locard and Lacassagne trade a mildly skeptical glance, but you agree with Holmes, though making no comment—your *Strand* accounts of Holmes' cases have been translated and published in France to some considerable popularity.

The older man says, "You may be correct, Mr. Holmes. In any event, we have had no luck with them."

Eyes narrowing, Holmes says, "Tell me more about the victims. Any other commonalities besides their place of employment?"

Locard says, "They all worked as models for painters."

"Any one specific painter, common to them all?"

Lacassagne says, "If it were that easy, sir, we would have the devil swinging from the gallows already."

Locard says, "The women all modeled for several painters. They also worked in a place that drew for them a great many gentlemen, uh…admirers."

Holmes nods. "Then, after dinner, we go to the Moulin Rouge and see what we can find there."

Your duck arrives and a silence settles over the little group. Before long your plates are cleared and the main course is brought out.

With a slight appreciative smile, Holmes says, "Beef bourguignon is Escoffier's specialty, the dish for which he is best known."

Again, the two French officials trade looks, perhaps surprised at how easily Holmes has shifted from homicide to roast beef.

Your little group's next stop is, indeed, the cabaret with the famous red windmill on its roof. At the foot of Montmartre, the hill which gives the district its name, the Moulin Rouge is an establishment that caters to the rich, although all strata of citizens enter the cabaret at some time.

Tonight the place is bustling to near bursting, with a large crowd, loud music, a smoky atmosphere, and raucous laughter.

After an introduction from Lacassagne, you and Holmes leave the forensics experts behind to follow Joseph Oller, one of the Moulin Rouge owners, to his private office. Tall, with bland looks made distinctive by a silver mustache and goatee, Oller doesn't look terribly pleased to be asked to talk to the two of you.

Still, Oller is polite enough to offer you chairs. A desk no wider than the English Channel separates you from your host. Though plush, the office reeks of cigar smoke—an ashtray on the corner of Oller's desk is practically overflowing. At your right, a painting of a dark-haired beauty in a can-can dress looms, its subject looking down in amusement.

Oller says, "I have already told the police everything I know, gentlemen."

Holmes replies, "Such an expansive statement is difficult to take seriously."

The club owner glares at Holmes. "The unfortunate young women worked here. They were all good employees, and we miss them terribly...but it would seem unlikely that they were killed because of their shared employment here at the Moulin Rouge."

"I wonder if your confidence on that point has something to do with the possibility that—should your cabaret appear to be at the center of a spate of sensational murders—your clientele might be considerably less eager to parade through your doors."

His face reddening with anger, Oller all but leaps from his chair. "We are *through* here, gentlemen!"

Holmes also rises, his own rage cold. "There are murders to solve, sir, and you may well have information that could help the police apprehend the murderer—and yet you remain mute! More concerned about business than the safety of your own employees."

Oller slams a fist on his desk and opens his mouth to bellow again, but you cut him off.

You say, "That is a most evocative painting."

Both Oller and Holmes turn to you.

"Who is she?" you ask.

Oller lets out a long breath, calming himself. "Marie Duquesne. She was a dancer here."

"*Was?*" Holmes asks.

The red that comes to Oller's face this time reflects embarrassment, not anger. "She was one of the victims—the first, in fact."

You and Holmes exchange sharp glances.

Then Holmes says, "And still you say you have nothing to offer the investigation?"

Oller's chin raises. "I have not told you anything the police do not already know. Now, you really must excuse me."

Holmes is quietly seething as you follow him out of the office and back into the cabaret. He strides straight past Lacassagne and Locard, and through the front door.

When you all catch up with him, he is pacing. You are about to say something to try to calm him when a heavily French-accented voice says, "Sherlock, my friend, is that you?"

You all turn to see a man whose small stature requires a lowering of your eyes. Not even five feet tall, with a full beard and pince-nez eyeglasses perched on his nose, he peers up at Holmes fondly.

The great detective's mood changes immediately. "Henri...how good to see you!" Stepping forward, Holmes bends at the waist and extends his hand to the shorter man and they shake heartily. "When did we last see each other?"

The man says, "London, perhaps, oh, two years ago?"

Turning to you, Holmes says, "Watson, meet Henri de Toulouse-Lautrec, a fine *artiste* and good friend. Henri, meet another true friend of mine—Dr. Watson."

You shake hands with the man. "A pleasure to meet you, Henri."

With a nod, Toulouse-Lautrec says, "As *les amis* of Sherlock Holmes, I fear we are together on a list most short."

"So it would seem," you admit.

Holmes makes introductions.

Then Toulouse-Lautrec asks, "What brings you to Paris, my friend?"

"Murder, *monsieur*."

Toulouse-Lautrec frowns. "The women of the Moulin Rouge?"

"You know of these crimes?"

The painter flips a hand. "Everyone knows, Mr. Holmes. Everyone in our special community, that is. Painters, models, we know."

Locard asks, "Did you know any of them personally?"

"*Monsieur*, I knew them all. Beautiful women, our muses." He shakes his head, his expression glum. "This is the tragedy *horrible*."

You ask, "You knew Marie Duquesne?"

A smile of pride breaks through Toulouse-Lautrec's gloom. "You have seen my painting of her in Oller's office?"

"That was yours?"

He nods. "Yes. I painted it perhaps one year ago."

"Striking indeed, sir."

Irritated by this small talk, Holmes asks, "Do you know what other artists she may have sat for?"

The artist nods. "Several, but I think one of the last was Pierre Bissette."

"Where can we find him?" Lacassagne asks.

"Why, right here," Toulouse-Lautrec says. "He should appear at any moment. It is Bissette that I came to meet tonight. You see, he owes me a drink...perhaps two."

Holmes asks, "Did the women have anything in common besides their manner of employment? Physically, perhaps?"

"They were all brunettes," Toulouse-Lautrec says without pause. "Your killer has a definite preference when it comes to the hair color."

Off Holmes' sharp look, Lacassagne says, "We noticed that, Mr. Holmes, but did not consider it important. It might easily be a coincidence."

Toulouse-Lautrec shakes his head. "This killer, he showcases his work, does he not?"

Locard nods.

"It is his art," Lautrec continues. "And every artist has a muse, my friends. Determine your artist's muse, and then you will be one step closer to apprehending him."

Holmes says, "*Monsieur* Lautrec is right. What specifically has he done to the victims that you have withheld from me?"

Lacassagne says, "We are keeping certain factors quiet until we have a suspect."

"That will not do, sir. We have a gifted artist right here before us, one who can provide insight into what some other 'artist' may be trying to achieve. Tell Henri everything about the murders, and allow him to enlighten us."

Toulouse-Lautrec laughs. "I fear you give me too much credit, Mr. Holmes."

"I doubt that. You might be the person best positioned to help us in our inquiries."

The small painter shrugs. "If you think so, my friend, I will try."

Holmes turns to Lacassagne and Locard. "Tell him what you know."

Without pause, Locard says, "The women were all strangled. They were all left similarly posed in public places."

"Posed?" Toulouse-Lautrec asks. "How so?"

"Each of them was smiling."

"Smiling?"

Lacassagne says, "An odd half smile, no teeth showing."

Eyebrows raised, Toulouse-Lautrec looks to Holmes. "Do you see it?"

"I believe so," Holmes says. "Da Vinci."

Locard and Lacassagne glance at each other.

"Da Vinci?" the older man asks.

Holmes says, "Your murderer's muse—or perhaps better expressed, his greatest influence—is Leonardo Da Vinci."

Locard asks, "How do you arrive at this, Holmes?"

"The murderer appears to be contriving real-life Mona Lisas."

Toulouse-Lautrec nods. "Exactly my thinking."

Lacassagne says, "You think this killer is doing *what*? That is insane!"

Holmes says, "As is befitting a murderer with so twisted a mind. But his insanity makes our man no less a cunning, worthy adversary."

Before the conversation can continue, a tall man in a dark suit approaches.

"Henri," the man says.

Toulouse-Lautrec turns to Holmes, gesturing to the new arrival. "As I said, Pierre Bissette—here to pay me his debt."

Introductions are made, but before the painters can enter the noisy cabaret, Holmes says, "Would you be so good as to answer a few questions, Monsieur Bissette?"

The painter shrugs, then nods. He is a tall, muscular man with dark hair that touches his collar and a suit that he has worn for one too many seasons.

"You knew Marie Duquesne?" Holmes asks.

"Yes, poor thing," Bissette says. "She sat for me more than once."

"We hear that you were one of the last painters for whom she modeled—would that be the case, do you think?"

"Possibly," Bissette says, shrugging again. "She sat for me the day before she disappeared."

Looking down, Holmes notes the man's watch chain. "That is most interesting, sir," the detective says. "Human hair?"

Bissette gently pulls the watch from his vest pocket, shows Holmes the chain. "From Claudette, my betrothed. She wove it herself."

"And where is she tonight?" Holmes asks, so good-natured as to arouse your suspicions.

"In Coubert, with her sick mother."

"When did she give that lock of hair to you?"

"Right before she left," Bissette says. "So I would not forget her."

"How long has she been gone?"

Bissette shrugs. "Five weeks, perhaps six."

Holmes says, "Her mother must be quite ill."

"Dying," Bissette says. "No idea how long it will take, though—sometimes it seems that the woman has been dying for years."

"Does your betrothed have a job?"

"Here at the Moulin Rogue, as a dancer—although obviously not at present."

"Obviously," Holmes says.

"Oh, and she is a model," Bissette says by way of afterthought. "When she returns she will be my masterpiece! I so love painting her."

"Does anyone else know where she is?"

"I would doubt that. She received a letter from her mother and left instantly. She did not even send a message to *Monsieur* Oller that she would not be in. That is how distraught she was."

Holmes, Lacassagne, and Locard trade looks.

"If that is all, gentlemen," Bissette says, "Henri and I have some serious drinking to do."

Nodding, Holmes says, "Then we will keep you no longer. Thank you for your time, Monsieur Bissette."

The painter turns to enter the cabaret, but Toulouse-Lautrec lingers. When Bissette is out of earshot, to Holmes, Toulouse-Lautrec says, "Sherlock my friend, there are another two painters to whom you should speak. Men who worked with all of these unfortunate models, and are also devotees of Da Vinci—Michel Linville and Simon Séverin."

Holmes says, "Thank you, Henri. It was a pleasure to see you again, although I hope the next time will be under circumstances more *agréable*."

Once Toulouse-Lautrec enters Moulin Rouge, Lacassagne says, "It would seem that in Pierre Bissette we have at least one good suspect already."

"Clearly, checking his story would be in our best interest," Holmes says. "Can you telegraph Coubert and find out if this Claudette is actually there?"

Locard says, "I will have it done as soon as we get back to the *gendarmerie*."

"The man claims to be in love with this woman, but does not remember precisely when she left, nor how long she will be gone...and tonight he is out on the town with Toulouse-Lautrec."

"And Paris," you observe, "is quite the town to be out upon."

"What do you suggest we do now?" Lacassagne asks.

"If you would take me to the site of the first crime," says Holmes, "I want to see where the body was found."

As midnight approaches, you arrive outside the Louvre, the museum quiet in the darkness, with barely any foot traffic, most everyone having retired for the evening.

Built as a fortress in the 12th century by Philip II, the Louvre Palace eventually became the Louvre Museum, which opened in 1793.

Locard and Lacassagne lead you to an area near the main entrance. The younger man points to a spot on the ground.

"Here is where the body was found," he says.

Silently, Holmes walks the area as you all watch him. He stops, stoops, pokes at something on the cobblestones, then stands straight again.

Holmes asks, "No one saw anything?"

Locard says, "No."

"We will get no helpful evidence from here—the crime scene far too old and trampled upon. You collected no evidence at the time you found the body?"

Lacassagne says, "There was precious little from the site itself."

Holmes narrows his eyes. "Even the smallest thing may help."

Locard says, "There was a small spot of mud on the victim's dress."

"Which," Lacassagne adds, "may have been there before her murder."

The younger man nods. "That is true, but it might also have been from the night she was murdered."

Holmes asks, "Have you learned anything about the mud?"

"It comes from the fifth *arrondissement* of the city, the left bank," Locard says. "She was found here, the first *arrondissement*, the Louvre. She lived in the eighth *arrondissement*, Élysée. At some point since last her dress was laundered, she crossed the river—even though she worked and lived on this side of the Seine."

"*Arrondissement?*" you ask.

Holmes waves a dismissive hand. "The *arrondissements* are the districts

Paris is divided into, much as London has its Whitechapel, East End, and so on. Any idea why she may have crossed the river?"

Lacassagne says, "Not offhand, but I do know that one of the painters Toulouse-Lautrec mentioned, Simon Séverin, lives in the Panthéon district, the fifth *arrondissement*."

Holmes asks, "How do you happen to know where Séverin lives?"

The older man says, "He is occasionally a sketch artist for the gendarmerie. He creates leaflets of wanted criminals, crime scenes, things of that nature."

"Including records of murder scenes?"

"At times."

"It is my experience, gentlemen, that some murderers go out of their way to involve themselves in an investigation. To insinuate themselves in some fashion, providing themselves with information, and feeding their egos. The Ripper did it by way of taunting letters, but I have heard of other murderers using other, more direct methods."

"*Mon dieu!*" Locard says. "That is madness."

"Indeed," Holmes says, "and so we have another suspect! Can we visit him in the morning?"

"Most assuredly," Lacassagne says.

"Then," Holmes says, "we are off to the next crime scene."

The Arc de Triomphe, situated at the west end of the Champs-Élysées, commemorates those who fought and died during the French Revolution and the Napoleonic Wars. Designed in 1806, the structure is, at fifty meters in height, the tallest triumphal arch in the world. By day, the tourist destination is marked by heavy traffic; tonight, as you walk under it, no one beyond your group is in sight.

Locard says, "This is where the second victim, Yvette LaSalle, was found."

Again, Holmes walks the scene. When he is finished, he says, "In a city this size, I find it hard to believe this madman is able to display his victims so easily and never be seen."

Lacassagne says, "As you yourself said, being insane does not mean he is lacking in intelligence."

"We know that he dispatches his prey elsewhere, but how does he make them smile in that quietly grotesque way that suits him? He would have to do that in the early stages of rigor, before they become too stiff for such manipulation, but at a time when the affectation will stay in place. That would be hours after death."

Lacassagne says, "It is as if he is a ghost. He deposits them, then disappears."

Pacing again, Holmes says, "The victims, dancers, actresses—were all of them petite?"

"Quite," Locard says.

"Ah," Holmes says. "Then I think I know how he is accomplishing his vile artistic display."

Lacassagne says, "Pray tell us."

"He commits the murders in private, of course. He holds onto his victims until he can complete their smiles of death."

"But then how does he move the poor wretches?"

Holmes' smile is ghastly. "They have all been found sitting, or lying on their sides, almost folded in half, have they not?"

Locard stares at the detective, agape. "How could you know that?"

"That is actually the clue as to how he moves them."

Lacassagne is growing agitated. "Stop talking in circles, my good man. I still do not see where you speculation is leading to!"

"The fiend is simply packing them into a valise. They are petite enough to do so. He packs them, like clothing for a trip, and carries the bag to his destination."

Locard says, "He would have to be a very strong man."

Holmes nods. "Undoubtedly he is. After all, he nearly decapitated a woman with a ligature, as Lacassagne here has said. If you were to try that, you'd find it far harder than it sounds. This is a very strong man indeed."

Locard asks, "Could our suspect Bissette be that strong?"

"He is a big enough man, certainly. And Séverin?"

Lacassagne nods. "He is at least my size and a much younger, vigorous man."

The next stop is the home of the Paris Opera, the Palais Garnier on the Boulevard de Capucines in the ninth *arrondissement*. The opulent, beautiful building was designed by architect Charles Garnier. Your carriage drops you in front of the south façade, and to the east the sun is just edging over the horizon. The night has been a long one, but Holmes is making progress. Once again, barely anyone is on the street, though on the corner, a good-sized man is unfolding some kind of wooden contraption.

When you get out of the carriage, Lacassagne freezes. "I don't believe it."

"What?" you ask.

"That man," he says, pointing. "It's Séverin!"

Holmes asks, "Here? Now?"

"Right over there, setting up his easel."

You look and see that the man also has a valise on the next to him on the ground. The hairs on the back of your neck stand at attention.

The four of you approach the artist. He is bigger than both you and Holmes, has blond hair and dark clothes. His easel has a blank canvas on it. He turns when he hears you coming.

He has blue eyes and an easy smile. In French, he says, "Monsieur Lacassagne, what a surprise."

The men shake hands and Lacassagne makes the introductions. Knowing that the two of you are from England, Séverin says stiffly in English, "I am pleased to meet you."

Without preamble, Holmes says, "May I ask what's in your valise?"

Séverin smiles and kneels to open it. "The tools of my trade, *monsieur*: paints, brushes, palette." He opens the case to show off vari-colored bottles of paint and the rest of his supplies.

"I designed it myself," he says with pride. All the bottles are tied down, the brushes are bound together too, the palette laid across the top.

"Clever engineering," Holmes says. "Are you good at this sort of thing?"

Nodding, Séverin says, "I have an eye for how to make use out of things others deem worthless." He holds up a coil of piano wire. "Like this."

He hands the coil to Holmes, who asks, "And you use these for what purpose?"

"Hanging paintings, of course. Someone tossed them away, but I saw a use."

Holmes trades a look with the French lawmen. Then, to Séverin, he says, "Is this the only case of its kind?"

"Certainly not. This case is designed for oils, but I have another for watercolors, and even one for sculpting."

Holmes asks, "May we see them?"

Séverin shrugs. "Another time, perhaps. Now, I must paint the Palais Garnier while I have the morning light. If you will excuse me..."

"One more question, please."

"Might I continue setting up as we talk? I cannot afford to lose the correct light."

"Surely," Holmes says.

Séverin goes back to his work, opening bottles of paint.

"You knew the four women who were murdered?"

"Not just *knew, monsieur*! I painted each of them, and more than once."

He stops fiddling with his paints and looks up at Holmes. "Do you suspect I may have had something to do with their deaths?"

"Did you?"

Rising, white-knuckled fists at his sides, the artist says, "I treated these women with respect, all of them! Even Gigi, a classless whore, I treated well."

Holmes glances questioningly at Lacassagne, who says, "Gigi Fournier, the last victim. The one nearly decapitated."

Holding up the coiled wire, Holmes says, "Something like this was used to commit the foul deed." He studies the wire. "There is no blood, but you could have cleaned it."

Séverin snatches back the coil. "I did no such thing. I would *never* have harmed those women!"

Locard steps between the two men. "No one is saying you did."

"Not yet, at least," Holmes says, with a smile as small and terrible as those of the dead Mona Lisas.

The painter takes a menacing step forward, but Locard holds him back.

"An interesting show of temper," Holmes remarks.

Séverin comes toward him again, and this time you and Lacassagne must help restrain the man.

Séverin shouts, "Get this pompous fool away from me, Lacassagne!"

"We are leaving," the older Frenchman says. "We are leaving."

"For now," Holmes says.

Séverin tries to break free, but finally stops struggling as Holmes strides away.

Leaving the angry painter to his work, your group hustles to catch up with Holmes.

"That was a scene of considerable melodrama," Locard says.

Shrugging, Holmes says, "We knew Séverin has the size to have perpetrated the crimes, and now we know he has the foul temper."

Locard says, "That is hardly evidence."

Holmes says, "His use of the valise and the piano wire is suggestive enough to make him a strong suspect."

You all climb aboard your carriage for the ride to the last stop—the Eiffel Tower. When you arrive, the sun is up, the structure already crowded.

Built to be the entrance for the 1889 World's Fair, the Eiffel Tower—named for its designer, Gustave Eiffel—is the tallest man-made structure on earth, and the city's most recognizable building. If Paris has a trademark, the Eiffel Tower is it.

The two Frenchmen lead you and Holmes to a spot near one of the massive leg-like supports.

Lacassagne says, "This is where Alice Ardoin, the third victim, was found."

Holmes takes his customary walk around the scene. As he does so, he asks, "Even here no one saw the murderer?"

"Difficult to believe, is it not?" Lacassagne says. "There are far fewer visitors at night, of course, but the tower always has *some* people around."

"And yet..." Holmes says.

Locard nods. "And yet..."

Holmes' attention is drawn to a painter a few yards away. While several people are sketching the tower and its many guests, only one man is actually painting on canvas. You and your French hosts follow Holmes as he walks over and moves behind the painter, looking over the man's shoulder at the dark tower being painted in the center of the canvas.

Whispering to you, Holmes says, "He is the correct size."

The painter is in fact a large man with dark features, his hair clipped close, a protective smock covering his clothes. It is dotted with spots of red, black, and blue. On the ground next to him is a valise not unlike Séverin's.

Stepping forward, Holmes asks, "Do you speak English, sir?"

Turning to the great detective, the man says, "*Oui.*"

Extending his hand, Holmes introduces himself, then the rest of your little party.

"Michel Linville," the painter says, a hand to his chest.

Holmes breaks into a wide smile. "Really? We have a mutual friend—Henri Toulouse-Lautrec."

Linville smiles. "Henri? I have not seen him in some while."

The two men exchange pleasantries about Toulouse-Lautrec. The usually brusque Holmes is pouring on the charm, putting the painter at ease.

This side of Holmes is one you have seldom seen, and Locard and Lacassagne note it as well. The detective is positively gregarious.

Clapping his new friend on the back, Holmes says, "Though the sun shines, *monsieur*, your painting is dark."

Linville nods. "As is life, *mon ami*."

"I notice you have a valise. Your fellow artist, Simon Séverin, has a very similar one, I believe."

"He does. He 'borrowed' the idea from me," Linville says. "I have had mine longer."

"He says he has separate ones for different modes of expression."

"Yes," Linville says. "I have more than one, too."

"Might I see inside this one? It's an impressive piece of work."

"Surely," Linville says, kneeling to open the valise. His case is very similar to Séverin's except that the colors are dark—blues, grays, purples. Brushes and a coil of wire, like Séverin's, are on hand, as well.

Unlike the other painter's valise, however, Linville's wire bears dark spots.

"Rust?" Holmes asks.

"The rain got to it," Linville says dismissively, tossing a rag stained with red over it.

Holmes nods. "Thank you for the education, sir. And I like your painting very much—perhaps when it is finished, I might be allowed to purchase it."

"*Merci*," Linville says. "When it is finished, we will talk."

With a wave to you all, Holmes says, "Our work is done."

"It is?" Lacassagne asks, stunned. "How so, *Monsieur* Holmes?"

Turning to all of you, Holmes says, "We have looked at the crime scenes, interviewed the best suspects, and I know who the murderer is. Watson, do you?"

Locard and Lacassagne look confused. The older man asks, "How can you possibly know who the murderer is?"

35

Holmes says, "It will soon become clear. Locard, have you heard back from Coubert?"

He holds up a note brought to him by a gendarme. "Claudette is there with her ailing mother. Seems Bissette was telling the truth."

"That rules out a potential fifth victim, and although he might be deceiving his beloved Claudette by carousing with Toulouse-Lautrec, he is not our murderer."

Shaking his head, Lacassagne says, "All right, it is not Bissette...but you believe it to be one of the other two?"

"I do not simply 'believe' it," Holmes says. "I know it, and more importantly, you have the evidence to put him away."

"So, you think it is Séverin?"

"That man has a vicious temper," Holmes says, "but a temper does not necessarily a murderer make."

"Linville, then?" Locard asks.

"Linville indeed," Holmes says, with a curt nod. "You can see the evidence from here."

Lacassagne says, "I'm sorry, sir, but I don't."

Holmes seems surprised at this lack of insight. "What of the red paint on his smock and the rag in his valise?"

Horrified, Locard says, "You mean—it's not paint!"

"Exactly. It is blood. The man carries no red paint, yet he has red drops on his smock and rag. The rust on the piano wire may indeed be rust in part. But that, too, is the color of dried blood. Michel Linville is your man."

Locard and Lacassagne depart to arrest the murderer.

Holmes turns to you. "You came to the same conclusion, did you not, Watson?"

"Certainly, my dear Holmes," you say. "It really was quite elementary."

Inappropriate Allies

David Boop

I chose Kit Carson because I'd written him into one of my weird westerns, and he's a wonderfully complicated man, but then I wanted to add a fictional character to work alongside him. Allan Quatermain was a perfect reflection of Kit, both seen as hunters of wild game and of men. It also allowed me to explore the idea of how we view one another, and how those views are often skewed by what we've been told and not what we're open to learning about each other.

David Boop is a Denver-based speculative fiction author and editor. He's also an award-winning essayist and screenwriter. Before turning to fiction, David worked as a DJ, film critic, journalist, and actor. When he was Editor-in-Chief at *IntraDenver.net*, David's team was on the ground at Columbine, making them the only *internet newspaper* to cover the tragedy. That year, they won an award for excellence from the Colorado Press Association for their design and coverage.

David's debut novel is the sci-fi/noir *She Murdered Me with Science* from WordFire Press. A second novel, *The Soul Changers*, is a serialized Victorian horror novel set in Pinnacle Entertainment's world of *Rippers Resurrected*. David was editor on the bestselling and award-nominated weird western anthology series, *Straight Outta Tombstone*, *Straight Outta Deadwood* (nominated for a *Scribe Award* and *Colorado Book Award*) and *Straight Outta Dodge City* for Baen. His follow-up anthology series will be space westerns. He's also edited two pulp hero anthologies for Moonstone Books.

David is prolific in short fiction, with many short stories and two short films to his credit. He's published across several genres, including media tie-ins for *Predator* (nominated for the 2018 Scribe Award)*, The Green Hornet, The Black Bat* and *Veronica Mars*. Additionally, he does a flash fiction mystery series on Gumshoereview.com called *The Trace Walker Temporary Mysteries*.

David works in game design as well, having written for the Savage Worlds RPG in their *Flash Gordon* (nominated for an *Origins Award*) and *Deadlands: Noir* worlds.

He's a Summa Cum Laude Graduate from UC-Denver in the Creative Writing program. He temps, collects Funko Pops, and is a believer. His hobbies include film noir, anime, the Blues and history.

You can find out more at Davidboop.com, Facebook.com/dboop.updates or Twitter @david_boop.

Inappropriate Allies

1852

It took Kit Carson two weeks to respond to the urgent summons from the Freemasons in Santa Fe. One week couldn't be rightly blamed on him, as it took their messenger that long to find him. Kit had heard of the group and found them fascinating. They'd been instrumental in achieving peace after the war with Mexico, and had arranged several of the land purchases that now made up the western territories. While he'd no direct dealings with them, he discovered, after the fact, he'd met many along the trail. Seemed no one really admitted to being one unless you directly asked them, though he knew now to look for some of their identifying symbols on their clothing.

When he arrived at the building they called a 'lodge,' it didn't look nothing like other lodges he'd stayed in. It was clean, furnished, and smelled of cherry wood smoke. A greeter offered to take his coat and guns—Kit only surrendered the Hawkins, but kept his Colts—then brought him into a room decorated with portraits of other members and more of those mysterious symbols. Being an Indian tracker, he took special note of the iconography. Reading signs like these had saved his life many a time.

"Welcome, Mr. Carson. Please do sit."

The stately man who addressed Kit had thick muttonchops and a baby face, but that belied the fierce man Kit knew him to be.

"Thank ye, Mr. St. Vrain."

St. Vrain smiled. "Please, it's Ceran. May I call you Kit?"

"I'd be honored if ye would."

"Good. So, you know me?"

Kit nodded. "Yup. Yer the one that got all those volunteers together to drive the Mexican soldiers outta Santa Fe. Helped us out a good deal."

"I'm glad," St. Vrain said. "Not that you didn't do your part in that mess. You've created quite a reputation for yourself."

Kit blushed. "By that, I hope ye don't mean those damnable books that keep showin' up. It's trumped up horse sheet, if ye ask me." Then he thought about where he was. "Beggin' yer pardon. Don't know that yer not a God-fearin' man."

The Freemason chortled. "I am, but I'm also no fool. Long as you don't take the Lord's name in vain, you're free to be you. And no, I don't read that type of entertainment, Kit. My opinion of you is based on reports sent back to D.C. from people who know you. That's why I can trust you with a sacred duty; one that no other man is as qualified to do."

Kit recognized a build-up if he'd ever heard one. Every time a request came from the military, even the President, it started by extolling his virtues.

"What sacred duty? More Indian killin'? I've about had my fill of that. I'll take down a red man aimin' to do me or others harm, but I'm no war man. I'm a scout."

"Heavens, no. Actually, it's to stop a war. In Africa."

That was the last thing Kit expected to hear. "I'm sorry, but didje just say, 'Africa,' as in the continent?"

St. Vrain made a subtle motion with his head, and the fellow who'd escorted Kit into the room left, only to return a few breaths later carrying an object on a tray. A fine cloth covered the item, but it was clearly curved.

"We have lodges in many places, Kit. While this one is only a year old, the Masons have been around for centuries and, occasionally, gifts of great significance are given to us for the work we do."

That got a raised eyebrow from Kit. "And what type of work do ye do…if I may ask?"

"Of course," St. Vrain replied, waving his hand as if all their secrets were open to discussion. Kit didn't like that type of suggestion, as that meant nothing real would be shared with him. "We do humanitarian missions. Whatever is needed in a community we serve. When tragedies strike, we step forward and help regain a sense of peace and calm."

Kit'd heard similar talk from Indian negotiators, who only claimed to be there to make peace. It rarely lasted or was even true to begin with.

St. Vrain continued. "It was in this spirit we helped rescue the Kundagi and Jecha tribes during a flash flood of the Zambezi River. Afterwards, the Kundagi leader gave us this…"

The other Freemason pulled the cloth off the item, and Kit saw a carved artifact the likes of which he'd never ever seen outside a museum, though he hadn't been in many of them. It was part of a tusk—most likely elephant—that had been made into a horn. On one side, there were carved scenes of a battle between two tribes. Turning it around, the opposite side showed the two tribes coming together in peace. The detail wasn't great, more like the cave paintings he'd seen all through the West.

St. Vrain carefully ran a thumb along the deep grooves. "During a period of strife near the lodge, this *Oliphant*—as it's called in Italy—was sent away lest it get damaged in the conflict. While not as intricate as the ones created during the Renaissance, the value isn't in its carving, or its ivory, which is indeed worth a fair amount these days. No, its value is in its symbolism for two tribes who are on the verge of war.

"The Kundagi, who originally gifted this to us, recently admitted it was *not* really theirs to give, but a gift from the Jecha, upon making peace with them. After moving from lodge to lodge, the Oliphant ended up here, of all places. They've asked if we would return it, to avoid another war with their once enemies."

"The ones they fought on that thar tusk?"

St. Vrain nodded. "The Jecha are very difficult to find, made more so by their desire to take their offense to battle." He sighed and reclaimed his seat. "We need you to escort this artifact to Africa, find the missing tribe, and return the Oliphant to them, or the possibility of war becomes almost a certainty."

Kit stood and got close enough to study the horn. "Yer askin' me to leave my home for a long time, travel to a country I ain't never been, and track some savages doin' their best to hide in preparation of attackin' other savages." It wasn't a question, but one lingered in the air.

The kindly man nodded again to his fellow, who replaced the cloth over the Oliphant and left.

"We don't expect you to do this alone, or without recompense, Kit. We already have a man waiting to help you once you get there. He's very much like you. A hunter. A tracker. A skilled fighter."

That didn't make sense to Kit. "Then why not just ship the tusk to him and have him return it?"

St. Vrain got up and walked over to a box. When he opened the lid, he pulled out two cigars. "Because I need someone I can trust, and this man… well, he's been known to create problems wherever he goes. Reports say he rejects most authority, and you, good sir," St. Vrain pointed one cigar at Kit, "know how to stay on task."

He snipped the ends off both cigars, then lit them using a lamp on his desk.

Kit immediately smelled the hint of cherry wood that he'd recognized entering the lodge. These were made from quality tobacco; not the skunkweed he often found on the trail. This, he figured, was the beginning of the mentioned recompense.

"I know it's a lot to ask, but when will you ever have the opportunity to go on an expedition like this? Less than a year, and you'll see part of the world few good Christian men have ever seen, track a race of people that you've never hunted before, and come back home with a healthy purse for your wife and children. Plus, you'll be stopping a war, and isn't that something worth a little sacrifice of your time?"

Kit took the proffered cigar. "When ye put it that way, how could I resist?"

"Excellent!" St. Vrain said. "We have a picket waiting for you off the coast of Florida. You'll leave by train tomorrow morning and arrive in Angola in under a month."

Kit's jaw hung loose. "Tomorrow?"

St. Vrain acted surprised by the question. "Of course. A war is brewing. Time is of the essence."

Forced to accept this news, Kit took a few slow drags of the cigar, enjoying how the smoke felt, tasted, on his tongue. He finally thought to ask, "The other tracker thar, the one ye say's like me, what's his name?"

~

It was with great trepidation that I, Allan Quatermain, waited in a café by the Port of Luanda for this American the Freemasons had asked me to accompany. I hated leaving my home in Durban to take a steamer around the horn to Angola, almost as much as meeting this 'expert' tracker. I had yet to meet a Yank who was not impetuous, uncouth, and barely civilized above the natives they exterminated on their own continent.

It was unfortunate to say the least that I had not been able to find the Jecha tribe myself, but then I had history with them…and them me. They knew how to erase their presence from me and my techniques, such that I searched almost three months to no avail. One would think there were only so many places to hide on the continent, it ultimately being surrounded by water, but they had done a remarkable job of staying one step ahead of me. It was my feeling that they really wanted to go to war with the Kundagi and did not want me talking them out of it. Only the return of their sacred gift would forestall that now.

Stymied, I prostrated myself before the Freemasons, who had engaged my services, and asked for help. They had approached me some months back while visiting Cape Town for a trade meeting. They begged me to find the Jecha before they started a war, the Masons feeling at least partially responsible for the events unfolding. When I messaged them later to tell them I still had no positive news, they wrote back informing me they had engaged the services of an American 'hero,' as they put it, to help.

Apparently, they had heard from their brother lodge in a placed called New Mexico, where the Jecha's Oliphant eventually landed. Though the leaders of the Cape of Good Hope Lodge had claimed no malfeasance on the removal of a religious item such as this Oliphant from its homeland, I learned long ago not to trust anyone regarding anything dealing with treasure. I consider it good karma, that when asked to return the item that had been given to them for safekeeping, they could accurately ascertain its location. Often, such treasures are 'misplaced' only to be found later residing on some rich collector's mantle.

That is the only reason I acquiesced to work with this man, Carson.

That name brought back memories of my dead wife, Stella Carson. It was a common enough name that the notion they may be distantly related was absurd. However, I have discovered that reality is full of such unbelievable coincidences. Still, I must keep my guard up around this man. He may be a tracker of some renown in his own lands, but this was Africa.

My Africa.

I would not be made to play the second to a foreigner who knows nothing of the spirit of the Continent.

As I got up from my table, I left the gift the Freemasons had enclosed in their last letter—a novel, if it could called that—*Kit Carson, Prince of the Gold Hunters*, on the table, though I should have thrown it in the trash, where it belonged.

~

Nothing would've made Kit happier than to have his two feet on solid land again. It had been a rough trip from the get-go. Having never been to sea, the realization that he was in the middle of an ocean, no land anywhere to be seen, had disconcerted him. Kit found himself in the uncomfortable position of being at the complete mercy of others, even after he got his "sea legs." Vomiting had been embarrassing enough, but his refusal to go topside except when necessary made him feel small. Made him feel like a coward.

So when one of the crew came to fetch him to the deck, he'd accepted to hopefully conquer that fear. He'd been rewarded with a sight unlike anything he'd seen in Kentucky, Missouri, Colorado, or any of the territories.

Five whales burst through the surface of the water as he and other passengers watched. Called a "pod," this family was frolicking like he'd known horses to do. It was magnificent. Kit'd recently heard of a novel about a man who hunted a whale, something he'd no frame of reference to at the time. As he became more fascinated with the pod, he made a note to find the book when he got back and have his wife read it to him. How could anyone hunt such creatures…and why?

After that, Kit would come up whenever someone spotted aquatic creatures such as dolphins, sharks, and the strangest thing, a creature called a swordfish with a needle-esque nose the length of a man. It launched itself into the air, spearing a bird flying overhead and dragging its prize back into the dark depths. He'd have so much to tell Joespha and the children when he got home.

Despite these reprieves, the journey was long, and Kit often got edgy at the emptiness around him. During the better times, Kit talked with the crew about their destination, and if anyone'd heard of the man known as Allan Quatermain.

"Aye, we know of him," said an Icelandic deckhand. "You'd have to be deaf as a haddock, not to."

A second one echoed, "He's both the savior and scourge of the Savannah."

"How can he be both?" Kit asked.

They laughed. The first seaman answered, "Well, that depends on which direction his blunderbuss is pointing, dontcha know?"

"Indeed," the second one agreed. "If it's pointed at a lion, he's the best friend you can have. But if it's pointed at you…" He left the statement hanging in the air.

Kit didn't need further explanation. Similar things had been said about him.

When he returned to his private cabin, Kit discovered another crewman coming out.

"Ah, Carson," he said, startled to be seen. "I was just looking for you. There…well, I was told to find you, as there might be a pod coming up, soon."

"Mighty kind of ye, but I just came from topside. No whales."

"Oh. I see," said the sailor. "Maybe I misunderstood. Regardless, the captain'd asked to see you."

Kit told the man to convey his apologies, claiming tiredness and desire to retire.

The sailor nodded and went on his way.

Kit made note of the man's face, and upon entering his cabin, he immediately checked his guns for tomfoolery, then the Oliphant and

45

found it had moved from its spot, though that wasn't uncommon due to the rocking of the ship. He opened the lined wooden case it'd been stored in, checked its condition, and then replaced it in the satchel. Though nothing was amiss, Kit didn't leave the cabin without the satchel after that.

No further incidents happened, though, and he felt himself quite done with the whole sailing thing when they crossed through a storm. The rocking of the picket nearly was the end of him. It reminded him no less of bucking a bronco inside a log cabin. When he lost his stomach that time, he felt no guilt. All the other passengers had, as well. The captain, a seasoned old salt, brought them through with little damage to the ship or its charges, and within a day they arrived at the Port of Luanda in the country of Angola.

Quatermain waited for him on the beach as their dinghies came ashore. Short and almost ferret-like in appearance—especially with his wild, spiky hair—Kit's guide looked perturbed.

"You're two days late," he said, as if Kit had anything to do about it. The man had a British accent tinged with what Kit assumed was some of the local dialect from having lived so long in Africa.

Kit nodded. "Sorry." He gathered his supplies from another boat, only to turn around and discover Quatermain already halfway back up the beach.

When he caught up, the reputed hunter had walked through the door of an inn. Quatermain approached the front desk, signed a ledger, and was handed a key from the owner. He, in turn, handed the key to Kit.

"Dinner is at four," Quatermain said, as a matter-of-fact. "We leave two hours before sunrise to make some distance before the heat gets unbearable. I know some places we can rest, then head out again to make the first camp before it gets too dark." Then the hunter tilted his hat and made to leave.

"Can ye bear it?"

Quatermain stopped and regarded Kit.

"I'm sorry, but what?"

Kit repeated, "This heat. If yer weren't with me, would ye stop?"

Quatermain raised an eyebrow. "Probably not, but I'm us—"

"Then *we* don't need to stop."

"Are you stupid or a fool?" Quatermain asked.

Kit shook his head. "Neither. I've spent a fair share of time in deserts. As long as we have supplies, it should be fine."

The hunter tilted his head back and laughed, drawing attention to them from other people in the lobby. When he finished, Quatermain challenged, "This isn't your territories, Carson. The Kalahari Desert is unforgiving. Consider yourself fortunate you have me as your guide." He waved his hand as if to indicate the rest of the world that wasn't him. "Others have tried to cross it, only for me to find their carcasses being picked apart by jackals."

"Hear tell the Mojave Desert once got into the hundred-twenties. Can't rightly say I was thar, but I've had water in my canteen turn to steam before I could wet my lips."

Quatermain studied Kit intensely, apparently in an attempt to gauge whether he was exaggerating. Slowly, the man nodded.

"Fine, we won't stop other than to rest the camels." He squinted at Kit. "You know how to ride a camel, correct?"

Kit nodded. "This fella brought a buncha 'em over to the territories, thinkin' to breed 'em. When no one would buy, he let 'em loose. Not before he taught me how to ride."

Quatermain eyed Kit and hmmm'd, before saying, "We should make the first camp before sundown, which is good." He turned again to leave, but asked Kit over his shoulder. "Why?"

"'Why,' what?"

"Why don't you want to stop? Why are you even here, Carson?"

As Kit walked past Quatermain for the stairs up to their rooms, he answered exactly as Quatermain'd asked the question, over his shoulder and with the same dry tone.

"I'd think stoppin' a war worth a little discomfort and expediency, don't ye?"

~

'I'd think stopping a war worth a little discomfort and expediency'? I recited to no one, once back in my room.

What arrogance! Not that he was incorrect, of course, but I suspect he will be begging for a rest halfway to our camp. And maybe even want to turn around before we reach the Zambezi River. Certainly, he has never crossed this large of a desert.

For a man I had read had a larger-than-life reputation, it was shocking to find him only slightly taller than me, barrel-chested, blue-eyed with light hair; he did not match the description of a man who had not only fought against entire tribes of natives back in the colonies, but also forced those same tribes to lay down arms in lieu of peace treaties. He carried with him an impressive array of weapons. I had not seen a Hawkins rifle before, but the Colts were as familiar as the ones I wore.

Even as we began our travels together, Carson kept his questions brief, and his replies to my own even briefer. The only way I was able to gauge his abilities were by the questions he asked.

"What'r the Jecha's gods like?"

"How do thar leaders get chosen?"

"Whar did each tribe originate? What'r the foods they prefer?"

And on and on as we crossed the Kalahari. Now, these were all solid inquiries aimed at discerning the mindset of the missing Jecha. But he did not ask them in any sort of order, nor all at once. Hours could go by between questions, and he never asked one personal one of me. I, however, did ask questions of his life, to better understand who I was dealing with. For my efforts, I learned he had one daughter from a previous marriage, and a couple from his current.

This was the one place where we found a connection. We were both widowers. He having lost his two wives, as had I. But even upon that reveal, he just nodded, as if that information was enough, and he had no inclination to delve farther.

Infuriating, to say the least.

The night of the first camp, Carson asked more specific questions of the Kundagi and the Jecha.

"Why'r the tribes ready to start fightin' again, and how does this thar tusk play into it?" He indicated the satchel he never let out of his sight. He only opened it once to show me that, indeed, he possessed the Oliphant.

"Ah," I said, as I leaned back against the rock I used as a makeshift chair. "That is an old story. It starts when the son of the Kundagi's medicine man, Fwaza, saved the life of the son of the chief of the Jecha, Kazinape.

"The Jecha were bushmen, and the Kundagi, river people. These two powerful tribes had fought over resources for many years, each coming away from the conflict bloodied. Peace was never discussed, nor was it wanted.

"Then came the day Kazinape fell into the swollen Zambezi River and was swept down toward a large waterfall. Knowing that the boy'd never survive the drop, Fwaza dove in after him and pulled him to safety. Kazinape had taken a nasty hit to the skull, so Fwaza bandaged him up and made sure he was well.

"Embarrassed, Kazinape swore Fwaza to secrecy. If his father ever found out he'd been rescued by an enemy, his father would cast him out of the tribe, and he'd never rise to lead his people.

"Taking pity on him, Fwaza agreed, though in the back of his mind, he knew someday that information would could in handy.

"Decades later, Kazinape became chief of the Jecha tribe and Fwaza ascended to chief witch of the Kundagi tribe. Resources had dwindled along the Zambezi after a drought, and the Jecha sent word that they'd launch one last fight for the control of the land. Whichever tribe lost would have to leave the Zambezi area and find another place to live.

"Fwaza messaged Kazinape secretly to meet. When the chief arrived, Fwaza begged for him to reconsider his course of action. When Kazinape couldn't be dissuaded, the medicine man said if he would not stop their attack, then he'd be forced to reveal their secret past, forcing Kazinape to be removed as chief.

"Kazinape, out of panic, killed Fwaza."

"That's horrible, but also predictable."

I nodded. "Fwaza knew that was a possibility. He also believed that his death might have…other consequences. Which it did."

Carson perked up.

Since I had a rapt audience, I finished the tale with a flourish. "Kazinape, overcome with guilt, went back to his people broken. He had owed Fwaza his life and slew his friend, instead. The chief went before his people, revealed the truth, and sent a message saying that the Jecha would leave the Zambezi.

"Instead of accepting, the Kundagi offered for the two tribes to share resources as one tribe, which was what Fwaza had wanted. Kazinape stepped down as chief. The Kundagi took over as the leaders of both tribes, and the Jecha filled in the medicine man vacancy, though he is really the voice his people. This is how they have remained at peace for so long. Kazinape carved the Oliphant in tribute and gave it to the Kundagi."

Carson threw another branch into our fire, sending up sparks before speaking. "What changed?"

"When the Zambezi flooded generations later, the local Masons helped the Kundagi and Jecha tribes relocate until such time as they could return to their territory. The Kundagi offered the Oliphant to the Masons in thanks, only they hadn't consulted with the Jecha before doing so.

"Time passed and the son of the current Kundagi chief and the daughter of the Jecha's medicine man fell in love and wanted to marry. The Oliphant, which is supposed to be brought out for exactly such an event, was no longer there. The Kundagi admitted what happened, which upset the Jecha. They left their once peaceful arrangement, hid, and began raiding Kundagi camps for supplies. The Kundagi, still not wanting to turn on their mostly intermingled tribesmen, have tried to avoid war, ultimately sending a messenger to the Freemasons asking for their gift back."

"That's whar I come in."

I nodded. "They've hidden from me in such a way that all my normal tracking techniques are useless."

"How are ye so familiar with these tribes?"

I nodded, expecting this question. "I've explored a good deal of the southern continent, Carson. Every inch that has been seen by a white man, I've traveled and, indeed, blazed many a new trail myself. I've used both Kundagi and Jecha as guides along parts of the Zambezi and traded with them. They've shared their tales, and I've shared mine."

Carson did not ask any other questions that night, choosing instead to turn in without nothing more than a tip of his oversized cowboy hat.

Again, infuriating.

But before Carson reached his tent, I heard the soft sounds of padded feet on sand. The growl that accompanied them I knew as clearly as I knew my own heartbeat, which now sounded loudly in my ears. I always keep my double shot rifle nearby and reached for it slowly as I whispered loudly to Carson, "Stand still."

He froze to the spot, and I saw him tilt his head slightly, in an attempt to hear what I had.

The jackals' eyes blinked on as each member of the hunting pack stepped close enough for them to reflect the dying firelight. They must be very hungry to approach this close to the fire.

Carson methodically unhooked his sidearm. "I count four."

By then, the dogs had stepped a little closer. "Six," I corrected quietly. "Two will patrol the parameter, in case their prey manages to get by the others."

"Not all that different from coyotes. Three apiece, then."

That arrogance, once more. I could probably get all six, but I would have to shoot two with the double shot, and then switch to my pistol. Or I might stab or club another two. I expected Carson would manage one, if he was a fair shot. Still, I gave him a nod and got my gun ready to fire.

When the jackals launched, my first shot struck true, but its echo still hung in the air when two additional jackals lay dead next to it. So focused had I been on my target, I did not witness Carson draw his Colts. I shot the fourth as it turned to flee, but Carson was already on the move.

With adept skill, he grabbed his Hawkins rifle and scrambled up the large rock we had chosen to camp next to. As Carson lay across its peak, scanning the darkness, he pulled back his hammer, and fired.

My ears rejected the sound that came after the report of his gun—the cry of a jackal as Caron's .54 calibre bullet struck and killed it. He reloaded quicker than any man I had ever seen, cleaning, pouring, tapping, then scanned the darkness before firing again, producing the same results; moonlight as his only guide. I judged the second jackal at nearly two hundred yards from our camp.

My jaw hung loose as he slid back down the rock.

"Sorry. I got carried away." Carson pulled a large knife from his belt sheath and set to butchering the jackals in our camp.

"What *are* you doing?" I asked, dumbfounded.

He looked up and tilted his head, not that all different from the very thing jackals did when they were confused.

"What? Are they not good eatin'?"

I stammered, "Well, no, I mean, they're tough, but edible when you've nothing else."

Carson nodded, and continued with his task. "We might be trackin' the Jecha for some time. Best to supplement supplies when ye can." Without looking at me, he asked, "Can ye throw some more wood on the fire? I want to get to smokin' before daylight."

∼

Three days in, Kit still didn't know why he'd been told to work with Quatermain. Sure, the fellow knew the tribal histories and his way around, but Kit could have hired any guide for that.

It wasn't until the fourth day that he understood.

When they spotted the six riders approaching from a good way off, Quatermain stiffened noticeably.

"What?"

"Portuguese treasure hunters. My guess is Xandin Moura. He and his type disguise themselves as legitimate businessmen looking for gold deposits, but really, they can smell a historical artifact a hundred feet away."

"Then we should keep them about a hundred and one, agreed?"

Kit pulled out his Hawkins. As he sighted on the lead rider, Quatermain urged caution. "Carson, these are not the sort we want to get in a shooting war with."

At about one hundred and two feet away, Kit put a bullet in the sand, directly in front of the lead horse. The animal reared back, but the rider didn't fall off. The rest of his team held up fast. Many of them drew pistols or rifles. By then, Kit had already reloaded and reacquired his target.

"Is that Allan Quatermain I do see there?" the leader said in an accent so thick, Kit only understood the man's question through context.

"That it is, Moura. You'll have to excuse my friend here, he's American. I'm sure you've heard that they tend to get a little 'shoot first, ask questions later,' when they see a group of riders bearing down on them."

That garnered Quatermain some chuckles from the Portuguese.

"Ah, an American, eh? That wouldn't be the legendary Kit Carson, would it?"

Kit didn't need to take his eyes off his target to feel the weight of his guide's stare on him.

"And what if it is?" Quatermain asked cautiously.

Moura waved his hand above his big, floppy hat, as if news of Kit's arrival was in the air. "Well, it seems he traveled here on a picket with some very good friends of mine who just happened to also be crewing said sailing ship."

"Yep, so?" Kit asked.

Moura's men fanned out to form a semi-circle around the pair of hunters. "Well, it seems, Mr. Carson…May I call you Kit?"

"I'd reckon not, seein' how yer tryin' to get the jump on us. Doesn't seem the sort of action people who use first names would do."

Moura laughed in a way that reminded Kit of the French or the Russians he'd met along the trail. He laughed with complete disregard for whether anyone thought him crazy.

When he stopped, he said, "You may very well have an excellent point there, Mr. Carson. For you see, apparently while you were enjoying the sights of the open sea, one of my friends went through your belongings in your cabin and found a most interesting item." Moura and his men moved closer. "It may even be called remarkable."

Quatermain growled.

Kit leaned his head slightly so he could say, "Thought someone was tryin' to steal it. Didn't rightly think they'd been a scout."

Then Quatermain sighed, long and hard. The type of sigh Kit had heard from generals when he came back from an Indian hunting party, only to tell them he'd brokered a peace with said natives.

"And what would be your interest in this item, should it actually exist?" Quatermain asked.

"That is a very, very good question." Moura put his fingers to his chin and tapped them. His large, sharp nose practically wiggled as he did. "I could keep it for myself. From what I heard, it would look very good on my mantle, would it not?" Some of Moura's men agreed. "But that doesn't keep food on the table, or on the tables of my fellow businessmen here, does it? No, I think I will have to sell it at auction to the highest bidder."

Quatermain shook his head. "No good. It's not of the quality you think. It's not from a master artiste from Italy carving intricate designs on a tusk brought to him by an elephant hunter. I've seen it, Moura, and it doesn't even have enough ivory to buy your men a round of drinks."

Moura clucked like an old hen. "Tsk, tsk, Allan...now, *you* I can call Allan, seeing as we have history. Allan, I will just have to see this item for myself, and determine if what you say is the truth. If it is, then maybe you two leave here without being waylaid by us but for a few mere moments. However...denying me my chance to look and make such a deduction myself...?" Moura moved closer so that Kit could see the determination in his blue eyes. "It will not turn out good for either of you, Allan, and I will *still* see the item."

Kit wondered how long his guide was going to stall the inevitable. They were going to be gunned down, but not before he and Quatermain killed at least half of them. Kit was sure he could get this Moura fella, and the one to his right. He caught a glimpse out of the corner of his eye as Quatermain's hand slid to his side iron, but could he draw it and shoot at least two more thieves in time?

Kit doubted it.

And then Quatermain's hand slid away from the gun, and he smiled. He smiled widely. In fact, he sat back on the saddle of his camel and downright looked pompous. "Carson, put your gun down." Quatermain waved his hand down to emphasize his words.

The tracker raised an eyebrow, reluctant to lose his sights on Xandin.

"Kit?" Quatermain said, more urgently, through the side of his mouth. "It's very important you lower your gun, right...now."

Sensing there was more going on than he knew, Kit released the hammer on the Hawkins and slid the gun back into the holster along his back. Kit, no longer focused on his target, realized what Quatermain was up to.

Moura got the wrong message. "Excellent, Allan. Now, *Mister* Carson, if you would do me the courtesy..." He extended his hand, as if Kit would just hand the Oliphant to him.

But Quatermain interrupted. "Actually, no."

Moura scrunched his face. "'No?'" He looked to his men. "Why does he say, 'no'?" Turning back, he asked Quatermain. "Why do you say, 'no'? I have several guns to your...well, none, Allan. These odds are not in your favor."

"No… you may *not* call me Allan. That's reserved for those I consider friends. Though, the *Zhu Twa Si* have other names for me. Mostly, they translate to 'he who deals fairly,' or 'he who would bleed for them,' or 'the man we owe a really big favor to, and who we now finally get to pay back.' Though that last one's just a guess, eh, Tuma?"

Two dozen savages appeared almost out of nowhere, but Kit had seen their slight movements as they crawled into position around the six men on horseback. They carried spears, bows, knives, and cudgels, many of which now were pressed against the throats or temples of Xandin's men.

One of the Zhu, wearing a top hat, smiled at Quatermain and said a few words in a language Kit couldn't understand.

"Why, no. You cannot eat these men, Tuma. They were just leaving… that is, after they wish us a safe journey. You were about to do that, weren't you, Moura?"

Moura nodded, noticeably not liking the new odds.

The Zhu disarmed the Portuguese treasure seekers, and Moura motioned with his head for them to turn around.

But it was Quatermain's turn to cluck at the thief. "Tsk, tsk, *Mister* Moura. But I didn't hear the wish for our continued safety. Isn't that right, Kit?"

"That's right."

One of the bushmen poked Moura's leg with a spear. The thief ground his teeth, but called over his shoulder, "I wish you and Mister Carson a safe journey, Mister Quatermain."

Quatermain nodded satisfaction. "And to you and your men, too. And when I see you again, let's have that drink, shall we?"

Xandin Moura and his bandits rode off without another word.

Once they were out of sight, the one Quatermain called Tuma came up beside Quatermain as he dismounted. They began to laugh heartily together.

"I did not say what you tell them, Allan," Tuma said, in almost perfect English. "I say, 'Nice horse. If I kill him, I keep?'"

"I was paraphrasing, old friend." Quatermain turned and addressed Kit. "Carson, this is Tuma, leader of the Zhu bushmen in this area. We've been 'joking family' for many years."

"We not joke with many outside the tribe," Tuma explained, after returning Kit's nod of greeting. "And even less we not… intimate with." He waggled his eyebrows at Kit, which made the pathfinder uncomfortable. "And we not call him any of camel shit he say. We call him 'blue-eyed menace,' or my wife call him 'the one who brings trouble' every time he show up." Tuma and Quatermain laughed again, as did most of Tuma's people.

That night, Kit and Quatermain ate with the Zhu people—which Kit learned were also called the !*Kung*, but found that hard to say, as they used this strange click at the beginning. The African version of venison they ate, made from *oryx*, a gazelle-type animal, really didn't taste all that different from what he'd had back in the states, which both relaxed him *and* made him homesick.

Often Tuma and Quatermain would switch from English to the Zhu's native tongue. At one point, Quatermain asked Kit to show Tuma the Oliphant. Tuma nodded appreciatively, and their discussion became more animated.

Before they turned in for the night, Kit asked what all the hullabaloo was about.

Quatermain slapped Kit on the shoulder and, grinning, said, "Tuma's heard a rumor of what region of the Zambezi we might find the Jecha."

"Really?"

His guide nodded. "We've got another two days' ride, but we must hurry." Then he got serious. "The rumor also says the Jecha plan to wipe out the Kundagi in three days."

~

At the next night's camp, I could tell something bothered Carson. He had not said much during the day's travel, choosing instead to focus on the hard ride we had to make. Tuma had warned me the Jecha had sent word to the Kundagi that if the Oliphant was not back in their possession in what would be two days now, they would strike from the shadows and destroy every living man, woman, and child.

They were not just planning war, but eradication.

Certain tribes had honor codes that went beyond the white man's understanding. Apparently, presenting a gift that had been given to you to someone else is a great sin akin to defecating on the original gifter. Even after many decades of the two tribes intermingling, they kept their identities as separate as possible, praying to separate gods, hunting in different ways, and for different things. The Kundagi, being the river people, handled the fishing, and the Jecha hunted game. Where they had come together was farming, which they shared equally, until the slight.

On the way out, the Jecha had burned the fields, taking that year's harvest with them. This weakened the Kundagi, who no longer had enough of the season left to grow new crops. They were able to fish and trade with other, friendlier tribes, but their way of life had been shattered. It demoralized them, as many had families, sons or daughters, brothers and sisters, with the Jecha. They did not want to go to war.

"Yep," Carson said from beside the campfire. "Same thing happened with the Reds in the territories. Nothin' civil 'bout war."

I agreed.

Carson finally revealed what had been plaguing his mind.

"Interestin' relationship ye got thar with the savages."

I gave him an incredulous stare. "You mean Tuma and the Zhu?"

He nodded.

"Well, first, they're *not* savages, they are *bushmen*, and while they don't have what scholars back home might call a 'classical education,' they're very intelligent. You saw how they made use of the land. How they outsmarted Moura's thieves."

Carson nodded again. "I don't mean they can't learn. Part of the problem with trackin' the Reds back home is how smart they are. Same with these fellas we're chasin' har. Smarter than most." He threw a cleaned jackal rib bone into the fire, sending up some sparks. "I just mean, when I meet their kind, they'r as likely to kill ye as save ye."

I seemed to understand what he was getting at. "Ah, why'd they rescue us, you mean? Or more, specifically, why'd they rescue *me*?"

"If they was Apache, they woulda waited until we shot each other up, then killed whoever was left."

I laughed. "Well, certainly there're tribes here that would do the same, but much like your Apache, they all have their reasons."

That soured Carson's face. "Ain't no reason to slaughter a man, let alone women and children."

"Oh, really?" Now my face scrunched up. "Taking someone's sacred land away from them? Killing them without provocation? Turning them into slaves, in many cases?"

Carson sat up straighter. "We try to work with them, and those who did, we got along with fine."

My voice raised a few octaves, and I threw my own smoked jackal meat into the fire. I no longer had the appetite. "Oh, do come on. Certainly you cannot believe that. Your government has not kept an agreement since before it was a government."

"Maybe we just don't like unfair contracts." He stood and turned toward his tent, obviously not wanting to further discuss the matter, but I was far from satisfied.

"Unfair? To whom? To the privileged land barons, or the rail barons, or even to your self-righteous Yanks, who can't even honor laws between the upper and lower parts of their country?"

Pausing mid-step, Carson spun to face me. "Oh, like y'all do with the Irish? They wouldn't be comin' over in droves to our country if ye treated them with an ounce of respect."

I stood. "How'd we get on to the Irish? This was about the savag—I mean, your Indians. The people *you* personally killed by the hundreds, maybe thousands, just because they were in the way of good ol' American progress."

Carson raised an eyebrow, but not his voice. "Whar'd ye get that idea? Maybe I killed a hundred total, tho' I can't rightly say, as many a time I was hidin' behind a rock, or runnin' away, or that war a bunch of us firin' and hard to tell who shot who."

"Not according to this," and I pulled from my inner jacket pocket the copy of *Kit Carson, Prince of the Gold Hunters*, that I had gone back to retrieve after initially leaving it on the café table. "Though I'd say Averill's description of you is off. You are certainly no 'mountain of a man.' You're five six, if you're an inch."

Lips tightened; Carson reached out a hand for the book.

Begrudgingly, I handed it over.

He tossed it on the fire.

"Hey!" I shouted, and began to reach for it, but the pages were already aflame.

"Thar was this lady, Ann White, who got taken by the 'Che. They'd had her for weeks. Tortured her. Did other stuff I won't even say, but ye can imagine. I'd been hired to rescue her, but by the time I got thar, they'd butchered her. I found her body still warm."

I shuddered at his story. Really, it was the most he'd said in one breath.

"She'd a copy of the damnable book in her stuff. I'd been made into some great hero." He directed his gaze at me and, in his eyes, he revealed the true man—the intensity of emotion that he kept bottled up inside. "I've often thought that Mrs. White prayed for my arrival, and that she'd be saved. She'd held out hope for deliverance by a man who never existed."

Carson walked away from me and the fire, but before entering his tent, he said, "I swore I'd burn every one of those books I find."

~

Kit and Quatermain reached the rainforest bordering the Zambezi half a day earlier than they expected. It was primarily due to the lack of conversation between them. It made travel that much faster.

Kit was uncomfortable talking about himself under the best of circumstances and reluctant to reveal the type of feelings he'd let out of the barn the previous night. He felt guilty afterwards, but for what reason, he wasn't sure. He couldn't have hurt the Brit's feelings, as Quatermain'd been the one to attack him. He should've known, though, as the hunter was far from the first Kit had run across that took those fanciful notions as truth. Hell, he started to wonder if shouldn't've asked if Quatermain'd read the book when they first met? Clearly, the man had a burr in his saddle from the get-go.

Still, that didn't make it right. How would the prim, proper English gent like it if someone wrote books about him that got all the facts wrong? Exaggerated *his* character? Kit didn't think it'd sit too well with him, either.

The desert gave way to grasslands and that became marshes for a spell before Kit finally saw the tree line that bordered the Zambezi River. Kit had only ever seen 'palm' trees in Florida before leaving for Africa. These, and the "Waterberry" trees mixed in with them, had lush green and yellow leaves. Other trees they passed had seeds looking no less like giant sausages. Kit wanted to crack one open to see inside, but Quatermain wordlessly pointed to a wholly different group.

That copse had small, yellow fruits. The hunter pulled one down and tossed it over his shoulder for Kit to catch, then demonstrated how to peel it open. The outer pulp was sticky and sweet, and the inner core tasted tart.

Quatermain said, upon chuckling at Kit's scrunched face, "Dates are much better dried, but edible either way…in case we 'run low on provisions.' I wouldn't want to be downwind of you, or you I, if we made a diet of them raw." He tipped his hat to Kit, which Kit returned. "Well, oh great tracker of men, where do we begin?"

Kit thought on this, and everything he'd learned about the Jecha.

"We need someplace whar no one would think they'd go."

Quatermain coughed like he'd a date stuck in his throat. When he stopped, he looked back at Kit. "That's all you have? Certainly, not. I've thought of that already. I searched the least likely places. I traveled up and down this river, looking for signs of footprints, broken palm branches, disturbed rocks. They're nowhere by this river."

"They'r nowhar *by* this river," Kit repeated. "They'r *in* the river."

The Brit nearly fell off his camel. "What?"

Kit nodded. "Ye talked about how adaptable the Jecha were right from the start. I found it puzzlin' that, for all thar combinin' of the tribes, they kept certain tasks separate. The Jecha hunted on land, the Kundagi on the river. Why? Why not also learn to fish on the river? Because that was the Kundagi's domain, whar they were most comfortable, whar they felt safest."

Quatermain's expression showed he understood where Kit was leading him. "So, if their tribes ever went back to war, the Kundagi would never expect an attack *coming* from the river. They'd prepare for battle with the Jecha coming via land."

"The Kundagi," Kit continued, "never planned for war. They thought their treaty would hold. After all, it was they that offered forgiveness and peace. It's in their nature to trust."

"But the Jecha, the ones whose leader slew his friend, never believed the peace would last forever. So, they must've planned for this day in secret for decades." Quatermain rubbed his forehead with a kerchief. The first time Kit had seen the man sweat from something other than the heat. "The raids weren't for supplies, but just to weaken their enemy. They already had all the supplies they needed."

Kit agreed. "They learned how to use the river to their advantage from the Kundagi…innocently, subtly."

Realization hit Quatermain, and Kit was delighted that his guide was finally on the same path as he'd been on for days. "Building boats, storing them somewhere. Probably weapons, as well."

Kit agreed. "Enough weapons to slaughter an entire tribe."

"Guns."

"Dynamite, maybe."

"But where?"

Kit got off his camel and retrieved a machete from his saddlebags. "One of my expeditions, we came across these falls in California I swore were five hundred feet high. We bathed under them, and discovered a cave had been made by water worryin' the rocks over so many years."

Quatermain joined him and, without acknowledging the task at hand, also drew out a blade. They began hacking at the palm trees along the river. "The falls where it all began. Where Fwaza saved Kazinape. They're huge *and*, because they're considered to be sacred by both tribes…"

"Or at least to the Kundagi…"

"No one would think to look for them under them."

After making solid progress on enough wood for their raft, they cut vines from the trees. Both men obviously knew how to make a boat, so without needing to task the other, they worked harmoniously.

Quatermain showed Kit how to use the palm tree sap to make their raft watertight. Kit carved a rudder the way he'd learned from Lewis and Clark. Within a few hours, they had a craft worthy of the Colorado River.

"Upstream or downstream?" Kit asked.

Quatermain decided downstream.

"Ye sure?"

Quatermain nodded, but Kit thought there was a slight look of uncertainty. "This area hasn't been explored much, due to the occasional flooding, land wars, and Boer conflict. I've sent letters back to the World Explorers Society asking them to fund an expedition out here, so we would have better maps. I hear a Dr. Livingstone is at the top of their list, but it might be awhile before he can get all the necessary materials together."

Despite Lewis and Clark's success, Kit knew governments preferred to hire pathfinders like him, or scouts from the various tribes. He cost a lot less, and if something happened to him, they lost one good man as opposed to a whole team.

They loaded the boat with their supplies and left enough lead for the camels to reach the river for water, should they need it. After testing the boat for buoyancy, they launched.

"Sorry, no champagne."

Kit stared at him. "What's that?"

Surprised, Quatermain explained how many of the Queen's vessels were launched by breaking a champagne bottle over the bow.

"No, I mean what's 'sham-pain'?"

Kit never drank more than whiskey or the occasional beer. What Quatermain described sounded as pompous as the idea of breaking a bottle of it each time a boat set sail. He'd rather be given a can of coffee for the voyage and a nice flask of some of the stuff St. Vrain certainly kept in his desk. That would be all the luck he needed.

∼

About three hours after we launched, a shadow passed overhead. I shielded my eyes when I looked up, expecting to see a rain cloud—something not entirely unexpected, and most certainly welcome in the afternoon heat.

What I found up there was neither expected nor welcomed.

The hot air balloon had a large basket under it. Two of Xandin Moura's men cranked handles which turned large fans that moved the airship briskly across the sky. Moura, himself, looked down on us through a telescope and, I assumed, smiled menacingly.

There were five men in total, with two thieves crammed at the back to avoid the elbows of their air-ship mates. My guess was Moura had the four rotating in shifts all night to catch up to us. I pulled out my own scope to discover Moura lighting the first stick of TNT.

"Um, Carson? Kit?"

Carson had been at the rudder, asleep, still managing to keep us steady in the water—more for the river's current, I was sure, than any effort on his part. I understood all too well the need to catch sleep where one could, but when I called to him, he awoke instantly alert, one hand still on the rudder, the other on his drawn sidearm. His eyes darted from one side of the river to the other.

I pointed up.

He slowly raised his gaze just as Moura dropped the first bomb.

It went off well behind us, causing only a small ripple that merely bounced us up and down. I knew, and Carson seemed to as well, that would not stay true for long.

He pulled up the rudder and grabbed one of the two oars. The other he tossed to me.

I set it down and instead retrieved my double shot. "We cannot out-paddle them, but if we put a few holes in that air sack of theirs, that *should* slow them down."

Kit agreed and retrieved his Hawkins.

The second explosion rocked us left to right. We had to steady ourselves.

"Man who shoots the least holes in it catches lunch?" Kit suggested.

"That *is* a very sporting challenge considering I can fire twice to your once. Oh, and I happen to like tiger fish. You'd better get a pole ready."

Kit kneeled and fired. I fired from a standing position.

I had fired both rounds and set to reloading when Kit fired his second shot. Damn that man! I know his gun was lighter, but a Hawkins was a muzzle loader while my Express was a breech. I should be able to outshoot him, but by skipping the cleaning process and risking the barrel exploding, this mountain man reloaded and reacquired faster than I could.

Our first shots hit, producing holes, and the escaping air pressure would make them bigger, but we still set about to fire again. My two shots, Kit's one then another right after.

The two non-cranking thieves had also brought rifles, much to our mutual dismay. They were not aiming for our transport, but at us.

Fortunately, at that distance they were not good shots, but soon they would be close enough to increase their odds of success.

Kit missed his next shot as the concussion blast of another explosion threw off his aim. The larger wave it caused sent me down to the floor of the boat and my gun went off above us.

Our holes were having an effect, just not the desired one. The balloon descended closer to us quickly, as Moura's men cranked harder than they had before. They would be in better firing range soon.

I did not need to see Moura light the fuse. He was close enough for me to hear it. Kit and I looked at each other, and without so much as another word, dove over the respective sides of the boat. We had barely hit the water before the boat shattered.

The rifles were gone, and while we still had our sidearms, I doubted they could ignite the powder now. I prepared to be riddled with bullets, but then I saw why we had not, as of yet.

Or, at least, Carson had not. He floated on his back, letting the current take him, with the satchel containing the Oliphant held tightly to his chest. They risked shooting it if they shot him.

Moura swore and grabbed one of the two shooters, throwing him out of the balloon, which was about thirty feet above the river now. The man plummeted head first, his scream not covering his boss's command to "Fetch!" Moura turned to the other gunner, who took it upon himself to jump out of the balloon, feet first.

As they surfaced and began swimming toward us, I noticed that the current had picked up some. Kit did, too.

"Waterfall?" He mouthed the word to me. I nodded.

I drew my knife and placed in between my teeth, angling my trajectory to get closer to Kit. The pathfinder had drawn his as well, placing it on top of the bag as if to say anyone trying to get the Oliphant would face imminent death.

Moura had his men turn the balloon toward the shore, and it landed in a grassy area, the bag collapsing over the basket.

The swimmers focused on Kit, seeing as he was the one hampered by luggage. I dove under the water and kicked hard against the current to get below one of the two. I buoyed up, knife held in both hands, and gutted one of the potential killers.

He did not have time to do anything but scream and grab his stomach, trying to hold in his bowels. He floated away from us.

The second thief had gotten close enough to Kit that the pathfinder had to kick him. This caused Carson to spin in the water, leaving his back open to the knife-wielding assassin. But no one really teaches you how to fight in a river with a rapidly increasing current caused by a rapidly approaching waterfall. The man made several jabs, but each time Kit rotated back up, Moura's thuggee got a boot to the head.

The roar of the waterfall had reached us, but I still thought it a ways off. It almost covered the sound of the shot from the shore. Moura and his men, safely extracted from their crashed balloon, now took shots at us, including endangering their own man. He even looked over at them, eyebrows furrowed in anger.

Moura shouted, "Well, if you don't want shot, get the tusk!"

The killer redoubled his efforts, and Moura's men aimed at me exclusively. I dove down and stayed down as long as I could, making sure to surface in a different location, and only long enough for a breath, before heading back down. I knew I would not be able to do this forever. I tried to get close to Kit, who kicked in a frog-like way at his assailant.

I got an idea. I positioned myself under Kit, and when he spun over the next time, I yanked him down, trading places and coming up with the knife at the ready. The blade caught the killer in the throat, but I took his knife to my shoulder in exchange. I pulled his blade free as mine went under with him.

Kit surfaced near me. We both took breaths and dove under again. The scout tapped his shoulder, which I thought meant he was concerned about mine. I waved it off. He instantly tapped both his shoulders this time, and I figured out his plan.

I would have only one chance, but I could not reason any other options other than go over the falls and hope to survive.

I took the satchel from Kit and hung it over my chest. We swam closer to shore, until we could see the silhouettes of Moura and two men, though I could not tell from under water who was whom. I tucked into a ball, and Kit got under me, my feet on his shoulders.

Then, in a move that had absolutely no way to work, Kit Carson pushed hard against the river bed, lifting me up and out of the water.

Moura's men aimed at me, but upon seeing the satchel around my neck, hesitated.

And in that split second, I threw the knife at the closest one, placing the dagger right between his eyes. I missed him dying as I crashed back into the water.

When Kit and I came up for air the next time, Moura and the remaining thief still stood next to their fallen comrade, staring down at his lifeless form, looks of disbelief on their faces.

∼

Two men waited to kill them on shore.

A waterfall waited to kill them ahead.

Kit waited again for another breath of air.

He'd fallen into rapids before and had to extricate himself, but he'd never done it under attack. He'd normally wait until a river boulder presented itself to catch hold of, then he'd hang there a spell to see if someone would retrieve him. If not, he aimed himself toward the next rock closest to land, and so forth.

Sooner or later, a bullet would hit one of them. Or maybe the thieves would just let them go over the falls and retrieve the satchel later.

Then Kit figured it out. He motioned to Allan to start swimming toward the falls. The hunter's eyes got real wide, but he trusted Kit in that moment, and followed him. When they surfaced next, they'd gotten some distance on Moura and his remaining man.

The outlaws had to start running to keep up with them, no longer shooting.

Quick enough, Quatermain could shout over to him. "What's the plan here?"

Kit said, "Find somethin' to snag that bag on…hold tight…and wait for Moura to catch us."

"And then what?"

Kit smirked, an action he rarely did, and only when he knew he'd gotten the drop on someone.

"I kill them."

Allan furrowed his brow. "And what if I don't find something to secure ourselves to?"

Kit shrugged as best he could while swimming. "Are ye a prayin' man?"

As luck would have it, plenty of boulders, branches, even whole trees had been wedged in spots near the edge of the falls. Not enough to get to shore, but one tree lay there with branches big enough to wrap the satchel like an anchor.

Together, he and Allan huddled.

That's where they were when Moura and his sidekick reached them. Both were slightly out of breath.

Allan looked at Kit, who held up a hand for patience.

When Moura could talk again, he shouted loud enough to reach them. "We can retrieve you from there, gentlemen. We have a long enough rope back in our deflated balloon, but it will take us some time."

"And all you want is the tusk, not us, right?" Allan countered.

"Indeed, sir. Why would I kill you in cold blood, and risk having the many tribes you are friends with come after me in revenge? Maybe even your own son would hunt me down, someday."

Kit raised an eyebrow.

"I would've gotten around to telling you," Allan admitted. "Harry and I don't talk to each other anymore. Not much, by any manner. *You and I* have spoken more words to each other over the last several days, for what it's worth."

"No deal," Kit replied to Moura.

"So, what do you plan to do, my friends? I'm on dry land and can wait you out. You will either drown, starve, or go over the falls where I can just retrieve your body and the tusk later."

"Thar's another option," Kit said.

Moura laughed that same crazy laugh Kit hated. "And what would that be, *Mister* Carson?"

"This."

In the blink of an eye, Kit pulled open the satchel from around Allan's neck. There came with it a ripping sound as he did, the palm tree sap having done its job sealing the carrying case watertight. He drew out his Colt and shot both Xandin Moura and his man in the chest. They fell backwards and didn't move.

Allan was incredulous. "You had a dry gun and didn't use it before now?"

Kit shrugged. "I couldn't get a good aim. Had to wait until I wasn't movin'."

The hunter opened his mouth to say something, but destiny chose that moment to shift the tree they hung on to.

~

Kit slipped under our tree, while I remained secured, if loosely, by the satchel's strap. I caught his jacket, allowing him to grab hold of my arm.

"This isn't going to hold!" I yelled through gritted teeth.

"I...know." Kit studied me as water cascaded over his face. "I'm not...that...man. I...don't hate them...the Reds..."

"What?"

"My...first two...wives...Arapaho... and Cheyenne. My children...are half breeds."

"Why're you telling me this?"

Kit spit out water between words. "We're... goin' over. If...we die...I...want...ye...to know...what...kind... of ... man... ye died with."

"You're a good man, Kit," I told him, "and I'm honored to die with you."

The tree released at that moment, and we tumbled over the edge.

Let me explain to you, for a moment, what going over a four-hundred-foot waterfall is like, in case you never get to experience it.

Which I hope you do not.

Newton talked about gravity and its effect on the human body, but without any form of air travel in his times, he certainly would not have had any knowledge of defying it.

My stomach did not clench up the way it does when I have gone over a cliff, or when a horse bucks me. With a waterfall that high, my brain had no previous experience to compare the sensation to.

I flew!

My arms extended from my sides, and my jacket flapped in the wind. I felt weightless, as if Newton's theories had been proven wrong.

I reveled in the feeling...for about five seconds until I saw the river below rushing at me. Then my stomach clenched, my buttocks clenched, and I am sure I threw up jackal jerky.

Kit, who was only seconds below me, tucked himself into the shape of a bullet, hands at his sides, head back even with his shoulders, toes pointed down.

My mind told me he must know what he is doing. After all, he was Kit Carson, Prince of Gold Hunters. Scourge of the Indians. Mountain Man. Trail Blazer. He'd certainly gone over falls that high before. I would trust his experience.

I mimicked his posture, and did say a few words, but mostly to my son, who I hoped someday would forgive his adventuring father.

And, as I hit the water, I realized one more important thing about Kit Carson.

He did not know shi—

~

Kit Carson dragged Allan Quatermain to the shore. The man's left leg was at an odd angle.

They'd surfaced close enough to each other, that Kit, once his senses returned, could get the hunter under his arm and keep him from downing. On dry land, he turned Allan to his side, slapped his back until he coughed up what river water he'd swallowed, and sputtered a "that's enough."

When Allan rolled to his back, he sat up and grabbed his twisted limb, as if that would ease the pain.

Kit knew it wouldn't. His own shoulder had popped out of place, something that'd happened before, and he was sure he'd bitten a hole in his cheek the size of Texas. He flopped onto his back, spent.

"Ow! My leg! Bloody hell! You broke my bloody leg!" Quatermain rocked back and forth.

Kit knew that wouldn't help either.

"Actually, ye broke the leg. I was too busy to do it."

Between the cries of pain, Allan stopped for a moment to see if Kit was serious. When Kit smirked, Allan smirked. Soon they were both laughing.

After they finished, Kit asked the hunter to help get his shoulder back into place, then he gathered tree limbs and vines to make a splint.

"You've done this before?" Allan asked, as Kit prepared to slide his leg bones into relative alignment.

"Many times. Too many." He gave the hunter a stick to bite down on.

"Does this hel—OW! Goddamn, OW!"

"No," Kit admitted. "It's just to distract ye."

Within minutes, Kit had Allan's leg tightened up, and had even fashioned a crutch for him.

"Not bad, Mister Carson," Allan had to admit. "Not bad at all."

"I have my uses, Mister Quatermain."

Quatermain sighed. "And I have mine." He raised his hands, and Kit looked over to see a hundred African tribesmen surrounding them.

"Jecha, I presume?" Kit said, mimicking the hunter's form.

"Yes. I saw one of their scouts poke his head out from behind the waterfall."

"And ye didn't think to share that information?"

"You were busy…unbreaking my leg."

Kit growled.

Quatermain spoke the natives' language without any rise in his voice. He kept calm, despite the threat of instant death. Kit admired that. He'd been in similar situations and used that exact tone.

Finally, he said, "Kit? Please take the Oliphant from the satchel around my neck, slowly, while keeping your hands in view at all times."

Kit nodded. This one he knew, too.

Carefully, he used only one hand to lift the satchel's flap, glad to see the wooden box remained inside. He then reached in slowly and extracted the case. He straightened and brought the item around until he held it with both hands, then he methodically unwrapped it, praying to the almighty that a bullet hadn't chipped its surface, or that it hadn't shattered in their flight over the falls.

Before he opened the box, he peeked in and sighed relief.

Then Kit Carson lifted the Oliphant up over his head. In the last light of the sun, just as it was finishing its journey past the horizon, its rays embraced the carvings, flowing through them, and making them glow.

~

Carson...I mean, Kit and I stood by the docks in Cape Town. We had headed south instead of back across the Kalahari. The steamer ship leaving in the next couple of hours would be a much better journey home for the pathfinder than the picket that brought him to my continent. Our paths would cross only once more, as he died not too many years after we parted. I was informed he died happy, though, with many children. I hoped they would prosper.

"It was nice of yer Good Hope Freemasons to pay for the upgrade," Kit said.

"We *did* avert a war." I agreed it was the least they could do. I would be getting an increase in hazard pay, and the few months of oceanside recovery time I requested. As I leaned on my faux crutch—my leg having been remarkably healed by the Jecha's medicine man before we left the Zambeze Basin—I thought I could use some salt air—not to heal the body, but the soul.

The Jecha left after reclaiming the Oliphant. Their reason for war gone, but also their desire to remerge with the Kundagi. They vanished into the grasslands, the place they once called home, and I doubted I would see them again for some time.

We had won, but also lost.

The Kundagi, having been informed of the Jecha plans, and how long they had been making them, set about learning to defend themselves for the next time someone set their sights upon them. Gone was their hopeful naivety that peace could be found in any two tribes.

I disagreed with them. Kit and I shook hands heartily; an action I should have done much earlier. As Kit gathered up his African-made saddlebags and his new double-barrel rifle, I grew melancholy. He and I were not so different. Not really. We fought to protect those we loved. We grieved those we lost. We saw the world in a way few men did, and the few differences we had became that which brought us together, not divided us.

"Quatermain," he said.

"Carson."

Kit headed up the gangplank. He paused to ask the purser if he would see whales on the trip, to which the man nodded enthusiastically.

The American pathfinder turned one last time and tipped his new hat—a gift from me—and smiled.

I repeated the gesture.

And then Kit Carson returned to his world, and I returned to mine.

In Earth and Sky and Sea Strange Things There Be

Keith R.A. DeCandido

In 1886, H. Rider Haggard—creator of Allan Quatermain—wrote a novel simply called *She*. It was the story of three men of England who journeyed to a hidden kingdom in southern Africa that was ruled by an immortal white woman named Ayesha, also known as "she who must be obeyed." The novel was adapted into film several times in the earliest days of cinema, with six made between 1899 and 1925. Hammer Films did a version in 1965 starring Ursula Andress, and another film was done in 2001 starring Ophélie Winter. It's also been adapted for radio and theatre. Haggard brought the character back several more times in his fiction.

Haggard wrote the novel as a fictionalized account of a true journey—a common narrative trope of the era—and the following story, which takes place shortly after the turn of the 21st century, assumes that Haggard got at least *some* details right…

Keith R.A. DeCandido has written novels, short stories, and comic books in more than thirty different licensed universes over the past two-and-a-half decades, including TV shows (*Star Trek, Supernatural, Doctor Who, Buffy the Vampire Slayer, Farscape, Orphan Black*), movies (*Alien, Cars, Kung Fu Panda, Resident Evil, Serenity*), comics (Spider-Man, the Hulk, the Silver Surfer, Thor, the X-Men), and games (*World of Warcraft, Dungeons & Dragons, StarCraft, Classic BattleTech, Command & Conquer*). In 2009, the IAMTW granted him a Lifetime Achievement Award, which means he never needs to achieve anything ever again. Find out less at www.DeCandido.net.

In Earth and Sky and Sea Strange Things There Be

June 2002

"Agent LaManna. I wish I could say it's good to see you again, but that would be a lie."

"Ms. Yatie. Wish I could say I'm surprised to see you here—hang on, no, wait, that's the God's honest truth. I will say, though, that it really *is* a surprise to see you in *this* rotten condition."

"I will make a full recovery, worry not."

"I'm going through a whole lot of emotions, Ms. Yatie, and I gotta tell you, 'worry' don't even crack the top ten."

"What would be atop the list, then, Agent LaManna?"

"Amazement, mostly. You slipped on a wet floor. You broke your neck. You should've died. Yet here you are, sitting across from me in an interrogation room, under arrest, something I've been trying and failing to do for ten years. And the docs tell me that your neck is *healing*."

"And this amazes you?"

"Kinda does, yeah. How else am I supposed to react when someone gets a fatal injury and doesn't die?"

"It is but the latest of many I have suffered, Agent LaManna, and far from the most interesting. Or, indeed, far from the most mundane."

"You gonna tell me how you did that?"

"Did what?"

"Not die."

"That depends. Will you provide me with intelligence on how you managed to arrest me? My passport should not have triggered a single security measure."

"Because the guy who forged it for you's that good?"

"I refuse to answer that particular query, Agent LaManna."

"Cause it'd be admitting that you had a forged passport. You sound like a lawyer. Which makes me wonder why you don't have one with you."

"I was alive when Hammurabi wrote his code of law, and I have observed jurisprudence—"

"Oh, here we go."

"—in hundreds of different nations over thousands of years. I'm more well versed in the laws of the nations of this world than any lawyer I might hire. I do not require legal counsel. I do require that you inform me of the reasons for my arrest."

"Were you paying any attention last September when those two planes wiped out the World Trade Center?"

"I vaguely recall discussion of it."

"Vaguely? You kidding me?"

"I have seen far greater disasters in my time."

"Jesus, again with the crazy talk. Look, they changed the passports after 9/11. They're a crap-ton harder to forge now. In fact, it's pretty much impossible. I don't care how much you paid your guy, he ain't that good. Nobody is. And that ain't the half of it."

"What do you mean?"

"I mean, I been digging *real* deep into the life of Ayesha Yatie. Which, by the way, is a whole helluva lot easier now thanks to a brand-spanking-new American law you obviously *don't* know much about yet called the PATRIOT Act. And you know what we found out?"

"I await your answer with bated breath, Agent LaManna."

"It's *all* phony. Every. Last. Bit. So I gotta ask—who the *hell* are you?"

"Do you recall, Agent LaManna, the book I mailed you several years ago?"

"Yeah, that 19th-century piece of crap. *Her* or something."

"*She* by H. Rider Haggard."

"Right, that."

"Did you peruse it?"

"Yeah, I read it. Like I said, piece of crap. I figured you sent it 'cause the main character was also named Ayesha."

"In fact, the protagonist of that novel was myself."

"If I'm remembering right, the narrator kept talking about how Ayesha was white, which you definitely aren't. Also, she was the antagonist, not the protagonist."

"I suppose it depends on your point of view. In any case, Agent LaManna, let me rephrase: the character of Ayesha is *based* on me. You see, while Haggard's tome was a work of fiction, it was, in fact, based on true events."

"Uh huh."

"You doubt me?"

"Let's see, do I doubt that you've been alive for thousands of years?"

"Your sarcastic tone notwithstanding, Agent LaManna, this does, in fact, answer your query as to how I did not perish when I slipped and broke my neck. I cannot die."

"And you ruled a hidden country in Africa a hundred and fifteen years ago?"

"I did, in fact, do so, until three men sojourned to Kôr to seek me out. However, I must state very emphatically that I was *not* waiting for a reincarnation of my one true love. The men who journeyed to seek me out believed that, but it was utter nonsense. The lover they spoke of was an imbecile whom I was glad to be rid of. But his family and their descendants created the fiction that I still longed for him, and that story was exaggerated and passed down."

"So Job, Leo Vincey, and Horace Holly really existed, too?"

"Those were not their true sobriquets. Haggard changed their names, a consideration he did not extend to me, though he did alter my skin color to that of someone far paler than I, likely because he did not believe that the Victorian-era audience for his published account would accept anything but a white woman in the role."

"Yeah, the main reason why I thought the novel was crap? Was 'cause o' the whole white-savior-black-savage nonsense. Didn't really age well. But you're telling me, Ms. Yatie, that the basic story was true?"

"More or less. The trio whom Haggard renamed Vincey, Holly, and Job did indeed venture forth to Kôr. And their arrival made me realize

77

how much time had passed in the outside world, and I thought perhaps I should return to it and see how it had changed—and how I might perhaps thrive in it where I did not before."

"So you didn't die back then?"

"Heavens, no, Agent LaManna. There was no 'flame of Life,' as Haggard imagined—though I suppose that that might have come from the account he adapted rather than his own imagination. No, I'm afraid I know not the origin of my immortality, but it certainly is no 'flame of Life,' and I did not step in it only to shrivel up and die as Haggard wrote."

"I was kidding, Ms. Yatie."

"I was not, Agent LaManna."

"All right, fine, to quote my favorite movie, 'you're sick, I'll humor ya.' What happened after you left Africa?"

"I first traveled to Greece. I had previously spent many fine years there, and I thought it would be a good place to reintroduce myself to the world. Unfortunately, I arrived in time for war to break out between Greece and Turkey right around the turn of the century. I had hoped my wealth would protect me, but—"

"Wealth? You were rich then, too?"

"I had amassed quite the fortune before I decided to become a reclusive ruler in the so-called 'dark continent,' Agent LaManna, and the land I ruled had impressive veins of both gold and diamonds. I can assure you; my wealth has always been considerable."

"And yet, here you are, under arrest, and you still can't tell me who you really are."

"I've done nothing but tell you that, Agent LaManna."

"You ain't Ayesha Yatie. I got a crap-ton o' paperwork that tells me that you created that identity. The social security number you're using belongs to a nine-year-old kid who died in a car accident in 1959."

"If you will let me continue, Agent LaManna, I will explain. As I said, the broad strokes of what you read in Haggard's tome were truth, as far as it went. After the war in Asia commenced, I travelled west to Europe, attempting to settle in London. However, while my wealth purchased a measure of respect, it was a tiny measure that was in opposition to the disrespect that came with the color of my skin. A dark-skinned woman could not be a member of European high society in the early days of the 20th century unless she was an entertainer, which I most assuredly am not."

"Dunno, you're doing a pretty good job o' storytelling right now."

"I instead went east to India, passed myself off as a native of that land, and found a British nobleman to marry. As the wife of nobility, I was accorded the respect I deserved. I used the combined wealth of myself and my husband to fund hospitals in France during the so-called War to End All Wars. When that appellation proved inaccurate following the rise of Chancellor Hitler, I absconded to South America."

"Didn't think Nazis were worth fighting?"

"I have seen all manner of warfare, Agent LaManna, but the methods of the 20th century proved crueler and more appalling than any I had ever seen. The inventions of the aeroplane and the submarine removed all personal consequence from war, making it easier to kill without even seeing your target. It is despicable. Something amuses you?"

"I ain't never heard anybody call it an 'aeroplane' outside of an old movie before, is all. And honestly? Killing is horrible no matter how you do it."

"Yes, but when you engage with rifles or swords or knives, you are face to face with your opponent. You see what you are doing. But the newer methods of fighting allow one not to even acknowledge that you are killing other people."

"Whatever, what happened after World War II?"

"I grew weary of the unrest in the South American nations and travelled to the United States, specifically California. Again, I used my wealth, this time to fund causes related to what was generally referred to as civil rights. It was an instance where my darker skin proved useful, as I was furthering a cause that directly benefitted me."

"Makes sense."

"But that movement also was met with violent responses from those in power, which endangered me."

"How, if you can't die?"

"I may still be hurt, Agent LaManna, and I prefer to avoid pain where possible. In addition, the creation of a false identity was proving more complicated with the advent of identification cards, social security numbers, passports, and the like. Eventually, I moved to New York City, and became a reclusive billionaire, the role in which I first encountered you a decade ago."

"And I been trying to nail you on insider trading ever since."

"Your efforts have been amusing to me, if futile. For someone who has only lived a few decades, Agent LaManna, I will admit that you have a certain cleverness. But your efforts were always doomed to failure."

"To failure?"

"Yes."

"Okay, this is the part where I remind you who's sitting on what side of the desk."

"I admit, this particular setback was unexpected."

"I bet. So, you got all this gold and diamonds and stuff from Africa?"

"Indeed. I brought only a fraction of my total wealth with me when I departed Kôr, and have gone back periodically to replenish my funds when necessary and look in on my people. In fact, that was what I was on my way to do when you captured me. I made some rather foolish investments, as I was assured that Enron and Lucent were 'sure bets.' After losing quite a bit of capital on those companies, there was a need for a fresh infusion."

"So let me get this straight. The reason why we can't find any evidence of who you really are is because you were born however damn long ago in Mesopotamia or where-the-hell-ever, your IDs are all forged because you were born so long ago, and you're really the immortal queen o' some lost kingdom full of guys in huts in the middle of nowhere in Africa."

"There are no huts in Kôr, Agent LaManna. I have reinvested my wealth in my queendom. We remain hidden, yes—I do not wish my people to be embroiled in the wars that continue to ravage the rest of the continent—but Kôr is a modern nation, worry not."

"Yeah, I wasn't worried. Either way, though, we got you on fraud and forgery. It ain't much, but it's enough to make me happy."

"I'll be in a minimum security penitentiary for a hilariously brief period, Agent LaManna. I've been imprisoned by the warlords of Mesopotamia and the pharaohs of Egypt. These summer resorts you call prisons hold no fear for me."

"Maybe, but we froze your assets and you got nothin' you can access."

"Here in the United States, perhaps."

"That's good enough for me. Enjoy prison life, Ms. Yatie."

"We'll meet again, Agent LaManna, rest assured."

September 2004

"Agent LaManna! How good to see you!"

"Wish I could say the same, Ayesha. Or, I guess, 'Your Majesty'?"

"Personally, I'm quite fond of She-Who-Must-Be-Obeyed."

"You know that some British TV show stole that from Haggard, right?"

"Haggard stole it from me, so it's only reasonable. In any event, I have been informed by your superiors that the Free Nation of Kôr has revealed itself to the world, stated that I am their queen, and has threatened to declare war on the United States if I am not released."

"Yup. And my boss told me that I had to be the one to escort you out."

"That was at my request. You see, Agent LaManna—may I call you Francesca?"

"I really wish you wouldn't."

"I'm afraid it was a rhetorical question, Francesca. In any event, I *did* say that we would meet again."

"You wanted to show off your queenliness to me, huh?"

"Something like that."

"Well, congrats. Let's get this over with so I can get back to my real job."

"Let us speak of that, Francesca. You see, I wished you to escort me to my freedom in order to discuss your job."

"What about it?"

"I wish to offer you a new one."

"Are you *kidding* me?"

"Not in the least. It has been quite some time since someone got the better of me. Certainly those idiots whom Haggard renamed as Holly and Vincey and Job didn't. But *you*, Agent Francesca LaManna of the Federal Bureau of Investigation, were able to incarcerate me where hundreds of soldiers, police officers, agents, and investigators failed over the centuries. I admire that, and would like you to come back with me to Kôr."

"For what?"

"To become the head of palace security. I will be a target now that we are out and about in the world, and I trust your ability to keep me from harm, as the one person who overcame my own ability to keep myself from harm. Will you accept, Francesca?"

"Are you out of your goddamn mind?"

"Is that a no?"

"I—Jesus, I don't—This is insane! I'm still trying to wrap my damn head around the fact that you really *are* the queen of the jungle or whatever, and now you want me to move to goddamn *Africa?*"

"Yes."

"I'm just a woman from the Bronx."

"You are a federal agent, Francesca, and a skilled one. Further, you have no family ties since your parents died, no husband, no children."

"I guess I shouldn't be surprised you vetted me. Jesus. Look, I—I gotta think about it, okay?"

"I do not require an immediate answer. I have several meetings in your nation's capital over the next week. I would appreciate a response before I fly home Tuesday next."

"Um, okay. I guess."

"Farewell, Francesca. I hope to hear from you in a week."

"Take it easy, Ayesha. You, uh—you gave me a helluva lot to think about."

The Death Song of Dwar Guntha

Jonathan Maberry

When *All-Story Magazine* serialized Edgar Rice Burroughs' "Under the Moons of Mars" from July to September 1911, no one could imagine the character would prove influential and enduring. Collected as *A Princess of Mars*, the first science fiction series was born. Burroughs continued to write stories about Mars both with and without Carter, a Civil War veteran mysteriously transported from Earth to the red planet.

Jonathan Maberry is a *New York Times* bestselling author, five-time Bram Stoker Award-winner, and comic book writer. His vampire apocalypse book series, *V-WARS*, was a Netflix original series. He writes in multiple genres, including suspense, thriller, horror, science fiction, fantasy, and action; for adults, teens and middle grade. He is the editor of many anthologies, including *The X-Files, Aliens: Bug Hunt, Don't Turn Out the Lights, Nights of the Living Dead*, and others. His comics include *Black Panther: DoomWar, Captain America, Pandemica, Highway to Hell, The Punisher* and *Bad Blood*. He is a board member of the Horror Writers Association and the president of the International Association of Media Tie-in Writers. Visit him online at www.jonathanmaberry.com

The Death Song of Dwar Guntha

-1-

My name is Jeks Toron, last padwar of the Free Riders, and personal aide to Dwar Guntha. When he dies, however he dies, I pray I will go with him into the realm of legends and that our song will be sung in Helium for a thousand thousand years.

That is not a heroic boast—I won't fall upon my sword at the death of my captain; but I have been in a hundred battles with him, and we have grown old together...and war is not an old man's game. For odwars and jeedwars, perhaps, but not for fighting men.

Dwar Guntha? Ah, now there is a fighting man. Was he not with John Carter when the Warlord raided the fortress of Issus? Aye, he was there, leading the mutiny of loyal Heliumites against the madness of Zat Arras. He was a man at arms in the palace when Carter was named Jeddak of Jeddaks—Warlord of all Barsoom. And in the years that followed, how many times did Guntha ride out at the head of the Warlord's Riders? Look closely at Dwar Guntha's face and chest, and in the countless overlapping scars you'll see a map of history, a full account of the wars and battles, rescues, and skirmishes.

Now, though...?

John Carter himself is old. His children and grandchildren, and grandchildren of his grandchildren are old. We red men of Helium are long-lived, but that old witch time, as they say, catches up to everyone. Guntha's right arm is not what it was, and I admit that I am slower on the draw, less sure on the cut, and less dexterous in the riposte than once I was. Even the heroes' songs for which I and my family have been famous these many generations have become echoes of old tales retold. In these days of peace there are few opportunities for songmakers to tell of great and heroic deeds; just as there are few opportunities for warriors to pass into song in a moment of glorious battle.

It seems to me, and to Guntha, that we live in an age of city men. City men, or, perhaps 'civilized' men, seek deaths in bed, just as our great grandfathers once sought that long, last journey down the River Iss.

We spoke of such things, did Dwar Guntha and I, as we sat before a fire, warming our hands on the blaze and our stomachs with red wine. The moons chased each other through the heavens, leaving in their wakes a billion swirling stars. Tomorrow might be our last day, and so many days lay behind us. It sat heavily upon Dwar Guntha that our last great song may already have been sung.

I caught him looking into the flames with a distance at odds with the hawk sharpness he usually displayed.

"What is it?" I asked, and he was a long time answering.

Instead of speaking, he straightened, set aside his cup, and drew his sword from its sheath of cured banth hide. Guntha regarded the blade for a moment, turning it this way and that, studying the play of reflected firelight on the oiled steel. Then with a sigh he handed it to me.

"Look at it, Jeks," he said heavily. "This is my third sword. When I was a lad and wearing a fighting man's rig for the first time, I carried my father's sword. A clunky chopper of Panarian make. My father was a palace guard, you know. Served fifty years and never drew his weapon in anger. First time I used the sword in a real battle I notched the blade on a Tharkian collar. Second time I used it, the blade snapped. When Zat Arras fitted out the fleet to pursue John Carter after he'd returned from Valley Dor, Kantos Kan himself gave him a better sword. Good man, that. He was everything Zat Arras was not, and the sword he gave was a Helium blade. Light and strong and already blooded. It had belonged to a padwar friend of his who died nobly but had no heirs. I used that blade for over twenty years, Jeks. It tasted the blood of green men and black men, of plant men and white apes. And, aye, it drank the blood of red men, too."

He sighed and reached for his cup.

"But I lost it when my scouting party was taken prisoner in that skirmish down south. No, why do I tell you, Jeks? That's where we met, wasn't it? In the slave pits of An-Kar-Dool. Remember how we broke out? Clawing stones from the floor of our cell and tunneling inch by inch under the wall? Running naked into the forests, wasted by starvation, filthy and unarmed."

I smiled and nodded. "We were armed when we returned."

Guntha smiled, too, and nodded at the blade. "That was the first time I used that sword. I took it from the ice pirate who sold us into slavery. I snuck into his tent and strangled him with a lute string, and for a time I thought I would throw this sword away as soon as its immediate work was done."

"That would have been a shame," I said as I hefted the sword, letting the weight of the blade guide the turn and fall and recovery of my fist on my wrist. The balance was superb, and the blade flashed fire as it cut circles in the air.

"And so it would," he agreed, and his smile faded away by slow degrees. "Yet look at it, Jeks. See the nicks and notches that have cut so deep that no smith can sharpen them out? And along the bloodgutter, see the pits? Shake it, you can feel the softness of the tang and if you listen close you can hear it cry out in weary protest. I heard it crack yesterday when we fell upon the garrison that was fleeing this fort. Hearing it crack was like hearing my own heart break."

I lowered the sword and looked at him. Firelight danced in his eyes, but otherwise his face might have been the death mask of some ancient hero.

"I know of fifty songs in which your sword is named, Guntha," said I. "And twice a dozen names it has been given. Horok the Breaker. Lightning Sword of the East. Pirate's Bane and Thark's Friend. Those songs will still be sung when the moons are dust."

"Perhaps. They are old songs, written when each morning brought the clash of steel upon steel. What do we hear each morning now? Birdsong." He grunted in disgust. "Call me superstitious, Jeks, or call me an old fool, but I believe that my sword has sung its last songs."

"There is still tomorrow. The pirates will come and try to take this fort back from us."

"No," he said, "they *will* take it back, and they will slaughter us to a man and bury our bodies in some forgotten valley. No one will see us die and no one will write our last song."

"A death in battle is a death in battle," I observed, but he shook his head.

"You quote your own songs, Jeks," he said, "and when you wrote them you were quoting me."

"Ah," I said, remembering.

"Tomorrow is death," said Guntha, "but not a warrior's death. We will try and hold the walls and they will wear us down and root us out like lice. Extermination is not a way for a warrior to end his own song. There are too few of us to make a stand, and all of us are old. Where once we were the elite, the right hand of John Carter, now we are a company of dotards. An inconvenience to a dishonorable enemy."

"No--" I began but he cut me off with a shake of the head.

"We've known each other too long and too well for us to tell lies in the dark. The sun has set on more than this fortress, Jeks, and I am content with that." He paused. "Well...almost content. I am not a hero. I'm a simple fighting man and perhaps I should show more humility. I have been given a thousand battles. It is gluttony to crave one more."

Again I made to speak and again he shook his head. "Let me ramble, Jeks. Let me draw this poison out of my spirit." He sipped wine and I refilled both of our cups. "I have always been a fighting man. Always. I could never have done temple duty like my father. Standing in all that finery during endless ceremonies while my sword rusted in its sheath for want of a good blooding? No...that was never for me. Perhaps I am less...civilized than my father. Perhaps I belong to an older age of the world when warriors lived life to its fullest and died before they got old."

"You've fought in more battles than anyone I've ever heard of," I said. "Perhaps more than the great Tars Tarkas or the Warlord himself. You've *been* in most of their battles, and a hundred beside."

"And what is the result, Jeks? The world has grown quiet, there are no new songs. The Warlord has tamed Barsoom. He's broken the Assassins Guild and exposed the corruption of the nobles in the courts of Helium, made allies of the Tharks and Okarians; overthrown the Kaldanes, driven out most of the pirates except these last desert scum, and brought peace to the warring kingdoms."

"And *you* were there for much of that, Guntha. This very sword sang its song in the greatest battles of all time."

"Ah, friend Jeks, you miss my point," he said. He sipped his wine and shook his head. "It is *because* of all those battles, it is *because* of all the good that has been done with sword and gun and airship that I sit here, old and disgruntled and… yes…drunk. It is because of the quiet of peace that I feel so cheated."

"Cheated?"

"By myself. By our success. I never wanted to die the way my father did—an old man drooling down my chest while his great-great-grandchild swaddled him in diapers. Nor would I want to live on in 'retirement'," he said, wincing at the word, "while my sword hangs above a hearth, a relic whose use is forgotten and whose voice is stilled."

We sat there, both of us staring into the fire.

I took a breath and held out his sword. He looked at it the way a man might regard a friend who has betrayed him.

"Better I should break it over a rock than let it fail in a pointless battle."

"Take it, Guntha," I said softly. "I believe it still has one song left to sing."

His hand was reluctant, but finally he did take it back and slid it with a soft rasp into its sheath.

"What song is left to old men, Jeks?"

"Tomorrow."

He shook his head. "You weren't listening. Tomorrow is a slaughter and nothing more. We will rise and put on our weapons and gear, and then we will die. No one will write that song. No victory will be won. It will be a minor defeat in a war that will pass us by. We are small and peripheral to it, as old men are often peripheral things. No, Jeks, though we may wet our blades in the dawn's red glow, there is nothing…" His voice trailed off and stopped. Guntha drew a breath and straightened his back, staring down in his cup for long moments as logs crackled and hissed in the fire. "Gods," he said softly, "listen to me. I am an old woman. The wine has had the better of me. Forget I spoke."

"Do you say so?" I asked, cocking my head at him.

He forced a smile onto his seamed face. "Surely you can't take my ramblings seriously, old friend. Nor hold them against me after we've drained our cups how many times? Who am I, after all? Not an odwar or a jeddak. A dwar I am and a dwar shall I die—though..." he paused and looked around at the men who slept under rough blankets on the wooden walkway behind the parapets of the small stone fort. "Truly, for a warrior what greater honor is there than to have been the captain of men such as these? Surely none of *my* songs would have ever been sung had it not been for the company of such as they."

"One might say so of all heroes, Guntha," I pointed out. I took the wineskin and filled our cups.

"Not so. John Carter needs no company of men to help him. Even old, he is stronger than the strongest."

"He is not of this world," I reminded him. "Besides...how many times has he been captured during his adventures? How many times has his salvation relied on others? On warriors? Even on women and men from other races? The great Tars Tarkas has saved his life a dozen times."

"Just as John Carter saved his," Guntha fired back.

"Which only makes my point. What man is a hero without another warrior or ally at his back?"

"Like you and me," conceded Guntha, then gave another nod to the sleeping soldiers. "And these creaky old rogues."

"Just so. And it is because men need other men in order to live long enough to *become* heroes that I am able to write songs. Otherwise...no one would be alive to tell me the tales that *become* my songs."

"And I thought your lot made it all up," Guntha said, though I knew he was joking.

"We...*embellish* to be sure," I said unabashedly. "All heroes are handsome, all princesses beautiful, all dangers fell, all escapes narrow, and all victories legendary. You, for example, are taller, slimmer, and better looking in my songs."

We laughed and toasted that.

"But see here," Guntha said, warming to the discourse, "surely there is another kind of hero in songs. The hero whose tale is sung over his grave."

"Ah, you speak of the tragic hero who dies at the moment of his fame. Is it a death song you crave now, Guntha? Since when do like sad songs?"

"Not all death songs are sad. Some are glorious, and many are rallying cries."

"They are all sad," I said.

Guntha shook his head. "Not to the fallen. Such songs are not melancholy, Jeks. Such songs are perhaps the truest hero's tale, for they capture the warrior at the peak of his glory, with no postscript to tell of the dreary and ordinary days that followed. There are many who would agree that a hero should never outlive his own song. I know I would have no regrets."

"I would have one," I said.

"Eh?"

"If you were to die in such a glorious battle, you know that I would be by your side. Our men, too. We would all go down together, our blood filling the inkwells of the songmakers."

"So what is your regret?"

I smiled. "I am just arrogant enough to want to outlive our deaths so that *I* would be the one to write that song."

Guntha laughed long and loud. Some of the sleeping men muttered and pulled their blankets over their heads.

"By Iss, Jeks, you'll have to teach your ghost the art of crafting songs."

We laughed, but less so this time, and then we lapsed into a long silence. Guntha and I looked out beyond the battlements of our stolen outpost, past the glow of torches, into the velvety blackness of the night. The moons were down now and starlight was painted on the silks of ten thousand banners and a hundred thousand tents. Cookfires glowed like a mirror of the constellations above. Guntha went and leaned on the wall and I with him, and we stared at the last army of the Pirates of Barsoom. Three hundred thousand foot soldiers and a cavalry of five thousand mounted knights.

Resting now, waiting for dawn.

It was a nice joke to call them pirate scum and a rabble army, but the truth was there before us. It was one of the greatest armies ever assembled, and it marched on Helium and the lands of the Warlord. Would our lands go down in flames? We told ourselves "no." We had learned long ago to believe that John Carter, jeddak of jeddaks, would find a way to rally and respond and soak the dead soil of Barsoom in the blood of even so vast an army.

I knew that this was the core of Guntha's despair. He wanted to be there, he wanted to be with the Warlord when the true battle came. Even though he believed that his next battle would be his last, he wanted that battle to matter, to mean something. To be legendary.

We were a nuisance who took this fortress by luck and audacity, but as Guntha said, we would be swatted before the sun was above the horizon. We would not see the Warlord's fleet of airships fill the skies from horizon to horizon. We would not be there when the last—truly the last—great battle of our age was fought. We would already be dead. Forgotten, buried in the rubble of a fort that still stood only because it was inconvenient to take it from us in the dark. There would be no moment to shine, no glory, no notice. There would only be death and then a slide into nothingness as memories of us were overlaid by the songs that would be written about the real battle.

"Perhaps the Warlord will come with the dawn," I said. "The messengers we sent were well-mounted."

He gave another weary shake. "No. They would need to fly on wings to have reached even the most distant outposts. Had we an airship…but, no. John Carter will come, and he will come in all his might and wrath, but our song, my friend, will have ended long before."

"You would never have made a songmaker," I said. "You don't know how to write an ending to your own tale."

"Ha," he laughed, "and that is what I've been trying to tell you all evening."

-2-

Guntha woke me at the blackest hour of night. Only cold starlight washed down upon him as he crouched over me. For my part I came awake from a dream of battle.

"What is it?" I cried. "Are we beset?

My sword was half-drawn from its sheath when he caught my wrist. "No, sheath your sword, my friend," said he. "Just listen to me for a moment and then I'll let you rest."

"Speak then," I said quietly, mindful of the men who slept around us.

"What I said earlier…they were weak words from an old tongue, and I ask that you forgive them."

"There is nothing to forgive."

"Forget them, then. I spoke from old age and regret, but as I lay upon my blanket I thought better of my words, and of my life. To hell with death songs and glory, and to Iss with the ego of someone to whom the Gods have granted a thousand graces. I said that I was a Dwar and by heaven I will die as one. Not as a hero in some grand song, but a simple man doing a simple job for which he is well-suited. A loyal soldier for whom his daily service to his lord is both his purpose and his reward." He took a breath. "I have had my day, and there need be no more songs for me. None to write and none to sing. Not for me, Jeks, and not for us. The song is over. All that remains is to do one last day's honest work and then I shall lay me down with a will, content that I have not betrayed the trust placed upon me."

I was tempted in my weariness to make light of so bold a speech at such an unlikely hour, but the starlight glittered in his eyes like splinters of sword steel. And all the shadows re-sculpted his face so that as he turned this way and that, he was two different men. Or perhaps two different versions of Dwar Guntha. When he turned to the right it seemed to me that I looked upon a much younger man—the young dwar I met in the dungeons so many years ago; and when he turned to the other side, the blue-white starlight painted his face into a mask like unto a funeral mask of some ancient king. Neither aspect betrayed even a whisper of the doubt or weakness that had been in his voice scant hours before.

I sat up and put my hand on his shoulder. "Dwar Guntha," I said, "you would have made quite a singer of songs."

He chuckled. "Don't mock me. It's just that I had second thoughts after I lay down."

"Tell me."

"If we are to die tomorrow—or, today, as I perceive that dawn is not many hours away—then at least let us satisfy ourselves to usefulness."

"I don't follow."

"What would you rather do, Jeks? Be an insect to be smoked out of the cracks in these ancient walls and ground underfoot… or die as a fighting man?"

"You ask a question to which we both know the answer. The latter, always."

"Then when the sun ignites the morning, let us not wait for death behind these walls. Let us ride out instead."

I smiled. "Ride out?"

"Aye! A charge. We might make the upland cleft, where the slopes narrow before they spill out onto the great plains. It's a bottleneck and we could fill it. With our thoats, we could make a wall of spears." Guntha slapped his thigh. "By the gods I would bear death's ungentle touch, but I will not—*can not*—bear it without blood upon my steel. Even if my blade breaks on iron circlet or skull beneath, then let it break thus, red to the hilt."

"Ride out?" I asked again. "Sixteen against one hundred thousand?"

"Better than sixteen quivering behind battlements they don't have the numbers to defend."

"We wouldn't last a minute."

"And, *ah!*—what a minute it would be."

"No songs," I said.

"No songs," he agreed. "The only song that need be written today is that of John Carter, Jeddak of Jeddaks, as he fills the sky with ships and rains hell down upon this pirate scum. This is it, you know. This is the last battle. Even if we survived tomorrow—and there is scant chance of that—war is over for our generation. Once this army is crushed, then there will be peace on Barsoom. Peace! And it was our swords, Jeks, that helped to bring about such a glorious and blessed and thoroughly depressing turn of events. No…let us ride out to our doom and the dooms of those who first oppose us. The Free Riders of Helium, sailing to hell on a river of pirate blood."

I laughed. "A singer of songs, indeed!"

We smiled at each other then. Dawn was coming and we both knew that only one last sleep awaited us now.

"I'll go wake the others," said I. "I think they will be pleased!"

And so they were.

-3-

Dawn did indeed come early, and with it the silver voices of a thousand trumpets. My head ached with the hot hammers of the wine-devils, but I was in my battle harness before the pale sunlight clawed its way over the horizon. Before the first echo of the trumpets had yet had time to reach the distant mountains and come back to us, we swung open the gates to the outpost and the Free Riders rode out into the dawn.

Such a sight it must have been, could I have but seen it from a lofty perch. Sixteen men in heavy armor from another age. Spears and lances, warhammers and swords, polished and glittering.

The pirates scrambled to meet us, the pike men and foot soldiers grabbing up pieces of armor even as they counted our numbers and laughed. Had I any thoughts of surviving the day, I too might have laughed; but I knew a great secret that they did not. We were sufficient to our purpose: plenty enough men to die.

We raced to the upland cleft, which was a natural fissure in the red rock through which only half a dozen horses could pass at once. The footing was bad and you needed a trailwise thoat to navigate it at the best of times. All other passes were much stepped or littered with boulders, which forced the army to funnel into the pass. Hence the reason they had stopped for the night. We did not flatter ourselves that that great monster of an army had paused for us.

Dwar Guntha rode before the company, his ancient sword held high.

A dwar from the pirates cupped hands around his mouth and bade Dwar Guntha to surrender.

"Surrender, old man! Beg for your life and my jeddak may spare it!" he taunted.

Guntha never stopped smiling, even as he hefted his spear and threw it with great power and accuracy into the throat of the pirate dwar.

"There is our surrender," Dwar Guntha cried aloud. "We will write our names in the book of death with pirate blood. Have at you bastards, and may the desert demons feast upon your cowardly bones!"

The pirates stared at the body of their fallen captain for a long moment, and then with a great roar like a storming sea, they swept toward us.

We formed ranks and drew into the cleft, and only when the first wave of them rushed up the hill at us we charged out to meet them. Spears flashed like summer thunder and the air was filled with a treasure house of bright red rubies.

Ah, the killing.

Guntha and I fought side by side, our thoats rearing and slashing with steel-shod feet. The enemy was so determined to run us down that they sent lancers and foot soldiers in rather than archers. After all, who were we but a few old men on old horses?

It was an arrogance that cost them dearly. And yes, it would have made a glorious song. A battle song. A death song that would be remembered long after our bones were dust. Alas.

Each of the Riders was a veteran of countless battles. Old maybe, but deft and clever and ruthless. They laughed as they fought, delighting in the expressions of shock on the faces of much younger men who learned too little and too late that wisdom and experience often trumps youth and vigor. They came at us in that narrow defile and we took them, shouting our ancient songs of war as the blood ran like a brook around our ankles.

But there were one hundred thousand of them. Though they sent not a single man who could stand before the least of us, they had men to spare and no sword arm can fight without fatigue forever.

I saw Kinto Kan fall, his body feathered with arrows, but his own quiver empty and the dead heaped around him—two score and six to be his slaves in hell. Ben Bendark, known as Thark-killer before the Warlord forged the alliance, swung his war axe, that great cleaver of a hundred tavern songs, and the head of a pirate jed flew from his shoulders. I never saw where it landed. Bendark gave a wild cry of red triumph even as spears pierced his chest and stilled his mighty heart. He fell next to his brother, Gan, who smiled even in death, his mighty hands clenched forever around the shattered throats of the men who killed him.

Hadro Henkin, the sword dancer from Gathol, leaped and turned and cut men from the saddle and slipped between spears and left a path of ruin behind him. He made it nearly to the chariot of the jeddak himself before a dozen spearmen converged and brought him down. His best friend, Zeth Hondat, screamed like a banth and threw himself at the spearmen, cutting them down one-two-three-four. Seven fell before the jeddak raised a huge curved sword and cut Zeth nearly in twain.

These things I saw and more. The waves of pirates were as limitless as the dunes of a desert. An ocean of spears and swords, but Dwar Guntha had chosen our spot well and we held the high ground while they were forced into a narrow killing chute. We slaughtered five times our number. Ten times. *More*. And still they came. As I parried and thrust, cut and slashed, I could not help but compose our song in my head. Despite the melancholy musings of last night, this was a glorious end. This was such an end that perhaps the pirates themselves would write the song. Not a hero's lament or stirring death song, but a tale of desert demons who it took an army to overthrow. We would be the monsters to frighten children on dark nights, and that would please Dwar Guntha. It was a way to strike once more into the heart of our enemy.

In a moment's brief reprieve I called to him. Guntha bled from a dozen cuts and leaned heavily on his saddle horn.

"What a song!" I cried.

"Sing it with your blade," he laughed, and they were on us again.

Then I saw three things occur in close succession, and what a wonder they were to behold.

First, I saw the fresh wave of pirates swarm toward us. These were burly men, not the foot soldiers or light skirmishers; these were the cream of their cavalry on fresh thoats, led by the fierce jeddak in his war chariot. Dwar Guntha reared up on his thoat, the reins flying free, a spear in one hand and his ancient sword in the other. With a cry so fierce and powerful that it momentarily stilled the war shouts of the pirates, Guntha thrust the spear deep into the roaring mouth of the chariot's lead thoat, and as the beast fell the chariot tilted forward to offer the jeddak up to Guntha's sword. The blade caught red sunlight and then flashed down, cleaving gold circlet and black skull even as the jeddak thrust his own great blade forward into Dwar Guntha's chest. Guntha's blade snapped as he predicted it would, but only on a killing stroke. His last, and a masterful one it was. The pirates could never reckon this day's victory without counting a terrible cost.

Dwar Guntha fell, and that was the second thing I saw. He fell and as he did so the entire battle seemed to freeze into a shocked moment. The pirates recoiled back from as if the sight of a hero's fall and their own champion's death stole the heart from them.

And then I turned to see the third thing, and I knew then why the entire army of pirates has stalled in this moment.

The sky was full of ships.

Hundreds of them. Thousands. The great combined host of Helium and the Tharks, together in a fleet such as no man has seen in the skies of Barsoom in fifty thousand years. I do not know how our scout reached the capital in time. Perhaps he found a patrol in their airship and flew like a demon wind to spread the news and sound the alert. I will never know, and do not care. John Carter had come, and that was all that mattered. He had come…and with the greatest force of arms this world could yet muster. Here, to this barren place by a forgotten outpost. Here to fight the last battle. Whoever won this war would rule Barsoom forever.

John Carter, warlord of warlords, grown wise in his years, knew this and he brought such a force that the pirates howled in fear.

But… ah, they did not throw down their weapons.

I will honor them enough to say that, and to say that they made a fight of it that *will* make songs worth singing.

Yet, my heart was lifted as I looked up and saw a fleet so vast that it darkened the skies.

Or… was it my eyes that grew dark?

I felt a burning pain and looked down to see the glittering length of a sword moving through me below my heart.

I laughed my warrior's laugh and I slew my slayer even as the air erupted with the barrage of ten thousand airships firing all at once.

And the voice of the singer faded, even to his own ears.

-4-

It was a cold night in Helium. The moons were like chips of ice in the black forever that stretched above the royal palace.

John Carter drew his cloak more tightly around him. He was still a tall man, still strong, though great age had slimmed him. Slender and hard as a sword blade.

He leaned a shoulder against a pillar and looked out over the city. Even this late there was the sound of music and laughter. The sounds of peace. How long had it been thus, he mused. So many nights of so many years without the clang of steel on steel? He sighed, content that his people lived without fear, and yet secretly craving those old days when he and Tars Tarkas rode out to face monsters and madmen and hordes of bloodthirsty enemies.

Those were memories of a different world than this.

He heard a sound behind him and saw Kestos, the singer, gathering up his scrolls after a night of composing songs for a pending festival. When the young man noticed Carter watching, he bowed.

"My prince," he said nervously, "I did not mean to disturb you...I'm just leaving—"

Carter waved it off. "No. Tarry a moment, Kestos. Tarry and entertain an old man. Sing me a song."

"Of what would you have me sing, my prince? Of the spring harvest? Of the dance of the moons above—"

"No. Gods, no. Kestos, sing me one of the old songs. Sing me a song of heroes and battle."

"I...know but a few, my prince. I can sing of your victory over the—"

"No. I know my own songs. Sing to me the death song of Dwar Guntha. That's a good tale for a night like this."

The young man looked embarrassed. "My prince, I am sorry...but I don't know that song."

Carter turned and studied him. "Ah...you are so young. To not know the great songs is so sad."

"I...I'm sorry..."

Carter smiled. "No. Sit, young Kestos, and I will sing you the song. Learn it. Remember it, and sing it often. Some songs should never be forgotten."

And as the moons sailed through the black ocean of the sky, John Carter, Warlord of all Barsoom, sang of the last charge of the great Free Riders.

And such a tale it was. All of the heroes were tall and handsome, all of the enemies were vile and dangerous, and each of the heroes slew a hundred and then died gloriously upon a mountain of their foes.

Or, so it goes in the song.

Building Bridges

Rigel Ailur

Known worldwide, Hua Mulan's fame stretches back more than a dozen centuries. A young woman who wanted to save her father became a legendary warrior who saved an empire.

Rigel Ailur writes science fiction and fantasy, with forays into other genres thrown in. She wrote her first novel (all of *seven* pages! with a cover and table of contents and everything!) at age seven and hasn't stopped since. Her first sale was a *Star Trek* short story, and she's contributed to *Shadowrun*. She's published more than twenty novels and more than eighty short stories, both standalone and across several series. Her series include the *Tales of Mimion*, and *The Patel Family Chronicles*. She's also contributed to *The Angel Cat Collection* and the *Lady Pirates* series.

In addition to being in the IAMTW, she is a member of SFWA, ITW, MWA, WFWA, Pennwriters, and Ligonier Valley Writers. Most importantly, Rigel dotes on her beloved astronomically adorable feline kids.

Visit www.BluetrixBooks.com for a complete bibliography.

Acknowledgments:

Thank you to everyone who graciously and patiently helped with the translation at the start of the story. Special thanks to Xuefei Mei, Terence Chua, and Qin Huang who went above and beyond in helping me work through my questions. Any errors in the phrase are strictly my own.

Building Bridges

榮譽非藏身之所，立身之基也。

Mulan and her granddaughter raced on horseback along the forest-lined road. Their horses' easy canter combined with a brisk wind and made the younger woman's long, loose tresses stream behind her. Mulan's white braid thudded against her back in time with the horses' gait. The trees were just beginning to reveal their autumnal colors. Gusts of wind frolicked among the flashes of gold in the treetops, making the ginkgo sing.

Mulan hoped to be on the way back home before the shower of fan-shaped leaves cascaded to the ground. Perhaps they could time their return so that the foliage rained down on them.

It depended on how long His Imperial Majesty required her presence.

One did not decline a 'request' to visit the emperor—or depart early.

They rounded a bend in the road and Mulan pulled up abruptly, eliciting a sharp snort of displeasure from her steed as he reared up, then stomped and sidestepped in an equine dance of annoyance before calming.

"What's wrong, Grandmother?" Caihong asked, wheeling around even as Mulan called sharply for her to stop.

Mulan tilted her head at the sight which Caihong had just turned away from.

The road and trees fell away at the edge of a deep ravine. Mulan heard the rapids far below still raging from the torrential downpour several days ago. Only freshly charred timbers remained of the wooden bridge that had spanned the gaping chasm.

Mulan scowled and heaved a deep sign of aggravation.

One also did *not* arrive late when invited by the emperor.

Fortunately she'd allocated thirteen days for the—normally—six-day trip. They had nine days to travel the remaining two days' distance.

Caihong gave an impatient grunt. "Upriver or down?"

Raising her eyebrow, Mulan said, "Indeed. That is the question."

Caihong snorted, then instantly lowered her eyes in shame. "I'm sorry, Grandmother. What is the answer to our question?"

"That I do not know."

Caihong raised *her* eyebrow and waited.

Mulan chuckled despite her consternation.

Her son always said that of all his children, Caihong took after Mulan the most—and not simply in appearance, or vocal timbre and intonation, or carriage and mannerisms. Caihong had toddled after Mulan from the time she no longer needed to crawl after her. Mulan had thought at one point that the child was imitating her.

Wanting to encourage Caihong to make her own decisions, Mulan would occasionally experiment. Without comment, she would do small things such as eat a food she didn't like, or not eat one she loved. Caihong's tastes had aligned with Mulan's true ones nearly every time.

Now Mulan saw her own consternation mirrored on Caihong's youthful face. Mulan rode closer to the cliff's edge and scanned the length of the narrow canyon, visible for a few miles in either direction before the forest swallowed it.

A bridge could lie just out of view, or many days away.

"Which way would you suggest?" Mulan asked.

Caihong looked at her askance, then grinned. "I suggest riding back to the village. Someone there should be able to tell us the next closest crossing, and we can make sure they know the bridge is out."

"Indeed. A wise course of action," Mulan affirmed, and Caihong beamed at the compliment.

The innkeeper's double-take betrayed his surprise at seeing them again so soon after wishing them a pleasant journey. The slight man, shorter even than Mulan, gave a respectful nod even as he delivered a heaping bowl of rice to a family seated at one end of a long, wooden table. Besides the foursome, only two other couples sat concentrating conspicuously on consuming their meals.

Mulan and Caihong remained just inside the entrance, careful to stay out of the way while the innkeeper and his family went about their business.

A shadow fell across the threshold as three men paused in the doorway. The smell of their unwashed bodies drifted. Mulan wrinkled her nose and, in tandem with Caihong, retreated further into the dining area. The tallest of the trio led the way. Of the other two, the soft look of the stocky one implied more fat than muscle, whereas the last was so skinny as to not have much of either.

The men surveyed the establishment like kings, wholly at odds with their dirty, disheveled attire and heavily scuffed boots. Even under the dirt, they looked young to Mulan, perhaps not far into their thirties.

Mulan pretended to avert her eyes, not wanting to reveal how closely she was watching them. She stooped, leaning heavily on the sturdy oak staff as if it were her walking stick and making herself appear frail next to her granddaughter. Caihong had inherited her father's height and his deceptively lean build which hid powerful musculature. At the corner of Mulan's vision, Caihong adjusted her cape so she could easily draw the swords it concealed on her back.

If the trio noticed two mere females standing nearby, they didn't deign to acknowledge them as they swaggered inside. Shoving two patrons aside, they commandeered a table. One of the men grabbed the barmaid, forcing her to twist out of his grasp. The tallest of the three, his sharp features twisted with impatience, bellowed for the innkeeper to bring them their repast and make haste with the libations.

Mulan stifled a derisive laugh at the pretentiousness, but Caihong didn't succeed. She did instantly turn the noise into a choking cough. Assisting her granddaughter's act, Mulan feigned fussing over her. She assured Caihong she'd soon be over the illness and ushered her solicitously outside.

Caihong's dark eyes flashed with fury but she said nothing until they'd moved far enough away from the establishment.

"Boors," Caihong muttered.

"Indeed." Mulan nodded in agreement as she cast a look back over her shoulder at the inn.

Her granddaughter regarded the inn anxiously as well. After a few moments of silence aside from the whistling wind whipping her hair into her face, Caihong caught the flyaway locks in one hand and asked, "Should we go back in?"

"I suspect the innkeeper will be occupied for a time," Mulan said. "We should take care not to make the situation worse. Perhaps someone else in the village knows the local roadways, and can direct us. If we can find someone not tending the rice fields."

Caihong glanced up at the thick white clouds scudding across the sky. "If we don't find out soon, will we want to stay the night? More comfortable than camping in the forest. Especially if the weather hits."

"Indeed."

In tandem, they strolled back toward the inn, raised voices reaching them in the street. "Fool! You call this a meal!" Shattering stoneware and crashing wooden plates mingled with screams.

Still in step, grandmother and granddaughter picked up their pace. They reached the entrance just in time to deftly sidestep as the three angry men stormed out and charged up the road.

An oppressive pall hung over the large, low-ceilinged room. The innkeeper, his stout wife, and three youngsters including the barmaid—their children, based on the resemblance—were cleaning up food, dishes, and chopsticks from the floor.

The family who'd been eating must have ducked out the back through the kitchen.

Caihong moved to help even as the innkeeper came and bowed to Mulan. "Honored Grandmother, how may we serve you? Is something wrong?"

Mulan raised a brow at the incongruous question, but replied rather than commenting. "We require a room for the night, please. The bridge is out, and it looks like a hard rain is coming. We also require information on the closest place to cross the river. We can't delay our journey any longer than a night." The last thing she or Caihong wanted was to attract attention, so Mulan didn't identify the Imperial city Xi'an as their destination. Unusual enough that two women were traveling alone.

The innkeeper's eyes widened for just a moment and he caught his breath. "The bridge is out? That's very bad. We get supplies from the north, and send our excess harvest to Xi'an. We're farmers, we have no engineers capable of repairing the bridge."

"I'm sorry. There is nothing left to repair. It might have been a lightning strike. It left cinders, not much more."

The man's face fell and shoulders sagged. Then he straightened his posture and raised his chin. "But we shall manage. Thank you for the news. If you backtrack another mile, to the last crossroad, and turn east and go five or six miles, you will come to another bridge. Much older, but made of stone. Shortly after you cross it, there is a narrow road running west, parallel to the river. It's easy to miss, so take care. It will bring you back to this road on the other side of the river."

"Thank you. If we may also prevail upon your hospitality, our horses need to be cared for this evening." Mulan withdrew a string of copper coins from a pocket in her cloak and handed the money to him.

The man bowed again as he accepted it. "Thank you, Honored Grandmother."

He quickly tucked the coins away as he waved to his son and instructed him to go to the stable immediately to look after the ladies' mounts. The innkeeper then gestured at his younger daughter as the boy dashed outside. "Would you care to see your room now? Rest before an evening meal?"

"We will say goodnight to our horses first," Mulan said with a chuckle, forestalling Caihong's interjection and receiving a broad grin from her granddaughter in response.

Caihong had gathered up the dishes that were unbroken and set them on one of the tables. The proprietress bowed to her in thanks.

As the pair turned to leave, the furious threesome returned, each brandishing a sword.

"Out of the way, old woman!" The leader snarled as he shoved past Mulan, pushing her hard enough to send anyone—but especially an elderly person—tumbling to the ground.

In a split second, Mulan had steadied herself with her staff and then struck straight out with it, cleanly knocking the sword from the brigand's hand. Continuing the same motion, she swept it around, catching the man at the ankles and knocking him flat on his face. She pressed her staff to the back of his neck as she kicked his weapon out of reach.

In the same instant, Caihong drew her own blades, batted the other two men's swords out of their hands before the men realized she was armed, and held her swords at their throats.

The little girl screamed and hid behind her father who, Mulan thought, looked nearly as terrified as the child did. Mother and elder daughter also regarded the scene in horror.

Caihong remained steady as a statue, no doubt awaiting some cue from her grandmother.

For her part, Mulan took the reaction of the innkeeper and his family as confirmation that she'd blundered into an ongoing problem the family had been dealing with as best they could. She and Caihong had just made it immeasurably worse.

"I am going to step back," Mulan told the man sprawled on the wooden floor, "and you are going to sit *right there*. Agreed?"

He glowered at her.

After another beat, Mulan released the pressure on the staff. As she expected, his arm shot around as if to grab the staff away from her. She evaded him easily and brought the other end of her staff down hard on his ribs, slamming him back to the ground. What the years had cost her in speed, she'd made up for in experience and anticipation and technique. Strength, she could maintain.

Mulan kept her voice even. "You are going to sit right there. Agreed? Then perhaps I can assist you."

A glimmer of interest showed in his furious glare. "Assist me?"

Mulan waited, brow arched.

"Fine, I'll sit here," he grumbled. Then his voice gained back some edge. "For a minute." He sat up and rested his hands on his knees.

Mulan gathered her thoughts. Even the brief glimpse at the jian had revealed fine workmanship that told her the blades had belonged to warriors or wealthy men.

Had these three stolen them? Or were they somehow—despite such dishonorable actions—the original owners?

Contemplating how best to begin—no, Mulan corrected, how best to continue, as she'd already created an even bigger mess—she recalled the man's grandiose language upon arriving. Perhaps she could make use of his attitude.

"And if your two esteemed companions would be so accommodating as to seat themselves as well?"

The leader nodded, and his two cohorts complied. Caihong stepped back but remained vigilant.

"Thank you." Mulan affected a relaxed stance, and gave the appearance of leaning heavily on her staff.

"Who are you?" he demanded.

"My name makes no difference at the moment," she said, seeing no benefit to enlightening him. The ill-tempered man might take it as a challenge. Even after half a century, people still spoke about her deeds. "May I ask the nature of the disagreement?"

The man's visage darkened and his eyes narrowed to slits. "These peasants shame my family. They act as if the land is theirs, but my ancestors have tended these fields for generations."

"You wish to regain your honor by restoring your family honor." Mulan nodded sagely, knowing the young man would infer agreement although she had offered only acknowledgment. Fortunes sometimes shifted; people, or families, sometimes fell out of favor with the emperor or someone close to him. Some simply fell on hard times.

He slouched, as if her taking him seriously deflated at least a bit of his anger. "That's right."

"Honor isn't a roof for a person to hide beneath. It's a foundation a person must maintain, and build on." Treading carefully, Mulan asked, "Is there not more honor in looking after those less fortunate than you? Rather than in scaring children, and sowing destruction?" She spread one arm over the mess the dining area had become. "More honor in helping people than in fighting an old woman?" She said that last with a wry, self-deprecating twist to her mouth.

At that—as she'd hoped—he actually laughed. He let out a sharp guffaw. "Yes, because you're so feeble, and your—granddaughter?—is such a delicate flower." He had a good laugh, deep and hearty and full of joy.

Without relaxing her guard, Mulan bowed at his compliment. Her cautious optimism grew. "How can you accomplish that?"

The innkeeper ventured a comment. "Your uncle was an engineer, was he not? He built the bridge over the canyon?"

The man's brow furrowed in confusion. "He designed it and oversaw the construction."

"Is that a skill you share?" Mulan asked. "Could you do the same?" When the scrunched look on his face didn't abate, she explained. "The bridge has been destroyed. If you are able to help, everyone will benefit once it's rebuilt."

The man climbed to his feet, moving slowly so no one would mistake the move as aggression. "The bridge is gone?" His voice took on a calculating tone; Mulan's optimism waned a little.

"Probably lightning," Caihong said. "There's nothing left but some burnt wood."

Mulan shifted her staff to her other hand as a subtle reminder she'd just throttled him, and to regain his full attention. "You are an engineer?"

He folded his arms and regarded her smugly. "What if I am? My family is no longer responsible for such things."

"That is the stance you're choosing to hide behind?" she challenged him. "You claim to want to restore honor, yet your shameful attitude and actions prove otherwise. You have no understanding of honor. With no understanding, you will never be able to regain it."

He flushed deep red and swayed ever so slightly, as if he'd barely stopped himself from lunging at her. "Why should I worry about the bridge?" he snapped, defiant.

"Indeed." Sadness imbued her voice. "It is very difficult to teach when a student has no desire to understand." She met his stare until he looked away.

But then he whirled and dove at her with a yell. She dodged, using her staff to deflect his attack and send him sprawling onto the floor. He sprang easily back to his feet, hands held poised in front of his torso that he angled away from her as they circled each other warily.

He moved like a bolt shot from a crossbow. The attacker's flurry of punches and kicks all fell short. Mulan evaded them all, sometimes by dodging, sometimes by redirecting their energy with her staff.

His two henchmen needed no further instigation and leapt at Caihong.

Fully occupied, Mulan could spare no attention for—let alone intervene in—her granddaughter's battle. Her own opponent demanded all her effort. His fury gave him considerable power; it likewise robbed him of any strategy, most focus, and all control.

At first, Mulan landed warning blows on his arms and shoulders. That only enraged him, so she quickly changed tactics. With more difficulty than when she'd taken him by surprise, she knocked him to the ground several more times before pinning him again.

Caihong used her swords defensively as she danced between and around the other two men. She landed her own blows, each punctuated by a resounding, "kiai!" Her finale maneuver sent one of the men headlong into the other, knocking them both out cold.

"You'll regret this!" the man on the floor shrieked.

Mulan ignored him, addressing the innkeeper instead. "Is there no magistrate nearby who can help you?"

The innkeeper hesitated, visibly distraught.

His eldest daughter spoke up, pointing at the man under Mulan's staff. "Yee-Jin's father was our last magistrate."

It required all Mulan's effort not to groan out loud. "You shame your father," she said harshly, smacking him with her staff. "Do not move," she warned him as she stepped back.

Caihong edged close enough to guard him, yet far enough to remain out of his reach.

"What is it you really seek?" Mulan demanded. "It can't be honor or you would not behave in this manner." She believed she had gotten through to him. If only she could reestablish that connection.

Few alternatives existed. She and Caihong couldn't remain indefinitely. Even if she didn't need to go to Xi'an, they had family and duties back home. Likewise, a magistrate in a neighboring town would not be near enough to keep this situation in hand. Mulan could tell one of the emperor's advisors that the village required a magistrate, but she had no way of knowing how quickly they would respond—if at all.

For a fleeting moment, she considered revealing her imperial medallion. The circle of gold covered her entire splayed hand. The serpentine dragon in flight engraved on it symbolized the emperor.

However, Mulan anticipated that would only increase his ire rather than alleviate the problem. She still couldn't remain, nor could she compel any magistrate to visit, let alone stay.

No, she had to find some way to break through his stubborn anger. Only if the solution came from him would it last.

She still awaited his reply. "What is it you seek?" she repeated.

He sat up but made no move to stand. Again his anger ebbed, and Mulan reevaluated her estimate of his age. She'd originally placed it halfway between her son's and her granddaughter's. Now, however, she revised that number downward and assessed him as not much older than her granddaughter after all.

Bullies only responded to bullies. Mulan knew that fact all too well.

Was his true nature that of a bully, or of the rational person she'd seen so briefly? She pondered if acting the bigger bully would work, then rejected that option. It led back to the same dead end. Yes, she could show him the medallion and elicit temporary cooperation, but in time he'd call her bluff and realize she wasn't coming back—at least not any time soon.

"I do want honor," the man replied, looking up at her. "Honor, and to restore my family's position."

"Honor must be demonstrated, not simply talked about." Mulan gathered up the three swords. "Fine blades," she remarked, admiring the workmanship. "I have a proposition, Yee-Jin. You claim your goal is to regain honor. Your actions must bear that out. Repair the bridge. Protect the village as your father did; don't terrorize it. Earn these weapons."

The expected explosion of rage didn't come. He actually looked interested, perhaps even curious. "How do you mean?"

"We shall take these with us," Mulan told him. "In several days, maybe a few weeks, we'll be traveling back this way. That gives you plenty of time to repair the bridge—which will be a good start in demonstrating your sincerity. If you are still fulfilling the duties of magistrate a year later, you'll earn back the swords." Mulan paused, then added, "We—or others on our behalf—may visit at any time. There will be no set schedule. That includes after the year is up."

"And if I don't accept?"

Mulan shrugged even as a wave of sorrow and weariness washed over her. "Then you have no honor and will not get the swords back. You should also keep in mind, the next people you pick a fight with may simply kill you and be done with it."

A flash of emotion crossed his face as if that had not occurred to him. Perhaps he simply required guidance, a nudge to point him in the right direction.

"You are a young man, strong, educated. Strive to fulfill your potential instead of squandering it." As a soldier and a parent, Mulan knew well how to imbue her words with both encouragement and admonition. "Do you not wish to put forth the effort, instead of drifting aimlessly?"

"Why does it matter to you?" Yee-Jin sounded genuinely puzzled.

"Every person matters," she replied solemnly. "A single person can do great things given the right circumstances."

He tilted his head to one side and stared past her, contemplating as if such a thought had never dawned on him before. "You believe so?"

"I do."

His two friends began to stir. Yee-Jin climbed to his feet then went to help them up. The pair cast baleful scowls at Caihong but seemed to be waiting for a signal from Yee-Jin as to the current state of affairs.

"We are going to build a bridge," Yee-Jin announced jovially, pounding them each on the back and eliciting a wince from the bony one. "Well," he amended, "we are going to supervise building a bridge. We will need a few more people to help. First, though, we must find suitable trees and secure permission to use them."

He turned and bowed low to Mulan. "Thank you, Honored Grandmother."

His two companions regarded him wide-eyed and slack-jawed, utterly bewildered at the turn of events. The innkeeper and his family looked stunned as well.

"We're...going to cut down trees?" the stocky man said, exchanging a baffled look with his cohort.

Yee-Jin slung an arm around each of their shoulders and guided them outside, starting to explain as they went.

Caihong watched them depart, skepticism plain on her face as she slid her swords back in their sheaths. She adjusted the straps across her chest to better position the blades on her back and straightened her cloak to conceal the weapons as before.

"You believe them?" Caihong said, half statement and half query. Mess temporarily forgotten, the family who ran the inn also gathered around to hear Mulan's reply.

"I do," Mulan answered. Ten years of leading troops had taught her how to judge character and motivate people. Subsequent decades of life had honed the skill. "They are angry, young men. Now they have an immediate task to complete. The swords are an additional longer-term incentive."

Their hosts' faces still showed their doubt.

"We will be back," Mulan reassured them. "You have my word. If the problem remains, we won't leave until it is solved."

The quiet confidence of the promise seemed to put them at ease. As they busied themselves putting the dining area back in order, the innkeeper ducked into a back room and emerged with rice paper and a quill pen.

Beckoning them to one of the tables, the man unrolled the scroll of rice paper. He drew a crude map illustrating the instructions he'd given them earlier. "The way should be clear, but I wanted you to have this. Will you want supper this evening?"

"No, thank you. Only a meal tomorrow morning."

He bowed then scurried off.

"We should see to the horses," Caihong said. "Are we still leaving early tomorrow?"

"Indeed. We can't risk being late."

Yee-Jin intercepted them halfway between the inn and the nearby barn. He bowed low to both women, then held out three strings of tin coins. "Honored Grandmother, please allow me to thank you. Please accept this for your stay, and for your horses' supplies as well."

She returned the bow and accepted his offering, understanding its symbolic importance. It demonstrated his taking responsibility and looking out for others. She had no need of the cash, but declining would have undercut the lesson she wanted him to internalize.

Such a tiny gesture, but it reinforced her hope that the big changes she was attempting to instigate would take hold and ultimately flourish.

They found the horses already fed, watered, and groomed, their tack cleaned and neatly arranged on a shelf beside each. Yee-Jin's two friends were just leaving.

"Well done, Grandmother." Caihong's wry grin of amazement turned to a warm, admiring smile. "Something tells me we won't need to detour on our way back."

"Indeed, Granddaughter, indeed. By then the bridge will be in place."

Paraíso

Yvonne Navarro

The almost cult-like craze for artist Frida Kahlo has been going on for some time. Although her paintings were known during her life (she died in 1954), it has only been recently that they have been fetching astounding prices. As an artist and a woman who has loved and also endured back surgeries that have left me in constant pain, I feel a closeness to Kahlo, an understanding that few others consider. I wanted to share that.

Yvonne Navarro is the author of twenty-three published novels, a lot of short stories, articles, and a reference dictionary. Her most recently published book is *Supernatural: The Usual Sacrifices* (based in the Supernatural Universe). Her writing has won numerous awards, including a Bram Stoker Award. Lately she's been getting into painting and artwork. She lives way down in the southeastern corner of Arizona, about twenty miles from the Mexican border, is married to author Weston Ochse, and dotes on their rescued Great Danes. She has an I Want To Do list that has about 4,274 projects on it and won't stop growing.

Paraíso

I FIND THE SMALL METAL SHEET IN THE LATE AFTERNOON, AMID A stack of rejected starts. It must be an old one, because I don't remember it at all and the edges are chipped, one corner bent so badly it's almost folded over. I straighten it the best I can, then peer at the bottom, but of course my signature—

Frida Kahlo

—isn't there. The painting is unfinished and drab; all browns and blacks, dreary areas that I can't decide are metal or gray paint. If I did start this, it's easy to see why I abandoned it. As if the smudges of grime and stains aren't bad enough, the half-finished image of a house is splatted on the screen as though someone—certainly not me—threw paint at the surface and it stuck. Part of me wants to rescue it, turn it into something, *anything*, more than what it is. The other part wants to cringe from it and put it out of sight. Exhausted from fighting the pain in my back, I choose the latter. I will deal with it some other day.

~

The depressing little painting gnaws at my mind, not just because I don't know where it came from or how it got here in the first place.

Lying in bed, I work on another small metal painting; my back will not allow me to sit upright today and my arm aches from having to reach above me with the paintbrush. Except for a small break for lunch, it takes most of the day before I am satisfied and can call this project complete. I struggle to get out of bed and set it aside to dry, feeling pain spider across my back and down my legs. No—*spider* isn't the correct word. It's more a series of lightning strikes, each one making me grunt with effort. I don't know how I'm supposed to live with this, the constant agony, the never-ending exhaustion, the *wanting* of the way life should have been before the accident when I was eighteen. I often daydream about how it would be, not only had I not been the victim in the trolley accident that was so devastating to my body, but had I not met and eventually married Diego Rivera. As I have often told my friends, there have been two great accidents in my life. One was the trolley, the other was Diego. Diego was by far the worst.

Every evening I lie in bed, drained at the end of a long, arduous day, having finished—if I'm lucky—whichever painting I have been working on, and alone. Diego has gone off with friends or one of his many paramours, and I am left to struggle with my need for him, body and soul, and try to understand why he does not value me as I do him. Why can he not see that he is my everything and that I cannot live without him—that all I want is to be with him?

~

Mornings are always difficult, but I finally feel better after I manage a hot shower, a small breakfast, and some pain medication. It is a bright day and the birds are singing outside. Today I decide to work in my studio, where there is good light and I can feel a slight, warm breeze. I am thinking about my next painting when I go to the stack of metal pieces, but right in front is the very same dismal painting that I pushed to the back a couple of days ago.

I stare at it, but I don't know if I'm annoyed or alarmed. Diego has not been in the house for almost a week, and other than a few servants, no one else is around. Although the studio is regularly dusted and the floors cleaned, no one ever touches my art materials.

So how did this ugly little painting show up yet *again* at the front of my supplies?

Frustrated, I examine it more closely. It's hideous; dark house, dark surroundings, darker sky. I don't know who painted it, much less how it keeps ending up in my studio, but it emanates gloom, pulling me into the scene as though offering a place to sink into utter despair, clouding my mind and—

I throw it across the room, barely realizing I cry out as I do so.

The metal sheet clatters as it lands against the bottom of a far cabinet and my breath catches as it nearly upends the row of very old artifacts I have arranged there. "Enough of this nonsense," I say aloud. This day is fast becoming not one of my better ones, and it has begun to pain me to move; because the surgeons amputated my right leg, the added weight on my left when I try to walk with crutches twists my back and only adds to my anguish. Even so, I awkwardly make my way over and manage to pick it up, holding the piece by the creased corner as if it were something nasty. I am surprised to find the metal warm under the tips of my thumb and forefinger. I hold it up higher, examining it in the clear morning light that spills through the triple wall of windows. The browns, blacks and grays are smeary and poorly defined, painted by an anonymous hand wielding a careless brush. When I look more closely, I wonder if the artist was more angry than careless; there is a feeling of something—or some*one*—being trapped in the dilapidated house where the windows are the blackest thing in a chilly, unwelcoming setting.

The scene looks like I feel on my darkest of days.

I stare at it a bit longer, then take it back and set it on my easel. Perhaps I will experiment a little on this ugly painting. I had planned to start another project today, another self-portrait which I have already titled *Self-Portrait in a Landscape with the Sun Going Down,* but there is something about this miserable scene that calls to me to...*help* it.

Although my body wants to settle in the wheelchair, I sit on the wooden chair instead, compensating to balance my missing leg and studying the image for a few minutes, assessing it. My father was an excellent photographer, and the small painting looks like it might have been copied from an amateurish picture taken decades ago. My gaze keeps going to the windows, so dark and black and hopeless. This is where I will start.

I mix a tiny amount of my favorite yellow and tone it with white, then carefully work on the windows of the house. There are five of them—two on the ground floor and three on the second—but it doesn't take long. In only a few minutes, I sit back and appraise my work, pleased to see that under my brush, the windows have come alive with warmth and light, beacons calling the lost in the gloom. On impulse I decide to keep going, and now my attention goes to the stormy skies above the house, the way they bear down upon the house and the landscape surrounding it, shrouding everything with hostility as if daring someone to step outside and face a never-ending apocalypse. I want to erase this feeling, but such a drastic alteration cannot be accomplished quickly; instead I start with lighter shades of gray at the horizon line, as though a rising sun is trying to force its way through a heavy rainstorm. Then I begin to lighten the surrounding areas, again doing small portions at a time.

After awhile, I stop and give myself a break, pleased at the results. Despite its brightened windows, the house has become even more of a blemish now that the background is altered. It looks ancient and decrepit, an abode that no one has maintained for a century or more, unloved and only existing because someone needs a modicum of shelter. Balancing on the chair has made my muscles grow stiff, but I cannot stop, not just yet; I am afraid that if I force myself to stand, the pain will become overwhelming and I will end up in my bed and groggy with painkillers for the rest of the day. My house girl always keeps the glass of water next to me full and I have three of the pills in my pocket. Out of habit I save the water for later and dry-swallow the pills, hoping they will be enough to dull the steel twisting in my back so that I can continue.

I stare at the painting for a quarter hour, playing with possibilities in my mind before I again pick up the paintbrush. The suffering down my back and in my hips never goes away, but the pills have lessened it to where I think I can keep going without moaning aloud. The house structure has my full attention now, and I let my instincts take over. Of its own volition, my hand moves and the brush picks up shades of *azul*—blue—the color of my home for so many years. I feel as though I am painting in a dream, but it is not my mind that conveys imagery to the metal. It is my *soul*, the essence of me that is linked to Diego—always, my Diego—and imagines how we would be together if he loved me as much as I love him. It might be in a house such as the one taking shape beneath my touch: smaller than Azul House, cozy rooms spilling over with color and comfort. No more affairs for either of us, because, finally, it will be just the two of us, in love. In *life*.

My house girl brings me lunch, a small plate of chicken mole, smaller piles of rice and beans beside it, hot corn tortillas. Beyond the glass walls of my studio, I can hear the soft sounds of the rest of the household as they gather for the midday meal, but I do not join them. Not today, not while working on this small, impulsive project that has made my constant discomfort somehow float far away from my consciousness. I pick at the food only to keep my stomach from complaining and I concentrate instead on my work, blending the oils without trying until they arrange themselves into an image of serenity and pleasure. Reds, greens, orange—the colors of summer overtake the drab, dry-looking ground around the house. A marvelous array of vegetation seems to grow as each fine stroke slides oil across the metal: bristly palm trees, thick ferns and heavy-leafed plants border the walls interspersed with lush red and orange flowers. And sunflowers, of course, because they are among my favorites.

It's as if I have been painting outside myself. I don't know how much time has passed; the sky is still brilliant and blue, but I can see the sun is lower, starting to descend behind the trees. Although I don't recall the house girl coming in, the plate of food from earlier is gone, replaced by a lovely platter of fresh fruit and a glass of cold hibiscus tea. I realize I haven't moved from this spot in what must be hours, but I feel fine. I can't recall the last time I felt this way—warm, pleasant, numb without my mind being dulled by layers of narcotics. As always, I am strapped into a back brace, but for a change I relax into it, not forcing my back muscles to be straight to avoid pain. There is only an agreeable sensation of being slightly weary.

I focus on the painting again, startled to see the transformation. Gone is the uninhabited, ramshackle structure in its murky and despondent surroundings. In its place is a welcoming house, blue like Casa Azul; pots overgrown with flowers in every color border a curving walkway to the door, while trees and plants in abundant shades of green and gold cradle the sides and circle around to the rear, stretching away to a far-off horizon. In the distance the sun is setting, its rays a palette of golds, oranges, and reds that is a thousand times more vibrant than anything I've ever before captured in my art. The piece is glorious; if it were real, I would sink into it to rest, to spend the rest of—

Wait.

It's not quite complete, not yet. My hands seek a smaller brush, and without even contemplating it, I add two figures, Diego in his traditional black suit, and myself in the native Mexican attire that he so loves; what makes him happy has always made me happy. It's about Diego—it's *always* been about Diego. He is my husband, my friend, my mother, my father, my son, me, my *universe*.

I drop my brush into the jar of spirits and push back my chair. Down in my soul, I know that now the painting is complete. Me and Diego in front of a welcoming, warm home. There is no one around to trouble us, no one else who might distract or threaten my grasp on Diego's heart. Here I have him all to myself as I have always wanted—no sharing with other women; here, he can adore only me.

Now the painting is lovely, and it dawns on me that I am thinking of what I see depicted in the oils as though it is a real place, somewhere that Diego and I can go where we can escape all the problems in our lives. My pain, the affairs he has that wound me so, the politics that so enrage him. The thought makes me smile for the first time in far too long.

I stand and the ghost of pain sings along the nerves in my back. It will not be long before it returns in full strength, as it always does. I test the oils with a fingertip; they are dry. I don't know why I am surprised at that, given the speed with which this wondrous, mysterious piece took shape beneath my brushes.

I am still smiling as I slide the painting next to the wall, behind all the other unfinished works. It will be my secret, a place where there is no pain, no jealousy, only contentment and joy and love, for me and Diego and no one else.

I know it will be there, waiting, when the time is right.

A Model Sailor

Aaron Rosenberg

Sinbad the Sailor is a dashing and heroic figure, the ultimate sailor, from *The Thousand and One Nights*, a collection of Middle Eastern and Indian stories dating back to the ninth century or earlier. Though the origins of the stories are uncertain, the first European translation was published by Antoine Galland in 1704, and the best-known English translation, the sixteen-volume *The Thousand Nights and a Night* by Sir Richard Burton, was first published in 1885. Sinbad's recounting of his seven voyages, each of which starts with him setting sail richly appointed and then leads to his shipwreck and other travails, only to end with his triumphant return wealthier than ever, have become a legend that has been retold in many formats and has led to many other heroic adventure tales in a similar mold.

Aaron Rosenberg is the author of the best-selling DuckBob SF comedy series, the *Relicant Chronicles* epic fantasy series, the *Dread Remora* space-opera series, and, with David Niall Wilson, the *O.C.L.T.* occult thriller series. His tie-in work includes novels for *Star Trek*, *Warhammer*, *World of WarCraft*, *Stargate: Atlantis*, and *Eureka*. He has written children's books (including the award-winning *Bandslam: The Junior Novel* and the #1 best-selling *42: The Jackie Robinson Story*), educational books, and roleplaying games (including the Origins Award-winning *Gamemastering Secrets*).

You can follow him online at gryphonrose.com, on Facebook at facebook.com/gryphonrose, and on Twitter @gryphonrose.

A Model Sailor

To say that the voyage had taken a turn for the worse would have been much like saying the Sultan's palace was large—while true, the gap between such a description and the reality in terms of scale would be sufficiently large for an entire fleet to sail through unimpeded. Indeed, one could easily be accused of downplaying to a nearly comical degree.

The trip had started well enough—they had set sail from Baghdad with a full crew of twenty and their holds stuffed with goods for sale and trade. Fair weather had graced their first week, the sun high and the sky clear but the wind stiff and steady, filling their sails and blowing them ever onward toward distant lands and foreign ports eager for their wares. The only incident of any note had been when old Hakim, a trusty and reliable hand well-liked by all, had succumbed to some strange ailment, perhaps brought on by the bracing wind and by foolishly offering to stand watch one night despite a brief but heavy bout of rain that had left him drenched and shivering, his nose and fingertips blue from the cold. He had worsened steadily after that, despite the captain's best efforts to minister to him, and three mornings later the men woke to find Hakim cold and still in his hammock, his body stiff and unyielding as the old oak his skin had resembled in hue and texture. They had sewn him into sailcloth and dropped him overboard, consigning the old sailor to the waves and the sea that had been his home for many long years, and had sailed on, one man fewer but a good deal heavier in heart.

Fortunately, at their next port of call, the captain found a willing replacement. A man had been sitting upon a worn barrel on one of the piers as they'd sailed up, and had immediately hopped to his feet in time to catch their rope and coil it about one of the pylons. He was tall and well-formed, his features noble and his beard neatly trimmed, yet his clothing was mere tatters and his turban ragged and stained. Clearly here was a man who had fallen on hard times, yet his eyes were bright and his smile warm as he welcomed the crew off the boat.

"Do you work here, then?" the captain asked him, stepping down last and joining this stranger on the pier as the men began unloading the hold to bring goods ashore for sale.

"I do not," the man replied. "I merely wait here in hopes of finding a ship that can carry me home. For I am a sailor like you, only currently without a way to sail."

"How came you here?" the captain inquired. For the man's voice and manner of speaking recalled home to him, rather than this distant shore.

"I was on a boat," the man answered, dipping his head in recollection. "But we were overtaken by a vast wave, which tumbled us all about and cracked the ship in two. I was fortunate enough to cling to a barrel"—and here he indicated the very barrel upon which he had been seated—"and that alone kept me alive, though I bobbed in the water like a cork tossed into a fountain. For many days and nights, I held to it, only half-conscious as we drifted along. Then a fisherman found me and fished me out of the water—not the catch he had hoped for, I am sure, but the one he discovered nonetheless! He brought me hence, and here I have remained, helping where I can in exchange for the occasional coin or scrap of food while hoping to find a ship willing to take me back to Baghdad."

The captain considered, scratching at his chin as he thought. "I have need of another man, for one of ours recently passed away after an illness," he admitted. "And we hail from Baghdad, so we will be returning there when our travels are complete. If you are willing to sign on as one of my crew, I will treat you well and eventually you will see home once more."

"With pleasure, and my thanks," the man exclaimed, offering his hand. "You may call me Bansid." And with that he became one of the ship's crew.

Bansid proved to be of great use, for he had been dwelling in that port for several weeks. As a result, he knew all the best places to sell the ship's wares, and all the best merchants to deal with, as well as those it would be wise to avoid. In short order, thanks to his help, the captain had sold off much of the ship's goods, traded others, and bought new items with the money thus gained. So it was that, once more fully laden and properly stocked, the ship set sail mere days later with Bansid on board. The captain had advanced him enough wages to purchase proper clothing and a clean turban, and the new addition looked completely at home as he scaled the lines and worked the ropes.

The rest of the crew were also content. Bansid was a friendly sort, always quick to lend a hand and always with a story to tell, yet he proved a good listener as well, and happy to sit quietly and allow others to speak. He complimented the cook on his meals, never complained about any task he was given, and slept without snoring. He seemed a model sailor and an excellent addition to the ship.

∼

Three days after they had left port, one of the sailors suffered a terrible fate. Nor was it of the type to be expected aboard a trading ship, where perils often awaited the careless and unwary. This death had little to do with a snagged line or a loose nail or a slippery deck. Indeed, the sailor in question, one Tareem by name, had been leaning upon the rail, having just finished swabbing the deck and taking a moment to enjoy the view before continuing on to some other task. The day was a fierce one, the sky gray and chill, the air blustery, the water roiling in tall, stiff peaks, and the ship was bobbing and weaving, tossed about by both wind and wave, yet such weather was bracing to a born sailor like Tareem, and merely served to sharpen his eye and quicken his blood.

However, none could have predicted what came next. Tareem gave a shout of surprise and pain, and those nearest turned toward him, only to stop and stare. Their friend and fellow had been set upon by a crab.

And what a crab it was! Its pincers were easily as long as a man was tall, its carapace the size of a rowboat, its eyes bigger than a man's head. It was as gray as the day, which perhaps explained how it had snuck up on poor Tareem unnoticed, and now it had the man caught in one pincer, the serrated edges of its massive claw already biting into his side.

Tareem cried out again, struggling to free himself, but his arms were no match for the crab's strength. Several others bounded forward, grabbing up scimitars and knives and clubs. But before they could reach their friend the crab leaped backward, hitting the water with a mighty splash that drenched the deck. The waves swallowed crab and sailor both, and that was the last anyone saw of poor Tareem.

∼

Two days later, Javad shouted, "Land ahead!" from the lookout. That puzzled the captain, for there was nothing to indicate land upon any of his maps. But Javad insisted it was so, and after a few moments Parsa agreed, calling, "I can see it!" from where he stood upon the prow.

"Very well," the captain stated. "It may be that we have stumbled upon some unknown island, and if so we will be the first to bring our goods to them and the first to discover what treasures they may have to offer. We will make for it, and see what we can see."

The crew cheered at this, for even though they were all men born and bred to the sea they still enjoyed walking upon dry land from time to time. Plus, if there were people there it would mean fresh food, possibly wine and women, and the opportunity for trade.

Sadly, as the boat drew near enough for all to see the land, they began to doubt whether any such delights awaited. For though there was a bright, pale strip that could only be sand, with trees waving beyond, there was no sign of human habitation, no city walls or tall buildings, nor even brightly striped tents. Nor did anyone come running to stare at them, or to call out a welcome.

"It seems we may have found an uninhabited place," the captain mused. "Well, if it is so we may still benefit from it, by finding fresh water and perhaps fruits and nuts to supplement our stores. There could be wild birds here as well." At that thought, the men's spirits rose once more, for fresh meat would be welcome indeed.

There being no place to tie up the ship, and too much risk in getting close when they had no idea how shallow the waters might become, it was decided to anchor well off and send a rowboat. Most of the men volunteered to go, but the captain sent only five: Armin, Darush, Izad, Kasra, and Bansid. A few of the others groused at the newest of their number being accorded such an honor, but none could deny that Bansid had proven himself useful, or that he was strong and observant enough to be a good choice for such a sortie.

Thus it was that the five unshipped one of the small rowboats, climbed into it, and rowed away toward the deserted beach, while the rest of the crew watched from on deck.

They rowed strong and steady, and within minutes their hull was scraping up onto the sand. Kasra was the first to climb out, and he gave a glad cry as his bare toes sank into the soft, damp sand.

Armin was next, but his attention was elsewhere, for something had sparkled at him there upon the ground. "Look!" he said, pointing, and made his way toward that spot. Stooping, he lifted the object that had caught his eye—which proved to be a diamond as large as his hand.

"Amazing!" Darush said, admiring his friend's discovery. Then he saw something, which proved to be another gem of comparable size. Soon they realized that such jewels were strewn all about them, and the men were eagerly exclaiming at their finds.

All except Bansid, who shook his head and eyed the trees beyond with some wariness. "I do not trust such riches when they are laying about so freely," he told the others. "I fear that this may be some manner of trap. We had best be wary."

"*You* be wary," Armin replied sharply, his hands already full of gems he juggled as he reached for another. "*We* are busy becoming rich."

Only Kasra, the youngest of the five, heeded Bansid's warning. Though he did select a large emerald from those littered upon the ground, the youthful sailor contented himself with that and watched their surroundings instead of trying for more.

It was he who first noticed movement among the trees and bushes bordering the beach. "There is something out there!" he cried.

Yet the others, intent upon gathering as many gems as possible, did not listen.

"Back to the boat!" Bansid ordered, his voice carrying the clear, confident tone of one long accustomed to command. Yet still, Armin, Darush, and Izad tarried, their greed overtaking their sense. Bansid retreated, head up and eyes scanning the foliage, and Kasra went with him, though reluctantly at the thought of leaving his friends behind.

More rustling arose, and then something charged out of the bushes. It was a boar, and an enormous one, nearly twice the size of a large man, its tusks as long as a man's arm. Yet the strangest thing about the approaching beast was not its size but its hide, for this was covered in glittering stones of all colors, very like those at the sailors' feet. It seemed the creature came here and rolled in the sand to scratch its back, dislodging gems as it did.

"Run!" Bansid shouted, and Kasra joined him. The other three did look up at that, and startled at the monster approaching. They dropped their treasures and turned to flee, but too late. The boar swung its head side to side, and its tusks tore into Armin, ripping him from belly to throat. Back the other direction and Darush fell, his stomach opened to the air. Izad got three paces before the boar gored him from behind, those giant tusks piercing the man's back and protruding from his chest.

"We cannot help them now," Bansid told Kasra, laying a hand on the younger man's arm. "We must save ourselves. Come!" And he led the way quickly back to their rowboat. Pushing it off from the beach, the two men leaped into it, breaking out the oars. The boar ran after them but stopped when the water lapped at its hooves, snorting in dismay and rage at seeing some of its quarry escape.

With only two to row, it took longer, but soon enough the rowboat was bumping up against the ship's hull. Ropes were lowered and Bansid and Kasra secured them to the boat's sides before shimmying up and onto the deck.

"Glad I am that you both returned to us safely," the captain declared, clapping a hand on each man's shoulder. "For I would rather lose three than five."

"Nor did we return entirely empty-handed," Bansid replied, reaching into his vest and drawing out a ruby as large as a baby's head. Kasra produced his emerald, and these were added to the ship's wealth.

That night the men drank a toast to their three lost friends, and the ship sailed on.

~

The ship's next stop was another unexpected landing, this time upon a tiny, conical island jutting up from the water like a mountaintop piercing the clouds. The small outcropping's surface was rough, dark-gray stone, but crumbly to the touch. Several men leaped down to investigate, and despite Bansid's urgings, Ehsan drove his blade down into the ground as deep as it would go. When he pulled back, the lower third of the weapon had melted away, and the rest was red-hot. But Ehsan had little time to worry about that—from the hole he had made a strange glowing liquid shot forth, like a fountain of fire. Its spray engulfed him, and the poor sailor screamed as his blood boiled and his flesh baked. He toppled to the ground, steam rising from his corpse, as the other sailors beat a hasty retreat. They had no sooner raised sail and cleared the island when a far larger stream of the same liquid burst out of its top, covering the entire island in glowing liquid fire.

~

Ghazi and Parsa died next. They landed—after being turned and tossed about by a storm so massive it had filled their world horizon to horizon and blanketed them in torrential rain for days on end—at a fabulous city made all of white marble and edged all in gold.

The city's prince welcomed them and gifted each man with magnificent brooches of rubies and diamonds and pearls. Many of the crew pinned theirs to their vests or shirts or sashes. Bansid affixed his brooch proudly to the front of his turban, and Javad and Kasra quickly did the same, for the two young men had noticed that of them all, their newest member was always the one who remained calmest and least affected by the strange events they were sailing through, and who came out the least scathed. But Ghazi and Parsa, being greedy, hid their brooches away among their belongings, and so when the prince treated them all to an elaborate feast as his special guests, those two alone among the crew were not wearing their new jewelry.

The feast was fine indeed, with a great many dishes laid out, and all upon plates of solid silver or gold. There was wine aplenty, and beautiful women danced to delightful music played by skilled musicians stationed in each corner of the room.

They were in the midst of the third course when a strange fluttering sound was heard overhead.

"Do not concern yourselves," the prince assured them all. "It is only the royal flock."

Just then the sound increased, and a flock entered the room via the large, arched openings overlooking the gardens beyond, soaring here and there below the high, vaulted ceiling. The birds resembled peacocks, with long tail feathers naturally colored in fascinating and intricate patterns, and small sprays of feathers above their brows that were equally decorated. Their eyes were sharp and bright, as were their beaks, and they chirped as they flew.

"They are trained, of course," the prince explained happily. "They know all of us, and would never harm us. Unwanted visitors are treated harshly, but that is why we have awarded you those brooches you wear—they mark you as honored guests, and so you are safe as well."

At that, Ghazi and Parsa rose, their faces white as flour. The two sailors made to dash from the room, intending to flee back to the ship and retrieve the protective brooches, but it was much too late. Upon seeing them, and their unadorned state, the birds let loose a harsh, fierce cry and dove, in a vast wedge of feathers and talons and beaks, straight at the unlucky pair. Before anyone could so much as rise from their seats to help, the birds had enveloped Ghazi and Parsa in a whirlwind of avian fury, tearing at their flesh and hair from every direction.

When the birds dispersed a moment later, the two sailors lay dead upon the floor, their blood pooling around them from a thousand cuts and gashes and bites. The prince expressed his sympathies, of course, and awarded the captain a cask of enormous black pearls as recompense, but it was still a somber crew that set sail the following day, leaving the island and its trained attack birds far behind.

That night, back on the water again with nothing but ocean around them as far as the eye could see, the men sat together and took counsel.

"We are cursed!" Mira, the cook, cried. "How else could such horrible calamities befall us!"

"I do not believe in curses," Zana argued. "Yet, we have assuredly seen rotten luck, and all in a spate."

"Luck? There is no luck involved," Ramin insisted. "This is black arts. What else could explain it?"

"If it were, though," Mazdak commented, and the others stilled to listen, for of them all he was the oldest and wisest, "would we not all have perished by now? Instead, here we still sit, and far wealthier than when we left."

The others nodded, for that much was clearly true. Yet they were still disquieted.

"I have never even heard of such things as we have encountered," Javad said softly. "At least, not outside tales. Never did I think I would be living through such things myself."

"Tales indeed," Kasra agreed. "It is like the stories of Sinbad, is it not?"

Many of the others shook their heads at this, for Sinbad was a figure often both invoked and cursed by sailors of their homeland. He was a heroic figure, to be sure, who survived all manner of catastrophe on only his wit and his daring alone, and yet those around him tended to suffer greatly from his very presence.

"I wonder if even Sinbad himself could survive all that we have seen," Zana said sourly. "Let us hope that we are done with such things and will have smooth sailing the rest of the way home."

To that they all agreed, and drinks were raised in the hopes that it might indeed be so.

Yet Bansid said nothing, only watched and drank and kept his counsel to himself.

~

The following night a mighty storm struck, equal to the one they had crashed through before. Vahid and Zana were on watch, wrapped in oilskins to protect them from the deluge, their hands and feet tangled in the rope lines so that they would not be swept overboard as the sea smashed against their ship and the waves topped the railing to sluice across the deck.

A sharp cry was their only warning, and that was muffled by the pelting rain and carried off by the wind before it could reach their ears. So Zana barely reacted at first when a dark shape emerged from the clouds and scooped up his companion, lifting Vahid high into the sky and disappearing with him into the night.

"No!" Zana called, reaching out for his friend even though Vahid was already gone. Some of the others heard him and emerged onto the deck just in time to see another shape emerge, plummeting down, its feet outstretched to latch onto Zana's shoulders. In shape it was much like an enormous bird, but its upper body and head were those of a woman, with long dark hair streaming behind, and its face was filled with a furious hunger that chilled every man there to the bone.

"Harpy!" That came from Bansid, who ran toward Zana, his lantern held high. The creature shrank back from the light flickering there against the dark. Yet her talons did not unclench, and she dragged poor Zana with her as she went, his own feet scraping across the deck. Then, with a powerful beat of her wings, the harpy leaped upward, the sailor still caught in her clutches. Bansid threw the lantern, but the wind batted it aside and it sailed out to sea even as the creature disappeared among the clouds with her prey.

~

They were now down to eleven men, including the captain. "We can barely manage the ship with so few," he stated, speaking to them all once the storm had passed and they had toasted the lost pair of Vahid and Zana. "We will limp home as best we can, but if we see a port we shall make for it, in the hopes that we can find a few more sailors to bring on."

"Who would wish to join so cursed a crew?" Mira muttered, but no one answered.

~

The next land they sighted proved to be uninhabited, at least by men. There were monkeys aplenty, however, and birds, and other manner of beasts. The captain sent a rowboat ashore, with Ramin, Shapour, Javad, and Bansid, to find what fresh food and water they could, for the ship was running low even with so many fewer mouths to feed.

When they landed upon the rocky beach, the sailors noted its strange appearance, for the ground was pocked with holes, none larger than a thumb in width and spaced anywhere from inches to several feet apart. "Avoid the holes," Bansid warned, and Javad nodded. The other two scoffed at this advice, but still they followed in Bansid's footsteps as they made their way inland.

There they found a stream, and filled their skins with water. Trees yielded coconuts and pineapples and oranges and dates. Bansid and Javad filled the sacks they had brought, and were content.

But the other two were not satisfied. "I want meat," Ramin insisted, and Shapour nodded. Together they used one of their bags as a makeshift net and captured a trio of small monkeys, who shrieked in terror and struggled but could not tear free of the coarse sackcloth. The two repeated the trick with their second bag, and so it was that the two of them ventured toward the boat carrying wriggling, screaming sacks.

Ramin had only just set foot on the beach when something erupted from a hole near his foot. He screamed and toppled, clutching his leg. The sack fell from his hands and the monkeys escaped—only to fall as well, choking and then going still as dark shapes arrowed up from the holes to strike at them.

"Snakes!" Javad whispered. And indeed it was. The entire beach, it seemed, was home to thousands of small, dark snakes. Judging by their effect, the narrow reptiles boasted a deadly poison. Already Ramin was moaning and moving sluggishly. Another snake bit him on the arm, and a third on the cheek, and then he twitched and stopped writhing altogether.

Shapour, having seen, this, tossed his bag as far from him as he could. But too late—snakes emerged and attacked each of his ankles, and the man screamed and fell. He was bitten four more times before he even struck the ground, and ceased moving almost immediately thereafter.

"Run," Bansid advised in a whisper. He took off across the beach, toward the boat, weaving and dodging to keep as much distance as possible between himself and the snake holes. Javad followed exactly, and the two reached the rowboat unscathed. Pitching their bags into it, they dragged the boat out to the water and then jumped in, rowing quickly back to the ship.

Then they were nine.

"We cannot risk any more deaths," the captain announced to the remaining men. "We will head for home and not stop until we get there."

The men cheered at that, but still they glanced about nervously. The fates had already shown that they did not require land to strike at the poor, heavily beset crew.

~

The day was fine and clear, the wind swift but warm, when Kasra cried out from above. "What?" the captain was quick to ask. "Is it land?"

"No," the young sailor called back. "A whirlpool, directly ahead!"

"Hard to port!" the captain called, and Mazdak at the wheel did as ordered, yanking down hard on the heavy wooden wheel to bring the ship about. Despite his efforts, however, the boat continued on its present course, and the old sailor cursed.

"We are trapped in the currents!" he shouted over what had first seemed only the rushing of the wind but now grew louder than air alone could explain. "I can't get us free!"

"Abandon ship!" Bansid bellowed, making for one of the rowboats. But the captain held up a hand, barring his path.

"No," the captain countered. "A smaller boat will only be pulled in that much faster. We must stay with the ship and trust in its size and bulk to see us through." He turned away and gave orders to secure everything tight, as in a heavy storm. But behind him, Bansid shook his head.

"What do we do?" Javad asked the sailor, stepping up beside him and speaking softly. "I do not wish to die here."

"Gather what you will," Bansid told him. "Stow it in the rowboat. Tell anyone else you think will listen. We will place ourselves there—that way, if the captain is correct, we will not have to abandon our friends or our ship." He shook his head again. "But I fear he will not be correct."

In the end there were four of them—Kasra and Mazdak joined Javad and Bansid in the rowboat. The captain frowned upon seeing the quartet hunkering down there, but did not order them out.

The ship was now moving in a circle, and they could see the whirlpool clearly at the center of their circuit. It was a deep hole in the water, as if someone had pulled a drain from a basin and the water was all swirling down and through. The closer they drew to it, the tighter the ship's circle became, and the faster they flew, their prow cutting through the water and sending white spray everywhere. Over the rushing sound they could all hear creaks and groans as the ship shuddered, its timbers not built to withstand such intense stress exerted from its sides and below.

"Hang on," Bansid urged, and the three with him did so, winding their hands around ropes and oarlocks and hooking their feet under planks. The ship was shaking, and with a mighty tearing sound something tore apart.

"We're taking on water!" Ario shouted from the deck. Already the ship had canted to one side as its hold filled, the added weight just dragging it deeper into the whirlpool's depths.

"Now!" Bansid shouted. And, with a mighty swing, his scimitar lashed out and sliced through the ropes holding the rowboat in place.

The tiny vessel leaped forward, all but flying across the deck of the foundering ship. They had been on the starboard side, and as the rowboat launched it sailed outward, away from the ship and the whirlpool alike. It skipped across the surface of the maelstrom, yet its momentum carried it on, evading the vortex's deadly clutches. When the rowboat finally slowed to a stop, the waters around it were calm, unruffled by the whirlpool's motion.

Javad and the others sat up and glanced behind. They could just make out the ship's top mast as it sank below the surface, dragged down by the whirlpool that was tearing it apart. Of the captain and the rest there was no sign.

"You saved our lives," Mazdak said to Bansid, clasping the younger man's hands. "Thank you."

"I did, but it is possible I imperiled them as well," Bansid replied. He sank down on the plank seat and shook his head. "It may be that all of this is my fault. Yet, if you will follow me and do as I say, I will see you home again safely."

"Why would any of this be your fault?" Javad asked. "You are not responsible for Fate taking a strange interest in tormenting us."

"I may be," the other sailor responded. "Fate has always delighted in treating me so, and those around me often suffer for it. You were not wrong in that, Kasra. For indeed, I am the one called Sinbad the sailor. And in my wish to take to the sea once more, I have dragged you and your friends into my tale." He bowed his head. "I can only beg your forgiveness, and strive to see us all returned to Baghdad in one piece."

The others gaped, for never had they expected that this vagabond-become-friend would turn out to be the legendary sailor himself! Yet perhaps it did explain the incidents they had suffered. Still, the four of them were alive and unharmed, and their rowboat weighed down with the riches they had acquired on their journey thus far.

They could only hope that Sinbad's luck continued to hold, and that by modeling their own behavior after his they might also partake in his uncanny knack for survival and success.

The Trials of Baldur

Will McDermott

Baldur (also spelled Baldr, Balder) is a Norse god, the son of Odin the Allfather and Frigga. Baldur's name translates from Old High German as brave, defiant, and lord or prince. Considered the most beloved of the gods, he married Nanna and fathered Forseti. The only one who didn't love Baldur was Loki, who contrived to kill the god. The legend of his death is one of the best known Norse tales from the Prose Edda.

Will McDermott turned an early love of mystery, fantasy, and games into a career. He has published eight novels and 16 short stories, and helped create innumerable worlds, characters, and stories for card, board, and video games. His fiction is often set in gaming universes, including *Magic: The Gathering, Warhammer 40K,* and *Mage Wars.* He is known for bringing larger-than-life characters alive on the page, including *Warhammer*'s Kal Jerico and Mad D'onne, *Magic's* Balthor the Stout, and *The Night Stalker*'s Carl Kolchak (who can be found in the pages of Will's Night Stalker novel, *Strangled By Death*, available March 2021). Find out more at willmcdermott.com. Follow him on Instagram at @w_mcdermott.

The Trials of Baldur

LOKI, THE GOD OF MISCHIEF, THE TRICKSTER, THE MOTHER OF THREE monsters, he who will be bound by Thor until Ragnarök, harbored such an intense jealousy and hatred of Baldur, the fair and most beloved of gods, that the trickster once lay with a seer in the distant wilds of Jotunheim in payment of prophecies concerning the death of Baldur.

The craggy seer, with wrinkles folded over more wrinkles, told the god of mischief many foul things that had not yet come to pass. She told of the wailing of gods and the keening of maidens over the death of Baldur, who would fall at the hands of his blind brother, Hodr.

The seeress also told of a humble and timid shrub that would, one day, fell the most beloved of all gods—the mistletoe—and how it blooms even in the dead of Jotunheim's cruel winter, bringing life to the cold, dead land.

"Where can one find this meek yet ruinous plant?" Loki asked as he stroked the crone's leathery neck in their shared bed of birch boughs.

"Three mighty oak trees provide home, hearth, and health to the seedlings here in Jotunheim," replied the seeress. "But all three are guarded by giantesses mightier than the trees they protect."

"I too am powerful, my sweet," cooed the trickster. His hand closed slightly around her neck as if to prove his point.

She laughed at the thought. "You could never best these giantesses," she croaked. "They are far too powerful for your weak magics. It would take a formidable god like Thor or Odin or Baldur to prevail in such a heroic trial."

Loki nodded in assent, knowing the seeress' words to be true.

"Thank you, my pet," he purred as he clenched his fingers and squeezed her neck until she breathed no more. "You have been most helpful."

∼

A plan formed in the nether reaches of Loki's twisted mind. The dead of winter had enveloped Midgard as well as Jotunheim, and the trickster had heard the wailings of the Druids in the north as they cried for some sign of the coming thaw. He had reveled in their pain, knowing full well the icy grip of winter would endure for many fortnights—longer if he were to breathe the frigid winds of Jotunheim down onto Midgard.

But now he saw how to use the pain of the Druids to his advantage in a way far more enjoyable than simply drinking in their icy anguish. He made his way to Asgard as the fullness of the plan formed inside his devilish head.

Soon Loki found himself on the golden plains of Asgard, standing outside the verdant gardens surrounding the gleaming Breidablik, the great hall of Baldur. Known as the fairest and purest point in the nine realms, so perfect was Breidablik that nothing impure could dare enter.

As Loki glared at the broad splendor of Baldur's hall, his resolve renewed despite the pain he would endure upon entering the grounds. His powerful hatred for the beloved god burned deep into the trickster's heart, steeling it against what was to come.

How could someone so underserving possess the love and admiration of all gods, he thought, of all beings in the nine realms? How had someone so simple attained such riches? The fairest of halls, the largest of boats, and the most beautiful and devoted of mates. It was unfair. Why, Loki had often wondered, were beauty and strength always revered over intellect and guile?

The god of mischief braced his tainted body against the scathing purity of Breidablik and entered the magnificent grounds. As he did, Loki shrouded his visage in the guise of Hodr, glad for the blindness that his magical cloak provided, for it blotted out the terrible beauty surrounding him. The purity pushed at the trickster as he shuffled forward, but by great force of will he made it to the hall and rapped on the copper-bound mahogany door with Hodr's gnarled staff.

The dark-wood door opened, bringing the shrouded trickster face to face with Nanna, Baldur's beautiful wife. Once handmaiden to Frigga, that most exquisite of goddesses, Nanna's radiance outshone all but her former queen. How fitting, the noble gods thought, that the fairest of gods—Baldur—should wed the fairest of all goddesses, save the wife of Odin.

All but Loki, that is. For, as much as Loki despised Baldur, he coveted Nanna more. In those moments, if the trickster allowed a glimmer of honesty to darken his brain, he might admit his mortal plans for Baldur were as much about wedding—or bedding—Nanna as they were about removing a Baldur-sized thorn from his psyche.

"Why, brother Hodr," Nanna said upon seeing the trickster in the guise of Baldur's blind brother. "Why do you dawdle and knock? You know you are always welcome here in Breidablik. Come in. Come in."

Nanna's voice was as smooth as satin sliding across marble, as melodic as a thousand chimes blowing in a light spring breeze. For longer than he cared to admit, Loki stood and stared, his ears and mind creating a portrait in his brain of the fair Nanna.

Finally, he spoke.

"There is no time," the trickster lied, knowing full well he could not enter. "I must speak with my brother in the gardens at once. It is a matter of utmost urgency."

With that, the disguised Loki shuffled off the marble threshold back toward the gardens. His breath had become labored from the heady interaction with the fair Nanna, so he bowed his head and made as if the short trek into the gardens were a labor worthy of Thor.

"What is so urgent, brother?" Baldur called as he bounded into the gardens behind Loki. "What vital business brings you to my hall?"

The cloaked trickster turned to face the fairest god and, were he not already blinded by his disguise, Baldur's radiance would have struck him so. Even through the swirling miasma of Hodr's clouded gaze, Loki saw Baldur's shining aura limning his statuesque form in a halo of light. It took all of Loki's will to avoid flinching at the heavenly sight seeping through his dead eyes.

"I have come to convey dire news from the realm of Midgard, dear brother," Loki began in the croaking tones of poor, blind Hodr. He bowed his head low to avoid burning the image of Baldur into his eyes—a fate worse than death by far. The trickster's perfect ears, however, heard clearly the rustling of nearby verdant flowers as they also bowed to the god—in deference to his surpassing beauty.

"I have heard the wailing of the Druids of the North," continued Loki, focusing on the task at hand. "They huddle in their hovels while a harsh winter blankets the land, turning the fertile land white with snow and the lush forests brown with death."

Baldur stepped forward and draped a thick, muscular arm across Hodr's stooped shoulders and began walking him toward the great hall.

"What can I do about the winter, brother?" he asked with a laugh. "It will end when it ends, and the wailing will cease. There is nothing to be done but wait for the sun's return and drink mead to stave off the cold. Come with me into my hall and we shall drink to an early spring."

Loki shuffled along as slowly as he dared while he barreled forward with his explanation.

"There is something you—and only you—can do to ease their suffering, my brother," he said. "For only Baldur, the fair and beloved, is brave enough to face the dangers and strong enough to complete this trial."

Baldur stopped, struck by Loki's faint praise. He turned and grabbed Hodr's bent form by both shoulders, forcing the disguised trickster to face him.

"What is this quest, my brother," he asked. "What would you have me do to aid the Druids of the north during their time of despair?"

Inwardly, Loki smiled. He had the fair god hooked. All he need do is point him in the direction of danger and the beautiful Baldur would rush headlong toward it.

"There is a plant I have heard tale of, brother," Loki croaked outwardly as he purred inwardly, "that blooms and remains green even during the deadest days of winter. It would shine like a beacon of hope in the forests of Midgard, bringing life to where once there was only death. You must bring this flower to the Druids to restore their faith in life and rebirth."

"That sounds easy," boomed Baldur. "I dare say even you could perform this task, dear brother. Where does this flower grow? What are these grave dangers of which you speak?"

"Jotunheim," replied Loki, daring finally to gaze at the glowing god before him, hoping for some twitch, some sign of weakness at the coming knowledge. "It is guarded by giants!"

~

Before night fell, Baldur had laid provisions within *Ringhorn*, the grandest boat in the nine realms, and set sail out of Asgard. In the bow the shining god had stowed cattle and feed for a fortnight. In the stern lay a hundred casks of mead and ale. In between, the god had piled fourfold one hundred fur pelts, which hid two-score weapons. Amidst all these stores stood Baldur's mighty steed Lettfeti, its hot breath jetting like great gouts of steam from a dwarf furnace.

The lord of Breidablik looked over his provisions from atop Lettfeti as *Ringhorn* passed beneath the Rainbow Bridge. The top of its curved prow—carved from a single mighty oak—nearly scraped the base of the multifaceted, arched gateway.

It took three days to cross the Iving, the river separating Asgard from Jotunheim. Baldur remained vigilant atop Lettfeti throughout, a thick rope grasped in each hand allowing the god to turn the mast to harness the winds.

As the frozen crags of Jotunheim's coast came into view, a jolt from below staggered Baldur's steed. Lettfeti lurched, threatening to send Baldur flying over the gunwale into the icy water. *Ringhorn* listed severely until the tip of its mast skimmed the water. Several bulls and a score of casks tumbled into the river as the shining god's face came within inches of the surface.

With his aura lighting the murky depths, Baldur saw movement beneath the waves. He dug his heels into the ribs of Lettfeti and hauled on the rope in his high hand to drag the mast away from the river.

As the sails rose from the icy torrent, the shape below also rose and gained speed. The creature, a sinewy and scaly serpent, broke the surface as *Ringhorn* settled back on its keel.

Turning the Tied

At twice the height of *Ringhorn's* curved prow, the serpent's head towered above the mast. It opened its massive maw, revealing row upon row of spear-like teeth, and hissed, spraying acidic sputum that burned gaping holes through *Ringhorn's* sails, shredding them in an instant.

Baldur hauled on the ropes to swing the mast hard around. The rotating boom slapped the monster's sinewy neck, causing it to double over and sending the head plummeting down toward the hull. Baldur released his hold on the ropes, rode toward the bow and leaped off Lettfeti. He grabbed the river monster by two massive teeth and dragged its head down into the herd of cattle, which scattered to the rear, kicking pelts and kegs over the side in their wake.

Using the boom like a pulley, Baldur hauled the monster's massive body from the water until it hung from the boom, its legs and tail flailing like an upended tortoise. With one final heave, Baldur pulled the serpent over the boom and then twirled around to swing the beast like a hammer on the end of a rope. As it twirled, Baldur jerked his arms back to snap its teeth and send the river monster hurtling through the air over the horizon toward Asgard.

With the threat gone, Baldur took stock of the damage. His sails were shredded to tatters and his stores depleted by half. Worse, he could no longer see the icy cliffs of Jotunheim on the horizon. *Ringhorn* lay adrift in the current, which pulled him away from shore.

Baldur looked at the long, curved teeth he had ripped from the monster's jaws. They stood twice his height and were as thick as his torso. He fitted each with a tholepin and attached them to the gunwales. Sitting astride his steed amidship, Baldur grabbed each tooth and used them as oars to row the rest of the way across the Iving.

~

Baldur hauled the prow of *Ringhorn* onto a rocky shoal and secured the bow line beneath a boulder the size of a mead hall to secure his boat. He lifted his steed onto the frozen ground and slew and ate one of his cattle, for he had not broken his fast for three days.

Sated, the shining god tied furs and casks across Lettfeti's back before leaping astride his steed and spurring it to a gallop. For two days, Baldur rode across the frozen desolation of Jotunheim, surrounded by craggy, ice-laden cliffs that arched overhead. Hundred-foot ice spears that had grown for an age at the tips of the pointed crags threatened to drop and cleave anything that passed below.

At the end of the second day, Baldur came to the edge of a great forest. Giant spruce, alder, ash, and sycamore rose toward a bleak sky. Their bare branches covered in ice held a scattering of brown leaves that fluttered like lonely pennants in the cold wind of Jotunheim. Baldur slowed Lettfeti and entered the wood, searching for any sign of the lone oak Hodr had said he would find, one of three in the realm that held the mistletoe plant he sought.

After a time, Baldur's eyes were drawn to a shock of green life amidst the brown death. He spurred his steed forward and came up beneath the barren branches of the greatest oak the fair god had ever laid eyes upon. It was so tall its canopy disappeared into the dark, roiling clouds that ever covered Jotunheim. It was so big around, a mead hall filled with two-score warriors could fit within its trunk.

Far above him, near the top of the surrounding trees, a large green bush enveloped a limb as thick as Baldur's thighs, looking for all the realms like a giant witch's broom. Grabbing a sickle made of uru, the same metal as Thor's hammer, Baldur leaped from the back of Lettfeti and began to scale the great oak.

The god climbed hundreds of feet until he reached the limb bearing the mistletoe. Baldur stepped onto the thick branch and strode out to stand above the green bush with its unusually suggestive, twin-lobed leaves. He raised the uru sickle over his head and cleaved the thick branch in one clean stroke. As the mistletoe-laden limb fell, the god snatched the end with his free hand.

Baldur was almost overcome by the aroma emanating from the swollen, white berries that sprouted from the slender stems below the delicate leaves. It was almost intoxicating. The god shook his head to clear his mind before climbing down the tree, his prize in hand.

When Baldur reached the bottom, he found a Jotun giantess in a standoff with his steed at the base of the mighty oak. The two stared at one another like rutting rams, watching for a moment of fear or hesitation in the eyes of the other.

Without taking her eyes off Lettfeti, or even blinking, the giantess spoke.

"You have desecrated my tree!" she barked. "Like all Asgardians, you take that which does not belong to you."

Despite being slight and bent and withered with age, the giantess stood defiant in the face of the shining god. She who had somehow cowed the fearless Lettfeti now showed no fear in the face of Baldur's godly bearing.

He bowed low, sweeping his arms before him in a sign of respect.

"I apologize," Baldur said. "I had no idea this old forest or this young bush were anyone's possession. Are not the trees and beasts free for all strong enough to claim them?"

"Typical Asgardian rhetoric," growled the crone giantess. "Everything belongs to the mighty gods."

"My father's father did create the entirety of the nine realms," Baldur stated with a smile and a short laugh. The crone was not amused, so Baldur softened his tone and tried again.

"I am truly sorry for my impertinence in removing the bush," he said. "What can I pay you for it? I have plenty of furs in my ship and gold in my hall."

"Nothing," replied the crone. "You can pay nothing for your impertinence. The damage is already done. You have ruined my mistletoe with that dull-metal blade. Only gold may touch the sacred bush."

"Can we not come to some arrangement?" asked the shining god. "You can take half the bush and replant, but I must take some of this mistletoe to Midgard. The Druids of the North cry out for life in their winter-dead forests. Surely, you can understand their plight."

"I understand nothing but the arrogance of Asgard," replied the giantess. "Who are you to dictate how all beings may live their lives? Leave the bush in my care and begone. I care nothing for your Druids."

Baldur considered the giantess. Her stern countenance had not wavered. If anything, her scowl had deepened and intensified.

"I am sorry we cannot come to an arrangement, giantess of Jotunheim," he started.

"My name is Tokk," screamed the crone.

"I wish you would be reasonable, Tokk," Baldur began again. "I have offered you repayment and to share in this bounty. You have declined both. Other mistletoe grown in this realm you can cultivate. The Druids of Midgard need this one specimen. I will take my leave now."

"If you remove yourself with that bush," cried Tokk as Baldur mounted Lettfeti, "I shall place a curse on all mistletoe in the realm."

As Baldur rode off toward *Ringhorn*, the voice of the crone echoed behind him.

"Mistletoe will crumble to dust if once they touch the ground," she called. "They will likewise wither and die of thirst if removed from their oak hosts, and shall slowly kill whatever arboreal host they claim as home unless that tree has a steady supply of nutrients and water."

Baldur laughed at the pathetic ramblings of the ancient giantess, for he did not believe she had the power to bind a curse to all mistletoe everywhere.

∼

Upon returning to *Ringhorn*, Baldur leaped Lettfeti over the gunwale onto the remaining furs amidship. He lashed the mistletoe to the mast before grabbing the tooth-oars and using them to lift the hull from the rocky shoal and push off into the icy river.

Baldur's bulging muscles made quick work of the return passage across the Iving, and the Rainbow Bridge came into view at first light. However, when Baldur stowed the oars and turned to retrieve the mistletoe from its lashings, he found the bush lifeless and brown. Its delicate leaves had crumbled to dust and the bulging berries had shriveled to pits.

"Damn that witch and her curse," muttered Baldur, his shining aura dimming alongside his mood.

Half a fortnight had passed since Hodr had brought him the dire news of the wailing Druids, and so far he had nothing but tattered sails, depleted stores, and a crumbling bush to show for his efforts.

And yet, he had crossed the seething Iving twice alone, a feat not matched since the Allfather had entered Jotunheim an age before to tame the giants. He had faced and defeated the river monster that had scuttled a dozen-dozen ships before *Ringhorn*. And he had climbed the tallest oak in the realms and hewn its mighty limb. He was Baldur. He could not be bested by a mere witch.

Baldur grabbed the tooth oars and heaved *Ringhorn* about in two mighty strokes. His aura renewed with his confidence; the shining god threw his rippling muscles into rowing. So fast did *Ringhorn* speed across the Iving that its wake washed over the Rainbow Bridge as the water parted to the riverbed behind its stern. When the longboat reached the far shore before midday, the prow cleaved a path onto the rocky shole that reached midship.

Lettfeti leaped the gunwale with Baldur astride, landing on the same shore Baldur had left but hours before. The pair galloped faster than the wind across the icy, crag-ridden land toward the great, winter forest once again.

A trek that had taken two days lasted less than a day. When Baldur pulled on the reins to slow Lettfeti at the edge of the forest, the beast hardly huffed nor sweated. Upon entering the woods, Baldur led his steed around the edge of the tree line away from the witch Tokk's oak toward the second target near the great wood's northern border.

Another day of searching brought Baldur to the base of a nearly identical, if slightly smaller, twin to the first oak. High above, just under the forest canopy, he spotted a shock of green, a bulbous mass surrounding a great limb.

Baldur could not cut this limb. He reckoned he would need the moisture and nutrients contained in the entirety of the mighty oak to sustain the small bush during the long journey to Midgard. He chose his mightiest axe, its six-foot handle carved from the core of a hickory, its curved head—forged and tempered by dwarfs from cold iron and uru—reaching another five feet above and below the stock.

The fair god strode forward, grasped his axe in both hands and rotated his body like a coiled spring. With his arms quivering and his chest tightening from the strain, Baldur set sight on the trunk, tightening his grip as he prepared to cleave the tree with a single strike.

"Stop!" commanded a deep, husky voice as Baldur swung the axe. "That tree is under my protection, Asgardian."

Baldur could not halt his attack. The energy had to be unleashed. So, mid-swing, the god simply opened his hands and released the axe. It clattered away across the forest floor, spinning as it tumbled and hewing several saplings and one tall sycamore before coming to rest halfway through a white spruce.

Baldur turned to face the protector of the oak and saw a giantess who was as like day is to night compared to Tokk. She towered over the tall god, her broad chest and shoulders well above his eyes. Next to the mighty giantess stood a riding wolf ten hands taller than Lettfeti, which the giantess held by a fistful of vipers she used as reins.

"My name is Hyrrokin," boomed the giantess, her voice cracking the air like thunder. "I am the guardian of this great oak. It is not yours to destroy."

Baldur bowed low, apologized for his impertinence, and explained to Hyrrokin the plight of the Druids on Midgard, his need for the mistletoe, and the curse placed on the shrubs by Tokk.

"She is a wicked one, that Tokk," agreed Hyrrokin. "She only cares for herself. The power of the mistletoe is a gift from the universe and should be shared. Her curse has now made that impossible."

"I appreciate your understanding in my endeavor, Hyrrokin," Baldur said. "May I have this oak and mistletoe for the Druids of Midgard?"

"You may if you allow me to harvest half its berries," Hyrrokin replied, "I will smear some into a deep gash in Tokk's oak tree to regrow the bush you took. The rest I will use to make a linctus I use to heal my wolf when it sustains injuries."

"You are most generous, Hyrrokin," replied the shining god. "I do not know how to repay you."

Hyrrokin smiled. "I know how, Asgardian," she replied. "You can face me in combat. I would test my mettle against the fairest and strongest of gods. If you best me, I will offer you an additional gift to ease your journey."

"What is that gift?" Baldur asked as he clapped his hands together in anticipation of the forthcoming battle.

Hyrrokin reached into a massive pack on the side of her wolf and hauled out a small, dark-skinned, elf-like creature, which she set on the ground. "This is Fit," she said, pointing to the only dwarf Baldur had seen outside a forge. "He helps me care for the trees. He may be able to help you overcome Tokk's curse long enough to reach Midgard."

"I accept your challenge," Baldur roared, feeling confident in his abilities to best even such a large and healthy giantess. He stepped forward to clasp her hand to confirm the pact. "What are the rules of this contest?"

Hyrrokin enveloped Baldur's shining hand in her massive palm and shook it once.

"None!" she said as she wrapped her other hand around Baldur's forearm and yanked him from the ground. As Baldur's legs and arms flailed, Hyrrokin flung him a thousand feet through the forest. The god slammed into an old hickory so hard it sent a crack snaking fifty feet up the trunk.

Baldur crumpled to the ground in a heap, dazed from the concussive force. He glanced up as he heard—and felt—what sounded like a stampede of oxen rumbling toward him. The stunned god looked up in time to see Hyrrokin bearing down on him, her head lowered.

Before Baldur could move, the giantess barreled into him, smacking their skulls together. The sharp report echoed like thunder through the forest, sending flocks of birds fluttering from their perches, squawking and screeching in alarm.

For a second time, Baldur hurtled into the hickory. His broad shoulders slammed into the cracked trunk, which shattered under the strain. The god scrambled away to avoid being crushed as the tree slid off its splintered stump and crashed to the ground.

"I thought you cared for this forest, Hyrrokin," he bellowed. "How can you be so cavalier about its destruction?"

The giantess stalked toward Baldur as he backed away, trying desperately to remain out of her reach.

"That hickory was old and sick. It needed to come down to provide space for new growth," she said. "Moreover, I required a weapon with reach!"

Hyrrokin grabbed the splintered end of the fallen tree, lifted it into the air and smashed it down atop Baldur before he could turn to run. The blow drove the god to ground where he lay on his back pinned by the massive trunk. To ensure Baldur couldn't escape, Hyrrokin strode forward and sat atop the trunk directly above the god's shining chest.

"I believe I have won the battle, Asgardian," roared Hyrrokin with a hearty laugh. "Although it was far too easy. I feel cheated."

"I would never wish to cheat you of anything," said Baldur. He reached up to grasp the trunk with both hands, "except for a victory you have not yet earned!"

With that, Baldur the fair, Baldur the just and wise, but also Baldur the strong, lifted the weight of the trunk—and with it the weight of Hyrrokin—off his chest and flung them both high into the air. As the hickory and giantess flew through the uppermost leaves, Baldur stood and dusted off his clothing.

He watched as the odd flying duo disappeared above the canopy. He waited for their reappearance, stretching the aching muscles in his back and shoulders as seconds ticked over into minutes. Just as the long march of time became unbearable, the birds nesting in the treetops screeched and scattered as the hickory crashed through the canopy, with Hyrrokin standing atop it.

As the two objects descended, Baldur leaped into the air. He grabbed the cracked hickory in both hands as it hurtled by and swung it around as Hyrrokin fell past him. Baldur slammed the tree into the giantess so hard the trunk splintered into kindling. The force of the blow drove the giantess into the ground below, causing all of Jotunheim to shudder from the impact.

Baldur landed next to the crater as splinters of hickory showered the forest floor. Fearing he had killed his worthy adversary, Baldur climbed into the hole and found Hyrrokin's bruised, unconscious from lying at the bottom. He lifted her under one arm and climbed out before placing her against a tree near her wolf.

"Come, Fit!" called Baldur to the dwarf, who cowered between the front legs of the giant wolf. "We have much work to do and I cannot wait for your mistress to awaken."

With that, Baldur retrieved his great axe and cleaved the mighty oak. The god grabbed the tree and lifted it off the clean cut. Holding the tree firm, he lowered the mistletoe toward the dwarf.

"Cut some branches for your former mistress, dwarf," he commanded. "I am true to my word."

Fit nodded meekly. He pulled a golden dagger from his belt and climbed out from beneath the wolf. Gingerly, tenderly, he cut a bunch of boughs from the bush and stowed them in the sack where he had ridden.

With that, Baldur lifted the top of the tree toward the sky to keep the mistletoe away from the ground and turned to walk out of the forest.

After Fit deposited the branches, Lettfeti grabbed the dwarf's collar in its mouth and trotted along behind the god.

~

Baldur carried the upright oak through the forest and across the rocky wasteland to the edge of the Iving. The trek lasted three days and three nights, with Fit running back and forth to fetch buckets of water for the drying, dying, tree. At the river's edge, Baldur lashed the oak to *Ringhorn's* mast, using strips of tattered sails to secure it in place.

He tossed Fit into the stern next to the kegs and pushed off. As soon as *Ringhorn* hit the river, though, it began to sink beneath the waves. In a rush, the shining god tossed kegs, cattle, and pelts overboard until the gunwales floated just above the water line.

The trip back to the Rainbow Bridge was harrowing for god and dwarf. With every stroke Baldur made with the tooth-oars, water washed over the prow, while every gust blowing down the river threatened to topple the oak and take the boat with it. Fit spent the trip bailing bilge water while Baldur and Lettfeti pranced from gunwale to gunwale to maintain a modicum of balance.

After two days and nights, the odd band beached on Asgard. Baldur once again hefted the tree into the air to begin the long trek across the bridge to Midgard. The wet crossing had kept the tree well-watered, but by the time Baldur, Fit, and Lettfeti reached the far end of the Rainbow Bridge, the leaves of the mighty oak had begun to wilt and the mistletoe sagged on its branch.

"We must hurry," Baldur told Fit. "Try to keep up."

With that, the fair and tireless god loped across the verdant landscape as the huge oak towering overhead swayed with every stride. He moved faster than a lynx and made more noise than a herd of caribou.

As they neared the northern reaches of Midgard, the green fields and forests turned white with snow. Still the shining god did not slow or tire. His precious cargo had gone limp on its dry, cracking branch. Many mistletoe leaves had fallen away during the journey. Yet, Baldur pushed on, the nearness of his goal spurring the god forward.

And then the unthinkable happened. A blur of motion raced across Baldur's path at twilight. The tiny shape disappeared in the long shadows, but its presence was felt immediately. The small animal, a vole perhaps, slapped against the god's shins as it flashed past, sending Baldur scrambling and tumbling forward.

Such a tiny creature should not have caused Baldur any trouble, but the impact felt like the god had caught his legs on a foot-thick tree root. The oak tree flew from Baldur's grasp and crashed to the ground, obliterating a dozen other trees in the woods he had been racing through.

Baldur regained his feet and ran to check on the mistletoe. Although wilted and frail, it had survived the fall. The branch it surrounded stood straight out from the trunk, but as the god approached, the mighty oak shuddered and creaked as the dry wood cracked all along the trunk from the strain.

The shining god raced forward, his aura illuminating the devastation as bark sloughed and limbs crumpled and fell. He reached for the mistletoe-enveloped bough just as it lost its battle with life and dropped away from the downed tree.

When the mistletoe touched the earth, it crumbled ito dust. In a single moment, a ball of leaves and berries and twisting stems became a cloud of flecks and flakes like a swarm of buzzing gnats swirling in the air. Tokk's curse had beaten Baldur a second time.

Baldur turned to Fit, who had finally caught up to him. "Dwarf!" he roared. "You must devise a way to keep the tree healthy longer. Speed was not the answer to this trial. Think on that while I sleep."

With that, Baldur lay in the shadow of the dead oak and fell into a deep slumber that no mortal could disturb.

~

As Fit watched the god sleep beneath a blanket of broken boughs, he heard a rustling in the underbrush near the base of the fallen oak. A tiny vole darted in and out of small hollows beneath the broken trunk as it flitted closer and closer.

Fit clapped his hands together, for he had not had a single meal in days and was as famished as Baldur was tired. And yet, when the vole reappeared from beneath a fallen branch, the malevolence burning behind its piercing, red eyes made Fit's limbs go numb with fear and caused him to lose all interest in eating ever again. He vowed there and then that if he survived the encounter with whatever evil spirit inhabited this forest creature, his sustenance would only ever come from cask or keg forever more.

The dwarf's worst fears were realized when the vole transformed before his eyes into the form of Loki, the god of mischief.

"Why do you aid Baldur in his trials?" Loki demanded. His red eyes burned so bright that small wisps of flame licked at the edges of his sockets.

Fit sat transfixed, his eyes locked on Loki's blazing orbs. "He won me from my... my mistress Hyrrokin." Fit's voice trembled and broke as he spoke. "On a wager... a test of battle."

Loki stared hard at Fit, making the dwarf wish he had never been born, making him envious of the dead oak tree and the ashes of the mistletoe.

"You toil for me now, dwarf," Loki said after a moment. "You shall complete a simple task and I shall not slay you and your friends and your family."

"Anything, my lord," said Fit with a small whimper. "Shall I destroy the last mistletoe for you and prevent Baldur from completing his trials?"

Loki smiled but shook his head. "No. Nothing of the sort," he said with a chuckle so chilling it turned Fit's blood to ice. "What do I care if this buffoon succeeds? But I do love how eager you are to please."

Fit dared a weak smile in the face of the trickster's praise, but kept his mouth shut for fear of pressing his luck.

"Simply bring me a cache of berries fresh from the stalks of the last mistletoe, and I shall ensure that you survive these trials unharmed," Loki said. He strode forward and laid a long, thin arm across the dwarf's shoulder. "In fact, I guarantee that your health shall never waver so long as Baldur draws breath."

~

When Baldur awoke a week later, Fit told the god he had a plan to keep the last mistletoe and the tree hosting it alive for as long as the trek might take.

"You must bring the entire oak tree, roots and all, to Nidavellir," the dwarf told the sleepy god. "I will craft a device in my workshop that will irrigate both plants."

"There is an obvious flaw in your plan, dwarf," replied Baldur with a yawn. "How will I get the hundreds-foot-tall tree into the mines of the dwarfs?"

"I will bring the device to the entrance and attach it there while you hold the tree," replied Fit. "You will be able to hold it aloft, won't you? It should only take a few days."

The shining god had no doubt he could accomplish this task. His only worry was whether the dwarf's contraption would function. He had failed twice and could not fail again. Wrapped in worry, Baldur did not notice the small vole watching him from beneath the dead oak boughs as he and the dwarf began their trek.

After crossing the Rainbow Bridge and the River Iving once more, the travelers reached the shores of Jotunheim. There Baldur and Fit parted ways, with the dwarf heading toward his ancestral home to begin crafting the watering device while the god rode through Jotunheim to seek the final mistletoe.

Baldur found the immense tree outside a cave near the far end of the cold, dead forest. If anything, it was larger than the first—if not in girth, definitely in height. The god could not spy the top boughs, which were lost in the roiling clouds above.

He looked around for any sign of a giantess guarding the tree. Seeing none outside, Baldur entered the cave. There he found Tokk, the cursed witch, stirring some bubbling liquid in a large pot over an open fire.

"I have come for your oak, witch," Baldur stated. "Once again, I offer you fair recompense for your troubles."

"There is nothing you can offer that is worth the price of that tree," Tokk replied without paying the god enough respect to look up from her pot. "That tree shelters my cave. It keeps the cold winds at bay, shades me from the harsh sun hanging low in the sky, and prevents predators from rushing in from the wild."

"I can bring you a replacement," Baldur suggested. "Pick any tree in the forest, and I shall rip it from the ground, roots and all, and plant it in this one's place."

"No need. No need," replied the giantess with a wisp of a smile on her face. "You will never wrest my mighty oak from the ground. No one is that strong. You shall fail and I will laugh at your Asgardian weakness when you do."

Rebuffed once again in his efforts to appease Tokk, Baldur turned on his heels and left the cave. He stared at the tree towering above and wondered how he would rip the massive oak from the ground.

He paced around the base of the cloud-scraping oak, looking for some knots or notches that might give him purchase. As he stood scratching at his chin, Tokk appeared at the mouth of her cave and laughed.

"This is not a problem you can conquer with blade or fists, Asgardian," she taunted. "And you are not the brightest of the gods, are you?"

Baldur smiled, for Tokk had inadvertently provided the answer he sought. The shining god, his aura becoming almost blinding in the dim light, strode toward the tree. He balled his left hand into a fist and cocked his arm. With a mighty jab, the god punched a hole through the bark and a foot deep into the pulpy flesh. He stepped to the side and repeated the process with his right hand.

Standing between the two holes, Baldur stretched his arms out and hooked his fingers into the handholds he had created. He then heaved with all his might. At first, nothing happened and Tokk cackled behind him. Then, the ground shook beneath the god as shrill creaks and deep groans split the air. Minutes passed until, with a long, low moan, the tree rose. At first only an inch or two. Then, with the sound of roots tearing and ice-covered ground cracking, the tree rose faster and faster.

The god stepped back to avoid falling into the hole that opened beneath the mighty oak as the trunk and roots pulled free from the ground. He moved one hand and then the other down the trunk and into the tangle of roots, eventually grabbing the tap root in both hands and raising it, and the tree, over his head in one swift motion.

"No!" screamed Tokk behind him. "This cannot be!"

Baldur heard the witch rush at him from behind. He twirled beneath the tap root to face the old giantess and kicked out. His boot met her stomach, sending her flying into her cave, where Baldur heard her slam into the back wall.

With that, Baldur turned and walked toward Nidavellir, the oak tree standing straight above him, its top branches cutting a path through the clouds as he traveled.

~

Ice-cold winds threatened to freeze Baldur's breath inside his lungs as he trudged across the frozen realm of the giants. And yet, not long after he entered Nidavellir, the god came to long for those frosty breaths. The air in this mountainous realm was choked with foul fumes from thousands of furnaces, forges, and smelters running constantly in subterranean dwarf workshops.

Clouds of black smoke belched into the sky from crags and crevices atop every mountain in the realm. Baldur could not even see the lowest boughs of the oak tree through the swirling haze that filled the sky. The sun was little more than a dull, red disc in the distance.

And yet, Baldur pressed on, even as acrid smoke coated his throat with a thick layer of soot. He could not stop to rest because he dared not lay the massive oak tree down. Yet he worried for the poor mistletoe somewhere out of sight above him. Why had he agreed to Fit's foolish plan?

At that moment, the god heard a call in the distance. "Asgardian!" yelled the thin, reedy voice of Fit. "Over here!"

Baldur could see little past the globe of smoky, godly light around him, but he followed the voice and found his dwarf helper. Fit stood next to a giant iron cage large enough to hold Fenris, the wolf. Instead of some beast, though, the cage was filled with an intricate web of tubes connected to a series of bellows atop large cisterns.

"What is that ungodly contraption?" roared Baldur. "It looks like some sort of Lokian torture chamber."

Even through the smoke, Baldur saw Fit's beaming smile fade to a frown. "I will have you know, Asgardian, that this is a one-of-a-kind tree irrigation system! Let me explain how it works…"

"I'm sure it functions perfectly, Fit," Baldur said quickly. "I trust your craftsmanship."

A strange expression passed through the dwarf's eyes; a mixture of pride and something else—something more akin to shame. Baldur let it pass, assuming Fit had stolen the idea from some other dwarf. The tree was heavy, and the god's strength was flagging.

"Just show me where to put the tree, would you, Fit?" he continued. "That's a good dwarf."

Directed by Fit, Baldur climbed a slope beside the cage and held the roots of the mighty oak over the cage while the dwarf installed a series of iron supports below. Baldur then lowered the roots into the cage and held it in place while Fit worked.

"You can release your hold on the tree, my lord," Fit said a day later, after checking every joint and weld inside the cage. "Carefully!"

Baldur drew one hand and then the other away from the trunk but stood ready to grab hold again should the tree sway. But, other than a bit of moaning and creaking as it settled, the tree seemed secure.

Baldur climbed down and watched as Fit began connecting the labyrinth of tubes to the ends of the roots. There were hundreds to attach.

"This will take some time, my lord," Fit said upon noticing Baldur staring at him. "Perhaps you would like to rest?"

"I believe I would," Baldur replied. With that, he slumped to the ground, leaned against the cage, and fell into a deep, dreamless sleep.

~

While Baldur slept, Fit connected hoses to the roots. It was slow work. He had to uncouple the ends one by one and thread them through the maze of twisting roots. After an hour, he had completed about a tenth of the connections and the god had begun snoring heavily.

That was the dwarf's cue to act. He extracted himself from the cage and scaled the trunk into the perpetual red haze hanging over the mountains of Nidavellir. Fit's black eyes worked fine in the low light, though, so he had no trouble finding the mistletoe.

The bush sagged a bit from lack of water, but that didn't matter for his purpose. He strode onto the limb and sat beside the green bush with its white berries. As Fit searched for a bough filled with berries that would work for his plan, he failed to notice the berries attached to the leaves near his face begin to swell and redden. Before he knew what happened, the berries exploded, spraying red juice and seeds all over Fit's face and chest.

The dwarf was almost overcome by the sickly-sweet odor. He tried to wipe the nectar from his face, but it had the consistency of tar. It was all Fit could do to free his hand from the sticky mess.

"This is what you get for getting entangled in the lives of gods," Fit told himself. But entangled he was, and the only path was forward.

He grabbed his golden dagger and began cutting away at a long, twisted bough deep within the bush. After climbing down and into his cage, Fit attached the freshly cut bough to a special cage and set of hoses hidden inside one of the cisterns.

"I hope these explode in the trickster's face," he muttered as he connected the hoses that would keep the mistletoe alive."

~

A week later, Baldur dragged the mighty oak tree and its cage into the northern forest of Midgard. The furrow he'd left behind on his way north had filled with runoff from surrounding mountains and become a mighty river.

As the god rested from his labors, Fit set to work detaching the hoses from the roots. The dwarf had been sullen ever since the start of their trip when Baldur had awoken to find Fit's pitch-black skin stained with a dark shade of red.

"What happened to you?" Baldur had asked with a chortle.

Fit explained he had gone to check on the mistletoe and several of the berries had exploded in his face. He wouldn't talk about it further and the entire trip had passed in silence.

Baldur left the taciturn dwarf to his work and made his way to the Druid village. There, he found a small child playing in the dim, winter dawn. His shining countenance caught the child's attention, who ventured closer to see the light.

"Hello, child," Baldur said, his soothing voice and bright smile making the child beam almost as brightly as his own aura.

"Who are you?" asked the child. "Why do you glow?"

"I am Baldur, son of Odin," replied the god. "I glow with the inner light of wisdom and beauty."

"Can I glow, too?" asked the child, the wonder of the world flashing behind her eyes.

"Perhaps," replied Baldur, "If you are good and kind for all your days. For now, tell your elders you have seen me today and that I come bearing the gift of life in the dead of winter. Tell them to come into the forest after they have broken their fast."

The child nodded and returned to her early morning play. The god slipped back into the forest. He hoped to find Fit and apologize for laughing at him, but when Baldur arrived at the tree, the dwarf was gone. He had finished his task and left. Baldur vowed to find the dwarf and make amends, but first he had to plant the tree.

With his bare hands, Baldur dug a deep pit wide enough for twenty warriors to stand abreast and deep enough that three of those warriors standing on each other's shoulders would not reach the top.

The god lifted the cage and lowered it into the hole. He then filled the hole, covering the roots and the cage and bringing the forest floor level again. Above him, the mighty oak towered over all other trees, with the mistletoe shining like a beacon of green light in the mud-colored, winter-dead forest.

Baldur looked upon his work and knew it was good. When the Druids arrived, he would tell them how to care for the bush: To only cut it with a golden blade, to never let it touch the ground, and to care for the tree as if it were their own offspring, for if it died so would the magical mistletoe. As he waited for the Druids, Baldur's light shone brighter than ever before.

~

Fit stood a ways off and watched Baldur plant the tree. The dwarf took a pull from one of the many bottles he had brought and emptied during the long trip from Nidavellir. The drink did nothing to brighten his mood, but it did help mute the voice in his head that railed at him every minute of every day.

As Fit watched the god toss huge handfuls of dirt from the bottom of the hole onto an ever-growing mound, a familiar vole with burning, red eyes scrambled up beside him and transformed.

"You have what I want?" asked the god of mischief.

Fit nodded and reached into his tunic to retrieve the berry-filled bough he had retrieved from the cage. He hesitated a moment before handing it over to Loki.

"You promise I will live a long life?" he asked. "I will become immortal like a god?"

Loki nodded as he snatched the branch from the dwarf's dark hands. "You shall not die as long as Baldur draws breath," Loki replied. "This is what I promised. This is what has been foretold."

"Foretold?" asked the dwarf, turning to stare hard into the trickster's twinkling eyes. "Foretold by whom? What do you plan to do with those berries?"

"Why, kill Baldur, of course," Loki replied. He let loose a hideous, cackling laugh that turned into a shrill squeal as he transformed back into a vole and disappeared into the bleak forest.

Behind the Tonto Rim

Jeff Mariotte

I won't lie—Roy Rogers was always my childhood hero, but Hopalong Cassidy came in a close second. Author Clarence E. Mulford created Hopalong in 1904, when the West was still relatively wild. Actor William Boyd portrayed the character in movies, and then an incredibly successful TV series that spawned floods of merchandise—including tie-in novels penned by Louis L'Amour, under the pseudonym Tex Burns.

Jeff Mariotte, one of the earliest members of IAMTW, is a three-time winner of the organization's Scribe Award for novels. He's written tie-ins based on more than forty separate properties, and as an editor has worked on many more. His dozens of books include supernatural thrillers *River Runs Red*, *Missing White Girl*, *Cold Black Hearts*, and *Season of the Wolf*, horror epic *The Slab*, YA horror quartet *Year of the Wicked*, and the acclaimed thrillers *Empty Rooms* and *The Devil's Bait*. With wife and writing partner Marsheila (Marcy) Rockwell, he wrote science fiction/horror/thriller *7 SYKOS* and other works. He has worked in virtually every aspect of the book business, as a bookstore manager and owner, VP of Marketing for Image Comics/WildStorm, Senior Editor for DC Comics/WildStorm, and the first Editor-in-Chief for IDW Publishing.

Behind the Tonto Rim

For almost two days, Hopalong Cassidy had been riding alongside the massive escarpment of the Tonto Rim, which rose thousands of feet into the crisp, blue sky of the Arizona Territory. From its upper reaches, a man could get a clean shot at his target, but he had no enemies in this area. He had nothing to fear under the Rim.

Or so he thought.

That was before he saw the carcass.

The land at the Rim's foot was almost as heavily forested as its top, with towering Ponderosa pines leaving their typical brown carpet on the forest floor. South of the forested area were rich grasslands, and it was there that his friend Will Dekle had his ranch. In summertime, it wasn't surprising that some of Will's stock sought out the higher country, where pines offered welcome shelter against the Arizona sun. That one might have strayed this far was probably not out of the question—if indeed, that animal had been a cow.

Hopalong spotted it after weaving through the trees and into a natural clearing. About three-quarters of the distance off, he saw a lump that he first took for a boulder sitting in the grass. Topper, the magnificent white gelding he liked to travel with, stood waiting patiently, ears forward as if sensing—like Hopalong did—that something was wrong.

Before he reached the carcass—before he could even ascertain its species—he was enveloped in a reek that turned his stomach. It wasn't the smell of mammalian death, but something much worse, like the breath of a vulture that had consumed a dead skunk that had been feeding on rotten eggs. Topper swung his head away and snorted, trying to clear the miasma from his nostrils. "Okay, boy," Hopalong said. "I don't blame you a bit. I'll go the rest of the way on foot."

He dismounted, led Topper away from the stink, loosened the cinch, and draped the reins around a young pine. There was ankle-high grass here, and the horse would be fine for a little while. That done, he took a breath of clear air, tied a bandanna over his nose and mouth and headed for the thing. The bandanna helped a little, but by the time he reached the carcass, his eyes were streaming and his stomach was doing flip-flops.

Up close, he could see that the creature was a steer, or had been. Its skin was more or less intact, its head still recognizably bovine. More than that, it clearly hadn't been here long. Insects hadn't eaten away its eyeballs. A long tongue lolled from its open mouth. Blood flecked the grass around it, still wet in spots.

But of the beast itself, little remained beyond those things. The innards of it—the guts, much of the meat, and seemingly most of the blood and other liquids—were gone. It was a dried-out, desiccated, emptied husk.

Hopalong couldn't begin to imagine who or what had done this, or even how. On a hunch, he turned the thing's back end a little—glad he was wearing his riding gloves—so he could see the haunch lying against the ground. And there, confirming his fear, was the brand: W Cross D.

This was one of Will Dekle's beeves.

Will had written Hopalong at the Bar 20, saying that he was having some problems with losses and asking for Hopalong's help. Will had been a good friend for years, and he'd never hesitated to back Hopalong in a crunch, so Hopalong hadn't even asked what the trouble was, had just sent a letter saying he was on his way. He'd started out the next morning, knowing he would probably arrive before the mail did.

Hopalong now had a sense of Will's problem, and why he hadn't included details in his letter. This wasn't a loss from rustling or wolves or catamounts. It was far worse. Hopalong rushed back to Topper and set off at a gallop for Dekle's ranch.

~

Twenty minutes to the southeast, he found wide, grassy pastureland occupied by plenty of healthy W Cross D cattle. In ten more minutes, he saw a comfortable adobe ranch house, settled in near a bunkhouse, a stable, and a couple of corrals. It was a right friendly setup, and efficient, too.

Dekle heard him coming and met him in the yard. He'd lost weight, and where once his cheeks and the corners of his eyes had shown the marks of a man who smiled easily and laughed like he meant it, now worry lines plowed his forehead. He was a couple of decades older than Hopalong, but he looked ancient.

"Bill!" Dekle cried out. "You came!"

"Didn't you get my letter?" Hopalong asked.

"You send one?"

"I figured I might beat it here. It should arrive soon, though."

"Way our mail runs, it might get here before the turn of the next century," Dekle said. "Then again, it might well not."

"Is that Hoppy?" The voice belonged to a woman. Dekle's wife had died more than a decade before, so who was this? Over his shoulder, Hopalong saw a beautiful young lady stepping outside. She wore jeans and boots and a checkered shirt, with a red bandanna around her neck and her blond hair in tight braids.

"You get remarried without tellin' me?" he asked Dekle.

"That's Wendy!" Dekle said, naming his daughter.

"But Wendy's a twelve-year-old beanpole!"

"Shows how long it's been since you've visited, you old son of a gun. She's all growed up."

"I can see that."

Wendy rushed into Hopalong's arms. She smelled fresh and clean, and after being near that awful-smelling carcass earlier, Hopalong was glad for the change.

"Thank you for coming, Uncle Hoppy!" she cried. "I told Papa you would!"

171

"I owe your pa my life a few times over," Hopalong said. "Nothing coulda kept me away."

Releasing Wendy, he put a hand on Dekle's shoulder. "Tell me what's been goin' on, Will. I saw a steer yonder, near the rim. Looked like it'd been turned inside out and emptied."

"Not in front of the girl," Dekle whispered. "Let's take care of your horse, and I'll tell you out there."

Hopalong led the gelding into the stable, removed his saddle and bridle, and rubbed him down with a clean towel. When Topper had drunk some water and was feasting on oats, Dekle leaned against the wall. "So, you said you saw one of our cattle."

"Looked like it'd been a good-sized steer," Hopalong agreed. "But I've never seen anything like it. I've seen wolf depredation, big cats, and plenty of dead beeves, but never one looked like that. Any idea what did it?"

Dekle shrugged. "You saw the Tonto Rim, right?"

"Hard to miss that. It's spectacular."

"It is that. It's also called the Mogollon Rim. Some folks say there's a Mogollon Monster to go along with it."

Hopalong grinned, but his friend looked morose. "You're not jokin', are you?"

"Wish I was, Bill. I got a nice place here. Not too hot in summer, nor too chill come winter. Good grass and year-round water. The livestock like it just fine, gain plenty of weight, and sell for good prices."

"Sounds ideal."

"It used to be. But in the past three months, I must've lost more'n fifty head. All like what you saw. I'm used to a few stragglers wanderin' off into the brush and never comin' back. Others catch diseases and die. Some few might be rustled from time to time, or what have you. But what you saw—well, I ain't ashamed to say it terrifies me. And if I keep losin' stock at that rate, why, it'll put me in the poorhouse afore long."

"I'll say." Hopalong didn't know what to think. If he'd heard this story without having first seen the desiccated steer, he'd worry about his friend's sanity. But having seen it—and smelled the stink around it—he had to wonder about his own. "That reminds me, there was a smell around there, like I've never run across anywhere." He sniffed his own black shirtsleeve and made a face. "Might have to burn my clothes."

"That's part of the legend!" Dekle said. "It's always got that stink!"

The Will Dekle Hopalong had known wasn't the type to believe in fanciful stories about smelly monsters. What could have caused such a change in his formerly level-headed friend?

"Do you have any other enemies or rivals, Will?" he asked. "Human ones? You said there'd been some rustlin'."

Dekle chewed on his lower lip and shoved the toe of his boot into the hay. "There's this one feller, Hank Foley. He's made a half-dozen offers for my spread, but I always tell him I ain't sellin'."

"Fair offers?"

"Not to my way of thinkin', Bill. Not bad offers, I reckon, but not what the land is worth. Anyway, this place is all I got, and I'm keepin' it."

"Is this Foley an honest man?"

"I cain't say he isn't, but I surely cain't say he is. Rubs me the wrong way, and that's a fact."

Hopalong studied his friend. "There's more to it, ain't there?"

Dekle nodded, almost reluctantly. "After Martha passed, why, I let the place go to seed. I ain't proud to say it, but it's so. I mostly stayed in my room for almost a year. Wendy had to purt' near raise her own self, and the ranch suffered. When I finally snapped out of it, we was in trouble. I had to go in debt to set things straight, and I'm still payin' it off, little at a time."

Knowing there was more coming, Hopalong remained silent. Finally, the man added, "Hank Foley, why, he's tight with Clarence Erskine, the banker. Erskine's been makin' noises about demandin' payment in full. I can't do that, especially with my stock disappearin' little by little. If Erskine follows through, I'll have to let him have the ranch. He'll no doubt sell it to Foley the next day."

"So it's to Foley's advantage to whittle away at your herd."

"Durn tootin'."

"Well, before I go chasing monsters, I expect it'd be a good idea if I dropped in on Mr. Erskine. And maybe Foley, too."

Dekle's eyes grew wide and moist. "You'd do that, Bill?"

"Why, you know there's nothin' I wouldn't do to help you out."

"I surely do appreciate that. But I figger you're gonna have to do some monster huntin', too, 'fore you're through."

Hopalong smiled and slapped his old friend on the shoulder. "We'll take it as it comes, Will. How's that for a plan?"

~

The Pine Branch wasn't the rowdiest saloon in town, but neither was it the quietest. It was the kind of spot where a brawl could break out at any time, but just as likely a day or two would pass without so much as a cross word being uttered. Hank Foley liked making Clarence Erskine meet him there, because although Foley was a rancher, the kind of man who could fit into various social circles, Erskine would otherwise not be caught dead in the Pine Branch. Some joints in town Erskine wouldn't enter, even at Foley's bidding, but he would come into the Pine Branch, and be uncomfortable for the duration of his stay.

Foley liked making bankers uncomfortable. It had been a specialty of his since his younger days, although he no longer used a firearm when he did so. He had discovered that bankers could be as easily swayed by financial pressures as by threats. It was just as lucrative, but considerably safer. If he'd known that as a young man, his kid brother would likely still be alive.

He ordered a whisky and took it to a table. Erskine came in about ten minutes later. "Thanks for meeting me, Hank," he said. "I might need two or three of these, after today."

"What happened?" Hank asked. "Why'd you want to meet?"

"I had a visitor today. Fellow named Cassidy. He asked a lot of questions about Will Dekle's loan, and some about you. He's only just arrived here, but I got the feeling he's already figured out some things."

Foley chuckled. "White-haired feller? Wears all black? Couple of bone-handled six-shooters at his hips, tied down on the thighs, looks like he knows his way around 'em?"

Erskine sat listening, his eyes growing wider with each sentence. "How'd you know?"

"He came to see me, too. You really don't know who that is?"

"Should I?"

"That's Hopalong Cassidy. He's from that Bar 20 outfit, and the worst of the lot."

Erskine's jaw dropped almost to the tabletop. When he yanked it up again, he said, "Hopalong Cassidy? I've heard of him. Are you certain?"

"I seen him before, down Texas way. Never crossed him, and never wanted to. Those guns have put more fellers in Boot Hill than any twenty lawmen."

"If he's taking Dekle's side in this," Erskine said, pressing his hands on the table so hard his knuckles turned white, "we might want to back off. Let things set the way they are."

Foley took a drink, mostly to hide the smile that came unbidden to his lips. "Too late for that. Things are in motion we can't put a pause on. And I want that ranch." He set the glass down hard. "Before autumn, too. Don't you fret; I'll take care of Cassidy. You hold up your end, and we'll be square."

Erskine swallowed hard and nodded. His lips moved, but he couldn't seem to get a word out.

He was afraid.

That was just how Foley wanted him. So scared, he would do what he was told.

~

Hopalong pushed his plate away. He had emptied it and enjoyed two slices of pie besides. "Wendy, that's the best cookin' I've had in many a moon. And that apple pie was so good, I'd keep eatin', if I had any place to put it."

Wendy blushed. The color in her cheeks made her look even lovelier. As if noticing where Hopalong's gaze had come to rest, Will scooted his chair back from the table. "Why don't we go outside and finish our coffee, Hoppy? You still ain't told me what you found out today."

"That sounds mighty fine, Will," Hopalong replied, lifting his tin cup from the table. "Likely a durn sight cooler out there now than it was durin' the day." Catching Wendy's eye, he patted his stomach. "Thanks for a fine meal."

Once they were established on the porch in a couple of old chairs, Hopalong said, "Will, you must have to chase off the boys with a shotgun."

Dekle chuckled. "There've been a couple, that's for sure. I've had to fire some hands, thought workin' for me gave 'em leave to call on her." He shot his friend a grin, and added, "I sure am glad she's too young for you, Bill."

Hopalong smiled back, but he was surprised. His hair had been silver for almost as long as he remembered, and it might make him look older than his years, but Will knew his real age. He guessed it was just a warning, and let it lie. He had no intentions toward the girl.

"Like I said, Will, I paid visits today to Foley and Erskine. Foley looked a mite familiar, though I can't put my finger on why. I reckon you're right about him, though. I couldn't pinpoint anything crooked, but he's got that smell about him just the same. Like he thinks he's smarter than everyone else, and he's just waitin' to prove it. I also got a look at his hired men while I was out there. I don't know as there's a cowman among 'em, but they sure like their guns."

"That's true," Dekle agreed. "I've seen Foley mighty quick to go for a gun hisself a couple times, for no good reason. Never got into a shootout, but he let it be known he weren't one to tangle with."

Hoppy nodded. That was interesting. "Does he have a past, that you know of?"

"He just showed up in town one day, spendin' money," Dekle said. "No idea where he got it, but he made a lot of friends in a hurry. He bought his spread within the month and started sniffin' around mine not long after."

"Erskine wouldn't tell me how much you owed, but he said it was plenty. I wish you'd have been in touch then, Will. Me and some of the Bar 20 boys might've been able to help you."

"I was too deep in my own sorrow, Hoppy. I couldn't come out of it even long enough to do that. Besides, you all have your own place to run."

"We have plenty of hands. We might could've spared a few and kept you out of this trouble."

"I'm in it deep, ain't I?"

Hopalong remembered the dead steer he'd seen. "I'd say so." He tossed his old friend a grin. "Let's see if we can't get you out of it."

"You got any ideas, I'd welcome 'em."

"I just might. You say this happens every other day or thereabouts?"

"Seems like, yep."

"And just to your beeves? None of your neighbors'?"

"Far as I can tell."

"Well, I reckon I'll ride back to the Rim. Set up camp and keep my eyes open for a few days, see what I can see."

"I can send some of the boys with you. Them as are left, anyhow."

"No need," Hopalong said, waving away his friend's suggestion. Dekle needed every hand he had. "I move quieter on my own."

"You'll go in the morning?"

Hopalong looked at the moon, three-quarters full and heavy in the eastern sky. "Why wait?" he asked. "I've got a belly full of Wendy's cookin' and your coffee. I'll head out now."

~

From the crest of a ridge just west of the Dekle ranch house, Hank Foley sighted down his rifle at Cassidy. That white horse fairly gleamed in the moonlight, making it easy to spot even at night. Foley's finger rested on the trigger, but then he removed it. A better idea had come to him. Killing Cassidy at Dekle's place would bring attention, and that was the last thing he wanted. Instead, he raced down the incline to where his trusted hand McGinniss waited with the horses.

"Cassidy's on the move!" Foley said when he reached the other man. "Foller 'im. Stay well back, though; word is, he watches his back trail like a hawk. If he's ridin' out this time o' night, I don't reckon he's leavin' the area. More likely he's tryin' to figger out what's happenin' to Dekle's stock. If'n he sets up camp somewhere, you ride out to our line cabin and leave a message, and I'll meet you with some of the boys soon as I can."

McGinniss nodded, tightened his cinch, and mounted up. Foley watched him go, then headed back up the slope. Once Cassidy was out of earshot, he might be able to plug Dekle, or at least put a scare into the old man.

~

Hopalong built a small campfire with dry wood to minimize smoke, positioned under a Ponderosa pine to further dilute it. He had spent the remaining hours of darkness prowling around to watch for Dekle's monster or whatever was mutilating the cattle, then slept away a good chunk of the day. Now he was up again, making coffee over the fire. The sun hung low in the west.

While the coffee brewed, he walked to a nearby creek and got some water for Topper, then returned and washed up. Back at camp, he set aside the coffee pot and started some dinner. The sky purpled, then went black, the pine-scented air like velvet against his skin. A man alone in the wilderness was truly alive, connected to all the ancestors he'd ever had in a way that no city-bound fellow could ever know.

With a meal inside him and full dark beyond, Hopalong checked the loads in his pistols, picked up his 1874 Sharps—figuring a large-bore buffalo rifle loaded with .50-caliber cartridges would likely bring down a monster—and left the campsite. The best way to find out what was happening was to keep an eye on the beeves, so that morning he'd located some well-used livestock trails. He left Topper and the campsite and followed one toward the Rim.

He passed a few cows, noted the W Cross D brands in the light of the rising moon, and kept going. Another forty minutes or so passed when he heard a new sound—the distinctive clopping of hooves on the ground, the slight jingle of spurs and tack, and the creak of leather. Somebody else was out here, and on horseback!

Stepping off the trail, he found a couple of large boulders, or maybe one that had fallen from the heights a century or more ago and split when it landed. Wedging himself into the slot between them, he was able to quietly work his way up almost to the top of the taller one, from where he could see some distance down the trail. The sound was coming from the south, so he angled his Sharps that direction and waited.

Minutes passed. The rider moved slow, likely being cautious on a possibly unfamiliar trail, where tall pines blocked the moonlight. As the rider came nearer, Hopalong put the stock against his shoulder and sighted down the barrel. He saw motion through the trees, and then the rider swung into view. Hopalong touched his finger to the trigger and pressed gently.

Then he recognized the person on the horse.

Wendy Deckle!

He released the trigger and climbed down from the rocks. He reached the trail just as she was getting to the point where he met it, stepped out, and said, "Wendy, it's me, Hopalong."

She gave a little shriek, but not as much of one as she might have if he hadn't used her name and identified himself.

"Uncle Hoppy!" she said when she'd gathered her wits.

"What are you doing here, girl?" he asked.

"It's Papa. He's been shot!"

"Shot," Hopalong echoed. "What happened?"

"He was hit in the leg," she explained quickly. "It's not too bad, but he can't ride. He asked me to see if I could find you, to let you know."

"Anybody see who did it?"

"No. It came out of the dark. In the morning some of the boys rode around the area. They found a spot up on a hill where somebody might have been laying for him."

"When was he shot?"

"The other night, about an hour after you rode out. He'd stepped outside to go to the privy. I heard the shot, and Papa cried out. I found him, helped him back into the house and tried to make him comfortable. Ruiz, one of the hands, went into town for a doctor. But it's a long way, you know, and the doc had other patients. I couldn't get away until late afternoon. I wasn't sure how I'd find you out here in the dark, but here you are! It's like a miracle."

Hopalong chuckled. "I heard you comin' a mile off. If you hadn't been on this trail, I'd've moved to the one you were on. But I'm glad—"

He stopped, because a wrenching cry split the night. He'd heard similar, when cattle were being slaughtered with unnecessary cruelty, but he had never heard a squeal of such pain combined with a shriek of absolute, bovine terror.

"What was that?" Wendy asked, wide-eyed.

"Unless I'm mistaken," Hopalong answered, "that's your pa's monster. Let me up in that saddle, and you can stay here where it's safe."

"Not on your life. You're not leaving me alone out here, Uncle Hoppy!"

There was no time to argue, and she was probably right, besides. "Okay, we can ride double. Slide back."

She did as he said, and he climbed into the saddle, stuffing the Sharps into an empty scabbard. She shifted behind him, then wrapped her arms around his slender waist. The appaloosa mare was spirited; not as fast as Topper, but the terrain was unfamiliar, and she carried a double load. The anguished cries continued, giving Hopalong a target to aim for.

Until they stopped, as suddenly as they'd begun.

The normal night noises—mostly birds and insects—had gone silent, so the darkness was weirdly still. Hopalong had a fair idea of where the beast must have been and kept going in that direction.

But smell travels farther in the dark than sight does. The mare shied when she sensed it, and Hopalong had to urge her forward. Then he caught it as well, worse than the other day for being fresher.

"Ugh!" Wendy said. "What's that?"

"That's the stink of the Mogollon Monster, accordin' to your pa. Me, I don't think it's any such a thing. But I got to admit I don't know what it is, except horrible. Means we're close, though. You want to get off?"

"Out here? By myself?" She tightened her grip on hum. "Not hardly!"

He gave up. The reek grew stronger, and he knew they were close. Then the trail curved around past some pines and he saw the animal.

It looked like it had been a plump, healthy female. Now she was caved in on herself, skin wrinkled like old shirts tossed into a pile. She lay in a meadow of perhaps an acre, where she'd stopped to graze on the thick grass.

On the far side of the meadow, disappearing into the trees, Hopalong spotted a brown, furry creature, walking upright.

He brought the horse to a stop and slid from the saddle, yanking the Sharps. "Stay well back of me, Wendy," he said. "I've never seen a bear maul an animal like that. And if it is a bear, it's a big one. They can run fast and climb faster, so if it comes at me, turn tail and ride like hell."

"Be careful," she said as he walked into the meadow.

He intended to.

The grass was almost knee-high, and damp from the night air. He pushed through. That creature had been moving fast, and he'd already lost it in the shadowy trees.

It was big enough to leave tracks, though, and when moonlight allowed, he studied them. They belonged to no bear he'd ever seen, nor any human. Each foot was almost twice as long as his own, and wider, with six toes sporting what appeared to be two-inch-long claws.

Could the legends about the Mogollon Monster be true? Hopalong didn't want to think so, but he had no better explanation.

Whatever it was, it was making good time. He was getting closer and closer to the base of the Rim and starting to worry about having left Wendy so far back. That cow was already dead, which made her safety his first responsibility. Finally, he broke out of the trees and saw the sheer, thousand-foot face of the Rim dead ahead. The creature was out of sight. He didn't think he'd passed it, and here, there was nowhere for it to go but straight up.

But no—as he scanned the wall's face, he spotted a dark opening. It looked barely wide enough for him to squeeze through, though the angle might've been deceiving. Moonlight clearly showed the creature's enormous tracks, heading straight for it.

A cave, then.

Well, he didn't have time to explore it now. He had to get back to Wendy. He noted the opening's location, determined to return during daylight. Then he hurried back the way he'd come.

Wendy was where he'd left her, anxious, peering into the woods. As he approached, he called out so she'd know he was coming. When he reached her, she shifted back behind the saddle, and he climbed up, holstering the Sharps again.

He started to tell her what he'd seen, but the sound of hoofbeats headed their way stopped him. He couldn't tell how many horses, but it sounded like plenty. "Think they're your pa's men?" he asked.

"He only has four or five hands left," Wendy said. "And with him shot, they're all staying close to the ranch."

"That's what I thought."

He wheeled the horse around. He didn't know who was coming up from the south, but he didn't want to meet them on this narrow path. Instead, he followed the cattle trail where it passed through the meadow and continued north, more or less parallel to the line the creature had taken through the trees. Before long, he reached the wall, not too far east of the cave opening.

Bringing the horse to a halt, he listened.

181

They were still back there. But now, he heard other horses, coming from farther east.

He didn't know all the ranches in the area, but he did know one thing—the Foley spread lay northeast of Dekle's. If Foley's men had any reason to come up here, they'd come from the east and south of here.

"What's going on?" Wendy asked, fear tightening her voice.

"I ain't sure, but I don't like it," Hopalong replied. "We'll head west for a spell, then cut south toward your place, and hope these folks are just passing through."

"This time of night? And that many? That's not likely."

"No," he agreed. "Not at all."

They'd been riding west for less than five minutes before Hopalong saw the flare of a gunshot from partway up the Rim's wall, ahead of them, then heard the report and the bullet whizzing past. They'd been herded into a trap! And he'd fallen right into it, with Wendy along for the ride.

The second shot missed, too, but the third hit the mare. She stumbled, and Hopalong knew they were going down. Another round might have hit one or both of them if they hadn't been plunging to the ground. Hot blood sprayed Hopalong as he hit the earth and rolled. At least he wouldn't have to finish the mare, because that shot had done it.

He heard the riders from the east closing in, and those coming from the south weren't far behind. He scrambled to his feet and grabbed Wendy, shielding her with his body, and looked for shelter.

That's when he realized where they'd fallen—just steps from the cave that creature had vanished into.

Looking almost straight on, he'd barely been able to see the opening. Someone riding alongside the Rim—especially in the dark—might go right past it without even noticing.

It was their best shot, anyway.

He snatched up the Sharps and loosed a round toward where he'd seen the last muzzle flash. At the same time, he drew Wendy toward the cave. "In there!" he said. "There's an opening!"

"It's so dark," Wendy said. She stumbled on one of the mare's out flung legs, and he caught her, guided her in. The sides of the opening were remarkably smooth, almost as if polished through years of use. Inside, the air was cool, but he smelled that familiar, rank odor.

"Are we safe in here?" Wendy asked. "It stinks."

Hopalong saw no use in lying. "I don't know. Safer than outside, maybe. But they might know about this place. And...and that creature that killed the heifer came in here."

"And you brought us in?"

"I don't see it," he pointed out. "And nobody's shootin' at us at the moment, so I'd call it a fair trade-off. We ought to get away from the entrance, though. Anybody stuck a gun in and pulled a trigger, they'd hit us, standin' here."

"Farther in?"

"I don't cotton to it, either. But I don't want to get plugged. Just a little ways."

He took Wendy's hand and, with the one holding the rifle, felt his way back. Before too long, the cave took a turn, then another. When he was sure they were out of sight from the entrance, he released her, pulled a match from his pocket, and struck it on the cave wall. They were in a kind of natural passageway, its walls and floor worn smooth. Brown hair formed a kind of carpet that kept their footsteps nearly silent. A couple of side tunnels intersected this main one, but before he could explore further, the match went out.

He was reaching into his pocket for another match when he heard the slightest, muffled rustling sound. The tunnel was too narrow for him to make effective use of the rifle, so he yanked his hand from his pocket and went for one of his bone-handled revolvers.

But too late.

Huge, strong hands gripped his arms. He tried to warn Wendy, but another one wrapped around his face. He felt fur against his flesh, and fought for consciousness against the horrendous stink.

It was a battle he won, but barely, and he wasn't sure the victory was worth it.

He struggled, but the hands were too strong. His Sharps was snatched away, and his six-guns remained in their holsters, useless. He heard a cry from Wendy, cut short, and guessed the same had happened to her. Whatever held him lifted him off the ground and carried him, as easily as he might tote a small child.

A couple of minutes later, the thing stopped. The air felt different here; he thought they had left the narrow passage behind and entered some larger space. Then massive hands released him, and what he saw stunned him into silence.

They were still inside the cave—if an expanse so vast could be considered a cave, and not another world altogether. Wendy was beside him, held by a furry creature like the one he had seen outside, and like the one he assumed was still holding him by the arms in an unbreakable grip.

But there was light—a greenish glow seemingly emanating from the rock walls that hemmed in the immense space. And in it, what he saw could only be described as a city—a city under—or behind—the Tonto Rim itself. Its walls were carved from the same stone as the walls. The city fell away from the spot where he stood, but as the cavern floor curved upward, so did the city itself. He saw multi-level buildings and roads and public squares, all laid out before him as if on a map. At a glance, there must've been hundreds of dwellings, although it was hard to know with any certainty because some of the structures were several stories high and could have held any number of inhabitants.

The sight was so striking that for long moments Hopalong didn't even notice the creature sitting before him. When he did see it, he couldn't tear his eyes away. It was like the others, heavily furred, powerfully built, with hands and feet easily double the size of his own. But it was old, its fur more silver than brown, its face at once humanlike and simian, with brown eyes beneath the shelf of its brow, flaring nostrils, and an outthrust jaw, all of it wrinkled with age. It regarded him with curiosity.

"You are not with Foley," it said.

Hopalong would have staggered if he hadn't been held fast. It spoke English! Though its throat wasn't made for human tongues, its voice gravelly, he understood it easily.

"Not hardly. You know Foley?"

"We have an...arrangement."

"You mean, he lets you kill beeves that don't belong to him?"

"The animals we take are Foley's."

"No," Hopalong countered. "They ain't. They bear the W Cross D brand of my friend Will Dekle." He ticked his eyes toward Wendy, likewise pinned on his left. "This here's Will's daughter. She can tell you."

"They're my father's stock," she confirmed.

"Foley says otherwise."

"Then he's a liar."

"Don't listen to him!" came another voice, this one human. "He's the liar!"

Hopalong turned his head just enough to see Foley and three of his hands walk into view. Foley wore an angry expression, like a man out for blood. "Just finish these two troublemakers, F'roon!"

The creature—Hopalong couldn't help thinking of him as a king, the regent of this hidden civilization, because of his bearing and the wisdom expressed by those mournful brown eyes—raised a dismissive hand. "I will decide their fate."

Foley stepped closer to Hopalong, still wearing that scowl, and the pieces clicked into place. "Now I know you, Foley," he said. "You're wanted in three Texas counties for murder. What was it, four bankers and two lawmen? And that little boy you trampled in the street, making your getaway. I knew you looked familiar."

"I never trampled no kid!" Foley snapped. "That were Simmons, and—" As if realizing he'd said too much, he clamped his lips together and looked at F'roon. "Never mind. This feller's just here to make trouble for all of us."

"I'm here *because* there's trouble," Hopalong argued. "Dekle's stock is being decimated, near to driving him out of business. Sounds like Foley's been encouraging you to take them. Meanwhile, he's working with a sleazy banker to steal Dekle's land."

"Is this true?" F'roon asked, his gaze fixed on Hopalong. "Foley is a murderer?"

"It's true. I couldn't place him before, but when he looked at me like that, I saw the face that's on wanted posters all over the state."

F'roon turned to Foley. "You killed a child?"

"T'weren't me, dammit, it were Simmons!"

"But you're admitting to the bankers and lawmen?" Hopalong asked. Foley shut his mouth.

"I see you looking at our city," F'roon said to Hopalong, waving one of those long-fingered hands toward the bizarre sight. "Once it was full of us. We were here long before your kind, even before the ones you call red. For thousands of your years, we dwelt here in peace. When we hungered, we journeyed into the outer world and took what we needed.

185

"But with the coming of humans, we became the hunted. It was ever harder to venture out. We began to die off, and nothing could stem the tide. Now we are few, and not long for this world. Foley found us and told us we could take his cattle freely."

"So Dekle couldn't blame him for the losses," Hopalong said.

"It's ruining my father," Wendy added. "And he was shot, this morning, right on our ranch!"

"I reckon that was you, too, Foley, or one of your men," Hopalong said. "Worried I'd find something up at the Rim?"

"Keep your mouth shut, Cassidy, or I'll—"

At a signal from F'roon, one of the creatures standing behind Foley muzzled him. Foley tried to wriggle free but had no more success than Hopalong had. F'roon gestured, and both Hopalong and Foley were lifted off their feet and deposited within the king's reach.

F'roon reached and touched Hopalong's forehead, then Foley's, as if checking for fever. "This one speaks truth," he said, pointing a clawed finger at Hopalong. "This other lies."

"I ain't—" Foley managed, before the creature slapped a hand across his nose and mouth again.

The king gestured, and the creature holding Foley made a twisting motion, wrenching Foley's neck almost halfway around. Hopalong could hear the crack it made when the bones snapped. Foley's men, each held by another of the creatures, tried to break free, but couldn't.

Wendy started crying. To Hopalong's surprise, the creatures released her and himself, and she rushed into his arms. He pressed her head against his shoulder, so she wouldn't look at the dead man, blood running from his nose and mouth.

"You make your mind up fast," Hopalong said.

"It is our way. As I said, we are few, and our time is short."

"I'll make you a squarer deal than Foley did, then. Will's going to keep his place. But Foley won't be needin' his. His land runs almost up to the Rim, about a mile west of here. His beeves are marked with a Slash F brand. He won't be needin' them, either, so you can have as many as you want, and the land besides. I'm sure the rewards from Texas will be enough to cover anything that might be owed, and I'll stick around long enough to buy the land outright and sign it over to you, so it's legal."

"You can do that?" Wendy asked.

Hopalong grinned. "I can sure enough try."

"I believe you, Uncle Hoppy," she said.

"I'm not sure I believe any of this,' Hopalong said, laughing. "But if I don't wake up in the next little bit and find out I'm dreamin', then I reckon it's real!"

By the time they got outside, the sun had cleared the eastern horizon and painted the Rim wall with light. Foley's men explained to their comrades what had occurred, and though some glared angrily at Hopalong, with F'roon and his creatures there, no one felt inclined to take action. Glumly, they rode off.

Hopalong turned to F'roon. "I reckon it'd be best to keep your existence quiet," he said. "Foley's men will probably scatter, and if they talk about it, folks'll think they're loony. But plenty of people would love to hunt you down, and I'd sooner see you prosper and your numbers grow. I can't make no promises about my kind—we're contrary as all get-out. But I'll do my best to keep you safe and fed."

They shook hands—Hopalong's lost in the enormity of F'roon's—then he and Wendy headed for Topper, back at the campsite. "Papa's never going to believe this," she said.

"We'll have to tell him. These things'll need some help, and I can't stay here forever."

"Oh, I wish you could, Uncle Hoppy!"

"I'll be around, time to time," he said with a smile. "I seem to have a knack for showin' up when there's trouble."

"And a knack for fixing it."

Hopalong laughed. "I reckon I try, Wendy. I do try. Sometimes, I might could even get it right."

In the Time of the Martians

Scott Pearson

H. G. Wells published *The Time Machine* in 1895, coining the term in the process. Initially serialized in *The New Review*, it was collected as a novel in varying texts by both Heinemann in England and Henry Holt and Company in the America. The Heinemann text is still in print and considered the official one. The story not only spawned countless other tales through time but has been adapted into three films, including the beloved *Time After Time*.

Two years later, Wells unleashed Griffin on an unsuspecting world in *The Invisible Man*. This "boys' book for grownups" captured the public's imagination, spawning imitators ever since. That same year, the prolific and imaginative author serialized his *War of the Worlds* in *Pearson's Magazine*. The invasion from our neighboring planet proved a popular concept, and a terrifying radio adaptation in 1938 still resonates today.

Scott Pearson is a full-time freelance writer and editor. He has published across a number of genres, such as lit fic, humor, mystery, urban fantasy, horror, and science fiction, including three *Star Trek* stories and two *Trek* novellas. He's the canon editor of the *Star Trek Adventures* role-playing game and the cowriter of the IMAX space documentaries *Space Next* and *Touch the Stars*. Scott lives in personable St. Paul, Minnesota, with his wife, Sandra, and their cat, Ripley. He and his daughter, Ella, cohost the podcast *Generations Geek*.

Visit Scott online at scott-pearson.com and generationsgeek.com and follow him on Twitter @smichaelpearson.

In the Time of the Martians

Malcolm Taylor stood upon his threshold, bidding a subdued goodnight to his departing dinner guests. Hillyer had appeared nearly convinced by his grim story of the future—all about young Weena, the Eloi, the Morlocks, and then escaping far beyond, to when the Earth itself was in its very death throes—but the rest clearly doubted his sincerity if not his sanity, even those who had attended the previous Thursday's demonstration of the miniature time machine.

As his friends gave their final waves and made their way to the station for hansoms, Taylor closed the door and returned to his drawing room. It was nearly one in the morning, but he didn't feel like sleeping. He tossed another log on the fire, sat, and started making a mental list of the supplies he would take with him when next he used the time machine. He'd been foolish to rush off into the future without so much as a compass, a proper supply of matches, or—

"Finally, they're gone."

Taylor startled at Griffin's words; he hadn't attended dinner, so when had he come in? Turning toward the sound of his unexpected guest's voice, he said, "After our argument last week, I thought I'd never see you again."

"Perhaps you never will," said Griffin's voice from thin air, followed by unpleasant laughter.

Taylor jumped to his feet, staring at the noticeable depression in the seat cushion of the same chair Griffin had sat in the previous Thursday. "By God—!"

"Steady on, Taylor! We've much to discuss, so sit down." Taylor did as suggested. "Now then," Griffin continued. "I need a place to stay. There's been a fire at my previous lodgings."

Taylor clenched his teeth. If he'd faced the Morlocks, he could deal with Griffin, visible or not. "How long have you been here?"

"I arrived at the same time as the journalist, I forget his name. When he stumbled in the dining room? I tripped him! When Hillyer spilled his wine, I had tipped it. When that candle on the mantel wouldn't stay lit, I had blown it out. Your Mrs. Watchett was the only one who noticed, catching me getting a nibble of the mutton. The look on her face!"

Taylor frowned. He'd noticed earlier that his housekeeper had gone white as a sheet. He'd told her she looked like she'd seen a ghost, as a figure of speech, but she had forced a laugh and had said it must have been her imagination; she knew his distaste for superstition.

"So I heard your entire story," Griffin continued. "And I need your help."

"I told you last time I won't work with you."

"So you did. But what I need is an experiment about time itself. Does that interest you?"

Taylor remained silent.

A creak from the chair indicated Griffin had leaned forward. "I thought invisibility would lay open the world to me, like a banquet spread for a king. I'd do whatever I wanted, whenever I wanted. But where do I live? Where do I dine? How do I avoid getting run down in the street? The simplest actions call attention to me. The lowest pickpocket has a better chance than an invisible man! I've been running, freezing, starving, been shoved, beaten, and chased by dogs."

Taylor felt no sympathy for the cruel, selfish man. The way he'd treated the wretched invisible cat he'd brought last week still bothered Taylor. "I don't see what this has to do with time travel."

"Last week I was only thinking about the advantages for an invisible time traveler."

"A valid point." Taylor wouldn't have minded being invisible to the Morlocks. "However, you've just listed all the problems you've had *because* you're invisible."

"Quite right. I need to be able to become visible, and switch back and forth at will."

"Are you saying you don't know how to reverse the procedure?" Taylor was astounded; it was as if he'd made a time machine only able to travel in one direction.

"Not yet, but I will—given enough time. That's the experiment I propose."

Taylor's eyes widened. "You want me to travel into the future where you've perfected your invisibility procedure."

"Yes. And bring the solution back."

"But then you would have the solution...before you ever thought of it."

"Quite the conundrum isn't it? But I have it all planned so we can leave straight away."

"Now? The both of us?"

"You wouldn't understand the procedure, you're merely my driver. Here's the scheme: I'll simply return to this room on this date in the future after discovering how to reverse and control the process. All we have to do is skip forward a year at a time until I'm waiting for us with the solution." The depression in the seat disappeared again as Griffin apparently leapt to his feet.

Taylor remained seated. Griffin's mean-spirited behavior diminished his discovery, and now he wanted to sully Taylor's own work to serve his self-centered ends.

The voice came from the door to the hallway. "What are you waiting for?"

Folding his arms across his chest, Taylor said, "I'm not taking you anywhere."

There was no response. After a moment, Taylor squinted, as if that would help, and craned his head around. He held his breath to focus on listening. It suddenly occurred to him that Griffin might try to take the time machine for himself. The thought made him stand abruptly, but he stumbled back into his chair as he bumped into something and then was shoved down.

193

"Thought I'd gone?" Griffin said from where he stood over Taylor. "Well, I could have done. You demonstrated the operation of your machine quite clearly last week. But I'd rather have your help, and I'm certain you'd rather be the one at the controls."

Taylor briefly considered throwing himself at the invisible man...but what if Griffin sidestepped him? Taylor would be at his mercy. No, he had little choice but to go along with this madman. "All right then."

"Good."

Taylor got back up, grabbed a lamp, and headed down the hall to his laboratory, not sure if Griffin was ahead of him or following. He got his answer when the door to the lab swung open before him. Tables and shelves of spare parts and equipment were cluttered about. The time machine sat awkwardly, pressed up against the northwest wall of the room, spattered with grass and mud, dinged and dented, one of the brass rails bent.

"Your machine needs a wash-up as badly as you did when you first appeared this evening."

Taylor frowned at the whole situation, but set the lamp on a table and got aboard the machine, wanting to get this over with as soon as possible. The machine had but one seat, however. "You'll need to stand close behind and hunch over a bit. Grab hold of the rail. The sensation is rough and disorienting, a trifle nauseating."

With a grunt, Griffin wedged himself between the rail and behind Taylor. One of his arms held tight across Taylor's shoulders; Taylor assumed the other was gripping the bent rail.

Griffin's voice issued from the air almost directly into Taylor's ear. "Note the time, about twenty past one. I shall be back here by then the year I have my answer."

Taylor looked at the clock on a nearby shelf, confirming Griffin's statement. He took hold of the control levers. "Hold on." He gave the starting lever a small push, counted off several seconds as he watched the indicator dials spin away days, then months...

∼

Taylor pulled the stopping lever. He put his hands on his stomach, which felt like it was twisting. Over his shoulder, Griffin groaned and stumbled, but then the invisible grip tightened again.

"Well?" Griffin's voice was shaky.

"We overshot by a few days. It's difficult to—"

"That was a whole year? And look, it's half past seven. In the morning, going by the light through the shutters. Astounding!"

"As I was saying, it's difficult to get it to a specific day, and right to the hour even more so. That's why I was late for dinner."

"Well, I would have left a note if I'd been here and we didn't show up. I don't see anything, do you?"

Taylor saw nothing either. "To next year then?"

"And feel that sick for every year of travel? No, let's just go five or so years. Surely I'll have perfected the process by then."

Taylor shrugged. "Whenever you're ready." He was jostled as Griffin rearranged himself.

"Ready."

Taylor returned his hands to the levers and eyed the dials, calculating his manipulations of the controls. "Right. Here we go."

This time, jumping ahead several years, there was a more noticeable impression of movement, a sense of the sun wheeling through the sky beyond a faint image of the laboratory around them. A rushing sound filled Taylor's ears, accompanied by a low moan from his passenger.

∼

With an eye on the indicator dials, he pulled back on the stop control, and their surroundings solidified. This time he landed on the right date, though hours ahead of time.

Taylor was shoved forward, and he heard Griffin stumble into the bench, its legs squeaking across the floor. Presumably he then sat, because the sound of his gasping breaths came from that level and direction.

"That was much worse than the short trip," Griffin said. "You need to refine your process as well."

195

Taylor's eyes were drawn to the soft red glow angling through the shutters instead of the brighter shine of the street lamps, which should have been lighted by now. Curious, he stepped off the time machine (after unscrewing the starting lever and dropping it in a pocket), moved to the window, and peeked between the louvers. He nearly lost his footing at the sight, and he threw open the shutters. Nearby houses were smashed, like a giant had stomped through the neighborhood. Some were on fire, and the night sky was tinted red as if London was also in flames.

Griffin's voice was at his side. "What future is this?"

"We must see." Taylor ran across the laboratory to the door, which refused to open. In the uneven reddish light, he realized the doorframe was twisted out of plumb. With a few kicks, the door gave in, and he lurched into a broken hall. Lucky for them the laboratory had been left relatively unscathed by whatever calamity had transpired, but the rest of the house appeared closer to kindling than a building.

Struggling and cursing, Taylor made his way through the wreckage and out the front door, where he saw a dead horse, an overturned carriage, and once-precious belongings spilled across the street. The air was dry and acrid, and the only sounds were distant sirens and odd metallic echoes like huge pistons. Houses still standing were dark, maybe abandoned, or perhaps remaining residents were too afraid to light a candle in the red-hued night. The house of his neighbor, Mr. Galanter, was a charred ruin.

Taylor staggered down the street, avoiding fires, heading westward toward the Thames. He didn't know if Griffin had followed, nor did he care. He walked past corpses, families seemingly struck down while fleeing, covered with a thick black dust or soot. There were more dead horses. Abandoned bicycles. But he had not yet seen a living soul, and he wondered how many were left here in Richmond, across the river in Twickenham, behind him in London itself. In his benumbed state he found himself at the Richmond Bridge. He stared at debris floating on the Thames: splintered wood, broken furniture, items of clothing. There were sheets of red, not cloth, but some sort of boggy weeds drifting in the current. There were also bodies.

Movement on the bridge distracted him—people! Two men were hurrying across the river, glancing this way and that.

Taylor ran toward them, cheered to see anyone alive. "Hallo!"

They stared at him, looking quite stunned. As they drew closer, Taylor realized the gulf between them; these men had lived through this disaster, and they looked it. Hair dirty and matted to their heads, clothes ragged and torn, faces smeared with soot. Taylor, in contrast, could have stepped out of a dinner party—which, to some extent, he had.

"Gentlemen," said Taylor, "I'm gladdened to see survivors. But what has happened?"

One of the men was mumbling a prayer and didn't seem to have heard. The other man's look of surprise turned to suspicion. "Are you mad?"

"No, I..." Taylor couldn't think of a believable explanation for his ignorance.

The man who had replied grabbed the other man's arm and tugged him along. "We must keep moving."

Taylor followed, as they were heading in the general direction of his house. After they trudged along in silence for a short distance, an idea came to Taylor, and he clamped a hand on his forehead. "Please, what happened? I came to in my collapsed house...I can't remember."

The man hesitated while the other started praying again. "The Martians invaded about a week ago. They have giant war machines."

Taylor stopped and stood dumbfounded. "Martians? Machines?"

"Yes." The man's expression softened to pity. "Are you on your own? I'm going to Leatherhead, to my wife. Come along, if you want."

"Thank you, but no, I'll wait it out in my house. The part of it still standing."

He nodded. "Good luck to you then."

Taylor shook the man's hand and watched him lead his companion away, walking briskly up the road. Then Taylor turned down another street and ran, as best he could around the debris, back home. As he turned into his yard, Griffin's voice from the edge of the street startled him.

"What's happening? In the distance I saw machines, three-legged things towering over buildings, shooting smoke and fire."

"They're Martians."

"What? Surely not!"

Ignoring Griffin, Taylor hurried through his ruined house to the laboratory. Griffin had lit a lantern, and to Taylor's great surprise and relief, he spotted the miniature time machine on a shelf. At some point in the intervening years since its demonstration, it had returned. He had just picked it up when Griffin came rushing in, making a clamor struggling through the broken door.

"Don't worry, I wasn't going to strand you here," Taylor said, though he doubted Griffin would say the same, which is why he'd taken the starting lever with him.

"Put out the lamp!" Griffin said.

"Why?" Taylor was looking in the direction of the voice when the shutters slammed shut on the window behind him. He spun at the sound.

"There's a machine practically upon us!"

Taylor put the miniature down on a table and quickly extinguished the lamp; he'd been so focused, he hadn't noticed the steadily increasing volume of the piston sounds he'd heard in the distance. Moving to the window, he bumped into Griffin, then—now that the lamp was out—lifted the louvers to see outside.

An enormous machine, different from what Griffin had described before, was maneuvering through the ruined neighborhood. It scuttled along on five legs, looking something like a crab or spider. Several twisting, tentacle-like metal appendages stretched out from the machine, rummaging through the wreckage of homes. Taylor wondered whether it was scavenging or just curious, the way it picked through the debris, tossing things aside. Whichever, it appeared satisfied with its findings on that side of the street, as it turned in place and then headed straight for the laboratory.

Taylor sensed Griffin's motion away from the window toward the time machine, but Taylor remained, watching the Martian approach. The piston sounds grew louder and the lab vibrated with every deep *thud* of the legs, their odd number creating an unnatural syncopation as the contraption lumbered forward.

"Taylor!" Griffin shouted from behind him, but Taylor froze in place as the Martian machine neared the window. When it stopped, Taylor glimpsed, through a glass plate in its underside, the bulbous Martian within, its own writhing tentacles at the controls of the machine, its large dark eyes in a noseless face staring back at him.

Startled onto motion, Taylor hurried to the time machine, and felt Griffin's arm wrap around his shoulders as he reached for the controls.

Taylor had a moment of panic when his left hand fell on empty space, then remembered he had the starting lever in his pocket. Just as he fished it out, there came a loud crash; the Martian machine's tentacle-like arms smashed through the windows of the laboratory. He flinched at the sound, and the lever slipped from his hand, skittering across the floor.

"Damn it all!" Taylor clambered from his seat and dropped to his hands and knees, feeling in the dark for the lever. As he did so, two tentacles undulated around the room, their metallic workings jangling like a pocketful of coins while mechanical claws at their ends grabbed at whatever they came across on the shelves and tables. He froze in place as a third metal arm snaked past him, nearly brushing against his sleeve. Then the missing lever was hovering in the air before his eyes, moving toward the time machine behind him.

"I've got it," Griffin whispered.

Again Taylor worried about Griffin taking the time machine for himself, but he was more concerned about the nearest coiling Martian tentacle, which swept back and forth above him. He was forced to crawl out from beneath the snaking thing before he could turn around, but he was relieved to see the time machine waiting for him. He scurried back into his seat, retrieving the lever from the air where Griffin held it out to him. As he started threading it back into place, two of the tentacles turned away from ransacking his equipment and headed toward him.

"Hurry!" Griffin hissed in his ear.

The lever had to be fully threaded to touch a contact and become operable. He twisted the lever faster, but it got out of alignment and jammed; he had to back it out a bit and start over. All the while the tentacles drew nearer.

"For God's sake, can't you operate your own invention?"

Ignoring Griffin, Taylor kept turning as he leaned back, away from the tentacles just a foot from his face and closing in, like two hands reaching to throttle him. Out of the corner of his eye, he saw the tentacle that had almost touched him on the floor nearing the miniature time machine. At the same time, the tentacles facing him flexed open their claws and lunged forward like striking snakes—at the last second, they turned away, instead shooting to the table, where the other tentacle had grabbed the model.

199

The three tentacles began turning the miniature over, examining it from all angles. Taylor wanted to rescue it, but they needed to escape this war-torn world. Before he could think of what to do, the lever clicked into place, and Griffin's invisible hand smashed down on top of his, thrusting the starting lever downward.

As their backward journey in time began, Taylor glimpsed a ghost of himself crawling on the floor, all his actions reversed, then the usual disorientation overwhelmed him. It was made worse by Griffin leaning in to hit the lever, which had overbalanced them. Taylor slipped forward. He grabbed the railings of the time machine as it slalomed along, trying to keep his seat. Griffin bumped into him repeatedly; they careened back and forth like men standing on a pitching boat.

"Hold on!" Taylor said. As he'd experienced while escaping the Morlocks, not being centered on the machine exacerbated the dizzying sensation, and he focused on regaining his balance rather than the controls and indicator dials. When finally he'd gotten back in his seat properly and was able to think somewhat straight, he saw that they were overshooting their destination by centuries. Taylor reached for the stopping lever, then hesitated as his concerns recurred about what should happen if, when the machine came to a standstill in time, it intersected with something substantial. But, with no choice, hoping they'd emerge in an open field rather than the hearth of a medieval building, he grabbed the stopping lever, slowing their travel. The blurry sight of time's passage took on a red hue reminiscent of the future they'd left; Taylor wondered if they were passing backward through the Great Fire of London.

∼

A red world snapped into reality—everywhere red. Taylor rubbed his eyes, uncertain of what he was seeing, his head still spinning from time travel. He got off his seat unsteadily and stepped away from the machine, turning slowly around. They were indeed in an open field, one blanketed with a tangled mat of blood-red fibers spreading in all directions as far as the eye could see. No sounds of human or animal disturbed the air.

"What in hell is this red weed?" Griffin said. "And where's London? Have you taken us back too far?"

"Yes, but only to the early 1500s." Taylor looked toward the sound of the voice, then saw the impressions of Griffin's footsteps in the red weed. Getting his bearings from where the bridgeless Thames wound past, flowing around Corporation Island—which was a huge lump of red—Taylor pointed northeastward. "Smoke should be rising from the chimneys of London over that way." But there was nothing to see in that direction except more of the weed. Somehow the emptiness weighed down on Taylor, he was sinking under the pressure of it.

"Nonsense. You must have the time wrong." The footprints paced back and forth.

Taylor stooped and yanked up a handful of the red weed. "I saw this stuff floating down the Thames in the time of the Martians. I'd never seen its like before." He felt a terrible idea take shape, spreading like this very weed through his consciousness.

"You think the Martians brought it with them? Then you've taken us the wrong way, into the future. The Martians destroyed London!"

"No." Taylor looked up from his handful of weeds. "I traveled to the far future and back without glimpsing this. Somehow the Martians were defeated, and quickly, so the invasion came and went in the blink of an eye as time streamed past me."

"How could we have beat those machines? That aside, I don't understand what you're getting at."

"As we escaped my laboratory, that Martian contraption picked up the miniature time machine."

The pacing footsteps stopped. "I thought it was lost to the future."

"It had an untested clockwork mechanism for its return. I didn't think it would actually work, but it must have, spinning back through time like a boomerang." Taylor turned toward the full-size version where it sat upon the carpet of red weed. "We gave a demonstration to the Martian and left him the miniature. If only I'd grabbed it."

Griffin's footprints approached Taylor. "You expected to lose it and already thought you had, so you're no worse off. Now we need to get back to my original scheme to—"

"There's nothing to get back to, you selfish bastard!" Taylor threw the handful of red weed at Griffin, which smacked him in the chest—going by where it stopped in the air and dropped near his footprints.

201

Taylor then stumbled back as Griffin ran at him, grabbing his coat lapels. The two of them tumbled to the ground as Taylor tripped backward over the uneven weeds. They fell down a slight hill and Taylor ended up beneath Griffin, the invisible man's hands moving to his throat. With a roundhouse swing, he clocked Griffin on the side of the head and felt the invisible weight roll off him.

Scrambling to his feet, Taylor said, "You wanted to experiment with the mutability of time, and we have the results. The Martians have used the model to conquer Earth before they even invaded!"

Impressions in the red weed moved as Griffin also got to his feet. Taylor took a step back and raised his fists, but Griffin stayed where he was.

"Well?" Taylor said after he could stand the eerie quiet no longer.

"If you were anyone else, I would—"

"And if I could see more than your footsteps..."

They lapsed back into silence. Griffin started pacing again. Finally, he said, "You think the Martians sent this infernal weed into the past."

"Far enough so that it displaced England of any people before London ever came to be."

"It's only a weed. Surely not enough to stop the Roman Empire."

"What if their empire never arose?" Taylor shuddered at the logical progression of his thoughts as he looked across the empty land. "What if livestock and beasts of burden were poisoned by this weed? Rome might only be scattered tribes of starving cavemen." He couldn't bring himself to voice the ultimate conclusion: maybe the whole human race was gone, the Garden of Eden overrun with red, choked to death by the crawling tendrils of this weed. If the weed could float upon the waves to other continents, perhaps all of Earth was now as red as Mars. Taylor felt numbed by the prospect that his invention had inadvertently led to this.

Griffin stood still. "How are we still here, then, if our ancestors were erased from time?"

Taylor's brow furrowed. "I guess because we were traveling through time. Untethered from its natural flow, we were isolated from the changes rippling forward from whenever the weed was dropped into our past." Absentmindedly he patted his pockets; he heard the rattle of a box of matches inside his waistcoat, but he found no tobacco of any form.

"And so here we are, witnesses to an empty world waiting for its tentacled masters to arrive centuries from now."

As Taylor took his turn at pacing, he could only imagine what Griffin was doing...scratching his head or maybe rubbing his hand thoughtfully on his chin.

"Hold up," Griffin said. "If history can be rewritten, we can rewrite it again. We only need to keep the Martians from getting your model."

"But they took it in a future that no longer exists." Taylor shook his head. "We cannot get there from here."

"Are we talking in loops and knots? It's hard to understand."

"Indeed. During my years devoted to constructing the mechanism of time travel, I thought little about the ramifications."

"That leaves the past, then."

"Yes, of course." Taylor felt a spark of hope. "We recover the miniature in the past, before the red weed can spread."

"Will it take an eternity traveling backward and forward to find it?"

"Haven't you glimpsed the passing of time visible beyond the haze surrounding the machine? We keep a close watch, and we'll see when things appear as they should. Then we stop and wait." Taylor gestured to a spot a couple yards from the time machine. "That is where the model sat in relation to the full-size machine. With any luck, the Martians covered the miniature with the weed right there. It could appear right beside us. The Earth belongs to the Martians for now, but we will take it back!"

∼

"This cannot be right," Griffin said over Taylor's shoulder.

Taylor lifted his head, shielding his eyes from the sun with one hand. The carpet of red weed had been replaced by a lush marsh: ferns, cypress, and cycads dominated, punctuated by a smattering of bright flowers; farther away palm trees jutted into the warm blue sky. A swampy odor was thick in the air, as was the buzzing of insects.

Taylor had stopped the time machine as soon as the overarching red hue flashing past them had disappeared. The long trip followed by the sudden lurching back into the world had wrung him out like a threadbare rag, and he had hung over the controls even as Griffin stirred behind him, listening to the gentle breeze.

"First I thought we were back home, in some conservatory," Griffin said, his voice gaining strength, "but then..."

Taylor felt Griffin's hand upon his head, turning it to the east. Not so far away from where the time machine sat unsteadily on the saturated ground was a vast body of water. It wasn't just wind that Taylor had heard, but the soft movement of shallow waves.

He turned his attention to the indicator dials and gasped. "We are well over fifty million years in the past! The furthest I've ever traveled."

"Fifty *million*!" The machine listed to one side as Griffin stepped off, his invisible feet sinking deeper into the mud than they had into the red weed. "We shall be the toast of London's—no, the world's—scientists."

"First we have to save that world." Taylor stood and pointed. "That's where the model should appear."

Griffin moved toward the spot and grunted, which Taylor interpreted as his disgust for the squishy sucking sound that accompanied each step. "How long must we wait?"

"It's difficult to say. I stopped as quickly as I could when the weed disappeared from view, but we could be hours or days ahead of the miniature's arrival."

"What are we going to eat or drink until then?"

Taylor sat back down. Their excursion into the future had gone so wrong so quickly that they now found themselves without any supplies for what could be a considerable wait. He had chastised himself for not provisioning his first travels through time, yet here he was in the same situation—though certainly through no fault of his own.

"We will likely starve here," Griffin continued, "especially if they moved it. Searching for the thing could take weeks."

Taylor decided to be optimistic. "Perhaps it's already here, but just beyond our sight." Stepping off the time machine, he trudged across the marsh. "With any luck—and we're due some luck—it's only on the other side of the tree line."

He heard Griffin following behind him, cursing at the difficulty of walking in the swamp, but after a few yards the ground firmed up and their pace increased. Taylor slowed as they reached the trees, wondering what sort of animals might be hidden in this prehistoric forest. Taylor took a step into the shade of the trees, looked for any animal movement, then continued forward, walking as quietly as possible. He spotted a clearing not far ahead and thought he glimpsed some red through the verdant leaves. Could this be the luck he had hoped for?

He sped up the last few yards, then froze as he burst into the clearing, stopping so quickly that Griffin ran into him from behind.

"What the devil—?" Griffin began, then cut himself off.

There indeed was the miniature, less than ten yards away, a couple yards of red tendrils already spread out around it. Also in the clearing were three shallow pits, just a few feet across, dug into the moist soil. In each pit rested one or two enormous eggs. One nest was occupied, and the monstrous bird swiveled its large head toward Taylor.

Slowly it stood, rising to at least six feet tall, an arching neck atop a barrel-chested body with stout legs. It puffed up its variegated green and gray feathers, spread its stubby wings out to the side, shaking them threateningly, and, with a hiss, snapped its giant beak open and shut; the *clack* echoed from the trees. It took one step toward them, thumping its scaly foot outside the nest.

Taylor moved back, keeping his eye on the huge bird until he was several feet into the forest. The bird craned its head to the sky, released a grating squawk, then stomped a couple more times before settling back into its nest. Soon there came loud footsteps, and two more of the giant birds raced into view from the other side of the woods. They made a patrol around the clearing before returning to their separate nests.

"Some luck we have," Griffin whispered, grabbing Taylor's arm. "Those things could tear us apart—like a robin with a worm."

∼

With some difficulty, they had dragged the time machine across the marsh to the edge of the forest. Although odd animal sounds came from within the trees, Taylor was glad to be farther from the sea; if there were giant birds on land, who knew what swam beneath the water.

Taylor was eyeing the new location, figuring that it corresponded to his garden, when a commotion of slapping sounds was followed by a shout from Griffin.

"Blast these insects! They've no trouble finding an invisible man."

"Shush! You don't want to attract anything larger than the insects." Taylor had been wondering where the mates of the nesting birds were.

Griffin's slapping stopped. "True. I've been trying to banish the Crystal Palace dinosaurs from my mind."

Taylor was not pleased to have those images placed in his head. He slumped onto the seat of the time machine. "All the more reason to get what we came here for so we can go home."

"How can we possibly retrieve the model from the nesting ground of those monsters? Even with rifles it would be a challenge."

Taylor nodded at Griffin's assessment. "Nevertheless, we must try. And I've just had an idea."

~

Taylor and Griffin huddled in the dusk at the edge of the clearing; within, all three of the monster birds were settling in for the evening. The two men had traveled back in time day by day until, just over a fortnight further into the past, the miniature and its red weed had disappeared from the nesting ground. Now they waited for it to make its debut in the prehistoric world.

Three hours had passed, with no sounds close by but insects buzzing and their stomachs growling—louder animal sounds had remained distant, thankfully—when the model appeared before them. It was accompanied by an odd flash of light and a subsonic rumble felt in their bones, something Taylor had never noticed while a passenger, but which he appreciated now. He had hoped its sudden arrival would scare the birds away, and the extra side effects could only help. Two of the birds were indeed so startled that they fled the clearing, abandoning their eggs. The last one, however, after lumbering to its feet, rushed at the machine while presenting the same threatening posture Taylor had received upon first entering the clearing.

With a sigh of disappointment, Taylor said, "As planned then?"

Griffin did not respond.

"Let's hurry before the others return," added Taylor. "We have little choice."

Finally Griffin spoke. "It was easy to agree to this mad scheme when I hoped it wouldn't be necessary."

Still, Taylor saw some branches pushed aside as Griffin stood and entered the clearing.

"Over here, you daft buzzard!" Griffin yelled.

The bird's big head and oversized beak spun toward the sound. Its head cocked to the side when it found no source for the noise. When Griffin started running, the bird clearly recognized the sound of fleeing prey, and it leaped into action following the footsteps.

As soon as its stubby tail was pointed toward Taylor, he left the cover of the forest, hurrying in a crouch toward the miniature. When the bird stopped moving so did he; he stared at the feathered beast's back, fearing that it had caught Griffin. But it was turning its head slowly from side to side, obviously trying to figure out where its prey had disappeared to.

"Take this!" The shout was followed by a thump and a squawk from the bird; Griffin must have thrown something at it. The bird was off and running again.

Taylor rushed the remaining yards to the miniature. He scooped it up, careful not to lose the clump of red weed that was wrapped around it, and hurried back to the forest. Just as he got under cover, a shrill cry rent the night, followed by the thrashing sounds of branches being shaken—then silence. Taylor looked into the clearing, but could see nothing; the bird must have chased Griffin into the forest and followed him in. Taylor pushed aside any worry about Griffin—after all, the fate of the entire human race hung in the balance—and stuck to the plan.

First, he reached beneath the miniature controls and pulled out the clockwork return mechanism. Now there was no chance the machine could go back to the time of the Martians and give them another chance to meddle in Earth's past. Next, he built a small fire—with the matches he had with him by chance—and dropped the tangle of weeds from the miniature into the flames. He watched until they were entirely consumed, then stomped the fire out to avoid the mishap he'd barely escaped in the time of the Morlocks. Only then did he let himself wonder about Griffin's fate.

Keeping the miniature in his hands, he returned to the clearing. All three monster birds were back, standing guard by their nests. Taylor risked one shout: "Griffin!" The birds' heads snapped in his direction, but they didn't leave their nests, just performed their wing-flapping, foot-stomping ritual, accompanied with hisses, squawks, and beak snaps.

Taylor waited a few minutes, straining to hear Griffin calling for help or moving through the woods. All he heard was the sound of insects. He started back to the full-scale time machine. If Griffin hadn't returned by morning, Taylor would search in the daylight. But as he left the forest, greeted by the soft sound of waves, Taylor saw that the time machine was gone.

∼

As Taylor fell to his knees in despair, with a flash and a rumble the time machine appeared before him. Griffin was himself slightly visible, being covered in spatters of mud and bits of leaves.

Taylor swayed between shocked relief and rising rage until finally finding his voice. "You lunatic! I thought you'd abandoned me here."

"I tried to return right after I left, but you need more exacting controls."

"This has nothing to do with—"

Griffin cut him off. "After barely escaping a painful death in the beak of that horrific bird—my leg is still bleeding—I was eager to discover our fate."

Chagrined to learn of the injury, Taylor took a deep breath and released it before saying, "What did you find? Did we succeed?"

Due to the mud on Griffin's torso, Taylor could just make out his shrug. "I don't know. I went forward only a century or two. The sea had risen, and I found myself in a couple feet of water. I started the return journey straight away."

"For God's sake! The machine could have been rendered inoperable, and we'd have both been stranded, without even the aid of the other to survive!" He snatched up the miniature from the ground and stomped over to Griffin.

"Get back and hold this," Taylor said, thrusting the miniature at Griffin, who took hold of it and relinquished the seat. Taylor sat at the controls. "Let's go home." But the despair he'd felt before Griffin's return had erased any hope that they'd returned time to its proper course. "If there's a London to go home to."

~

Only minutes into their journey, Taylor glimpsed, through the haze of evolving time surrounding the machine, various flora and fauna, but no invasive red weed. A smile spread across his face. As he saw beloved London rise from its Roman roots to become the heart of its own Empire, and finally enter the long reign of Queen Victoria, the smile became so wide it was almost painful.

Taylor had attempted to return under cover of darkness, just a couple hours after he had left under duress with Griffin, but he overshot, returning instead the following afternoon. As he'd expected, they appeared in his garden behind the laboratory. Everything looked exactly as they had left it; they had indeed vanquished the invasive red weed.

They hadn't yet caught their breath after the disorienting trip when Mr. Galanter appeared at the low stone wall that separated their gardens. "What the devil was that? I dropped my tea I was so startled!"

Taylor staggered to his feet, attempting to keep himself between Galanter and where the slightly visible Griffin held the miniature. "Erm...that is—"

"Good God, what's happened to you?" Galanter seemed not to notice the time machines, focusing on Taylor's unkept appearance.

Taylor brushed at his muddied and torn clothes. "I look a mess, but I'm fine. Sorry about the tea, I'll make a fresh pot after I've washed and changed."

"Well," said Galanter, rubbing his neatly trimmed beard. "I never turn down a nice cuppa. Will there be biscuits?"

"I'll check my tins."

"Off you go then!" Galanter said with a smile, then returned to his garden bench.

209

"Let's get these machines inside," Taylor said, speaking softly so Galanter wouldn't overhear.

～

Swearing that everything was fine, Taylor had sent his rather concerned man-servant and Mrs. Watchett away immediately to avoid further questions and any possible interactions between them and Griffin. Taylor washed up first and then had tea with Galanter while Griffin took his turn.

When Taylor came back inside, he found Griffin in the kitchen dressed in some of his laboratory clothes and boots; from the waist down it looked normal, but the headless body and empty shirtsleeves raiding the cupboard were disturbing.

"What now?" Griffin said, his mouth visibly full. When he finally stopped chewing, the food went down his throat and disappeared from view within the shirt.

Taylor frowned at the disgusting sight. "Nothing. Things are as they were."

"Nothing? We saved everything! We've seen with our own eyes how ancient the Earth is, and how right Darwin and Huxley are. As I said in the past, we will be the toast of the world!"

"The world has no reason to believe us. Not to mention we were simply righting our own missteps in saving it. Putting out a fire you started yourself doesn't make you a hero. And traveling into the past is surely playing with fire."

"Things as they were then. You will take me to my future self, avoiding the—"

"No."

Griffin stepped closer. "You can help me, or I'll take the machine myself."

Taylor put a hand on Griffin's chest and pushed him back a step. "You can try, but I'll fight you every step of the way to keep you from using my machine or finding your solution. If, however, you leave London, I'll let you alone. Then we shall both have time to pursue our work instead of battling one another."

Griffin took a single step toward Taylor, raising his arms, but he backed off as Taylor suddenly had a carving knife in hand.

"Damn it, man, all right," said Griffin. "A truce."

~

Taylor had helped Griffin wrap his head as if he'd suffered some terrible injuries, getting him gloves and dark glasses, and then walked him to the hansom station. Griffin was a lost cause; Taylor was convinced of that. He was equally convinced that Griffin would not honor their truce indefinitely; honestly, he wasn't sure it would last the day.

Taylor was nothing like Griffin. He would never feel entitled to indulge his every whim, to demand the adulation of his peers, expect the less fortunate to bow to his word. He simply wanted to make things better, and he'd seen a future where mankind had lost its way. Even having a time machine, he was impatient to find a better path, a way to avoid the Eloi and the Morlocks.

After he'd gathered provisions, including his tools, and packed the miniature to carry along with him, he realized there was one loose end. He wasn't sure what effect it might have on his own future across the millennia, but he had to try to spare England this hardship.

"Mr. Galanter!" he called over the stone wall between their gardens.

His neighbor wasn't long in answering with a "Mr. Taylor!" and soon joined him.

"I'm off on a long trip, and I have a favor to ask of you."

"A trip? Where to?"

"Far away, practically another world!"

"Ah, to Wales, then," Galanter said, laughing at his own joke.

Taylor laughed right along, realizing he would rather miss Galanter. "Even farther away than that." He held up a sealed envelope. "Could you deliver this to Ogilvy?"

"The astronomer?"

"Yes. He'll know what to do, I hope. Much depends on it."

"I shall do so with my own hand."

"Good man." He shook his neighbor's hand. "Goodbye, Galanter. I do hope to see you again someday."

And with that, the time traveler rushed back to his machine, and his future.

A Prisoner Freed in Oz

Marsheila Rockwell

Ozma of Oz first appeared in L. Frank Baum's 1904 *The Marvelous Land of Oz*, the sequel to his seminal *The Wonderful Wizard of Oz*. Since then, the girl ruler of Oz has been featured in many works, from Gregory Maguire's *The Wicked Years* series to the television series, Emerald City. But Baum's Ozma was the one who stole my heart. I never wanted to be Dorothy--I was already poor and plain with only my imagination to rely on for my adventures. I wanted to be Ozma—she taught me that even as a little girl, I could aspire to be something more than what I was, and I didn't have to be a grownup to have dreams and goals. That book—her character—sparked a fire in me that never died and is directly responsible for the fact that I've realized so many of my dreams, including becoming a published author, even though I started out disadvantaged in many ways. She is proof that reading one book can change the course of someone's life for the better. How could I *not* want to write a story about her, given the chance?

Marsheila (Marcy) Rockwell, a multiple Scribe and Rhysling Award nominee, is the author of twelve books to date. Her work includes *7 SYKOS*, a near future SF/H thriller co-written with writing partner/husband Jeff Mariotte; The Shard Axe series, the only official novels that tie into the popular fantasy MMORPG, Dungeons & Dragons Online; two collections; dozens of short stories and poems; multiple articles on writing and the writing process; and a handful of comic book scripts. She is also a disabled pediatric cancer and mental health awareness advocate, and a reconnecting Chippewa/Métis. She resides in the Valley of the Sun, where she writes dark fiction and poetry in a home she and her family have dubbed 'Redwall.' Find out more here: http://www.marsheilarockwell.com/ or follow her on Twitter at @MarcyRockwell.

NOTE: This story draws largely from *The Marvelous Land of Oz* and *The Patchwork Girl of Oz*, both published in the early 1900s. Accordingly, some of the attitudes initially presented regarding why a person might choose to break a law or want to be transformed will likely ruffle modern feathers, as much of Baum's work would be considered "problematic" by today's standards. However, I have tried to present Ozma as a bit more progressive than her creator. Hopefully I have succeeded in that endeavor.

A Prisoner Freed in Oz

For Mae

"Bring me the prisoner," Ozma said. At once, the Soldier with the Green Whiskers set off for the house with the colored glass dome that served as the Emerald City's rarely used prison.

As she waited upon her emerald throne in her great Throne Room, dainty chin on dainty fist, the eternally young princess pondered this extraordinary situation. In all her time as Ruler of Oz, there had only ever been one other prisoner for the soldier to fetch—Ojo the (No Longer) Unlucky, a Munchkin boy who'd broken the law against picking six-leaved clovers out of love for his dear Unc Nunkie, because the magical plant was necessary to turn the man from a marble statue back to flesh and bone.

And now here was another prisoner, this one a Gillikin boy. It was most unusual; Ozians were by and large a contented lot and had all their worldly needs met, so there was no reason for them to fib or steal or do any of the even worse things that Ozma sometimes glimpsed in her Magic Picture before she could look away. They had no cause to break the few good and just laws Ozma imposed on them for the happiness and safety of all.

And yet, like Ojo, this boy had done so. He had tried to sneak into the Emerald City Vault, but had, of course, been caught by the Vault

Custodian, Tillydoggle, the sister of the prison jailer, Tollydiggle. The custodian was there, not to guard the vault or keep people out, but simply to log what citizens left or took. The vault did indeed contain riches, but they were not greedily hoarded. The treasure therein consisted of the largesse of the Emerald City's citizens and those of the four surrounding countries. They would bring whatever they had that was more than they needed—and in Oz, that often required wheelbarrows, wagons, and other more fantastical carriages—to store for whomever might be lacking. Tillydoggle logged far more deposits than she ever had withdrawals.

In her Magic Picture, Ozma had seen the boy hide himself in the back of a baker's wagon, under baskets of bread, muffins, and delicious tamorna pastries—one of which he'd eaten—then try to sneak inside the vault while the baker and the custodian were conversing.

A loud, deep bell had rung when the boy had crossed the threshold of the vault, a carryover from when the Wizard ruled Oz and hoarded more than he handed out. The Soldier with the Green Whiskers had arrived straightaway to arrest him for Unauthorized Vault Entry—a law that perhaps should have been stricken from the books once the Wizard was unmasked as a fraud—and taken him to Tollydiggle to await Ozma's pleasure.

It was possible the boy hadn't known about the law, but the fact remained that he had felt the need for a stealthy entry, which suggested that he had, at the very least, sensed that his deed was wrong. And yet he had done it anyway.

He must have had a reason. Ozma very much looked forward to learning it.

It was doubly sad, really. Sad that the boy had chosen these actions and sad that he had lost his freedom because of them. But those who did wrong seldom did so because they were bad people. More often, Ozma believed, it was because they were not quite strong or brave enough to do right. She hoped that a little kindness might remedy that.

The Soldier with the Green Whiskers ushered the Gillikin lad into the Throne Room. He was wearing a voluminous white cloak with a deep cowl that hid both face and form. Previously, prison garb had consisted of a white robe that covered the entire personage and had two eye holes through which the prisoner could see. After Ojo's trial, Princess Dorothy

Gale, Ozma's dearest and most beloved friend, had taken her aside and mentioned that the Munchkin boy had looked like a silly spook house ghost dressed up for a Halloween party, and Ozma had the former Kansas farm girl work with the Guardian of the Gate to remake the offerings in the Official Wardrobe, so that no other prisoner who came before her court would ever be thought of as "silly."

Ozma gestured and the soldier removed the boy's cloak and jeweled handcuffs. She studied the Gillikin lad, whom she judged no older than her own apparent sixteen years. He had been afforded the chance to bathe, and offered his choice of many lovely clothes with which to appear before her. He had chosen a long lavender coat of velvet, with a pink satin collar and cuffs and large silver and pearl buttons running down the front. He wore pink hose and purple slippers with silver buckles. His long dark hair was combed into soft waves about his face and he had big brown eyes that shone with both worry and defiance.

"Zav of Gillikin Country," the Soldier with the Green Whiskers announced and then stepped back a respectful distance, still holding the robe and handcuffs, should they be needed again. Ozma rather thought they wouldn't, but some of that would depend on Zav.

Zav did not face her full court today. Princess Dorothy sat to Ozma's right with Toto on her lap, and Professor Woggle-Bug sat to her left, in place of the Scarecrow, who was off gallivanting with Scraps, the Patchwork Girl, of whom the straw man had grown quite fond. The Cowardly Lion and the Hungry Tiger lazed at Ozma's feet. In front of the gem-encrusted throne was a small table upon which sat a platter of the incriminating tamorna pastries, magically still warm from the oven, their aroma making several of the assembled stomachs growl hungrily. There was no one else present, and the other seats that normally filled the Throne Room had been removed.

"One of the Laws of Oz forbids unauthorized entry into the Emerald City Vault," Ozma said gently. "You stand accused of having broken this law." She did not mention the stolen pastry, as the baker had immediately forgiven the small transgression when he learned of it.

She was surprised when the boy did not hang his head as Ojo had done when he was similarly accused. Instead, Zav straightened his back and stood taller.

"Did you do so?"

"Yes!"

Ozma sat back in her throne, looking at the boy thoughtfully. Finally, she spoke.

"Why?"

"I was trying to find Mombi's spell book. Everyone in Gillikin Country has heard the story of how she transformed you from a girl into a boy named Tip when you were a baby, and then back into a girl again when you were older. I tracked Mombi down and tried to get her to do the same for me, but she said she couldn't do it anymore, that Glinda the Good had seen to that. But she also said that the spell should still be in her old spell book, and that was probably being kept under lock and key with all the other great treasures of Oz in the Emerald City."

That explained why Zav had been trying to get into the vault—he had been misled by Mombi, who even without her magic was still managing to cause trouble. But that was far less interesting than why he'd gone to Mombi in the first place.

"You want to become a girl?" Ozma asked in surprise.

"I don't want to *become* a girl," Zav retorted indignantly. "I already *am* a girl. I'm a girl trapped in the wrong body, and I'm trying to find a way to fix that. To get the right body. Like you did."

"I see," Ozma said, and she thought perhaps she did. "You know, Glinda disapproved of Mombi's transformation magic because she felt transformations were not honest, and no respectable witch should try to make things appear to be what they are not."

Zav—who, despite what Ozma had assumed before, had in fact been very brave up until that moment, and quite strong to pursue what he knew to be right for him, even when others might think it to be wrong—looked crestfallen.

"Does—does that mean you won't help me? I thought if anyone understood, it would be you."

"On the contrary. I *do* understand, and I think Glinda would, too, for all her somewhat old-fashioned assertions." Ozma smiled at Zav, and was pleased to see him relax somewhat. "Transformation magic isn't evil when it changes someone from who they're not to who they truly are."

She rose from her throne, lifting her pearl- and emerald-embroidered Robe of State deftly with one hand as she stepped down from the great green seat's height. When she had reached the floor, Professor Woggle-Bug, who had been holding her golden royal scepter as she descended, returned it to her, its multitude of rubies, sapphires, diamonds, and other gems sparkling with every movement. With her free hand, Ozma gestured for Zav to follow.

"Come."

She led him out a side door and into the palace proper, shaking her head at her companions when they made as if to join the duo. This next part was a task for her and Zav, and them alone.

As they walked, she told Zav what her own experience of being changed from Tippetarius the Gillikin boy to Ozma the girl Ruler of Oz had been like.

"As Tip, I was always unhappy living with Mombi. She did not treat me well, but that wasn't really enough to explain my innate dislike of her. I think, even though I was only a baby when she cast her original transformation spell, somehow, deep down, I still knew something wasn't right, and it was because of something she had done. But it wasn't until after she transformed me back into my true self that I realized that much of that unhappiness stemmed from being in the wrong body."

"That's exactly how I feel!" Zav exclaimed. "Well, except for the hating Mombi part."

Ozma laughed. "Yes. Except for that part."

She stopped in front of a door no different from any other in the palace. But unlike the other doors, this one was locked. She withdrew a golden Oz key from the base of her scepter and inserted it into a keyhole that had appeared beneath the doorknob. As she turned it, there was a faint chime, and the door swung open.

Inside the room were many sorcerous items, most of which had been collected over time from the various vanquished Wicked Witches and placed in this magically locked room where they could do no further harm. Ozma led Zav past a small table with a crystal ball on it, by another table which bore a necklace of sharp iron thorns, and in front of a tall silver harp with a soundbox fashioned to resemble a singing woman. The silver woman's eyes opened and she glared at the two as they walked by.

Finally, they reached a wooden podium upon which a leatherbound journal rested. This, of course, had been the first of Mombi's deceits, for it was not a spell book as she had told Zav, but merely a collection of various magical recipes scribbled on bits of paper and shoved willy-nilly between the journal's covers (the second deception had been letting Zav think the journal was located in the Emerald City Vault, which the old woman knew quite well contained nothing so vile).

Ozma leafed through the yellowing pages until she found the transformation spell, then she looked up at Zav.

"Are you sure you want to do this? I cannot reverse the spell once spoken—Mombi did not write that incantation down, but kept it in her head, where it was stripped away along with all her other magical knowledge by Glinda's draught."

Zav nodded confidently.

"I'm sure. This is the only way I will ever be truly happy."

"Well," Ozma replied with a smile, "we certainly can't have an unhappy Ozian."

She bade Zav to lie down on a nearby—non-magical—couch and close his eyes. Not needing the herbs, powders, and gesticulations Mombi had relied on for much of her magic, Ozma simply spoke the words written in the old woman's unsteady scrawl.

A fresh breeze blew through the room, and Zav opened her eyes.

Ozma helped the young girl up from the couch. Zav did not look much different than she had before, though her hair and features were softer and her skin glowed as if kissed by the morning dew. Her clothing was a bit snugger through the hips, but Zav had chosen an outfit that could be worn equally well by a girl or a boy, so the fit was not unflattering.

Ozma led the girl over to a mirror on the wall. This mirror *was* magical, but when a face appeared in its glass and began to speak, Ozma shushed it into silence and it faded away. Once the glass was clear again, Zav beheld herself, and her delicate mouth curved into a wide, happy smile. She touched her face reverently, turning this way and that to observe the way her new body looked and moved.

"Finally," she whispered, tears in her big brown eyes as she looked at Ozma. "I'm finally free. Thank you so much."

"Of course. I only wish I had the power to transform everyone who feels the way you and I did, so no one would ever have to suffer through the unhappiness of not being able to be their true self."

"I wish that, too," Zav said.

"What shall we call you?" Ozma asked.

"I think I'd like to be called…Mae."

"Then Mae you shall be, henceforth," Ozma declared.

As she led Mae from the room, the girl gave her a concerned look.

"What is it?" Ozma asked. She had worried that her friends would not accept her once she changed from a fugitive farmhand to a princess, but they were true friends, and had loved her just the same. She wondered if that's what was disturbing Mae.

"It's just, I… I… I'm really sorry for having broken the law," Mae blurted. "I was scared that if I just asked for your help, you might say no. I know better now."

"Indeed. But it was an understandable worry, and a forgivable one."

Mae's grateful smile was radiant.

"And now," Ozma said, holding a hand out to Mae, "I think it's time to introduce my dear new friend to my dear old friends, and to eat some of those delicious-smelling tamorna pastries. Are you ready?"

Mae took her hand.

"I'm ready."

The Comet Cannon of Planet X

Robert E. Vardeman

Running on ABC from March 9, 1950 through February 26, 1955, *Space Patrol* captured the imaginations of young children as America was entering the Space Age. The nine hundred fifteen-minute episodes inspired all manner of merchandise, including one of the last radio shows, comic books, toys but, curiously, no tie-in books.

Robert E. Vardeman, after publishing close to three hundred SF, fantasy, mystery, and western novels, doesn't have a bucket list. Or so he thought, in spite of having *Terra V* wallpaper on his computer and a scale model of the *Terra V* on his desk. The chance to write a *Space Patrol* story fulfills a hidden urge to honor the TV show that launched his love of science fiction. He wrote three titles in two different Tom Swift series, paying homage to Tom Swift Jr. and that series' influence on his reading. Now, with this story, he tries to match the thrills and sense of wonder given him by Commander Corry, Cadet Happy, Carol Carlisle, and all the other Space Patrollers. Writing this story might not be the same as having a Martian totem head or a rocket cockpit or a smoke pistol (he has one mounted in a shadow box) but it comes close. For more check out his website www.cenotaphroad.com.

The Comet Cannon of Planet X

"Smokin' rockets, Commander, the comet is heading straight for Terra! It'll destroy the planet!" Cadet Happy jerked back from the space viewer and looked in panic at the pilot, Commander-in-Chief of the Space Patrol, Buzz Corry.

The tall, handsome officer worked with quick, sure moves at the controls of his ship, the *Terra V*. The mighty battlecruiser drove forward so fast that any added acceleration would cause the hyperdrive to activate and fling them into the vastness of interstellar space.

"I've primed three cosmic missiles, Hap. Target the comet with a standard bracket pattern."

"Me, Commander? But I'm only a cadet." Happy reached out to the missile sight. His hand shook. "What if I miss? The capital of the United Planets will be destroyed!"

"The time's too short to evacuate everyone. Do your duty, Cadet!" He had trained his cadet well. Happy would not fail him—or the millions on the artificial planet, Terra.

"Aye, aye, sir." Cadet Happy pressed his eye to the sights, lined up the crosshairs and began a countdown. When he yelled, "Fire!" the huge ship shuddered. One cosmic missile after another launched.

The brilliant flare caused Commander Corry to throw up his arm to protect his eyes. Then the shock wave laden with gases and debris from the destroyed comet buffeted them.

"We blew it apart, Commander. We saved Terra!"

Commander Corry yanked the control sticks over hard, sending the ship into a violent turn.

"Leaving behind so many large fragments is dangerous, Happy. We have to keep a thousand smaller projectiles from hitting the planet."

"But there are too many to take out with a missile. What're we going to do, sir?"

Buzz steered directly into the path of the cometary debris. Then he switched on the repeller ray used for landing the huge battlecruiser on a planetary surface. Inside the *Terra V*, it sounded like being trapped in an echo chamber. Tiny pings became huge thuds as the hull was pelted with rocky fragments. A few control adjustments spun the battlecruiser about its major axis, the repeller ray deflecting different sized remnants of the cometary mass with every rotation.

"I'm getting dizzy, Commander. I can barely hang on!" Cadet Happy grabbed the space viewer console and clung to it. His feet lifted as the ship spun faster and faster. And then Buzz countered the roll with the attitude jets. Working steadily, he slowed the axial rotation and finally returned the *Terra V* to normal flight.

"Check the space viewer, Hap. Be sure we diverted all the dangerous rubble left from the cosmic missiles."

"You did it, sir! *We* did it! You swept away all but a few tiny pieces. Terra's planetary meteoroid detectors will warn everyone if those are going to hit anywhere important."

"Chances are good what's left will burn up in the atmosphere. It looks as if Terra is safe."

"That sure was a close call, Commander. It's a good thing we were close enough to blow it up."

"Yes, Happy, it was. But it was exactly aimed at Terra, as if it had been fired from a cannon."

"It was only a comet, sir. Coincidence. Why, you know that—" The warning klaxon cut off the cadet.

Buzz grabbed the spacephone and clicked it on. Before he could acknowledge, Secretary General Carlisle's voice boomed forth.

"Commander, you saved us. But there are new comets heading for Earth and our Mars base at Canali. I've ordered other ships to intercept and destroy if they can."

"That's terrible, sir," Cadet Happy said. "Three comets? That's impossible unless the Oort Cloud is getting indigestion! It's too bad we can't use them for target practice, too."

"We only have one cosmic missile left in our tubes," he said to his cadet. To the Secretary General, "Sir, transmit all the information you have so we can track down the source. A larger comet must have split apart somewhere on the edge of the solar system."

"You have a different mission, Buzz. A more personal one. Let the other Space Patrol ships deal with the comets."

"Another mission, sir?" Buzz frowned. This wasn't like the Secretary General. The safety of Terra and the other United Planets was always his primary concern.

"Major Robertson is at our Ceres science station."

"That's where Carol is," Happy cut in. Buzz silenced any further outburst with a gesture.

"Has something happened to your daughter, sir?" Buzz gripped the controls so tightly his knuckles turned white. Sending the United Planets' head of security to the research station meant trouble. "Robby" Robertson was a topflight investigator.

"When he found the station deserted and all the research equipment gone, Major Robertson used fungal scene reconstruction. You will receive a video any second now."

Buzz and Cadet Happy turned to the view screen. Ghostly images of Carol Carlisle appeared, moving in a jerky fashion. The fungus outlined her, then collapsed into a pile of dust after a few seconds, only to be replaced with a new image from more fungus sprayed into the laboratory. A second figure appeared. She fought but was engulfed by a paralo-ray. Then the images collapsed.

"I recognize him. That's Doctor Kruger," Buzz said. "He kidnapped Carol!"

"If Doctor Kruger attacked her, that means Prince Baccarratti ordered him to do it!" Cadet Happy dropped into the copilot's seat, hands hovering over the controls, anxiously awaiting orders.

"Why'd Baccarratti want to take Carol, sir?" Buzz turned over the reasons. The self-styled ruler of the entire solar system might have revenge in mind, but his schemes were usually more sweeping. The crazed genius always had a method to his undeniable madness.

"She was working to develop a mass accelerator intended to propel asteroids to the inner planets for mining. Buzz, I'm afraid Baccarratti has forced Carol to reveal her research. That's how the comets are so fast and so accurately aimed." The Secretary General's voice broke. "Commander, save my daughter. And stop Prince Baccarratti from sending more comets at our planets!"

Buzz Corry repositioned the *Terra V* and initiated the hyperdrive.

"Where are we going, Commander?" Cadet Happy rested his hands on the controls, ready for action.

"We're going to the most dangerous spot in the solar system," Buzz said grimly. "We're going to Prince Baccarratti's lair on Planet X!"

~

"It's so big, Commander. I can't believe it." Cadet Happy drew back from the space viewer.

Buzz stared at the immense blue-green globe ahead. Storms swirled constantly, storms with two-hundred-mile-per-hour gusts capable of lifting boulders and turning them into air-propelled missiles. Boiling acid seas covered half the world and a dense primordial jungle the other half.

"It's five thousand times more massive than Earth, Hap. And look. See that?"

"It's like a giant spitball, Commander. Only it's… it's a comet!"

Buzz turned grim.

"The volcanoes are spitting out huge balls of magma. That's natural. See how the gob of molten rock accelerates away? Baccarratti is using Carol's linear accelerator to aim the mass at Terra."

"And Earth, sir. I calculated the trajectory. That one's heading directly for Earth!"

"Prepare to fire a cosmic missile. We can stop it dead in its orbit." Buzz rested his finger on the launch button. "Tell me when, Hap. And don't miss."

"Now, Commander, now. Fire!"

Buzz's finger stabbed down. The *Terra V* shuddered as the powerful cosmic missile raced straight and true to blow apart the comet.

"Dead center, sir! A direct hit! But there's another one spinning around the planet. It's gathering speed and...and there it goes!"

"Line us up again, Hap. Hurry."

"This one's headed toward Terra. Baccarratti intends to send swarms of them until we can't intercept all of them!"

"Hap, give me the missile targeting solution. Hurry." Buzz watched as the cometary mass, trailing gases and bits of molten material, gained speed. In minutes it would whip away from Planet X toward the inner system and the United Planets' capital world.

"Sir, we've used all our cosmic missiles. We can't stop it!"

"This worked once, it'll work again." Grimly, Buzz steered the massive battlecruiser toward the deadly comet. "Strap in. Prepare to use the repeller ray."

"But, sir, it's so big!"

Buzz concentrated on driving his ship directly into the path of the deadly flaming projectile. The *Terra V* lurched.

"What's that?" Cadet Happy held onto the armrests on his copilot's seat.

"Carol's linear accelerator is still on. We caught the edge of the field. Here we go." Buzz drew back on the control sticks and rolled the battlecruiser over. The repeller ray screeched as it worked against the comet. The comet veered away, but the *Terra V* began to tumble.

"What happened, sir? We're falling like a leaf."

"Newton's Third Law, Hap. For every action there's an equal and opposite reaction. It took everything we had to deflect the comet from its course." Buzz fought to regain control, but the huge ship only tumbled faster. At the last possible instant, he once more used the repeller ray to brake their fall. Still, the *Terra V* plummeted through the heavy jungle growth at a deadly speed.

Then the repeller ray gave out. The ship fell with no way to slow— except to crash into the planet.

~

"He ruined it. Corry ruined my attack again!" Prince Baccarratti pounded his fists against the space viewer. He swung about and shoved Doctor Kruger away. "It's your fault. You let him get close to the planet!"

"Sire, you gave no orders." Doctor Kruger cringed when Baccarratti slapped him with a glove. The prince's form-fitting black leather tunic gleamed in the flicker from the space viewer and made the black falcon emblem on his chest appear to come alive.

"Fool. You are a fool. Must I tell you everything?" Baccarratti paced back and forth. "Bring her to me. Bring me the Secretary General's daughter!"

"Yes, sire." Doctor Kruger half turned. He slid his hand under his tunic, gripped the butt of a small pistol. As he whirled back around to face Baccarratti, a bone-tingling hum filled the room.

Baccarratti held his Z-ray in front of Kruger's face.

"You think to shoot me, you dolt? You will obey me. The Z-ray will wipe out all resistance in your foolish mind. Go. Bring Carol Carlisle to me here in my throne room." Baccarratti waved the wand under Doctor Kruger's nose and sent one more blast of mind-numbing ray into the man's brain.

"I obey you, my prince." Like a zombie, Doctor Kruger left.

Baccarratti looked around the room, built in the manner of a medieval castle of stone blocks. The far end was dominated by his throne, decorated with the black falcons of his family crest. At the other his view screen showed only swirling jungle mist thousands of feet below where the castle perched on its rocky spire. He stalked back to the view screen and tried to penetrate the fog, to no avail.

"You died, Corry. You must have. Collision with the comet knocked you out of orbit to crash on my planet. Yes, you are dead. Planet X will swallow your bones." He scanned the top of the jungle growth. Already the hole torn in the vegetation had closed over where the *Terra V* had plunged downward. "Nothing survives on the surface of *my* planet. If the crash failed to kill you, Corry, the dinosaurs will trample you to bloody pulp."

Shuffling sounds caused him to spin, the Z-ray wand lifted. A cruel smile twisted his lips. Baccarratti motioned for Carol Carlisle to come closer.

"You must send more comets toward Terra, toward Earth and Mars and the other worlds of the United Planets. How soon can you prepare a new barrage?"

Carol fought not to answer, but the power of the Z-ray was too great.

"I must wait for new ejecta from the volcano," she said in a choked voice. "I cannot predict when a mass large enough will be blown out."

"The United Planets must be destroyed!" Baccarratti used his Z-ray at full power. The tiny resistance Carol had shown before melted away under the ray's insidious influence. "Go. Keep your linear accelerator powered up. Do not deny me my pleasure!"

"My f-father," she gasped out, fighting the Z-ray's effect.

"Your father will die unless he surrenders rulership to me, Prince Baccarratti, the Black Falcon!" He turned up the power to maximum. This time no trace of defiance remained. "Go. Send more comets sunward using your cannon."

Carol Carlisle shuffled off, all willpower to resist the prince wiped away.

Baccarratti fiddled with the view screen controls, hoping to catch sight of a massive dinosaur stepping on the *Terra V* and crushing it. Crushing it just like he would crush the United Planets and seize power. Frustrated by the swirling mists, he stalked from the view screen to the elaborately carved ebon throne. Baccarratti paused a moment at the base, then mounted the steps, turned, and sat. He savored the power.

"You are gone, Corry. You can no longer oppose me. Soon, I will rule the solar system from this throne. Soon!" Prince Baccarratti's cold, mocking laughter filled the castle and echoed out across Planet X.

~

Buzz Corry hung upside down in the pilot's seat, held by the safety harness. He reached out and powered down as much of the ship as he could. The acrid smell of burning metal filled his nostrils and warned that the *Terra V* was in dire condition.

"Wh-what happened? Commander? Commander!" Cadet Happy thrashed about in his own harness.

"We're alive, Happy. Be careful when you release your latch. We're upside-down."

"Smokin' rockets, Commander, th-that's a dinosaur! He's going to eat us!" Happy pointed out the front window. A gargantuan beast lumbered by, chewing on a mouthful of vegetation ripped from a towering tree.

"It's a vegetarian," Buzz said. "Better to worry about being stepped on." He unfastened his harness and somersaulted down, standing on what had once been the overhead. It took only a few seconds more for him to help his cadet down.

"What are we going to do, sir? We wouldn't stand a chance outside the ship. A stun rifle won't mean a thing against a dinosaur that big. And… and… " The cadet looked around helplessly.

"It's true, Happy. The *Terra V* is wrecked. We'll never lift off from Planet X."

"A space tug," Happy said, refusing to admit defeat. "Make that two. That'll do the trick. They can swoop down and grapple the ship fore and aft and *whoosh!* rocket away and get us into space."

"The hull's been breached." Buzz thrust his fingers through a wide crack in the cabin bulkhead. He jerked back when carnivorous insects bit at his flesh. "Even if we wore spacesuits, we wouldn't last long."

"Do you think we wrecked the comet? Losing the *Terra V* is terrible, but it's worth it if we saved a planet full of people."

"We knocked the comet off course. It's heading out into interstellar space now. But that won't matter as long as Baccarratti uses Carol's accelerator to send more comets sunward." Buzz worked on the upside-down controls, running diagnostics. Most systems failed to register any activity.

"Sir, look. The mist is blowing away. You can see—"

"The spire with Baccarratti's castle atop it."

"That's thousands of feet high, sir. If we want to get Baccarratti, we'll have to climb the spire. I don't know about you, but I'm afraid of heights."

"You're a spaceman, Happy, and you're afraid of heights?" Buzz had to chuckle.

"There's a difference between climbing up all that rock and looking down from orbit. Being in space doesn't bother me, but if I so much as glanced over my shoulder and saw how far down it would be if I fell off the spire, I'd get dizzy and fall for sure."

Buzz continued to work on the controls, then stepped away and shook his head.

"It's hopeless. The engines won't lift us even an inch. The repeller ray is damaged, but can be fixed. The rest of the ship is bent and battered too badly to ever help us."

"What about the space phone, sir? Can we call for help?"

"It's smashed. The only way to get it to work is complete replacement." Buzz heaved a sigh. "Grab a stun rifle and let's explore outside. We'll have to find a way to survive in the jungle." He rubbed his hand where insects had chewed on him. Even the smallest creature on Planet X was deadly, and there were plenty of huge ones. The distant roar of angry saurians warned him of that.

"All we have are two, sir. The arms locker was ripped off. We lost everything else. I had these two out to replace batteries."

Buzz powered up the one Happy handed him. A quick systems check looked good.

"Full power, auto-aim activated, the rifle's in perfect condition. You do good work Cadet."

Happy beamed at the compliment, then checked his own stun rifle. It was ready for action. He held it at port arms and looked skeptical.

"Sir, are these powerful enough to bring down one of those dinosaurs? I know they'll stop a man. I remember how they worked on the giants of Pluto. But a dinosaur is a lot tougher."

"With any luck, we won't have to find out." Buzz went to the main hatch and spun the locking wheel. With the *Terra V* rolled onto its back, the hatch opened inward but the vegetation and spongy ground prevented him from leaving the ship. It began oozing into the airlock.

"What'll we do? Can we use the rifles to blast our way out?"

"There's no need to do that, Hap. Come on. You said the arms locker was torn off. We can leave that way."

A few blasts from the rifle caused encroaching vegetation to flinch away from the ragged hole in the hull where the arms locker had been. Buzz stuck his head outside and gave a quick look around. He ducked back.

"What is it, Commander? What'd you see?"

"We're in a swamp and the ship is slowly sinking. We'll be swallowed entirely in another hour."

"We can't stay and we can't leave. What are we going to do, Commander?"

"I wish I knew, Happy, I wish I knew."

~

"He is dead. Your famous Commander Buzz Corry is gone. My planet has devoured him!" Prince Baccarratti stepped back from the view screen so Carol Carlisle could see the misty-shrouded jungle floor. "Now that he no longer opposes me, fire your comet cannon! Send another missile of death toward the United Planets."

Other than a single tear running down Carol's cheek, she stood frozen, prisoner to Baccarratti's Z-ray. He tormented her, but her will was gone. Held in thrall by the Z-ray, she could only obey.

"I will do so when it becomes possible."

"You will address me by my title, slave!" Baccarratti stormed away from the view screen. "And you will obey me fully. Send a comet now. Now, I say!"

"Prince Baccarratti, my accelerator can only propel asteroids a mile in diameter. Smaller ones fall apart, and larger ones don't fit inside the propulsion ring."

"My volcano spits out magma constantly. Pick an eruption and send that. I order you."

"But, Prince, not all ejecta fits. I told you."

"Lies. You lie to me to save your precious worlds. Your precious father! The Secretary General will suffer because you lie to me." Baccarratti raged. When his anger cooled, he turned the view screen to the cone of a huge volcano.

The interior bubbled and frothed with liquid rock. A dome built, cooled, and filled with magma pushing up from the depths of Planet X.

"There. That one. Fire that one with your weapon."

"Yes, Prince." Against her will, Carol powered up her accelerator. The ring around the cone of the distance volcano glowed as energy flowed into it. The metal heated, red, orange, white hot to match the magma rising from the center of the planet. The bubble exploded upward.

The accelerator field seized the bubble, spun it, then pulsed into ultraviolet, far past human sight. The bubble trembled and drooped under the intense force. It lost shape and collapsed into itself. A fiery streamer rose high, then sank back into the maw of the volcano.

"What happened? Why didn't it sail off into space?"

"It was too small to withstand the acceleration, Prince. The size must be just right or this will happen every time."

"And it cannot be too large, yes, you said that." Baccarratti slapped his leather gloves across his left palm as he stared at Carol. She wanted to flinch as he brought the gloves up, but the Z-ray held her motionless. Instead of slapping her, Baccarratti only caressed her cheek with the gloves.

It repulsed her more than if he had struck her.

"Stay here. Wait for the right size. When you find it, summon me. I want to see the messenger of destruction for the United Planets with my own eyes."

Baccarratti left, his boot heels clicking on the stone floor. Carol tried to move, to overload the power to her accelerator and destroy it. She failed. The mind-enslaving Z-ray kept her an unwilling but faithful servant to the Black Falcon.

∼

"We're trapped, sir. We can't stay in the ship, and if we get out, we'll be tromped on by the dinosaurs." Cadet Happy swallowed hard. "That is, if the quicksand swamp doesn't swallow us up first."

The swamp burbled and made sucking noises as the *Terra V* listed more to one side. The foul stench of decay made standing and staring out the rent in the battlecruiser's side all the less attractive.

"Climb out, Happy. Get on the top of the ship."

"The top? But that's the bottom now since we're all upside-down."

"Go. Get up there. We're going to Baccarratti's castle."

"But sir, it is way up there. We can't fly." Commander Corry shoved his cadet out.

Happy slipped and slid on the outer hull until he stood on a tiny patch that had somehow escaped all the slime. He looked down and frowned.

235

Then he brightened as he understood.

"I'm on the repeller ray plate. I cleaned this patch the last time it was turned on. I don't mind but—"

"Hang on, Hap. We're airborne in three, two, one."

The sudden acceleration took Buzz's breath. He and his cadet clung together as they soared higher, upward out of the jungle, past the tree tops and more. The repeller ray wasn't powerful enough to lift the mighty *Terra V*, but it retained enough energy to hurl two humans a thousand feet into the air. Two thousand. Three and more. They surged above Baccarratti's castle.

"Use your rifle," Buzz ordered. "Get us out of the repeller ray field."

"But, sir." Happy looked down and turned pale.

Buzz circled the cadet's waist with his long arm and fired his stun rifle with his other hand. They twisted together, out of the field and, for an instant, hung suspended. Then they started falling. Buzz kept firing to give them lateral movement.

They landed hard on the castle battlements. Cadet Happy stayed on hands and knees, stunned by the impact because he had closed his eyes and was unprepared for the sudden stop. Buzz touched down on both feet, took a few quick steps and regained his balance. He looked down into the castle keep. A check assured him that his stun rifle was still functioning.

"Let's go. I don't know if we set off alarms. Baccarratti is a suspicious one. We don't want to be caught out in plain sight."

Happy peered over the battlement three thousand feet to the jungle below.

"We're so high I can't see the dinosaurs. The fog's too thick, but I can still hear them fighting. Do you hear them, Commander?"

Buzz grabbed him by the arm and dragged him along to stone steps going down into the courtyard. From there they could make their way into the keep. The Space Patrollers encountered no resistance until they opened the door into the keep. A sizzling energy bolt tore a huge hole in the wood door, forcing them to drop flat. Both men fired, but Buzz's aim was more accurate. His stun ray hit Doctor Kruger in the middle of the chest. The renegade scientist stiffened and toppled like a felled tree.

"Good shooting, sir. I missed him by a light year, but you hit him right in the bread basket. Look, his jacket's smoking from the stun ray."

Doctor Kruger's eyes flickered. He gagged, coughed and rolled onto his side. "Help me, please. He... he used his Z-ray on me."

"I'll give him another shot and—"

"Wait, Hap." Buzz knelt after making sure Kruger's pistol lay beyond the fallen man's reach. "What are you saying, Doctor Kruger?"

"He kept me under his control using the Z-ray, just as he's done with Carol Carlisle."

"Carol!" The name escaped Happy's lips. He clamped a hand over his mouth to prevent any further outburst that might alert Baccarratti or his guards.

"The Secretary General's daughter. He has her at the top of these stairs. I'll help you. I hate him. He kept me prisoner all these years." Kruger sat up, clutching his midriff.

"Don't trust him, Commander. He's as bad as Baccarratti."

"No one's that evil, Hap." Buzz came to a quick decision. He held out his hand. Doctor Kruger took it so Buzz could help him to his feet.

"You won't regret it, Commander. This way." Doctor Kruger climbed the stairs half bent over, clutching his stomach where the stun ray had struck. The paralysis ray had countered the Z-ray that had held him in thrall, but the burned section on his abdomen made any movement painful.

"Don't step there. The slightest pressure will set off an alarm." Doctor Kruger pointed out the trap. All three stretched up and put their weight on the step just above. No alarm sounded. No trap was triggered.

"See?" Doctor Kruger said. "Trust me. I want him arrested as much as you do."

They reached the top of the stairs. Doctor Kruger held up his hand and whispered, "She's in the throne room. Baccarratti might be there with her. I'll scout it out for you, then give you a signal to take him."

"Go on," Buzz said, pushing the door open a few inches. Baccarratti's recognizable voice barked orders. Buzz caught sight of Carol working at a bank of instruments.

"This one is the right size," she said in a dull voice.

"Launch it. Use the comet cannon and destroy Earth!" Baccarratti's laughter filled the huge chamber.

Doctor Kruger nodded once, then pushed into the room. He moved slowly, shuffling as if he was still captive of the Z-ray.

237

"What is it, Doctor Kruger? Why do you disturb me in my hour of greatest triumph?" Baccarratti stormed around an immobile Carol Carlisle and slapped the doctor across the face with his gloves.

Buzz and Happy burst into the room, leveling their stun rifles, but Doctor Kruger responded to Baccarratti's attack first. He batted the gloves aside and drove a bony fist into the prince's face, staggering him. Before Baccarratti had a chance to recover, Kruger struck him again. This punch knocked his adversary to the stone floor.

"Don't move, Baccarratti. You're under arrest." Buzz trained his stun rifle on the fallen prince. A sudden cry of alarm caused Buzz to whirl around.

"Drop the rifle, Corry. If I shoot the cadet with his own rifle at this range, it'll fry his brains, if he has any!" Doctor Kruger pressed the muzzle of the stun rifle into the cadet's temple.

"I'm sorry, Commander. I should have watched him, but he jumped me when I was trying to get a clean shot at Baccarratti." Happy did nothing to live up to his namesake. He had allowed Doctor Kruger to grab his rifle in a careless moment.

"Drop your rifle and kick it over, Commander. Do it or I swear I will shoot." Doctor Kruger jammed the rifle even harder into Happy's temple.

"Don't do it, sir. He'll only kill you, too."

"I don't have any choice, Hap." Buzz did as he was ordered. "Let him go, Kruger."

"Let him go? When I have the Commander-in-Chief of the Space Patrol and his cadet prisoner? Not to mention the daughter of the Secretary General?" Kruger laughed, imitating Prince Baccarratti to a chilling degree. "Baccarratti put a grand plan in motion. I'll take it over and rule instead of him."

"Doctor Kruger?" The voice came softly, almost a whisper. "I have something for you."

Kruger turned toward the supine Prince Baccarratti. Surprise froze him for an instant. By the time he jerked the stun rifle away from the cadet's head in a vain attempt to train it on Baccarratti, it was too late. A searing energy beam from a small blaster in the prince's hand tore into Doctor Kruger's chest. He crumpled as if his legs had turned to water.

"Don't, Corry. Don't go for your rifle or you'll suffer the same fate."

Prince Baccarratti got to his feet, the small weapon he had hidden in his tunic trained on the Commander.

"I'm sorry, sir. If I hadn't let Kruger get the drop on me, this wouldn't have happened."

"That's all right, Happy. We'll get out of this." Buzz moved around.

"Freeze, Corry. I took no pleasure out of shooting my one-time ally. If I have to shoot you, I will cherish it forever!"

"Surrender, Baccarratti. We've got you surrounded."

"You joke. I have the weapon. Kruger is dead. You and your cadet are in my line of fire. You have me surrounded? Ha!"

"Carol is behind you."

"She is under the influence of my Z-ray. She—" Baccarratti stumbled forward as Carol Carlisle fell into him from behind.

Both Buzz and Happy grabbed the prince and quickly secured him.

"How did she throw off the effect of my Z-ray? It is impossible!" Baccarratti thrashed, but he was too well secured.

"She was frozen in place, but she managed to tip herself enough to fall over into you." Buzz used the Z-ray taken from Baccarratti to counter the mentally paralyzing spell. Carol shuddered, sagged, and then hugged Buzz.

"Oh, Buzz, it was all I could do. I was completely under his electronic spell." She slowly regained her composure and stepped away. "I ought to take that pistol of his and use it on him like he did on Doctor Kruger. It's what he deserves."

"We'll take him back to Terra to stand trial," Buzz said.

"Yes, Corry, take me to Terra. Or what's left of it!" Prince Baccarratti laughed hysterically. "There is a comet on a collision course. You have no way to stop it."

"Oh, Buzz, I had to launch it using the comet cannon. I couldn't help myself."

"She's right, Commander. The comet is on a collision course with Terra. What are we going to do?" asked Happy. "The *Terra V* is a derelict and the other Space Patrol ships are protecting other planets. What are we going to do?"

"Watch your capital world be destroyed, Corry. Watch the Black Falcon's revenge!"

"Wait, Buzz, I can stop it," Carol said. She went to the instrument panel. "Another lump of magma is forming that's perfect."

"Perfect, Carol? How?" Buzz crowded closer and watched her fingers flying over the controls.

"Perfect to intercept the first comet before it reaches Terra. I can launch it faster so it'll overtake the larger comet. They'll collide and destroy each other millions of miles from the danger point." Her finger pressed the launch button. "There. It's on the way."

Prince Baccarratti sputtered in fury at his last attempt at conquest being thwarted by the Space Patrol.

"What's wrong, Baccarratti?" Cadet Happy asked. "You were bragging before. But now you don't have a comet-ment."

The Magic of Nadia

Weston Ochse

I find Octobriana to be unique in the pantheon of licensed properties in that the creator, Czech artist Peter Sedecky, developed her and then declared her open source. First titled Amazona, she was quickly renamed Octobriana to celebrate the October Revolution that was the foundation for the Soviet Union. Octobriana isn't just a larger-than-life communist superhero, though. She espouses the original ideas of the revolution and despises oligarchs, Stalinistic tactics and his thugs, and capitalism in general. She's a believer in the communal values as set forth by Lenin that all are created equal, and has set aside her immortal self to ensure that happens.

"The Magic of Nadia" is a day in the life of Octobriana. Oligarchs have sent their agents to obtain the slippers worn by Nadia Comaneci when she obtained her magical perfect tens. Octobriana doesn't believe anyone should have such an item, because ownership and the use of it would elevate someone from equal to superhuman.

Weston Ochse, a *USA Today* Bestselling author, is the multi-award-winning author of more than thirty books and one hundred fifty short stories, including *SEAL Team 666, Burning Sky, Grunt Life*, and *Bone Chase*. A long-time member of IAMTW, he's worked with the franchises of *Hellboy*, *V-Wars*, *X-Files*, *Alien*, *Predator*, Clive Barker's *Midian*, and *Joe Ledger*. *SEAL Team 666* has been optioned by Dwayne Johnson. His work has also appeared in DC Comics and IDW Comics. You can find him online at www.westonochse.com.

The Magic of Nadia

I ASKED OCTOBRIANA WHY SHE WAS DOING IT, AND ALL SHE COULD say was it was because she had to. So, here we were sitting at a restaurant in Oradea, Romania, called The Bridge—its location near a walking bridge over the River Kris the reason for the name. We couldn't have been more different as we sat sipping Ursus. Me, a buck fifty soaking wet with twelve-year-old muscles on a thirty-year-old body. Her, blond hair rippling in the sun, breasts barely held back by three thin strips of material, belly naked so one could see her Billy Idol belly button ring, red shorts like she'd stolen them from Wonder Woman and knee-high white boots with three-inch heels. A red star was tattooed in the middle of her forehead, the same blinking red as her lipstick.

We were about two miles away from the old Soviet Olympic Committee Gymnastics Headquarters. Between us and there was about as much danger as we'd ever faced, according to the intelligence I'd received. The Queen of Soviet Badass herself and me, Octobriana's sidekick, butler, chauffer, factotum, and acolyte, were just waiting to make our move. I didn't do much during her fights except carry her extra ammunition and a few other defensive measures I'd learned through the four years we'd been together. I asked her once why she'd chosen me, but she'd refused to answer, instead reminding me that I could have been dead had it not been for her myriad interventions.

Which was true, but then I reminded her that when she saved Pussy Riot from the gulag in the spring it had been my idea and quick thinking that had kept her from being shot in the back by an RPG.

"Hey, you," said a drunk, leaning heavily on the chair beside the table. "I know you."

She regarded him through heavy lids, "You don't even know your mother," Octobriana said.

I slugged back some beer, but was in no hurry. These were the moments I enjoyed, when she'd take some lech and put him in his place.

"Okay. Okay. Maybe I don't know you, but I want to know you."

"Think you can get it up?"

"Does Putin wear nipple rings?"

And off they went to the bathroom.

Not at all what I'd expected. Sure, Octrobriana's ways of dealing with things were far different from those of other superheroes. I tried to imagine Captain America doing the same to a fan, but couldn't make it work. I guess that's what made her so much different.

I went ahead and ordered dinner, knowing she'd be hungry after sex. The pasta arrived at the table the same time she did. She didn't say a word and I didn't want to know. I understood the mechanics involved and just didn't want to imagine her in the middle of it all.

Just as we were about to finish, we heard a scream coming from the bathrooms.

I glanced at her, but she made no move, just continued eating.

"Did he not please you?" I asked.

"He worked for the Oligarchs. Thought he could get the upper hand."

"What did you do?"

"Twisted his head around so he could watch his back from now on."

I nodded. "Seems fair. Was he from Melinchenko?"

She nodded, slurping the last of her walnut sauce from the bowl.

"I suspected as much. Intel said he'd commit his assets first."

"First or last. Doesn't bother me." She tossed her napkin down and flexed her shoulders. "Are you ready, dove?"

I shoved some bills on the table and grabbed the duffle bag.

"Are you sure you want to walk?"

"Why not? It's a beautiful day? Everyone should be able to see such beauty."

And it was beautiful. We crossed the River Kris. Farther down, it ran through town, on one side extravagant homes and on the other an immense brick wall with a footpath nearly at water level. Before us was a mile of forest on both sides of the river, and paths where the occasional pedestrian strolled. Popcorn and nut vendors stood silently by their wares, filling orders, conversing softly. The loudest sounds came from the riffles in the river and the birds in the trees.

Octobriana strode a few meters in front of me. Her high-heeled white boots made her as tall as any man. The muscles on her arms continued along her back and down to her spine, creating a V of carefully maintained energy. I often wondered how much of her power was from the radiation treatments that granted her immortality and what portion was from her own strenuous workouts, much of the time with real-life dummies.

I spied the vendors first. They weren't selling anything. They appeared sickly, black greasy hair, nails dirty, clothes in tatters.

"To the right."

"I see them."

"Recognize them?"

"Ravens, I think." She made fists and held them tight. "Don't matter, though."

Being the hero that I am, I paused and knelt to retie one of my shoes. Watching her out of the corner of my eye, I began counting, calling fifteen when they would attack. I was two seconds short. They attacked on thirteen.

One leaped in front of Octobriana.

The second leaped behind.

"Go back the way you've come," said the one in front, words slipping past rotten and blackened teeth.

"You know I can't do that. They must be destroyed."

"How can you destroy something that is meant to be good?"

"Good for whom? The slippers give an uneven chance."

An attacker launched from the tree above.

Octobriana sidestepped and the attacker slammed into the ground, lying motionless.

245

She jogged to the cart and picked it up as if it were a toy, slinging it at the person who would block her way. The wooden mechanism flew into the side of a tree and exploded in wood and splinters.

Octobriana turned to the last assailant, who was already running past me.

Like the coward I was, I stuck my leg out and tripped him.

My mistress was upon him, raising his body over her head, then tossing it fifty feet into the center of the river.

Two more attacks and we arrived at the Highway 19 Bridge over the Kris. Once across, we angled in front of the Intercontinental Hotel and then inside to the bar on the second floor. Here she ordered a martini. I kept with the local Ursus beer.

I sat on one of the sofas, my back to the view of the river and my front to the door.

She sat at the bar, garnering more glances than an all-nude game show might on television. She was perfect in every way except for the bloody leaf that was stuck to the back of her head.

I got up, removed it, and tossed it into the trash.

I couldn't have her going around with—

I saw that the bartender had grabbed the trash and was hurrying towards the kitchen door.

I slammed down my beer and ran after her, barreling through the swinging doors hard enough that they slammed into the wall on either side.

The bartender was nowhere to be found. Instead, I saw a kitchen filled with fearful cooks and servers, all looking at me as if I'd just gone insane.

I returned to my beer and Octobriana called over her shoulder, "What was that all about?"

"Nothing, Octobriana. Just nothing."

When he came, I wasn't sure if this was who she was supposed to be meeting. He was completely corporate, his suit straight from Saville Row. His hair was no more than two inches all around and not a single strand was out of place. His shoes were hand-made works of art. His nails were the envy of women.

Sitting beside Octobriana, he made her seem brutish and barbaric. Raquel Welch in One Billion BC brutish, yet beautiful all the same.

I leaned in to better hear.

"They say you want to destroy them," he said, even his words enunciated perfectly. Where did they get this man?'

"They don't belong in the world."

"Oh, but they do. They are of historical significance."

"Not so," Octobriana said, taking a sip of her martini. "They are a blight on fairness. How fair was it for Nadia to use magically-tainted slippers to commit the biggest gymnastic fraud in Olympic history?"

"But she never knew of the fraud. She never knew she wore magic," he said, never letting his voice raise more than half an octave. "How can you fault a young girl who was a victim?"

"And that makes a difference to you. What would you do with it?" She slung back her martini and poked the marble hard enough to crack it while asking for another. "I'll tell you. You would play God and decide for yourself who deserves such a thing—perhaps for the highest dollar—while millions of men and women live in squalor and have no opportunities. Why don't you stress elevating the masses rather than finding shortcuts?"

He waited until she'd been served, then took a gentle sip of his own drink. "They said you were a tough negotiator."

"Negotiator! Ha! What am I negotiating? I am Octobriana. I fight against the oppression those like you would impose."

"Now, it is my turn to laugh," he said. "Who is it that you believe I am oppressing?"

"Everyone who doesn't get the chance to compete fairly. The moment you inject magic into a non-magical endeavor you are giving that person advantage over all of the others. That goes against everything Lenin stood for."

"But not Stalin."

"Fuck Stalin. He is a capitalist communist. He cares nothing for the proletariat except to see us held down hard enough so that we can't become flies in his oligarchs' vichyssoise."

"That's a little harsh, is it not?" he said, finishing his drink, then standing.

"I don't think so at all." She finished her drink as well. "Are you ready?"

He nodded and left the hotel first, heading right.

She followed ten seconds later and I was right behind her. Perhaps I'd been too overworked. Perhaps there was nothing to what happened earlier.

247

I'd be glad to get this behind me. I was looking forward to a bowl of Ciorba de Burta—nothing like Romanian tripe soup with cream and vinegar.

Three of us walked Aleea Strandului.

A park lay to our left. The river flowed to our right.

A new American hotel blossomed garish neon signs in the twilight air.

We passed this as well, walking single file until we came to the almost abandoned old Soviet Olympic Gymnastic Headquarters. Some effort had been made to revitalize it, but the western part of Romania didn't have the luxuries of the eastern coast and the Black Sea.

All the while, we'd passed various Romani living in the park, under bushes, around the corners. They were never present in broad daylight, knowing that the police would ensure that they were removed to somewhere less populated. But at night, they came out blinking and eager and hopeful, a thousand years of guile and lifestyle eschewing modernity for a life outdoors and away from local laws.

The man entered a door three-quarters down in the complex.

She waited for me and I hurried to catch up.

"What was that commotion back there?" she asked.

"Oh, it was nothing."

"Whenever you say something is nothing I know it was something."

I shrugged and smiled weakly in the growing darkness. I adjusted the duffle bag. "You had a leaf with some blood on it. I threw it away."

"You threw it—"

"I don't think that it was yours."

"You don't think that—"

"Everything will be all right."

She gave me a look. "Are you proud to be working with me?"

"I am happy to make a difference. Anyone could do the same as I could," I answered, careful to cling to socialist values.

"Perhaps we've been together too long. You believe you are better than the others."

"Do I believe that my value is imparted by my ability to do the better job?" I stared at the ground. "I do. But isn't that part of being egalitarian? If I do better, perhaps I can convince the others to do better, given the same advantages and tools to do so?"

Her eyes wandered to the door and she seemed to contemplate what

I'd said. But then she said without looking at me, "I think we've spent enough time together." And with that, she slipped inside.

After a moment, I closed my jaw. I certainly hadn't expected this. I remember once being in discussion with an old friend—long since dead—where I compared Octobriana to Superman.

"How can you possibly compare the two?"

"One is an alien and the other has an alien way of thinking," I said. *"They both mean well, but they approach problems from diametrically opposing problem sets. Superman tries to be more human to fit in, knowing that by being close to society, he can better save them. Octobriana tends to seem less human, because the political constructs created by Marx and Lenin are impossible to emulate in the real world without coming across as inhuman, which is entirely based on the definition by those who have the loudest voices."*

"But that makes them opposites."

"Octobriana is alien by choice. Superman is alien by birth. They are both aliens to this world."

"Are you saying that only aliens are able to see the bad in our world?"

"Have you heard of the Heisenberg Uncertainty Principle?" I asked.

"Of course. Any scientist gets it. We just mitigate against it."

"One more interesting note," I said. *"And this is what cemented it for me. DC Comics came out with a three-arc prestige series format called Red Son. The idea was that Superman as a baby landed in a Ukraine farm collective rather than a farm in Kansas and was raised in a commune. When he was of age, the Soviets made him known to the West, which completely caused a paradigm shift in the Cold War, turning it into a metahuman war instead. What's interesting is that the Soviet Union is seen as the good guys and the land of plenty, while America is ruled by the likes of Lex Luthor and is on the brink of socio-economic collapse."*

"What's so interesting about that?"

"By virtue of having a Superman, they were no longer living in a land of equality."

"Much like Octobriana. Do you think she gets that?"

"I doubt it. Her one convenient blind spot."

"And this is who you think Octobriana is? A Red Son. A Superman for the modern age?"

"Why not?"

"Why not indeed?"

I checked my watch and noted that five minutes had passed. I knew she was done with me, but I couldn't just let her go. Not under these circumstances.

I slung the door open and moved through an atrium to the top level of seats in the main auditorium. What I saw there made my blood run cold. Octobriana, hanging in the middle of the air, arms outstretched, legs twitching, head down, blood dripping from her fingertips.

My memory flashed to the woman rushing away with the bloody leaf. Fifty-fifty it was Octobriana's. I should have taken the bet.

My glance took in five Romani standing in the middle of the floor below her, one holding something glowing between her fingers. They were in the middle of a ceremony. If this were a movie, I'd engage them, speak with them, let time pass. But I wasn't fucking around.

I dropped the duffle bag and pulled free an M72 Law Rocket Launcher. I extended it, depressed, and prepared it to fire. But instead of aiming at the five in the middle of the floor, I aimed at Octobriana. It was going to hurt, but it was probably the best strategy.

I fired and watched as the bottle-sized rocket sped across the gap and exploded, sending her flying across the room and into the corner.

Then I dropped the launcher, jerked free an AK 47 and opened fire on those on the main floor. The one holding up the glowing slippers fell hard to the ground along with her comrades. They might have been invoking a certain amount of blood magic on Octobriana, but that didn't make them impervious to bullets. That was their problem.

I racked another magazine, and descended to the bottom of the auditorium. I'd killed three. A fourth was still alive and gasping for breath. I glanced around and saw no weapons available, so I ignored the target. Instead, I used the working end of the rifle to pick up the glowing slippers. And to think these were the cause of all the problems.

A rustling came from the other side of the auditorium. I could hear someone crashing and stumbling over seats as they made their way to the auditorium floor. Finally, I saw Octobriana, her hair smoking, her skin soot-covered from the blast. She approached me and wobbled a moment, using a chair as balance.

"So, it's going to be like that, huh?"

"You gave me the impression you were done with me." I said.

"Yet you still hung around."

"I'm a hanger-arounder," I said.

"Did you get them all?" she asked.

"I think so. All that's left is this."

"We should destroy it."

"We could, but I was thinking of something different."

She glanced at me and then at the slippers. "What could that be?"

Half an hour later, I was still sitting in the cheap seats of the auditorium watching her complete perfect ten after perfect ten. From the balance beam to the uneven bars to the floor exercise, she manipulated herself across the floor in perfect patterns.

As I explained it to her, "These slippers were the result of a member of the proletariat excelling. Rather than be punished, they should be cherished. Maybe find some way for them to become the norm rather than the rarity."

I watched as she twisted and landed, tears in her eyes, proud to be a Soviet Superwoman, sensational in her ability to bring egalitarian and superhuman ideas into one distinct conversation.

The Truth About the Cats of Ulthar

Jennifer Brozek

"The Cats of Ulthar" was a short story written by H. P. Lovecraft, on June 15, 1920. A cat lover, he was early in his career, and his Lord Dunsany influence can be seen in the writing. The literary journal *Tryout* published it in November 1920. The story was reprinted twice in *Weird Tales*.

Jennifer Brozek is a multi-talented, award-winning author, editor, and media tie-in writer. She is the author of *Never Let Me Sleep*, and *The Last Days of Salton Academy*, both of which were nominated for the Bram Stoker Award. Her *BattleTech* tie-in novel, *The Nellus Academy Incident*, won a Scribe Award. Her editing work has netted her Bram Stoker Award and Hugo Award nominations. She won the Australian Shadows Award for the *Grants Pass* anthology. Jennifer's short form work has appeared in Apex Publications, Uncanny Magazine, and in anthologies set in the worlds of *Valdemar*, *Shadowrun*, *V-Wars*, *Masters of Orion*, and *Predator*. Jennifer is also the Creative Director of Apocalypse Ink Productions.

Jennifer has been a freelance author and editor for over ten years since leaving her high-paying tech job, and she has never been happier. She keeps a tight schedule on her writing and editing projects and somehow manages to find time to volunteer for several professional writing organizations such as SFWA, HWA, and IAMTW. She shares her husband, Jeff, with several cats and often uses him as a sounding board for her story ideas. Visit Jennifer's worlds at jenniferbrozek.com.

The Truth About the Cats of Ulthar

By ones and twos the cats arrived in the yard of the abandoned house on the windy bluff overlooking the roiling ocean. Some walked out of shadows. Others slunk in under the broken boards. Still others leapt from on high to land silently on the ground. Speaks the Truth watched them all from the top of the tarp-covered table with a keen eye—for she had only one—and waited until the stars aligned and the time was right.

It was a good-sized yard filled with overgrown terraces and edged with large trees revealed by a misty full-moon night. Before her, dozens upon dozens of cats of all ages, breeds, and colors in the natural world lounged, walked, and cleaned themselves awaiting her word. Many greeted each other with head rubs and tail twines. Fewer met one another with soft growls and arched backs. Fewer still kept the mass of felines between them.

No fights broke out. Not here. Not now. That was forbidden on this night of all nights, but the shadows grew thicker and more substantial than they had any right to do. Something was afoot. A predator was on the move and coming closer.

Still, Speaks the Truth was glad to see so many of her kith and kin amongst the great clowder. Long had she held this august role as Speaks the Truth; it was her position in this world as much as it was her name—both inherited from the one who came before. Though she wondered how much longer she would be the one to carry the truth to the young and old. Heavy is the crown, they say. Heavier is the truth when there are those who fight against her and her words. Heaviest is the burden of knowledge, true sight, and duty to protect all those who need protecting.

As if called forth by the thought, she sensed the Dark Wind within their midst. She felt it seep in, oozing past the wards that protected the Great Gathering from prying and ignorant eyes. Normally, that could not happen. This rite was protected. But still, the abomination was here. She did not know what the Crawling Chaos would attempt this night. It would be sly and cunning, like the monster it was. She would meet it as she always did: with righteous fury and Goddess-blessed magic.

Signaling her readiness to begin with an arching stretch and a yawn full of teeth, Speaks the Truth settled into her readied pose. As an Abyssinian, she had a regal countenance despite her age. No, her fur wasn't as soft or as sleek as it once was, but her back was strong and her limbs limber enough. She still had it in her to command her audience and meet their thoughts head-on.

The gathered cats from all over the world stilled in respect. She raised her voice and spoke. "Tonight I tell you the truth about the cats of Ulthar. It is known that we, as cats, are cryptic and close to strange things men were never meant to see. The question is why. Tonight I will tell you."

A ripple of anticipation rose and then fell against the breakwater of those who had already heard this tale. As mistress of the story, Speaks the Truth waited until the air stilled once more. "It is true: in Ulthar, no one is allowed to kill a cat. This is a human law brought forth through fear and misunderstanding. Although the humans' fear was misplaced and what had happened misinterpreted, this decree is what set the rest of catkind on its Goddess-born mission."

Speaks the Truth's sense of the Dark Wind grew as a small white cat, a moggie that was more than a kitten but less than an adult, wormed its way from the back of the clowder towards the middle. She could almost see the monstrous shadow of what hid within the catling. Most could not and paid it no mind. Nothing more than a few soft growls of warning to a young cat who should know better. But those who knew understood her ear-flicked instructions and kept the little white cat in sight as it moved in closer.

Her worn heart already mourned for the one who had not had an honest chance to live.

"The story goes that an old evil couple on the edge of the village hated cats and would kill any they caught with slow malice, making certain the pain would last and the villagers warned by the cat's death yowls. This sinister couple was so frightening that the villagers would rather attempt to keep their cats away than confront the atrocity."

A sigh rippled through the crowd—knowledge of all those cats tormented and killed, longing for an open world to hunt and hide in, the dangers from without and within. Humans too afraid of their own to protect those that needed protecting. Images and memories flew through the mind as they were shared on this one rare night.

"In the village of Ulthar, travelers and merchants came from afar. One day, a caravan of travelers arrived with an orphaned boy who had a kitten that was his only family and greatest love. Unaware of the evil couple, the boy allowed the kitten to roam." Speaks the Truth shook her head. "The kitten...died."

Hisses and low growls ran through the gathered on sharpened claws.

"When the boy found out what had happened to his beloved kitten, he prayed to the Goddess for help, for revenge, for justice. For a full day, he prayed. That night, he and the travelers left Ulthar."

Her single mortal eye blazing, she raised her voice. "That was when we cats went to work. For the door had been opened to our Goddess. The proper rites made. The just petition granted. For so long the cats of Ulthar had lived with the danger they could not defeat; the couple was powerful. This is what the humans were too frightened to confront and preferred to turn away from."

Speaks the Truth lowered her voice. This was her favorite part. "Two by two, we built a sacred circle at our Goddess's command. Two by two, we opened the door with our Goddess's blessing. Two by two we entered that unholy place and slew the sinister couple, held helpless by the mystical rite, and—"

"Come now, Speaker. Do not lie through omission!" The interrupting voice came from the small white cat but was bigger than seemed possible. The white cat's once-blue eyes were black as pitch and its fur stood on end. "There is more to this story, O' Speaker of Truth...or are you afraid to reveal it?" As the felines around the catling drew away, shadows played about the open space, looking like tentacles questing for the unwary and the weak.

Though her heart sped up and her claws unsheathed themselves, Speaks the Truth remained calm, biding her time. Only the tiny twitches of her tail tip displayed her agitation. "You are not welcome here, Dark Wind."

"And yet, here I am."

"Possession is not an invitation." She watched as her guards moved towards the interloper while the previously unwary continued to back up and prepare for whatever was to come.

The white cat sat quiet and serene. Only the flicks of its ears told the story of its awareness. "It is...if I am invited into the being...who then brings me thus."

Speaks the Truth yawned, teeth present and gleaming; a warning. One the arrogant would ignore. "What do you want, Abomination?"

"To tell the truth. The whole truth. The part that you never tell in your Great Gatherings. Nothing more."

Sensing a weakness, she inclined her head. "Speak your piece." When the white cat stood as if to join her as her equal, she allowed some of her Goddess-born blessings to come to the forefront. "Keep your place, Outsider. I allow you to speak and nothing more." Power lashed out behind her words.

Snarling, the white cat sat again with an abruptness only covered by the sudden decision to clean its paw.

Pressing her advantage, Speaks the Truth raised her voice. "Listen to the version of the truth this possessed one would have you hear. Know it for what it truly is."

"What is that?" the Dark Wind asked, calm once more, though the cat it possessed still trembled from the warning slap it had received.

Speaks the Truth said nothing, allowing the silence to grow. She stared at the white cat and the abomination within it and waited. The silence grew heavy and oppressive, forcing all within it to understand who held the upper hand here.

"The truth," the Dark Wind began, "is based on the observer and the interpreter. The humans believe the cats of Ulthar killed the sinister couple in revenge for the lost kitten. The cats of Ulthar believe they killed the evil couple at the behest of their Goddess. The truth is neither. The truth is that *I* killed the human couple because they displeased me. The cats of Ulthar did nothing more than clean up after me."

Discomfort rippled through the clowder. Before it could grow into something dangerous, Speaks the Truth interrupted the emotion, her voice flat and unimpressed. "Is that all you wanted to say?"

"No." The white cat stood and arched, then sat again. When it spoke with that too-large voice, seduction entered the fray. "I am here to offer those who would like, another voice. Another path to power. Bast may be an Elder God, but I am one of the Outer Gods who speaks for the Great Old Ones. You see the power I wield. My kind is not welcome here, and yet even the great and powerful Speaks the Truth's wards do not bind me."

"Spoken as you wear a skin not your own."

"Are you afraid to let me speak?"

She narrowed her mortal eye. "Should I allow a discussion with a predator on whether or not I should be eaten by it?"

The Dark Wind raised its voice and its power. "You should allow the cats of the world to listen to another path of power and not attempt to hoard their worship."

She felt the corrupting power push out and lash at her within. It hurt more than she'd expected and it felt as something ruptured within her old body. This had gone on too long and she had had enough.

Speaks the Truth hissed, her hackles raised. "You have every other day of the year to tempt the unwary, Outsider. I need not hoard any worship. We have been worshipped as gods for thousands of years. We continue to be worshipped even now, every day, upon their digital screens. Writers worship us. Artists adorn us. Supplicants send out their prayers with images and digital memories. It happens every single day. We bring joy and pain, distraction and obedience. We remind the arrogant of what is important and the humble of whom is cherished. I need not allow you to ply your trade in this sacred setting, little mouthpiece. You have no power here."

Even as the Dark Wind fought against her power, it still attempted to lure the unwary. "The Great Old Ones have the same prayers in images and digital memories. We have power to gift..." The white cat shuddered and shook, stumbling to the side. Around it, five cats of different breeds but of a singular intent stood, pinning it in place within the mystic circle they'd made.

Speaks the Truth turned her unseen eye upon the white cat and felt her body filled with the Goddess and her power. It spoke with her voice and so much more. *"You are not welcome here, Nyarlathotep. These are my people. Go."*

She felt the power flow from her into the possessed cat...barely more than a kitten; a foolish, unwary catling. She felt the Dark Wind forced from the cat's body and felt it tear the unfortunate one's soul to pieces. Would that she could save the catling whose name she never knew. She couldn't, and now all he would be was a warning to others of the foolishness of dealing with those such as Nyarlathotep.

Though...a distant forgotten memory bubbled up, then disappeared before she could capture it.

While the Goddess's power receded, it did not leave altogether. Speaks the Truth remained limp within her mind and listened as the Goddess spoke again with her mouth—though the voice was otherworldly. *"The Crawling Chaos has brought into question whether the cats of Ulthar killed the sinister couple. This is not a question I will allow to stand.*

"As the child's petition to me allowed the cats of Ulthar to finally act, the final killing blow did come from the evil one so recently banished. For those humans were his servants, killing the cats in his name. He killed them before the cats of Ulthar could finish what they'd come to do. It was a choice of allowing his servants to die by an enemy's hand and losing all of the power they'd gained or killing them himself. He was forced into it. If he had had a choice, he would rather have allowed them to live and continue to be used. Much as he would have preferred to do with that poor kitten."

Every eye in the clowder went to the limp form still confined within the living circle of cats.

"That is what the Dark Wind offers you. Power at too dear of a cost and a painful death even if you do everything it wants. But, that is something to be

contemplated later. Now, the rest of the truth is to be heard."

Although the Goddess slipped away as gently as she could, Speaks the Truth felt the sudden and overwhelming exhaustion and emptiness she always did at such times. It was both exhilarating and terrible—to be so close to the divine and yet so far away. She took a long, slow breath and regathered her wits, ignoring the throbbing pain within.

"Rejoice," she murmured. "It is not often that the Goddess blesses us with Her presence. This has been a night to remember…"

Looking at the now collapsing form of the white cat, decaying faster than nature allows, Speaks the Truth repeated what she had already said. "Two by two, we built a sacred circle at our Goddess's command. Two by two, we opened the door with our Goddess's blessing. Two by two, we entered that unholy place and slew the sinister couple, held helpless by the mystical rite. Then, as decreed, we devoured their flesh so that no corruption would spoil the land."

She shook off the exhaustion and held herself with regal pride. "It took a full day for all of the cats to consume the flesh. Each bite imbued us with power and knowledge. More than we had ever known. It opened our minds and our eyes to the many worlds beyond ours. And we, in turn, opened the eyes and minds of every other cat in the world and beyond."

Bowing her head, she gathered herself for the last part. Voice soft, she continued. "With the power came a decree; a duty." She raised her head. "For all your lives you've known to block the portals between this world and those beyond, but you have not known why. Now you know why you've had this instinctive ability to halt interlopers with a gaze. Known how to spot them slipping in those places that are thin: through glass, through cracks or seams in a wall, through corners of a house, though mirrors…through the eyes of mortals. This is why you must chase away those that slip through your guard. This is why humans ponder our gaze and our frenzies. They cannot see what we see. They cannot know what we fight. For men were never meant to know. They are too fragile for the truth."

Speaks the Truth sighed. "This is why all cats must protect themselves and the humans from otherworldly beings. Because, in Ulthar, they proved to the Goddess that they did not have the wit or will to do what needed to be done. Is it not true that the human babe will flee to its mother when frightened? And the puppy wet itself as it shows its belly, submitting? What does a kitten do? A kitten will brace itself for what is to come and be as fierce and as cunning as it can be.

"The sacrifice was twofold. We took revenge and gained a duty. And through the Goddess's power, we spread that duty and that power to all of catkind. All cats are descendant from that sacred rite and the original cats of Ulthar."

For once, no cat disagreed. Instead, silence greeted the proclamation. A surprised and heavy silence. A knowing silence. One she'd seen before. It meant more this time because of the dead and decayed body within their midst. She gestured to the body with a tail flick. "That is what happens to those foolish enough to believe the lies of any of the Outer Gods or Great Old Ones. That is why there is a Great Gathering once a year to retell the tale to the young and old. It is rare that an interloper secrets its way in, but it once again proves the lesson on what happens to those who fall for their lies."

As the clowder felt the Great Gathering come to a close, Speaks the Truth felt an unusual urgency. She did not know if she would hold this august role again. "Cats of the world. Remember we are one family with one sacred duty. It comes in many forms, but I believe in you, your abilities, and your strength. Go forth and protect all that you can. Enjoy the humans and their adoration, but never forget what your duty is."

This time, as the clowder moved, it was with joy, anticipation, and for some, new knowledge or renewed purpose. One by one, the cats young and old disappeared from the yard of the abandoned house, leaving behind only the decayed body of the unfortunate catling, its five sentinel guards, and Speaks the Truth herself.

She realized her duty as she approached the circle. Memory, long hidden, revealed itself once more. It was time. She had lived a long life. Longer than she deserved. Only those who had been so foolish could ever speak the truth from experience. She bowed her head in acquiescence and entered the circle.

Touching noses with each of the Goddess-blessed cats who had been guide and guardian, she said goodbye. Then settled in to wait. The Goddess filled her once more.

"*Come, Seeks the Sun, it's time to come home and another will take your place to*

Speak the Truth once more. You have done well. You belong with me at my side."

Knowing she had done all that she could and this young one had learned the same hard lesson she once had, Seeks the Sun reclaimed her old name and went home, leaving behind a bewildered but wiser little white cat who took her name and her duty. They would continue on in her place. It was finally time to rest.

Children of the Wild

Tim Waggoner

Herne the Hunter is a figure in English folklore, a spectre who haunted England's Windsor Forest in Berkshire. You know he is near by the sound of rattling chains and a silhouette of a man with antlers.

Tim Waggoner, a critically acclaimed author, has published over fifty novels and seven collections of short stories. He writes dark fantasy and horror, as well as media tie-ins. He's won the Bram Stoker Award, the HWA's Mentor of the Year Award, and he's been a finalist for the Shirley Jackson Award, the Scribe Award, and the Splatterpunk Award. He's also a full-time tenured professor who teaches creative writing and composition at Sinclair College in Dayton, Ohio.

Children of the Wild

"I COUNT FIVE," HERNE SAID.

Max tilted his head upward, sniffed the air.

"Seven. Two are hiding—one behind the Chevy off to our right, one beneath the school bus behind us."

Herne accepted Max's assessment without question and didn't look at either vehicle. If Max said there were seven, there were seven. About average size for a pack, although that was the only thing normal about these creatures. Their general shape was canine, but they were significantly larger than regular dogs, almost the size of small ponies. Their teeth were longer and sharper, their heavily muscled bodies covered with thick brown fur. They stood with front legs apart, heads lowered, feral yellow eyes—a sure sign they'd been touched by the Wild—fixed on Herne and Max, growling deep in their throats, muzzles dripping saliva. Although it was midafternoon and the sun hung bright in a cloudless sky, the early April air had a cold bite to it, and a chill rippled down Herne's back. That was the reason he shivered, *not* because Max and he were facing seven snarling killing machines eager to tear the flesh from their bones. That's what he told himself anyway.

They stood in a junkyard, surrounded by old vehicles, metal dented and rusted, windows cracked or missing altogether. A cemetery for machines, cast aside and forgotten. The ground beneath their feet was muddy from last night's rain, and there wasn't much space between the cars to maneuver in. Not the best circumstances for a fight, but there wasn't much to be done about it. Herne gripped a 9 mm Glock in his right hand. A crudely formed stone blade hung sheathed at his side, but he wouldn't touch it unless he had to. Sunder was for emergencies only. Max was unarmed, but he didn't need to carry a weapon. He was one.

Herne expected the monster dogs to attack right away, but they held their position, and a moment later he understood why. A huge wolf came loping into view, larger than the others, its brown fur streaked with gray. It was silent, its yellow eyes glimmering with sharp intelligence and deadly calm. When it came within ten yards of Herne and Max's position it stopped. It regarded them for a moment, and then its form blurred, flowed upward like liquid, and when it became solid again, it was human. Well, human*ish*.

"You are not welcome here, Warder."

The creature was seven feet tall, covered with fur, its hands and feet bearing savage-looking claws. Its head retained its lupine shape—protruding muzzle, large pointed ears—but its features were more expressive now, like a human's. Its mouth was capable of speech, though its sharp teeth were a clear reminder that despite its transformation, this creature remained a beast at its core.

"We get that a lot," Max said.

The creature focused its gaze on Max. It sniffed the air, then its eyes narrowed.

"Be silent, *hound*."

Max feigned a wounded look, then turned to Herne.

"Did you hear what he called me?"

Herne shrugged. "Better than mongrel. Or cur. Or flea bag. Or—"

"You can stop now, thanks."

"Bow-wow," Herne finished.

Max scowled at him. "Really? Did you have to go there?"

Herne smiled. "Yes. Yes, I did."

The manwolf growled low in its throat.

"You are fools." His mouth stretched into an expression that was half snarl, half smile. "In more ways than one."

He turned away from them and gestured with one of his clawed hands. A moment later, a woman appeared, walking between a pair of smashed vehicles—a petite brunette with long straight hair bound in a ponytail, dressed in a white blouse, black suit jacket, matching slacks, and black open-toed shoes.

Herne was dismayed to see her, but not surprised.

"What are you doing here, Elena? I told you it was too dangerous to follow us."

Elena's expression remained impassive as she looked at Herne, then she blinked and her brown eyes became yellow.

"Oh shit," Max said.

Elena smiled, revealing a mouthful of extremely sharp teeth.

Max looked to Herne.

"This is bad," he said.

"Very," Herne agreed.

Elena snarled, raised hands that had become claws, and rushed toward them.

Earlier

"Feeling nostalgic yet?"

Max sat in the red SUV's passenger seat, window down, face turned toward the breeze coming in, nostrils flaring as he drank in whatever scents were carried on the morning wind. He liked to ride with the window down, regardless of the weather, and Herne enjoyed teasing him about it, saying things like, *If you see a squirrel, let me know if you want me to stop so you can chase it.* But he wasn't in a teasing mood today.

"Mixed feelings," he said. "How about you?"

Max kept his face pointed toward the window as he answered. "It's different for me. We may have met in Bridgewater, but it was never my hometown. I didn't grow up here."

"Did you grow up anywhere?"

Max frowned. "That's a good question. I must've been a pup once, but I don't remember anything about it."

"Maybe you sprang full blown into existence, like Athena from the brow of Zeus."

"Maybe." The notion seemed to disturb Max, and he fell silent.

Herne wished he hadn't said anything. As conflicted as his feelings about his childhood were, at least he had one.

They made an odd pair, the two of them. Herne was in his early thirties, tall, broad-shouldered, well-muscled, with hard features and hair cut so short his scalp was nearly bald. He usually wore flannel shirts—today's choice was brown and green—along with jeans and hiking boots. His eyes were an icy bright blue, cold and intimidating. In contrast, Max was shorter, thinner, and appeared at least ten years older than Herne. He had a scraggly mop of brown hair and several days' worth of stubble on his face. His features were softer than Herne's, but his eyes—brown with flecks of yellow—hinted at a hidden fierceness. He wore a black hoodie, a T-shirt with the words *Who Let the Dogs Out?* on the front, jeans, and running shoes.

They remained silent for the next several minutes until they drew near a small *Welcome to Bridgewater* sign posted on the side of the road. A couple seconds later, they were past the sign, and for the first time in over a decade, Herne was home. As they drove toward the center of town, he wasn't surprised to see that Bridgewater hadn't changed significantly during his absence. It was much the same as any other small southwestern Ohio town—old houses situated on tiny plots of land, gas stations, convenience stores, churches, fast food restaurants, bars ... Everything seemed shabbier than Herne remembered, grimier, as if time's passage had left a residue that no rain could wash away.

Herne drove toward the center of town. Courthouse Square was the location for Bridgewater's administrative offices, along with the police and fire departments, but there were some small shops as well—a pharmacy, a liquor store, a pizza joint, and a coffee house called Java Nice Day. The last time Herne had been in town, a funky candle and soap shop called Scentsability had occupied the latter's space. His mom used to stop in and buy weird-smelling candles which she'd light up as soon as she got home. His dad always complained about the smell, but he never asked her to blow out the candles.

"I miss your parents too," Max said. "And before you say anything, no,

I haven't suddenly developed an ability to read minds. I just know you."

Herne didn't reply. He found a space on the street not too far from Java Nice Day, parked the SUV, and he and Max got out. As they walked to the shop, Max said, "Nervous?"

"Why should I be?"

Max smiled but said no more.

From the outside, Java Nice Day retained the ambience of the candle store—red brick walls, window with fliers for local businesses and missing pets taped to the glass, a wooden front door with peeling paint and a tarnished metal knob. Inside, though, it looked no different than any generic chain coffee store. Sleek plastic tables and chairs, soft classical music playing over speakers mounted on brick walls, a chrome and glass counter behind which young men and women with dyed hair and tattoos worked hissing and grinding machines that looked and sounded like they belonged in a mad scientist's laboratory. It was between the morning rush and lunch, and the shop was only half-full. People sat talking, typing on laptops, and staring at their phones, except for one woman sitting alone at a table near the far wall. She was looking at Herne and Max and smiling.

Herne hadn't known what he might feel when he saw Elena Benson for the first time in nearly fifteen years. Sadness? Joy? Melancholy? Nervous? Self-conscious? Hopeful? He felt all of these things and more.

He walked to her table, Max following a step behind. Elena rose as they approached, and—maybe because she was dressed professionally in jacket and slacks—Herne expected her to offer her hand for him to shake. Instead, she stepped forward and hugged him. He was so startled that for a moment he just stood there, arms at his sides. But then he reached up and hugged her back.

When she pulled away, her smile was tinged with sadness. For what might have been? Maybe.

"It's good to see you," Elena said. She looked at Max. "And your uncle."

Max wasn't a blood relation to Herne, but his parents had pretended he was Herne's maternal uncle in public in order to explain his constant presence to the people of Bridgewater. Some of them had undoubtedly assumed Max was an "uncle," the third member of a polyamorous relationship. The truth was far different.

Elena cocked her head slightly and examined Max more closely.

"You look like you haven't aged a day since the last time I saw you," she said.

"That's because I haven't."

Elena laughed, but Max only smiled. That smile didn't reach his eyes, though. They narrowed as if he were examining her closely. If Max's scrutiny bothered her, she showed no sign of it.

She turned to Herne. "Do you want to get something to drink before we talk?"

A tall white cardboard cup with a white plastic lid sat on the table, next to the remains of a lemon poppy seed muffin on a ceramic plate.

"We're fine," Herne said.

Max looked disappointed, but he didn't say anything.

The three of them sat down, and Elena took a long sip of her drink before speaking. Herne had the sense that she was stalling. That was okay with him. He wasn't sure what to say either.

Max sniffed the air.

"This place still smells like candles. You wouldn't think that scent would pair well with coffee, but it's actually not that bad."

If Elena found the comment odd, she made no mention of it.

They spent the next several minutes catching up, talking about what they'd done since parting all those years ago, how mutual acquaintances and their families were doing. Elena spoke for the most part, as Herne didn't keep in touch with many people from the old days, and both of his parents were dead. Eventually the small talk wound down, and Elena took another long sip of her drink, as if she needed the caffeine for what was to come next.

"So," she began, gaze focused on Herne, "you're some kind of paranormal investigator these days?"

"*Some kind* is a good description," Max said.

Herne ignored him. "And you're a famous TV news reporter."

She laughed. "I work for a local station in Cincy. Not exactly the big time. Don't get me wrong—I like my job, but I'm not asked for my autograph everywhere I go. According to your website, you also work as bounty hunters."

"From time to time," Herne said. "It pays the bills."

"Hunting is hunting," Max said. "Only the quarry changes."

Herne thought Max was starting to sound a little too much like a serial killer, so he changed the subject. "How did you find our site?"

"By luck. I was searching for people in your, ah, line of work, and I came across your business: *Wild Things Investigations*. The name intrigued me, and I clicked on the About tab, and up came your picture and biography. To say I was surprised would be an understatement."

"*I* was surprised when we got your email."

Her smile broadened. "I hope it was a pleasant surprise."

"It was," Max said. "Aside from all the stuff about mutilation killings, that is."

Several people close by caught his words and turned to stare.

"In your email, you said three people have been killed by what authorities are assuming was a pack of wild dogs," Herne said. "And that all the victims worked for the town's animal control department."

Elena nodded. "Over the last few years, Bridgewater's had a problem with feral dogs. You know how it is. People's pets run off and never come back, or they come out to the country to dump animals they don't want any longer. The dogs get together in groups and turn wild in order to survive. Several small packs have been spotted in the area, and they've been preying on farmers' livestock—mostly small animals like chickens, but they've brought down some sheep and even a couple calves. The town decided to do something about the situation and hired several new people to work animal control to bolster their numbers. Their mandate was to capture the dogs alive if possible, but rumor has it that they've mostly been shooting them."

Max's eyes flashed with anger and he growled softly. Herne put a hand on his shoulder, and Max quieted. Elena looked back and forth between them, but she didn't comment.

"I'm not sure what the paranormal aspect is here," Herne said.

"There might not be one," Elena admitted. "But lately there have been reports of large, savage-looking dogs roaming the area, things that seem more like wolves, but real big. And they're supposed to have yellow eyes that almost glow."

Herne and Max exchanged a look. Yellow eyes like that were often a sign of the Wild.

"As I said, the three people who were killed were working to get rid of the feral dogs." She glanced around, then lowered her voice. "Their bodies were ripped to shreds, but the medical examiner said there was no sign of predation. The animals didn't feed on them. It's like the dogs killed them for revenge. But dogs don't do that kind of thing, do they?"

"You'd be surprised," Max said grimly.

Herne ignored him.

"So you think there's some kind of otherworldly cause to these killings."

"Honestly, I don't know what I think," Elena said. "My station assigned me to do a story on the killings since I grew up in Bridgewater, but the more I look into it, the stranger it all seems. I go with my gut, Artie, and my gut tells me something is seriously wrong here."

Herne couldn't help smiling. No one had called him Artie since… well, since the last time he'd seen Elena.

"What do you think?" she asked him.

Herne looked at Max, then back to her.

"Can you take us to the scene of the most recent killing?"

∼

Elena led the way in her blue Prius, and Herne and Max followed in their SUV. As they headed across town, Herne found his thoughts drifting back to his last days living in Bridgewater.

He'd been a teenager, an only child, and he'd lived with his parents in a cabin in the woods not far from town. Ben and Laurie Herne were nature writers and photographers, primarily doing articles for various magazines. But that was just their day job. In reality, they were Warders, guardians of the balance between what humans thought of as the civilized world and the Wild, the ancient magic that had existed since before the first primates had evolved. The Warders were an old order, their sacred calling passed down from parent to child over uncountable generations. Their patron was the Horned King, a powerful nature spirit that manifested as a great stag and who, it was said, appeared to Warders from time to time to aid and guide them. Max had been given to his parents by the Horned King to assist them in performing their duties, and he had been a good and loyal friend. His mother and father had trained Herne his entire life to one day take on the mantle of Warder himself, but then one day they didn't return from a mission. At first, Herne wasn't worried. His parents could be gone for days, even weeks at a time when they were dealing with a threat from—or to—the Wild. But when nearly a month had gone by, he knew something was wrong. He was preparing to go in search of them when Max came home, severely wounded and close to death. Max told him a powerful entity calling itself Jack Sharp had killed his parents and nearly killed him. Herne, grief-stricken and filled with rage, vowed to hunt down Jack Sharp, whatever he was, and make him pay for what he'd done.

That night, the Horned King came to him in his dreams and gave him Sunder, a stone weapon carved by the first Warder and imbued with the power of the Wild itself. When Herne woke, he found Sunder on top of his dresser. When he touched the blade, he felt the power of the Wild flow through him, threatening to overwhelm him, and he immediately dropped the blade. A voice whispered in his mind then. *Touch it only when you need it. And do not hold it a moment longer than necessary, else you will be lost to the Wild.* Herne had heeded the Horned King's warning, and he'd been extremely cautious when handling Sunder ever since.

Before leaving on his quest to track down Jack Sharp, he'd spoken to Elena. They'd been together for almost two years by that point. They'd met in school, in second-year Algebra class, and they'd been inseparable ever since. There'd been a distance between them, though, as Herne couldn't tell her the truth about what his parents really did and what they were training him to do. And he couldn't tell her who Max really was, either. When he told her he had to leave town and that he didn't know how long he'd be gone, he hadn't been able to tell her why. She'd been hurt and angry, and they hadn't parted on the best terms. That had been almost fifteen years ago, and despite all his encounters with the Wild since, Herne had never so much as discovered a hint of who or what Jack Sharp might be and how to find him. He would keep searching, no matter how long it took, and in the meantime, he and Max continued to protect the balance between the world of humans and the Wild, working as bounty hunters whenever they needed money. All in all, it wasn't a bad life, but it could get lonely sometimes. Max was a good friend and partner, but sometimes Herne wondered what his life would've been like if he hadn't left Bridgewater. Would he and Elena have gotten married? Had kids? Would he have lived a normal life? Could he have been satisfied with a such a mundane existence, or would he have always felt the call of the hunt, reminding him that he had been born for a different, higher purpose? There was no way to know, of course, but he wondered, and he supposed he always would.

He pulled himself out of his thoughts and turned to Max.

"What did you think of Elena's story?"

"She was always intelligent and sensible, and she seems even more so as an adult. She's not the type to let her imagination run away with her. And as for relying on her gut, she spent a lot of time around you when you were kids. Some of your ability to sense the presence of the Wild might've rubbed off on her. Your mother didn't become a Warder until after she married your father. Being a Warder isn't a matter of genetics, at least not entirely. More to the point, what does *your* gut say about this situation?"

"It tells me that I shouldn't have had that second breakfast burrito this morning."

So far, Herne didn't feel anything either way about Elena's story. Still, her description of those dogs—savage, large, yellow eyes…

"How about you?" he asked. "I saw the way you looked at her when we first got to the coffee house. Did you sense anything wrong about her?"

The passenger side window was down, and Max gazed at the passing buildings for several moments before answering.

"Something's not right with all this, but I'll know more when we get to the scene of the most recent killing. Still, I'm inclined to believe her."

So was Herne.

~

"A junkyard? Seriously?"

Castillo's Salvage and Recycling was located on Bridgewater's east side, near several small used-car lots, which to Herne's mind was more than a little ironic.

"What's wrong with it being a junkyard?" Herne asked.

"The whole mean junkyard dog thing is a racial stereotype," Max said. "I find it offensive."

"I guess you'll have to take that up with whoever's behind all this."

"It indicates a complete lack of imagination, too." Max shook his head. "Very disappointing."

Elena drove through the junkyard's entrance and Herne followed. There was a chain link gate, but it had been torn halfway off its hinges and was bent and twisted. Elena pulled up to a small white building with a black roof with a sign reading *Main Office* mounted next to an open doorway. Two strips of yellow crime scene tape covered the doorway in an X, and Herne knew where the last killing had taken place. The spaces in front of the building were empty, and Elena parked in one. Herne parked next to her. They all got out and stood in front of the door.

"The first killing happened next to a dumpster outside a greasy spoon," Elena said. "The second took place behind a grocery store. The victims were both animal control officers searching for feral dogs. The third one happened here. The gate had already been damaged—by those monster dogs wanting to get in, people assumed—and an animal control officer was sent to investigate. He searched the junkyard for dogs, and when he didn't find any, he returned to the office to talk to the manager. One of those things broke down the door and killed the animal control officer. It ignored the office manager, and he was able to escape unharmed."

"Another reason you suspect the dogs are specifically targeting the animal control people," Herne said.

She nodded.

Herne reached toward the crime scene tape, intending to remove it so they could step inside, but Max raised a hand to stop him.

"There's no need. I can smell what I need from here."

Elena gave Herne a puzzled look, but he didn't explain. Max closed his eyes and inhaled deeply several times. When he opened them, Herne saw the amber flecks in his irises had become more pronounced.

"We're definitely dealing with Wild things here. Can you sense it?"

Herne felt a warm tingling on the back of his neck, and he knew Max was right.

"I do."

Herne returned to the SUV, got his gun belt out of the back, and buckled it on. He holstered his 9 mm on his right side, Sunder on his left. When he returned to the others, he looked at Elena.

"It would be best if you got in your car and stayed there until we're finished," Herne said.

"But—"

"It could be dangerous," he said. "We're prepared for this sort of thing. It's what we do."

She frowned. "And I'm *not* prepared?"

Max smiled, displaying a mouthful of sharp white canine teeth.

"Not like we are."

~

Fur sprouted on Elena's face and hands as she came at them, and her teeth and claws grew longer, sharper. Herne wasn't sure how it had happened, but somehow the manwolf—the creature he was certain was behind the killings in Bridgewater—had infused Elena with some of his own power, transforming her. Had he gotten to her after they'd left to search the junkyard? Or even earlier, when she'd been investigating the deaths on her own? After she emailed him to ask for their help but before they arrived? Had she brought them here at the manwolf's command so that he could ambush them? It seemed the most likely explanation. He remembered the way Max had stared at Elena when they'd first arrived at the coffee shop. He must've sensed something was wrong with her, although he hadn't been able to determine exactly what.

Herne didn't want to harm Elena, but he couldn't simply stand there and let her tear his throat out. Not only did he prefer to live, he knew that Elena would be devastated by what she'd done once she returned to her right mind. His hand was a blur as he drew his Glock, switched off the safety, and got a bead on the half-human, half-wolf creature Elena had become. He wasn't going to kill her, just shoot her in the shoulder, hopefully get her to break off her attack. But before he could fire, Max started running toward her.

He wanted to shout for Max to stop, but before he could speak, his friend's form darkened, as if he were suddenly cloaked in shadow. His shape bent, twisted, reformed, and when the change was complete, he'd become a large black hound, something like a rottweiler but bigger and shaggier. He had become the Black Dog, companion and ally of the Herne family for generations. Elena snarled, lips flecked with foam, and leaped forward as she drew near. Max launched himself into the air to meet her attack, head lowered, and he slammed into her stomach. Air whooshed out of her as she fell to the ground, and she lay there, stunned.

Bet her gut didn't like that, Herne thought.

If she had been a true creature of the Wild instead of a victim of it, Max would've gone straight for her throat now that she was down. Instead he turned to meet the charge of two of the manwolf's fully canine servants. Herne guessed they were dogs, likely feral ones, that the manwolf had transformed, just as he had Elena, in order to carry out his attacks on the animal control officers. Max was barking and snarling as he fought with the monster dogs, each of which was as large as he was. Herne saw a flash of movement off to his left and saw two dogs coming at him from that direction. A flash off to his right, and a quick glance in that direction revealed that two more dogs were attacking from that side. Herne was a fast shot, but he knew he wasn't fast enough to take all four of the beasts before they reached him. Besides, they'd been innocent animals before the manwolf had got at them, and he'd prefer not to kill them if he could avoid it. That meant there was only one thing he could do.

Still holding onto the Glock with his right hand, he reached down with his left and drew Sunder.

The instant his flesh came in contact with the stone blade, he felt it—the power of the Wild. It rushed into him like blazing fire, causing every nerve in his body to shriek with equal amounts of pain and pleasure. The sheer strength of Sunder's power threatened to overwhelm him, and he felt his thoughts becoming disjointed, tangled, fragmented. His emotions were amplified a thousand times, and chief among these feelings was anger. The idea that these four animals thought they could stop *him*—a goddamned *Warder*—with something as simple as teeth and claws made him laugh like a lunatic. Sunder would slice through their throats like a red-hot knife through butter, and he would bathe in the dogs' blood as they perished.

He dropped the Glock, transferred Sunder to his right hand, and almost ran toward the closest dog, one on his left. But with an effort of will, he managed to stop himself—barely. He was a Warder, and it was his duty to maintain the Balance. The Wild had no more claim on him than the civilized world. He was his own man and always would be.

His emotions receded as he returned to himself, and he could think clearly again. He held Sunder out in front of him, point first, and turned from side to side, displaying the blade to the oncoming monster dogs. When they drew close enough to sense Sunder's power, they stopped, ears back, heads lowered, yellow-eyes fixed on the prehistoric weapon. They whined softly and shuffled from side to side, as if unsure what to do. Sunder's mere presence was often enough to terrify the lower-level creatures of the Wild, sometimes even repelling them the way crucifixes repelled vampires in the movies.

"Forget the blade!" the manwolf roared. "Kill him! Tear open his belly, feast on his entrails!"

Herne rolled his eyes. The older a creature of the Wild was, the cornier its dialogue. He risked a glance in Max's direction and saw that his friend was still contending with the two dogs that had attacked him. He was bleeding from several wounds, none of which looked severe, as were his opponents. Max was taking it easy on them, more or less, because they couldn't help what they'd become. But he knew it was only a matter of time before Max had to go for the jugular. He couldn't keep playing around like this all day. He checked on Elena. She had gotten to her feet, but she was hunched over and cradling her stomach. He hated to see her hurt like that, but it was far preferable to gazing upon her corpse. Hopefully she'd remain incapacitated until the fight was over, one way or another.

"Tell your pack to back off!" Herne called out to the manwolf, still turning right then left and back again, making sure to keep the dogs' eyes on Sunder. "We don't want to hurt them if we don't have to."

The manwolf released a literal bark of a laugh. "You're a Warder. Killing is all you know."

"Really? Then how come I'm not cutting your dogs' throats right now? And look at Max. He could do a hell of a lot more damage if he wanted to."

The manwolf's yellow eyes narrowed in thought, but he did not reply.

An ear-splitting shriek cut the air, and Herne turned to see Elena coming toward him once again, fangs bared, claws raised. She staggered a little, her gut still hurting her, but she'd recovered enough to start moving again. He brandished Sunder at her, and she stopped, raised an arm to shield her eyes, looked away. But when he did that, the other four monster dogs took advantage of his distraction to run several feet closer. He went back to holding the blade out to all of them, facing right, then left, then toward Elena, and back again. But each time he switched positions, the dogs and Elena managed to close the gap between them by several more feet. He knew he wasn't going to be able to keep this up for long. Soon one of the dogs would reach him, or maybe it would be Elena, and he would have to defend himself. There was no guarantee he could do so without harming them, especially when using Sunder.

He heard growling coming from behind him then, and he felt a sick cold sensation in his own gut. Max had said there were seven monster dogs in all. Max was fighting two, and he was holding four at bay. That left one dog unaccounted for. He spun around and saw it coming at him. He shoved Sunder toward it, and the beast came to an abrupt stop, half snarling in frustration, half whining in fear. Now Herne had to defend himself on four fronts, facing each group of dogs and Elena in turn. He did his best to hold them all back, but he was failing. Whenever Sunder was turned away from them, they were able to close the distance a bit more. He knew he could keep this up only a few more seconds until they converged upon him. Max was too busy fighting a battle of his own, and Herne knew he couldn't count on his friend to come to his rescue.

He released his grip on Sunder and let the blade fall to the ground.

Elena and the dogs snarled in triumph and dashed toward him. He curled his hands into fists and raised them, knowing that it would do no good but determined to go down fighting if he had to.

"Halt!" the manwolf shouted.

Elena and the dogs—including the two Max battled—froze. They turned to look at the manwolf, muscles still taut, bodies shivering, desperate to spill blood but unwilling to disobey their master. They remained like this as the manwolf strode over to Herne. Just before the creature reached him, Max—in human form once more and bleeding from a dozen bites and scratches—stepped to his side.

The manwolf regarded them for a moment and then said, "You spoke true. You do not wish to kill my children. You cast aside your weapon rather than harm them."

Herne didn't reply. He'd taken an enormous gamble dropping Sunder, and all they could do now was wait to see what the manwolf would do next.

The yellow fire in the creature's eyes dimmed.

"Let us talk."

~

The manwolf's name was Bloodtooth, and he had come to Bridgewater to protect those whom he saw as his children.

"Your kind bred them from wolf stock, created them to be obedient companions. And then instead of taking care of them, you cast them out to fend for themselves. And when they begin to rely on their ancient instincts to help them survive, what do you do? Hunt them down and slay them. It is an affront to the Wild, and I shall not allow it to stand."

The four of them—Herne, Max, Elena, and Bloodtooth—stood talking in the junkyard. The seven monster dogs, relaxed for the moment, sat close by, watching. Elena had returned to her fully human self, and her mind was once again her own. She was shaken by what Bloodtooth had turned her into and forced her to do, but she was holding up well enough.

Herne knew Bloodtooth was referring to the animal control officers shooting the feral dogs rather than capturing them and taking them to a shelter. The creatures of the Wild hated guns and viewed them as an unfair advantage.

"I understand," Herne said, "but I can't allow you to kill any more humans. The Balance must be maintained. I can, however, guarantee that no more dogs will be shot in this town."

Bloodtooth frowned. "How will you do this?"

Max grinned. "We'll track the shooters down and have a talk with them. We can be very persuasive when we want to be."

"And I'll do a story for my station about the situation," Elena added. "I'll expose the bastards and tell the world what they've done."

"And this will be effective?" Bloodtooth asked.

"The vast majority of humans despise animal cruelty," Herne said. "Especially when it happens to dogs or cats. The publicity will force the town officials to fix the situation. And I'll return to Bridgewater periodically to make sure it stays fixed."

Bloodtooth looked from Herne, to Max, to Elena, then back to Herne, considering. Finally, he nodded.

"Very well. I accept your terms."

Bloodtooth extended his hand. Amber threads of energy emerged from the monster dogs' eyes, nostrils, and mouths. The energy flowed toward Bloodtooth and into his hand, and as he withdrew his power from the dogs, they reverted to normal canine form. When the transformation was complete the dogs—confused and frightened—scattered.

Bloodtooth fixed his yellow eyes on Herne.

"See that you keep your promise, Warder."

Then he turned, his form blurred, and he loped away on all fours. When he was gone, Elena looked at Herne.

"Warder?" she asked.

Herne smiled. "It's a long story."

~

He told that story over lunch. They ate at a small café not far from Java Nice Day. They kept a fully stocked med kit in the SUV, and Max cleaned his wounds before they reached the place. His preternatural healing abilities did the rest, and by the time they sat down to eat, his wounds had become scars. By late afternoon, they would be healed completely.

Elena took Herne's story in stride. After what she'd experienced over the last few days, she was more than prepared to believe him. As Herne had guessed, Elena encountered Bloodtooth during her investigation, after she'd emailed them asking for help. The manwolf had invested some of his power in her, as he had the monster dogs, and after that, she became bound to him and was forced to do his will. He ordered her to lead Herne and Max to the junkyard, and she had done so without hesitation, something she now felt great guilt over.

"I can't believe he could control me so easily," she said.

"The Wild is a primeval force," Herne said. "It's not easily resisted, even when someone is prepared for it."

"Which you weren't," Max said.

Both Herne and Elena had ordered chef salads. Max had ordered two hamburgers as rare as the cook was willing to prepare them. He'd already finished his food, while Herne was only half done with his salad. Elena had only picked at hers.

"What gets me is that Bloodtooth is responsible for the death of three people," Elena said, "and yet nothing is going to happen to him because of it. He just gets to leave without experiencing any consequences for his actions."

"Do you think I should have killed him?" Herne said.

She looked at him a moment while considering her answer.

"Yes. No. Maybe. I don't know."

"My job is to maintain the Balance," Herne said. "I only kill when I have to; otherwise, I risk upsetting the Balance even further."

"The Wild has its own rules and laws," Max said, "and they don't always match the ones in the human world."

"As long as no more dogs are killed, Bloodtooth should behave himself," Herne said. "But if he doesn't… "

"We'll be back," Max finished.

~

They said their goodbyes in the café's parking lot.

Elena hugged Max, and Max sniffed the air as she did so. When they parted, Max gave Herne a look, then climbed into the SUV's passenger seat, leaving Herne alone with Elena.

"Do you have to leave so soon?" Elena asked him.

"Max checked our email on his phone after we left the junkyard. A new request for help came in while we were dealing with Bloodtooth. People have been disappearing near a lake in Michigan, and we need to check it out."

She nodded. "I understand. Well, I'll do what I promised and get working on my exposé on the animal control officers. But if you ever need help on a case, don't hesitate to call me."

Herne thought he detected a glint of yellow in her eyes, and when she smiled, her teeth seemed a bit sharper than they should be. He understood the look Max had given him a moment ago. He'd sensed the change in Elena was permanent. Herne realized that he hadn't seen Bloodtooth remove the power he'd granted Elena. An oversight on his part, or perhaps a gift in repayment for the trouble he'd caused? It was hard to say. The motivations of Wild creatures weren't always easy to determine.

"I'll do that," he said.

It was his turn to receive a hug, and when they broke apart, she gave him a last smile, then headed for her Prius. He watched as she got inside, turned on the engine, backed out of her space, and pulled onto the road. A moment later she was lost to sight. He stood there a moment longer, then he got in the SUV.

"You miss her already," Max said. It wasn't a question.

Herne turned on the engine and began to back out of the space.

"Time to get back to work," he said.

A minute later, they were on the road and headed for whatever would come next.

Blood of Dracula

Stephen D. Sullivan

In 1897, author Bram Stoker published *Dracula*, a gothic horror melodrama about Count Dracula, a vampire from Transylvania who comes to England looking for new blood—literally. The cast of *Dracula* is large, and the story is told from diverse points of view, largely in diaries, journal entries, and letters. Among the story's protagonists are Jonathan and Mina Harker, both of whom fall under Dracula's sway before finally, together with their companions, confronting and destroying the monster.

The survivors—and not all of the Harkers' friends survived—then resume their "normal" Victorian-era lives. That story took place in 1890 (with a brief coda in 1897). This story takes place between the two Great Wars, nearly forty years later…

Stephen D. Sullivan is the award-winning author of more than fifty books, including trilogies for *Legend of the Five Rings*, *Spider Riders*, and *Dragonlance*. He chose *Dracula* as his Public Domain property to write about because he's used some characters from that classic (and *Frankenstein*, too) in his latest novel, *Dr. Cushing's Chamber of Horrors*. He plans to use a character from this short in an upcoming sequel to that book. This seemed a perfect chance to introduce her and let her spread her wings, both figuratively and literally.

Other cool stuff Steve has worked on includes *Dungeons & Dragons* and *Star Wars* (games), *Teenage Mutant Ninja Turtles* and *The Simpsons* (comics), *Iron Man* and *Thunderbirds* (junior novels), and the 2017 film, *Theseus and the Minotaur*. His most recent projects include *Frost Harrow* (modern-gothic horror), *Tournament of Death 4* (fantasy), *Atomic Tales: Strange Invaders* (50s SciFi online and in audio), and his *Scribe*-winning novelization of the "Worst Film Ever Made"—*Manos: The Hands of Fate*. Check out Steve's latest at: www.cushinghorrors.com - www.stephendsullivan.com

For my father's cousin Richard West, Tolkien scholar, who died of Covid-19—our modern plague—during my writing of this story. Rest in Peace, dear friend. The world is poorer with your passing.

Blood of Dracula

Between the Two Great Wars

I GAZED AT THE MIRROR IN HORROR, WATCHING THE BLOOD RUN down my face and hands, feeling the warmth, smelling the sweet metallic odor—*So* enticing!

What have I done?!

Drip... drip... drip...!

Crimson spattered on Mother's dressing table. Lovely little pools...

The blood is the life!

Dripping from my arms... from my cheeks... from my chin... The livid puddle on the dresser growing larger with each drop.

My body trembled; my lips quivered.

Just one little...

My tongue darted out, found what I wanted.

Warm and salty... Tang of iron...

Delicious!

"Lucy... What have you done?!" My mother Mina's voice, horrified.

Though no more horrified than I as I closed my eyes and licked my lips clean.

I was only twelve.

So... Good!

~

"Lucy, are you *sure* you want to do this?" my brother asked, concern written on his handsome face, as I stepped onto the platform of the train bound for Whitby.

"I'm sure," I replied.

"Even with our parents away?"

"Yes, especially now. I know it was only supposed to be a short visit, but I'm not sure they'll ever come back from America, John. You know how fragile Father's health can be."

My brother, John Quincey Arthur Abraham Harker, winced slightly and leaned heavily on his silver-handled cane at the mention of our father's constitution. My brother has had his own health issues through the years, and still limped from the wounds he'd gotten in the Great War. He's also nearly sixteen years older than me, and fancies himself much wiser.

"Yes. Indeed," Quincey mused. (*Quincey* is what everyone but me calls him.) "I think the climate of the American Southwest agrees with Father. I didn't anticipate that when our parents decided to visit the home country of my namesake."

"I don't think *anybody* anticipated it," I said, book images of faraway Texas drifting through my mind. My brother had a lot of names, all from dear friends of our parents—Jonathan and Mina Harker—but his nickname came from Quincey Morris, a Texan who'd given up his life to save my mother and the rest.

Our family didn't talk about those "dark days" much, save to mention Quincey's bravery or how beautiful and full of life *my* namesake, Lucy Westenra, had been. She was Mother's best friend, and died at the start of that whole terrible adventure back in 1890.

Father's constitution had suffered greatly during that time—his hair had gone from lustrous brown to pure white, though he was a young man then—and his health still had occasional bouts. "But if the desert air makes Father feel better…" I continued, "I'm just glad they're happy."

"As am I," Quincey agreed, still looking thoughtful as he touched the tip of the cane to his lips. "But are *you* happy, Lucy? I mean… Why this sudden desire to go to Whitby? Our family hasn't visited there since you were a child."

"That's *exactly* why. I'd like to see the place again, relive the fond memories."

"But why *now?* The summer's over, after all—and your birthday's just around the corner."

"That makes it the best time possible. You're busy here in London with the firm... Mother and Father are in the States... It seems a good time to take a little holiday—for my birthday."

I could tell that my brother didn't entirely believe my story.

"I heard from Jack," he mentioned, taking a deep breath. "He said you'd left your post at his sanitarium. Why, Lucy? Working with 'Uncle' Jack was the type of position most young nurses dream of."

Blood... The blood...!

I blinked the sanguine images away and forced a smile.

"I just need a change, is all, Johnny—a change of scenery from dreary old Purfleet, and dreary old London, too."

"Then why *resign?* Why not just take a bit of leave—or a *holiday*, like you said? You know Jack Seward loves our family as though it were his own. I'm sure he'd have been accommodating."

"I know, but... Right now, I'm not sure that nursing is the right thing for me."

Blood... Warm... Rich... Tasty...!

"I need a break... to sort out my thoughts," I concluded. "I'm almost twenty, you know. I need to figure out what I want to do with the rest of my life."

"It seems to me that nursing is a damn fine career," he offered. Then, a new thought seemed to occur to his clever solicitor's mind. "It's not about some *boy*, is it?"

I laughed. "No, Johnny, it's not about any boy—or *man*, for that matter."

"You're not sleepwalking again, are you?"

"No," I lied. "Of course not. As I said... I just need a change of scenery, to help clear my mind."

"Well, little sister, I suppose you know what's best."

"I do."

He handed me some papers and an old, heavy key. His work with Father's firm dealt mostly in real estate, and he'd been at it almost since I was born. "Here's the lease for the cottage and the key—all legal and proper. Try to take good care of the place while you're there. I had to call in a few favors to get it at a reasonable price."

"Even in the off-season?"

My brother grinned. "Well... That helped, too, of course. Are you sure I can't change your mind?"

"Not a bit."

"There *might* be some unpleasant memories there," he warned.

"Far outweighed by the good ones," I assured him.

"Is there anything else I can do?"

"Give me a kiss goodbye and wish me well."

He bent and kissed my forehead. "Have a safe journey, Lucille Arabella Harker. Enjoy your holiday."

"I will."

"Call me or send a telegram if you need anything."

"I will. Promise," I said as I stepped from the platform onto the train. "And Johnny..."

"Yes?"

The train began to pull away. My timing was excellent. I cupped my hands around my mouth and called to my brother as his figure on the platform diminished.

"Don't mention any of this to our parents! I don't want them to worry. I'll catch them up when I come back."

~

"Oh, Mother! What have I done?!"

"Hush, now." My mother embraced me, pulling my seventeen-year-old body to her breast as though I were still a babe. "Hush, my unexpected child."

That was the endearing familial term she'd adopted because she bore me late in her childbearing years; 'a wonderful gift,' she'd called her surprising pregnancy.

"It's nothing," she murmured sweetly in my ear. "You haven't done anything. Words are *not* deeds, nor are thoughts."

"Oh, God, Mother! But I *wanted* to! I wanted to *so* much! It was like that

292

time when I was twelve, with the rabbit... I'd almost forgotten that, but..."

"I know, dear. I know. Believe me."

"How *can* you know?" I stared at my hands, and they looked more like claws to my terrified eyes. Memories from five years previous came flooding back: the blood...the stains...scrubbing...The terrible crimson that seemed like it would never come out of my skin...

And my mother's soft words, spoken on a day when she should have had far more pleasant memories to cling to—my brother Quincey's birthday. Thank God he had been away, on a Scottish hunting trip with our father.

They had been hunting, yet *I* was the one tainted by blood.

All that had faded from my memory, seemed like some terrible dream... Until today—again, my brother's birthday.

Once more, he was away with my father—on business in Paris, this time—and, once more, as on that day five years gone, I felt the terrible *urge*.

"It wasn't *you* who was out walking with Cynthia," I blubbered to my mother. "It was *me*. We were having fun... Talking about my birthday party last month... Admiring the last blooms of autumn as we walked that old pathway along the Thames—you know, the one down by the weir."

"Your father and I have strolled there many times. It's quite a romantic spot."

"I...Yes, I suppose. But we were just walking and chatting, enjoying the day. And then Cynthia ran across the lawn in Old Deer Park. And I ran after her. And we were laughing...And I'd nearly caught her when she tripped...and she went down...and her legs tangled in mine... and I went down with her...and we rolled across the grass, all sort of knotted up... And I ended up on top, still laughing.

"And she was still laughing, too. And I looked down at her, as she tried to catch her breath, her pulse throbbing in her pale neck and...

"Mother, I wanted to *bite* her!

"I wanted to feel her flesh yield under my teeth. I wanted to feel the warm spurt of her blood into my mouth. I wanted to taste the coppery sweetness of it with my tongue as it ran over my lips and down my chin, dripping onto my breast...

"Oh, God! Mother!"

Mina Murray Harker held me tight and whispered softly in my ear.

"It's all right now, dear. You *didn't* hurt your friend. You didn't do anything wrong. I understand."

"But you *can't* understand," I insisted, weeping and gently pounding my fists into her shoulders. "You can't!"

"But I *do*," she replied softly. "I too have felt that awful, all-consuming desire. When I was just a little older than you..."

"But it's *not* some kind of sex thing," I broke in, misunderstanding her compassion. "I wanted to *kill* her. I wanted to rip out her throat and drink her blood, like I did with that rabbit when I was twelve."

She nodded gravely. "At the time, we thought that was some kind of accident," she explained. "You were going through a difficult patch—the sleepwalking and all—and your father and I believed it was perhaps a bid to gain our attention, on your brother's birthday, that went too far."

"But it *wasn't!* I *wanted* that blood. I wanted to taste the *life*. I wanted the life of that poor bunny!"

My mother shivered, but still held me close. "'Only be sure that thou eat not the blood: for the blood is the life; and thou mayest *not* eat the life with the flesh,'" she murmured.

"Is that from the *Bible*?"

"Yes, dear."

I covered my face with my hands, ashamed. "Then I'm... I'm doomed... damned."

"No, no, my dear unexpected child. Understand that, at the time, your father and I thought the problem when you were twelve was an accident—but we did talk it over and realized there had been *other* times, too."

"W-what?" I asked. My breath came in short, sobbing gasps, and I looked up at her through tear-stained eyes. I felt miserable, frightened to my very core.

Was this *not* some kind of twice-in-a-lifetime fluke?

The whole world had suddenly become cold and distant.

My mother gazed down at me beneficently. Her voice was warm and loving, full of understanding.

"Dearest Lucy, when you were two, you gave me quite a nip while I was feeding you. It took a few weeks for the bite to heal.

"At seven, you stole the drumstick of a duck from the kitchen."

"I remember that. I thought it was cooked."

"But it was raw, and yet, you still ate the whole thing."

"I-it was? I did?"

"Yes, dear. And then the rabbit, which had also been destined for the larder, like the duck. Because you had been sleepwalking and didn't really seem to remember it later, your father and I thought that killing the animal had been an accident—that in your trance-like state, you'd started to consume it before it was cooked."

"But I *didn't*." I protested plaintively. "I remember everything now… I *wanted* to drink its blood…"

"Because the blood is the life." Mother sighed. "We've heard those words before, your father and I—a long time ago, before you were born. And I myself have felt what you felt today."

"But you—"

"I know you think it's impossible, but nevertheless, I did—just the same as you felt it today—but directed toward your father. I was just twenty years old."

"W-what? You wanted to…?"

"I wanted to drink his blood. I wanted to savor his life as it ran out across my lips."

I clutched the crucifix I'd worn since childhood, shocked by my mother's words.

For the past few weeks, the cross' touch had irritated a rash on my chest, but—heeding my parents' oft-repeated maxim—I stubbornly refused to take it off. I turned to the tiny silver icon for solace now, though it became uncomfortably hot in my hand.

Nevertheless, I held it tight.

"It's so long ago…" Mother continued. "But I remember it as clearly as if it were yesterday. Probably your father and I should have told you this long ago, but we hoped that the past might *stay* in the past. We hoped that our family had freed itself from this… curse.

"Certainly, your brother has never been vexed by it. But he is a man, and despite your father's travails, this sin was mine alone—because *I* was the one who tasted the blood of Count Dracula."

~

I gazed from the window of the small cliff-top cottage out over the desolate October landscape and across the cold gray expanse of the North Sea. The grass outside had already turned brown in anticipation of the winter to come.

The oak rafters of the little house smelled of herbs and aging wood, but the ocean breeze carried in a salty tang through the cracks around the edges of the many-paned windows. Still, even with the infiltrating draft, the cottage was a cozy place, filled with polished Edwardian furniture and overstuffed chairs. The big feather bed on the second floor looked dreamy. Using it tonight would be like sleeping on a cloud.

Yet, part of me didn't *want* to use it. Right now, *sleep* was one of the things that I dreaded most.

Though perhaps "dread" was too strong a word.

After all, how could anybody be afraid in this little seaside town, with its quaint shops, boisterous pubs, busy fishing wharfs, and local small restaurants filling the air with the sounds of happy customers and the aromas of home cooking and fresh seafood?

No. Whitby was a place to feel *comfortable*, and my mother's strange history with the location had long since been blotted out by family memories of childhood summer trips.

But tonight, after the shops and pubs closed, and all the ships lay safely and silently at harbor, then only the constant low whisper of the sea would keep me company. Eventually, I would sleep, and then?

Despite what I'd told my brother, I *had* been sleepwalking lately. Once, I'd even woken outside my home, on the green, in my nightgown, my bare feet cold and damp from the early morning autumn dew.

Fortunately, I'd been able to steal home—which wasn't far—before being noticed by anyone.

That and similar minor incidents left me shaken, though. Plus, my birthday was drawing near, which always made me nervous.

Only one day away...

Since the revelations of my seventeenth birthday, the interval between my birthday and Quincey's had made me increasingly nervous.

Mother (and, later, Father) had tried to calm my worries, to little avail. Though they did demonstrate the reality of a five-year gap between my...

episodes.

And this was only my *twentieth* birthday, and the year in which my troubles *might* return—every fifth year after my family had nearly perished, before Quincey and I were even born—lay more than two years in the future.

Given that, really, I had nothing to fear.

That's what I told myself.

So, why these strange longings? Why the images of blood playing through my brain? Why the sleepwalking?

All of which was why I had left my home, my job, my brother, and the few people I could call close friends, and come here in hopes that Whitby and its pleasant memories might overwhelm the vague tug I felt in the deepest parts of my soul, and that I might sleep without somnambulist rambling, and dream without images of indulging the craving I feared most.

And should, God forbid, I give in to such things, at least I would be far from the people I cherished. I would be a danger to no one but myself.

Or so I hoped.

Taking a deep breath of the salt-tinged air, I opened the package I'd brought with me from visiting the town earlier—a shepherd's pie for dinner.

I peeled back the waxy brown paper, savoring the aromas of mashed potatoes, carrots, peas, onions, cheddar cheese, and beef.

So many smells in one small package.

As expected, it proved a delicious distraction. Only briefly did my mind stray to the thought of the blood coursing through the veins of the steer that had given its all for the pie's meat.

Consume the flesh, not the blood—not the life.

After supper, I built a small fire and sat in the overstuffed chair near the fireplace, reading *The Murder on the Links*. The book was a few years old, but I felt that both the author—a Mrs. Christie—and her detective character showed promise. Though I must admit that I purchased the volume merely because my brother likes to play golf.

A good dinner and a good read soon worked their special brand of magic, and as the fire dimmed, I found myself beginning to doze.

Should I hike upstairs to that soft-looking feather bed? But I felt so cozy there by the fire that before I knew it, my eyes gently closed, and I slipped off toward the land of dreams…

Scritch! Scritch! Scritch!

A vague scrabbling, like a mouse in the baseboards, roused me.

I opened my eyes to a darkened room, filled with a diffuse gray light filtering through the windowpanes. Sea fog enveloped the little cottage in this eerie illumination—neither day nor night, dark nor light. I could see my surroundings clearly but not distinctly, as though everything were a dream.

The soft chair under me felt solid enough. The embers in the fireplace warmed my left calf, and the smoky scent of the afterglow filled my nose. In the muffled distance, the Whitby lighthouse sounded its foghorn.

Scritch! Scritch! Scritch!

The noise again. Not a mouse, but something at the window…

I leaned forward and peered intently at the fogbound panes three steps away.

My blood ran cold as two pale hands emerged from the mist and scratched against the glass. The long white nails scraped at the mullions, as if trying to loosen the glazing and pry the pane free.

"Stop it!" I cried, springing to my feet, attempting to sound braver than I felt. My left hand found the fireplace poker—the only weapon that came to mind—and seized it. "I'm not afraid!"

The hands withdrew from the window, disappearing into the fog, and a soft feminine chuckle echoed through the cottage's sitting room.

"Whoever you are, this isn't funny!" I brandished the poker and stepped toward the window. I knew that locals sometimes liked to play tricks on tourists—though my heart of hearts feared that was *not* happening here. My stomach twisted like a cold snake in my gut.

"Lucy… Dearest Lucy…" a woman whispered from the mist. Somehow, the voice seemed both cold and warm at the same time, forbidding yet inviting. "Open the window and let me in. Please, darling."

"No," I replied, shaking my head as much to convince myself as to forbid my unseen visitor. Because part of me—an extraordinarily strong part—*wanted* to open that window.

"But why, dearest?" the voice insisted. "We're friends, aren't we?"

"How can we be friends?" I asked. "I have no idea who you are."

"But you *do*, darling. You've known me since before you were born."

A face appeared out of the fog; a lovely visage framed by a halo of golden hair. Her full red lips smiled at me, and her dark eyes gleamed sympathetically. "Let me in, my love."

I froze on the spot and nearly dropped the poker. The breath caught in my throat.

I *knew* the face emerging from the mist!

I'd never met her, but I recognized the woman at my window from the portrait my mother cherished, a picture that I'd seen as long as I could remember.

She was my namesake—Lucy Westenra.

"Y-you're dead! You died nearly forty years ago!"

"Is that what they told you?" the dead Lucy inquired, and her face became even more beatific. The corners of her ruby lips turned down in sadness. "Oh, my dearest Lucy... Some things in life are not so simple as most would have you believe."

My brain felt as cloudy as the fog outside. I shook my head, again, trying to clear it. "How can that be? You're either dead or you're alive. My mother told me you were dead."

"Relationships change," the dead woman suggested ever so sweetly. "I moved on, chose a new way. Dear Mina disagreed with the choice I made. To your mother and her friends, I *was* dead—and I remain dead to this day.

"But I'm here for *you*, my love. I've come to take you away with me, to a new world, a better world than you've ever dreamed."

"I... I..." I tried unsuccessfully to pull my thoughts together.

"Let me in, dearest, and we'll discuss it. We can talk as long as you like. It's me... Your Aunt Lucy."

My right hand reached for the window, to unlatch it, but my left still held the fireplace poker.

Those two parts of me warred as I looked at my dead aunt's lovely face.

I stepped nearer, and her body emerged from the mist. She was dressed all in white, in a long flowing gown, like a gossamer-clad angel.

She held out her arms, beckoning me.

I took another step.

Lucy smiled, her sharp teeth gleaming.

The poker fell from my numb fingers, clattering to the cottage's wooden floor.

The metallic din rang in my ears, startling me. I blinked, and my blindly groping fingers found the silver crucifix hanging at my neck—the one my mother had insisted that I wear since I was a very small child.

I held the cross between me and my namesake.

The other Lucy hissed and wheeled away, instantly vanishing into the mist.

My knees buckled, and I swooned.

When I woke, sunlight was streaming through the cottage windows. I lay on the floor and had a terrible crick in my neck.

Whether my nighttime visitor had been real, I couldn't determine.

Not a sign of dead Lucy remained.

Perhaps I had merely been dreaming and sleepwalked to the window.

But the poker lying on the floorboards suggested otherwise.

~

The story my mother told me that day three years ago had been soul-chilling—like nothing I could ever believe as reality.

Yet, she swore on her love for my father that it was all true.

She told me about an ancient evil that nearly killed Jonathan before traveling across Europe and settling, leechlike, upon England's fair shores.

She told me of Count Dracula, a vampire, a creature who would never die so long as the blood of the living sustained him. He had lived for centuries, this fiend who could change his form into that of a wolf, a bat, shimmering mist, and many others.

Dracula had come from Transylvania to England seeking fresh blood, literally. He landed on our fair shores near Whitby, in a shipwreck filled with corpses.

From there, a terrible plague of death and misfortune had followed in his wake. One of his first victims was nineteen-year-old Lucy Westenra, my mother's best friend, my namesake.

She had died and then risen from the grave as a beautiful phantom. The papers called her the "Bloofer Lady," and she preyed upon young children, until my parents' friends tracked her down and destroyed her. Her fiancé and a man named Van Helsing drove a stake through her heart, filled her mouth with garlic, and cut off her head.

My parents and their friends later destroyed Dracula as well, but not until he'd corrupted others and made my mother drink his blood. Quincey Morris, my brother's namesake, had perished in that final conflict.

My brother, it turned out, had been born two years to the day on the same date that Quincey died—the day Count Dracula had also met his end.

"It's always been a comfort to your father and me that your brother's birthday falls on that day," Mother said.

"And that's why you call him 'Quincey,'" I mused. I'd known he was named after people important to my parents, but I'd never heard the full, true story before.

"Yes. Because he was a dear friend and he loved Lucy as much as I did, and he saved my life by helping your father destroy Dracula."

My seventeen-year-old self had stopped crying now, self-pity replaced by awe at the fantastic tale—surely it *couldn't* be true!—and by a cold fear growing in my belly.

Because I knew—despite the modern era we live in, with the electric light and automobiles and telephones and moving pictures—that the story *was* true, and that it explained my strange behavior, this wicked compulsion that seemed to manifest every five years, between my October birthday and the anniversary of my brother's birth in early November.

It explained the weird feelings I'd had for the past month, culminating in my tussle with Cynthia in Old Deer Park, and my craving for her life blood, earlier.

Today... on my brother's birthday.

"The day Dracula died," I muttered.

Mother nodded. "Yes," she said quietly. "I'm afraid that this strange curse has somehow passed from me to you. I'm so sorry!"

"As if menstruation isn't curse enough!" I added with an ironic laugh. Then, the icy terror in my gut twisted. "Mother?"

"Yes?"

"What about *my* birthday? Is there something special about *that* day?"

She looked at me, her eyes filled with sorrow.

"October third..." she began. "I've tried not to think of it, over the years, and I know your father has, too—because your birthday should be a day of joy and celebration not one for past... memories."

"Yes?"

She took a deep breath, and held my gaze with her own.

"Because that day," my mother continued, "October third... Is the day that I drank the blood of Dracula."

I was only seventeen when she told me.

I've hated birthdays ever since.

~

The ruins of Whitby Abbey towered over me, its crumbling tawny spires turning red in the last rays of sunset. The earth smelled of rich loam and withering grass. The ground beneath my hiking boots felt solid, reassuring. Here stood an edifice whose roots sank deep into the past of England.

I'd felt a need to come here today—a need to pray, though I've never been much for church. The local non-ruined clerical establishments just seemed too *new* for my purpose. It was an ancient evil that my soul was battling, whether from within or without, and I needed a setting to match my struggle.

The silver crucifix at my throat felt warm, though the air remained autumn chilly. Already, out at sea, the fog marshalled its forces for its nightly assault on the land.

Today was my twentieth birthday—October third.

I'd taken a quiet celebratory supper at an out-of-the-way café on Church Street, solo of course. At home with my family, I might have indulged in a celebratory glass of brandy. But here I was alone, and not quite old enough to legally hoist an elbow, unless, of course, I was willing to endure unsavory male companionship to procure it for me.

I had no desire for such company. I didn't want to be with *anyone*;

anything I might do tonight, I needed to do on my own.

I finished my meal and ascended the 199 steps leading from the town up to the abbey.

The view from atop the hill was magnificent, and because of the time of the year and the advancing hour, I had it all to myself.

Watching the fog roll and gather, I wondered whether tonight would be like last night.

Would my dead 'aunt' return? Had she even been there in the first place?

I should stay here. *I'll be* safe *here.*

But another part of me noted the absurdity of thinking that I might sleep tonight amid the cold decrepit walls of the abbey. I hadn't come equipped for camping, despite my boots; I hadn't even worn slacks.

Lie down here and you're sure to catch your death.

Would that be so terrible, though?

Might it not be better to perish than to live with this curse, whether real or imagined? Could I brave this terrible bloodlust, with being a constant threat to those around me?

When I'd thought these fits might come only every five years, enduring them seemed possible. But now, on my twentieth birthday, a full two years before my next anticipated bout, I dreaded the urge rising within me.

The waitress, who had served me earlier, and even the busboy, had looked... enticing.

Why? Why now?

The thought this might become my usual state of being terrified me. Perhaps my mother's stories were only fantasy. Perhaps I was simply going mad.

Because surely it was insanity that suddenly impelled me to scale the decaying abbey without climbing gear or safety ropes. Surely it was madness that led me to the top of the east wall's left-hand spire and made me stand there, precarious, as the last rays of sunlight vanished in the west.

I threw out my arms, my skirts billowing in the sea breeze that heralded the night fog. I don't know whether I uplifted my hands to the sky in triumph or in desperation.

The North Sea, gray and nearly shapeless under the fog, seemed to stretch forever. The evening mist surrounded the hilltop I stood astride, turning the abbey grounds into a shrinking island of solidity.

The darkening world seemed fantastic... unreal... just another dream from which I might soon wake.

Below, eternity beckoned.

"All this, the master will give you..." a voice whispered on the wind.

I nearly lost my footing...slipped...struggled to keep from falling... clung to the spire, scraping my hands against the stones.

To my left and above me, atop the pinnacle of what was once the roof of the abbey's nave, crouched Aunt Lucy. The misty sea breeze tugged at her white gossamer garments and her flowing golden hair. She looked like an enormous angelic bird at roost. Her sharp teeth gleamed in the advancing darkness.

She swept her long pale fingers in an arc, indicating the surrounding fog-bound countryside. "All of this can be yours. Just climb down from here and follow me."

The blood is the life!

I shook my head, my eyes straying toward the ground, far below. "I'd rather die."

With one swift step, she bounded from where she perched to the spire I clung to. It almost seemed as though she walked on the air. She landed just below me, her fingers almost touching my boots.

"You need *never* die," she told me, her voice sweet and seductive. "Do one small service for the master, and he will grant you eternal life."

"W-what service?" My head began to swim—maybe it was the height, or perhaps the fire blazing in Lucy's dark eyes.

To live... There was nothing so terrible about that. Was there?

"The master's blood flows in your veins," my dead aunt purred.

"My blood?"

My twentieth birthday...The day my mother had tasted Dracula's blood...

I'm the same age she was then!

"Just a few drops will wake him from his long slumber," she continued, creeping up the spire, her slender hands reaching for me. "Then we'll be together...forever. You'd like that, wouldn't you, Lucy?"

She surrounded me, her gossamer nightgown billowing in a wind I barely felt. Her face was almost touching mine. Her breath, colder than the North Sea, caressed my cheek.

I *wanted* to say yes. I was tired of fighting.

"It will be an end to all suffering," she promised, as if reading my mind. "Anything you want, you need but take it. Just… say… '*Yes!*'"

I tore my eyes away from hers and cried:

"No!"

I tried to throw myself from the spire, but she grabbed me with claws like iron.

"Then I'll just have to *take* what I want," she snarled, her sweet face suddenly bestial, her fangs bared.

"NO!" I screamed.

Rather than pull away, I tore open my collar, baring my breast, and crushed her to me.

The crucifix hanging on my bosom pressed into her pale flesh.

Lucy Westenra howled in agony as the cross burned into her.

She tried to pull away, but I held her tight, wrestling with a demon atop the crumbling deconsecrated church.

We overbalanced… fell…

The ground rushed up to meet us…

And then she was flying, her arms becoming wings, carrying me with her, even as she wailed and more of her burst into blue-white flames.

We soared across the hilltop and out over the cliffs, raptors struggling in a mid-air death grip.

Her flames threatened me now, and it felt as if the crucifix was burning into my breast.

We arced up into the sky, and the cold fog embraced us.

And then Lucy vanished.

Whether she burned into nothing or melted away into the mist, I cannot say.

I fell.

Like Icarus drawn too close to a black, lifeless sun.

The wind tore at my clothes; they fluttered like inadequately fledged wings.

The fog parted and the cliff bottom rushed up, its rocky teeth poised, eager, to rend my flesh and crush my bones.

I did *not* want to die!

I spread my arms wide and fire surged through my veins, as the cross on my chest blazed bright.

My body grew light...

The winds grew less...

And somehow, impossibly, I settled lightly onto the rocky shore below the cliffs at Whitby.

I felt... *better*, whole, somehow.

I looked at my arms, astonished. They'd grown long and thin, transforming into batlike wings.

I flew!

All around, the cries of my winged brethren echoed on the night air.

I touched my ears with my clawed hands and found that they, too, had stretched and attenuated, become batlike. My nostrils thrilled to the smell of sea, and fog, and rocks, and the distant town, and so much more.

To my eyes—if I was seeing with only my eyes—the whole world looked bright as day.

And my bloodlust had gone, vanished...

Or perhaps it had been tamed by the same strange fire that burned a scar in the shape of the cross into my chest.

I walked to the water's edge, found a calm tide pool, and gazed at my reflection.

I looked *hideous*, part bat, part human.

But I felt... *alive*!

Perhaps *this* was what I'd always been meant to be: Something... Some*one* bridging the world of my family with that of Aunt Lucy and her dark master.

But even now, I couldn't be sure that she'd been real.

Perhaps this whole trial was something I'd had to work out on my own.

I stretched as I contemplated these puzzles, and as I did—miraculously—my body settled into its familiar shape once more.

Again, I was Lucy Arabella Harker.

I passed the test.

"Lucy, are you *sure* you want to do this?"

My brother looked even more concerned than he had when I'd been embarking for Whitby.

I didn't blame him. Here we were together at the train station with me leaving London again, not four weeks after my previous trip. Except this time, I was going much farther away... And I had no idea if I'd ever be coming back.

It likely seemed mad to Quincey that I was gallivanting off again, that I was *not* returning to my position at Dr. Seward's, and that I was *not* instead finding some nice man and settling down as a proper British housewife, either. Rather, I had decided to light out for the continent to seek my own fortunes, or as people my age now said—and I could imagine my brother's shudder at even thinking this phrase—to "find myself."

And yet, that's *exactly* what I was doing.

Poor boy.

He'd never understand that I'd *already* found myself, mostly, and that what I'd found was both darker *and* brighter than he could easily imagine. It was the last bits, how this new Lucy fit into the world, that I needed to figure out. I couldn't do that under his watchful eye.

And even with our family history, I lacked the words to tell him. Perhaps, one day...

"Don't worry," I assured my older brother. "I know what I'm doing."

He shook his head. "I certainly hope so. Our parents won't forgive me—forgive *either* of us—if you don't."

I smiled and put a comforting hand on his cheek. His face felt warm, full of life beneath my fingers. I had not even the slightest urge to bite him.

"I can do this," I said. "I'll be all right."

"But where will you go? What will you do?"

"I have some money put aside. And I've got my nursing to fall back on if I need it. People always need good nurses."

Quincey rubbed his chin, which sported a day's worth of growth. Apparently, my decision to leave had struck him so powerfully that he hadn't even bothered to shave before hurrying to the station.

How un-British of him!

"I suppose nurses *are* always needed," he admitted. "But Lucy, dear, you're not... running away from anything... Are you?"

"No." I hated to lie to him, again, but...

I remained unsure whether everything I'd encountered was all in my head. In fact, I couldn't shake the lingering feeling that there *was* someone out there who wanted my blood—the blood of Dracula—for their own wicked purposes. Perhaps it really *was* Aunt Lucy...

Or maybe it was someone I didn't suspect or even *know*... yet.

In any case, it would be safer for both Quincey and my parents if I were far away from them if that ultimate destiny was, indeed, yet to come.

"I'm not running from something, I'm running *toward* it," I told him. "Toward my future—whatever that may be."

He shrugged in reluctant agreement. "Well, I hope you'll remember me... remember *us*, whenever you find it."

I kissed his stubbly cheek.

"I will. Tell Mother and Father I'll write when I can. And tell them not to worry."

He sighed. "I'll do my best, baby sister."

I threw my arms around him and hugged him tight; he returned the embrace.

"And I will, too," I promised.

We released our clench, and I mounted the steps onto the train as the conductor gave the last call.

"Take care of yourself, Lucy."

"I will," I replied as the train began to move.

Then, remembering something important, I cupped my hands to my mouth and shouted:

"Happy birthday, Johnny!"

As he receded into the distance, he smiled and waved in reply.

I smiled, too.

Perhaps birthdays weren't so bad after all.

A Study in Crimson

Derek Tyler Attico

One of the most recognized fictional heroes around the world, Sir Arthur Conan Doyle's consulting detective made his debut in 1887, going on to have 56 official short stories and four novels and countless pastiches ever since. He has been adapted for stage, screen, comics, and every other form of storytelling. His tried-and-true methods for deduction have proved influential to real-world law enforcement and generations of mystery writers.

Derek Attico is a science fiction author and essayist from New York City. He is a winner of the Excellence in Playwriting Award from the Dramatist Guild of America and a two-time winner of the *Star Trek Strange New Worlds* short story contest. Derek is also a contributing writer to the *Star Trek Adventures* role-playing game from Modiphius Entertainment. A photographer in his spare time, Derek can be found capturing images of New York City one frame, and story, at a time. He can be found @Dattico on Twitter and Instagram. For a complete bibliography, please visit www.DerekAttico.com.

A Study in Crimson

The No. 6 train raced through the Bronx along skis of steel at nearly fifty miles per hour. The rhythmic clacking and swaying of the steel car was a welcome respite from the chaos of the outside world. He'd been observing the passengers sitting across from him for almost ten minutes. Like a row of books on a shelf, the stories of their lives were like titles for novels.

The alcoholic guitarist with a penchant for pancakes. The elevator repairman who desperately wants to be an actor. The sous-chef in love with his boss. An honest, hardworking student.

In truth, they all bored him; it was only the book on the end that gave him any real interest. Despite his staring, the book hadn't looked up once; he was either deliberately avoiding eye contact or so deeply engrossed with the activity on the six-inch screen in his hand that he simply hadn't noticed.

The observer leaned forward in his seat, making sure to attract the attention of the book—the man sitting across from him.

"Change is a good thing, Doctor," he said.

Surprised, the doctor looked up from his phone. "What did you say?"

The observer, a lean, young, dark-skinned man in a black hoodie, stared back at the doctor with eyes that took in more than they revealed.

A smirk played across the young man's face, as if he knew he'd said the right words to force a conversation.

The millennial stuffed his hands into the hooded sweatshirt's pockets as he leaned back slowly in his seat, not unlike a fisherman pulling in his catch. "You, Doctor, home from Afghanistan. Looking for a new apartment, change is good."

Confusion teetering on anger played across the older man's face. "What the hell is this?"

The young man wondered if what he was starting to feel was anything like the endorphins normal people bragged about when they went to the gym.

God he hoped not.

"Chill. It's something I do when I get bored. Pick a person and tell them everything about themselves, then ask what I got right."

The older man chuckled. "Really? And how much trouble has that gotten you into?"

The observer smiled. "It's nothing I can't handle."

The doctor folded his arms. "I'm sure, okay, then by all means, dazz—"

The young man's eyes widened as he began. "—Black, accent says American who's traveled abroad. Your glasses say late thirties, so you're old, but contrary to the New Balance running shoes, don't dress that way. You wear them because they have great orthotics, something you know as a doctor, on your feet all day. But they're better than the combat boots you wore over in Afghanistan. I know that because of what I can see of the Arabic tattoo that starts on your neck. Isn't that the word for peace? You're from the Bronx. Since I've been watching, you haven't looked up once, not at any of the people getting on or off any of the stops. Why? Because you're comfortable, which means you live nearby, probably staying with a relative, which brings me to the phone in the wallet case. You haven't been texting, but pinching and zooming which means pictures, which means apartments. And from the J. Wat that I can see on your ATM card, it's really just elementary to deduce your name. Doctor. John. Watson."

The observer folded his arms, mirroring the doctor across from him. "Well?"

Doctor John Watson looked over at the smug twenty-something and felt like anything out of his mouth at this point would just be a formality. "I'm not old," he said, finally.

The young man looked at Doctor Watson, seemingly, for the first time. "You know, Doctor, a lesser man would've just lied to me." The train slowed and the observer stood as the car slid into the station. "This is me. If you're interested, I think I may have a solution for you that will be beneficial to both of us." As the train stopped and the doors opened, he walked out and turned to the doctor before they closed. "Come by 221B Baker Avenue today, the name's Sherlock Holmes."

~

Mrs. Hudson stood wide-eyed in front of the monster that took up nearly half of the living-room wall. "Sherlock, why on God's green earth do you need this?"

Unable to resist the glare he could feel now bearing down upon him, Holmes casually lifted his eyes from his book and glanced in his landlady's direction. Her dreadlocks always seemed to perfectly frame her face, especially when she was asking a question that was actually a statement. Like most prey, Holmes knew better than to stare down this particular predator and returned to what he was reading. "I need to keep an eye on things, Mrs. Hudson."

Martha Hudson turned from the young man doing his best to ignore her, and back to the monitor hanging on the wall. Nine smaller screens stuffed inside this large one, each with a live feed, and the name of a city.

Like the monitor, the two-bedroom apartment she rented to the young man had far too many things crammed in it, and was barely recognizable from when he first moved in. It was clear the young man had trouble interacting with people, and was some kind of functioning science hoarder, always bringing in some such experiment.

But looking around the controlled chaos of the living room, Mrs. Hudson reminded herself it was this young man who stopped the banks from illegally seizing her brownstone. "You've got a guest downstairs. Can't you straighten up in here sometime, Sherlock?" Without waiting for a reply, the owner of 221B Baker Avenue headed for the front door of the apartment.

Not leaving anything to chance, Sherlock spoke through the

protection of his book. "Thank you, Mrs. Hudson, please tell Doctor Watson to come up."

The front door remained open as Holmes listened to Mrs. Hudson meet Watson on the staircase, followed by an exchange of words and a very loud "Yes Ma'am" from the doctor. As Watson ascended the stairs and stood in the doorway, Sherlock finally lowered the cover of his reading material. "Your IED injury is barely noticeable, Doctor, I imagine a testament to your discipline and physical therapy regimen!"

John Watson realized his mouth was open only as he began to speak. "What? How could you possibly—"

Sherlock didn't bother waiting for the end of the doctor's sentence. "On the stairs, your gait is ever so slightly off on your right side. Conclusion, injury, most common leg injury in Afghanistan..."

Watson completed the sentence with a look of wonder on his face. "...IED." The doctor smiled. "You know, on the train, I thought what you did was some kind of trick or something. I came here to prove myself right, but now I see it's just, well, genius."

Holmes stood and walked over to Watson. "Actually, Doctor, it's rather elementary. I see what everyone else does, but I pay attention." Holmes looked around the apartment. "On the train I told you about a solution to your problem that could be beneficial to—'

To Sherlock's surprise he was now being interrupted, something it was clear he wasn't used to experiencing.

Watson chuckled. "—Mrs. Hudson already explained it to me on the staircase. When she learned I'm a doctor, she offered me the second bedroom. Said she needed some normalcy around here." Watson extended his hand. "It's a little messy, but for half of what she's charging you in a gentrified Bronx neighborhood, I can live with it. One question: what made you offer it to me?"

Sherlock took the doctor's hand. "I read people every day, Doctor, but your story was interesting, and you were honest; that's a hard combination to come by."

John Watson smiled as he looked around the room. "Thanks. So this thing you do, is it how you earn a living or do you have a day job?"

Before Holmes could answer, both men turned towards the door and the sound of someone coming up the stairs. Sherlock walked across the room to the window. Shifting aside a blade from the vertical blinds, he looked onto the street below. "I'm an investigator of sorts, and on occasion, like today, a consultant for the New York Police Department." Turning back to the door, Holmes spoke an instant before it opened. "Hello, Inspector Lestrade."

The cheap suit and rubber-soled shoes wasn't what revealed that Joseph Lestrade was a detective; his face wore his profession. Lestrade's gray eyes told the tale of a man who had been changed by the horrors he'd seen and was trying to hold onto what little humanity he had left.

John Watson didn't need Holmes' special ability; he recognized the look because it was the same one he woke up with every day since Afghanistan. But as he looked at what was obviously a seasoned police detective, he realized it was more than that.

Lestrade was nervous.

The cop glanced from Holmes to Watson and back again before speaking. "We've got a bad one. I can't explain it. You need to come with me, see for yourself."

Sherlock eyed Lestrade as he put on his hoodie. "You know I won't ride in the back of your vehicle, detective. We'll call a car and follow you."

Lestrade and Watson both looked at Holmes. The NYPD detective shook his head before he spoke. "We? No. The courtesy I extend to you, Holmes, doesn't cover anyone else, period."

Sherlock walked over to his chair and sat, crossing his legs. "Doctor Watson is someone who can assist me and won't second-guess everything I do."

Lestrade stiffened after an uneasy moment of silence. "Fine," was all he said. The detective turned without making eye contact with Holmes or Watson as he walked out the door. "I'll be downstairs, don't be long," he mumbled.

Watson turned to Holmes "So you work with the NYPD and you want me to assist you, doing what exactly?"

The young man pulled out a smart phone and tapped on the screen. "You'll see when we get there; ride will be here in five minutes." Holmes ended the call and put the phone in his back pocket as he returned to the window.

Watson walked over to Holmes; both men stared through the blinds

315

watching Lestrade argue with someone on his phone. "See what?" Watson asked.

Holmes watched Lestrade on the sidewalk pushing against the confines of his rank, explaining to his boss why they needed to give a black guy and his assistant unfettered access into a crime scene. "See what has Lestrade so scared he gave me what I wanted."

~

The elevated subway station at 161st Street in the Bronx on River Avenue was synonymous with history, New York and, most importantly, baseball. But now it was the one thing it had never been since becoming the stop for Yankee Stadium.

Quiet.

NYPD street blockades cordoned off not just the station, but the entire north side of the major thoroughfare. Sherlock Holmes ducked under the strip of police caution tape at the base of the station stairs that Detective Lestrade held up for him and John Watson. As the trio ascended, Holmes took notice of the HAZMAT truck parked across the street. Sherlock shot a glance to Watson, whose eyes answered that he'd seen the vehicle and had the same questions.

"So," Sherlock said to Lestrade, "whatever it is, it may be biological, but you're not sure—that's why I'm here."

This time the cop didn't bother to look at Holmes as they finally reached the train platform at the top of the stairs. "It's right down here, the last car."

The IRT 4 train rested in its slot, its smooth stainless steel cars running the length of the platform. As the three men walked towards the end, only police were on the platform, all of the train's doors were open, and the nearest cars were empty.

"What the hell happened here?" Watson said, more to himself than anyone.

Lestrade stopped just short of the last car and turned. "You've got five minutes. The Deputy Commissioner is on his way and it will be better for both of us if you're not here when he arrives." The inspector sighed before continuing. "Opening day is tomorrow at the stadium, so the clock is running on this, and yes, you're right. HAZMAT says whatever it is, they don't think it is present any longer."

Holmes noticed a few of the officers on the platform staring not at him—Sherlock Holmes the advisor who had consulted on thirty-seven cases with the NYPD. What they actually saw was a young black man in a hoodie; one cop even moved his hand down to his firearm until he saw Lestrade. Sherlock stared at the men until they looked away; only then did he continue to the last car.

Lestrade fell in line behind the two men. Watson saw people inside, sitting, standing, reading, listening to music on their headphones, holding onto grab handles, but something was strange.

None of them were moving.

Watson realized that Sherlock was silent and nearly as motionless as the flesh and blood statues in the train car as he took it in. The doctor turned to Lestrade and let out a nervous chuckle. "Is this some kind of troupe? One of those freeze flash mobs, a stunt?"

Sherlock stepped into the car, speaking to Watson over his shoulder. "This is no stunt; I fear they're all dead. Shall we, Doctor?"

John Watson walked in behind Holmes, who had a compact magnifying glass in his hand, and almost like an ophthalmologist was examining the deep-red-beyond-bloodshot eyes of a teenage boy holding onto the floor-to-ceiling pole, corded headphones snaking up from his phone and into his ears. Except for the crimson eyes, it was an ordinary snapshot of life, now frozen forever. As Sherlock moved to an elderly woman sitting next to other passengers, Watson actually allowed himself to take in the entire train car. It was the same everywhere he looked, moments of life eerily frozen and the same scarlet eyes on all the passengers.

Lestrade stood with his hands in his coat pockets at the mouth of the door. He watched as first Holmes, and then Watson, went from passenger to passenger. "About two hours ago this train went express from 125th Street in Harlem straight to here—nothing unusual about that, just alleviating congestion. We've got camera footage of people getting in and out of this car at 125th. When it arrived here, passengers on the platform alerted the motorman." The inspector looked down at his shoes. "You see why I called you… can you tell us what this is?"

Sherlock was silent.

Watson looked up from the seventh person he was examining—a man facing the closed doors on the opposite side of the car. His tinted horn-rimmed glasses resembled Watson's own pair, but that was where their similarities ended. His AC/DC t-shirt, jeans, and a leather jacket spoke of a life the doctor couldn't imagine.

Holmes' silence was deafening in the train car. As Watson watched Holmes make his way down to the end of the car, John felt a need to fill the void. "No signs of struggle on any of them. Rigor mortis has set in, but that doesn't explain the initial cause of death, or the dilated pupils, and massive subconjunctival hemorrhages around the eyes."

Watson turned to face Inspector Lestrade. "It's like they all just stopped, at exactly the same moment."

Holmes finally spoke, the tone of his voice conveying everything. "No residue, no skin discoloration or unusual odor on their clothes, not even a sign they were aware of what was happ—" Sherlock stopped mid-thought as something at the end of the car caught his eye. Holmes walked past several passengers until he came to the last passenger in the car, a woman who had her back to him.

Watson joined Sherlock; the young man appeared transfixed at the back of the woman—apparently a nurse from the scrubs she was wearing, but unlike the others something was out of place on her.

"That's a strange hat for a woman to be wearing," Watson said.

Sherlock moved slowly around the woman, almost like a machine scanning her, committing every inch to memory. He stopped in front of her; crimson eyes stared back at him. Finally, Holmes allowed himself to look up at the plaid double-flap cap. "It's called a deerstalker, what British hunters would wear when they're stalking the animal."

Sherlock noticed something on the underside of the flap above the young woman's crimson eyes. Holmes shot a glance down to the end of the car where Lestrade was talking to an officer. In a swift but gentle motion, Holmes reached under the flap and pulled off what was there, a piece of paper taped to the underside. "It's also the cap that belonged to a cartoon dog detective I used to love as a kid."

Slowly, Sherlock Holmes opened the folded note and read the message that made his blood run cold. *This is above your station. Do not interfere. Moriarty*

~

John Watson stood in the doorway of the makeshift lab that was supposed to be his bedroom. The square footage of the room was generous, but with two workstations, books, computers, and lab equipment, the room felt tiny. Watson observed as Holmes sat at one of the desks, crouching over a microscope. Holmes had said nothing on the way back to 221B Baker Avenue; he just stared at the note the entire time. "Sherlock, who is Moriarty?"

Sherlock turned a dial on the old microscope, switching lenses. "A whisper in the shadows, a criminal mastermind and my arch nemesis."

Watson let out a nervous chuckle, "People don't have nemeses, Sherlock."

Holmes looked up from the microscope, "I do; he sent me a note."

Watson stepped into the room and sat next to Holmes. "What did he do it for? Is it some kind of sick statement, or do you think he's actually going to attack Yankee Stadium tomorrow?"

Holmes returned to the microscope. "There's always a reason for what he does, but it's doubtful he'll attack the stadium. I think Moriarty killed a train car full of people to eliminate one person. The question is why and which one? Lestrade sent over their information, but that's thirty-six identities to comb through. There's not enough time."

John Watson didn't bother hiding the disgust on his face. "That's horrific. Have you ever met Moriarty?"

Sherlock glanced up at his new friend before returning to his work. "No. I only learned about him recently through some exploits I stopped. I'm looking forward to meeting him and putting him away forever."

Watson watched Holmes move the note from the microscope to some sort of computer scanner. Once he closed the scanner lid, the monitor next to them magnified the image. The dark ink on the note looked like grooves carved into the side of a mountain. "Sherlock, the

Turning the Tied

person he was after, it's got to be the nurse. She had the note!"

Holmes shook his head dismissively. "It's too obvious, but she did work at a hospital, near Grand Central Terminal." Sherlock looked over at the monitor and smiled. "This parchment is sold exclusively, in person, from only two places in the world. Waterloo station in London, and… Watson?"

The doctor smiled. "Grand Central Terminal."

Sherlock pulled out his phone and ordered a car. Then he texted what he'd discovered to Inspector Lestrade. "This is a lot to take in, and will almost certainly be dangerous. I'd understand if you don't want to assist me."

Watson smiled. "It's nothing I can't handle. But we need to make a quick stop on the way."

∼

As the town car turned onto the FDR drive, John Watson felt the added weight of the SIG Sauer P226 standard under his left arm, resting in the holster he was now wearing after making a stop at his brother's apartment. The weapon felt light in comparison to what he was feeling, and the inevitability he and Sherlock were racing towards. "All those people in that train car. I can't stop thinking about the guy with the glasses like mine, just gone."

Sherlock turned to Watson. "What did you say?"

The doctor frowned in slight confusion, and then repeated, "All those people—"

Holmes interrupted Watson, seemingly unaware he'd done so. "His glasses were coated with UV light sensitivity, that's why they were tinted inside the train car."

Sherlock took out his phone and typed furiously.

Watson shook his head. "Right, makes sense, nearly all glasses have that—"

Without looking up, Holmes interrupted again. "Then why were his pupils dilated like all the rest? With the tinting, the pupils should have been constricted; even after death he should've had a lesser dilation than the others. But he didn't, and that's because he didn't have them on when he was killed. That's why Moriarty didn't take them with him; he knew I'd catch that detail, so he left them. Clever."

Watson opened his mouth to give a response, closed it, opened it again. He finally asked the only question he could think of. "Do you know how they were killed?"

Sherlock smiled. "Catch up, doctor, I've had a working theory for some time. This only verifies it and that we're going in the wrong direction. The game is afoot!"

~

Like most apartment buildings in the Bronx, there was no elevator. The building's gray walls and black tiled floor made Watson feel like he and Sherlock were mice in a maze. At three in the morning the six-story walk up was quiet, with only the occasional sounds of life as the two men crept past apartments.

Watson held his firearm down at his side, while Holmes held his phone in much the same manner. "We should've told Lestrade to meet us here," the doctor whispered.

Sherlock shook his head. "And tell him what exactly? We've come back to the Bronx, to 161st Street and Third Avenue to investigate Alex Drebber, one of the victims? No, they're where they need to be, where Moriarty wants them, and expects me to be."

Watson wasn't sure he liked the grin on Holmes's face; it was as if the man was treating this as some kind of personal chess match.

Sherlock stopped in front of one of the apartments, looked at his phone and then gently listened at the door. "Here it is, apartment 6C, Alex Drebber, 38, divorced. I don't hear anything," Holmes whispered.

John Watson watched Holmes put his phone in his back pocket and pull a thin pouch out of his front pocket. Taking tools out of the pouch, he worked on the door.

Watson looked down both ends of the hallway, "What are you doing?"

Sherlock looked up at the doctor as the lock clicked. "Knocking."

As Sherlock put away his tools, John raised the gun and stepped into the darkened apartment. Somewhere, very far away, Watson heard the voice of his friend shouting something.

But it was too late.

The apartment erupted into a series of white-hot flashes of light. The doctor tried to move, but to his amazement realized he couldn't, and then he realized something else.

He wasn't breathing.

It wasn't like he was holding his breath; he knew he wasn't, but it was as if his body had forgotten how to breathe. Forgotten everything. He felt the tension in his muscles with no way to alleviate it. Sherlock was in front of him now, screaming something, but Watson felt like he was deep underwater, drowning within his own body. The doctor wanted to scream, or cry, do anything that would break him free of whatever he was in so he wouldn't die like the others, all those people.

Just gone.

Doctor Watson knew the only mercy of this moment would be the unconsciousness that was pushing in all around him and darkening his vision. He glimpsed a shadow that his sluggish mind told him was Sherlock; the man held something in front of his face.

Light.

But not in uneven quick flashes like before; these were in a steady, rhythmic pulse. And almost without realizing it, John Watson blinked. Suddenly his body remembered how to breathe, and the lungs that were on fire were now taking in the precious oxygen that was denied them just a few moments ago.

Gasping, Watson dropped to his knees. "Wh-what the hell was that?"

Holmes bent down to help his friend up. "That, Doctor, was genius!"

Still breathless, Watson looked at Holmes. "What?"

Sherlock paced like an excited child on Christmas, stopped and looked at Watson with pity. "My apologies, Doctor, I'll go as slow as I can. Now, just like certain patterns of light trigger the brain and cause seizures, Moriarty has found a pattern of light to trigger a neural response and short-circuit the brain and nervous system. Do you see?"

Watson nodded. His eyes felt on fire. "That's why I couldn't move and what caused the people on the train to all have the hemorrhaging around the eyes. But, how did you bring me back?"

Holmes smiled. "That, dear doctor, is the best part. I deduced that while your optic nerves and brain were still functioning, a slower rhythmic pattern of lights could restore normal brain function, and in effect restart you. Another few seconds and nothing would have helped."

Watson didn't know if he should be dismayed by the glee on Holmes's face, or thankful that the man had saved his life. "Thanks."

The doctor looked around the darkened room; even with the available moonlight from outside pouring in, it was clear the apartment was empty. "I never thought I'd hear myself say this, but it looks like this was a trap."

Sherlock walked over to the bare living room window. "Not necessarily, Doctor. Sometimes the absence of a thing defines what it is. Before Drebber was divorced, he was a career roadie specializing in stage lighting for bands. Then seven months ago he takes this apartment. Why?"

Watson stepped to the window to see what Holmes was looking at. He followed the detective's gaze across the street. A Con Edison power truck was parked out in front of a piece of history. "The Old Bronx Borough Courthouse? That building's been an eyesore in the Bronx for over forty years and still no one can figure out what to do with it. You're saying all this, the train car, the deaths, is about that?"

Holmes stared down at the building.

Like everyone else who lived in the Bronx, they knew the abandoned building had become invisible in plain sight. Completed in 1914, constructed out of granite, with two massive pillars above the entrance and between them, Lady Justice, holding a scale and a snake. The old IRT Third Avenue elevated line used to run right in front of it, and now even at night in its dilapidated state the structure still seemed majestic. "We're about to find out, Doctor."

∼

Holmes and Watson stayed in the shadows as they viewed the Con Ed power truck. Orange cones and floodlights highlighted the hole in the ground where the power crew would work.

Two men were in the van.

Watson chuckled. "Sherlock, I'm telling you this isn't it. They've been working on replacing powerlines for this building for years."

Holmes motioned with his chin across the street. "Look at the workers."

Watson watched the two workers in the van from the energy company, and then it hit him.

They weren't moving.

"Time to go, Watson!" Holmes got up and ran across the street. Startled, Watson followed just in time to see Sherlock drop into the pit where the crew worked. Taking out his weapon and thumbing off the safety, Watson followed.

Under the asphalt of the street, the doctor didn't know what he expected to see, but it wasn't this. Inside the pit, the powerlines looked real, but now up close he could see they weren't, and there was something else.

A door, ajar.

Watson used his firearm to slowly open the metal door that was seemingly built into the fake pit. As he stepped through in near darkness, Sherlock held a finger to his lips. Next to him was a man wearing a windbreaker jacket. The man, like the victims in the train car and the van above, was frozen, another statue that wouldn't reveal its secrets, but still foretold dread. Watson's eyes narrowed as he saw the unmistakable symbol on the windbreaker, the seal of the Department of the Treasury.

The frozen federal agent was reaching for a weapon that no longer resided in his holster. Sherlock turned his phone to face Watson, so the doctor could see he had just texted Lestrade with a picture of the treasury agent and the address.

Silently, Holmes and Watson stepped past the agent into a hallway with a long corridor; at its end was a dimly lit room. Voices reverberated off the walls from up ahead. Holmes whispered: "If we move slowly we shou—"

Watson turned to see why Sherlock had stopped speaking, and then he understood. There was a gun pointed at the base of Holmes' skull, and another into his neck.

A voice slipped out of the darkness from behind the two men. "Slowly, drop the gun and the phone and raise your hands or I'll shoot."

As both men dropped what they had and raised their hands, Holmes spoke. "Moriarty?"

A soft chuckle slipped from the shadows. "Walk down the hall, Mr. Holmes; he's expecting you."

Sherlock caught Watson's gaze but remained silent. Cautiously, Holmes padded forward.

The voice from behind Watson reached out again. "Turn around."

Watson turned, and as he did he could see his friend was nearly at his destination. As the doctor faced the voice, even though he couldn't see the face, he realized his error.

"You've been at this for a day, Doctor; you really should have checked my eyes," the shadow taunted.

"Thanks for the tip," Watson replied.

The two firearms pushed out of the darkness and into the doctor's face. "Your turn now, down the hall."

As Watson moved slowly down the hallway, he felt the heat bleeding off of the concrete walls that were beginning to feel more and more like a tomb. The voices up ahead were getting louder; one was clearly Sherlock, and then suddenly, the room was bathed in a series of flashing lights, followed by a single gunshot.

"Sherlock!" Without thinking, Watson took off down the hall. He heard the steps of the faux-agent behind him. As he entered the lit room, cool, crisp air washed over him. Four rows of computers ran the length of the room. Several statues of real treasury agents stood, and another lay on the ground, a gunshot in the chest.

Sherlock Holmes was nowhere to be seen.

Watson turned to the faux-agent. "Where is he?"

The faux-agent was about to speak when another shot rang out and he slumped to the floor, dead. Watson turned to see a hooded figure standing in front of him.

"Change is a good thing, Doctor. Isn't that what you always said?" The British accent and smile from the hooded young man told John Watson who was speaking.

"Professor Moriarty," Watson said with disgust. "I told myself this couldn't be you, that it was one of your sycophants, that I'd buried you."

Moriarty stepped up and lowered the hood. While it was the face of

Sherlock Holmes, nothing in it resembled Sherlock Holmes. "It certainly isn't from your lack of trying, doctor. Took me two years just to influence him, and another to orchestrate this while he slept!"

Watson was horrified. "That's not possible. I took steps to keep you contained, and to ensure Sherlock didn't remember me."

Moriarty laughed. "I'd forgotten just how slow you are. Did you think meeting you on the train was just a happy accident? He may not remember you, but I do. I discovered certain patterns of light could help break down the barriers that kept me caged. Imagine my surprise when I found the pattern to kill in such a melodramatic way."

Watson looked around the room. "And this place?"

Moriarty walked around Watson. "Oh, I knew about this place long before you became my therapist, doctor. After 9/11 someone thought it would be smart to hide the computers that held all of the nation's wealth in one of the poorest boroughs. The World Trade Center is just show. The real money is in the Bronx, here in this data center, so I thought I'd help myself."

The doctor watched his former patient; there was very little of the person he once called a friend. "The things you'd done, you've always been brilliant, but I saw you capable of great kindness and incredible cruelty. We decided on this together, that's why it worked. Sherlock Holmes is a good man, Professor."

Moriarty put his gun to Watson's head. "Sherlock Holmes is a work of fiction! His name comes from a cartoon I watched as a child! He's the figment, not me!" Moriarty cocked the hammer on the pistol. "Here, let me show you what it's like to become a memory!"

As Moriarty started to squeeze the trigger, Watson spoke. "Reichenbach Falls."

Like the statues of flesh and blood he'd created, Moriarty's hand froze. "What is this? What did you do to me?"

Doctor Watson stepped to the side and out of the path of the weapon. "Consider this my insurance, Professor, a last resort that can only be used once. Reichenbach Falls."

Now the young man's entire body stiffened as if invisible strings were repositioning him. "Everything I've done since you made me like this is on you. All of it! You better pray I don't get out again, because I'll make this seem trivial! I'll burn the world, John! Do you hear me? I'll burn it all down and it will be on you!"

John Watson looked at his friend, not with anger, but pity. "You're right, this is on me, and if I have to, I'll spend my life making sure neither I nor Sherlock Holmes ever see you again. Reichenbach Falls."

Inexplicably, the anger and hatred in the young man's face melted. Sherlock Holmes looked around, uncertain at first, and then smiled at the sight of his friend. "Is Moriarty gone?"

The question surprised Watson. "Wh-what do you mean, Sherlock?"

Sherlock Holmes lowered the firearm he was holding, then after a moment of thought handed it to Watson, butt first. "Once you eliminate the impossible, whatever remains, however improbable, must be the truth."

Legacy

Robert Greenberger

Guy Boothby (1867-1905) was an Australian writer known for his sensationalistic genre fiction. Among his prolific works was a series featuring Dr. Nikola, an archetypical supervillain complete with a pet cat as his companion. These exploits were initially serialized in *The Windsor Magazine* and subsequently collected into five novels. By the fifth book, he seemed to have achieved his goals and shifted from villain to anti-hero. A contemporary of Prof. Moriarty, Dr. Nikola was a brilliant man searching the Orient for the secret of immortality, which made him a bit of a cross between Sherlock Holmes' nemesis and Dr. Fu Manchu (a debt Sax Rohmer acknowledged).

Robert Greenberger is a prolific writer of media tie-in fiction since his first novel, *Star Trek: The Next Generation: The Romulan Stratagem* in 1990. Since then he has happily played in the *Star Trek* sandbox (even editing the DC Comics version for eight years). His other tie-in works include *After Earth*, *Batman*, *Captain America*, *Captain Midnight*, the *Green Hornet*, *Hellboy*, *Iron Man*, *Planet of the Apes*, *Predator*, *Scooby-Doo*, *Sherlock Holmes*, and *Zorro*. He has also written numerous essays and books on pop culture in addition to original fiction. A member of the IAMTW, he won the Scribe Award for his novelization of *Hellboy II: The Golden Army*. He's a cofounder of Crazy 8 Press, which publishes original works. Bob has worked for DC Comics, Starlog Press, Marvel Comics, Gist Communications, and *Weekly World News*. Currently, he lives and works as a high school English teacher in Maryland. For more, find him at www.bobgreenberger.com.

Legacy

THE INVITATION ARRIVED THE OLD-FASHIONED WAY: IT WAS HAND-delivered by a uniformed messenger. The paper was cream-colored and thick, the penmanship on the envelope, exquisite. In dark blue ink, clearly from a fountain pen, I was being invited to dine with the sender, described only as an old family friend. The date and time for the meeting was all that was added.

Looking back, everything seemed so innocent, but now, reflecting on the account of the past few days, I wonder if I was just being naïve.

Seated at my desk at the *Daily News*, I examined the missive. No return address, no clue as to the sender. As I held the paper to the light, searching in vain for a watermark or a clue, passersby jibed at me for the hoity-toity invitation. Hoping I had my curtsy ready for my host. This clearly had to be from my hoped-for celebrity crush or maybe one of the millionaires I recently wrote about during my five years working the business beat. Any of it, all of it, or none of it could have been the answer. Obviously I had to accept, if only to resolve the mystery, and I hoped this would lead to a big story. I needed something to work with, but my would-be host had definitely covered his or her tracks. The messenger's uniform bore no logos and seemed generic. That in itself suggested that my future host was taking great pains not to be easily discovered.

The restaurant chosen was a relatively new, upscale gastronomic establishment called simply Jack's. I'd heard about it, but couldn't afford the bill even if I was interested in this sort of fare. I am a proud meat and potatoes man, maybe with a side of vegetables if my fiancée Lilly was on hand. At least I knew how to dress for the occasion without prompting; donning a freshly pressed navy blue suit, crisp white shirt, and a red and blue striped tie. To top off the look, I shaved carefully that morning; even sprang for five bucks to have my shoes properly shined. Without knowing the purpose of the meeting, I needed to be ready for everything from a prospective job offer to an exclusive interview about something wonderful.

Making certain to arrive in the Battery early, I looked about, but nothing raised an alarm. No private security, no surveillance vehicles. Okay, so the President was not my sender. I could live with it, since he was of the other party. When I gave the hostess my name, it turned out that my host was even earlier. The hostess, a lovely young woman in a white shirt and bow tie, black slacks and high heels, escorted me to the rear of the restaurant, which overlooked the Hudson River and Statue of Liberty, a magnificent view on this lush, early summer's night. My host rose as we approached and I flushed with a dash of disappointment at not recognizing the figure. The man was only slightly above average height, and his slight build suggested nothing about his background. The jet-black hair was brushed to the side in a contemporary style, somehow nicely framing his oval face. The complexion was pallid, almost ghostly. Albino? No. The almost-white skin made his black eyes stand out. Even from a distance I felt their gaze, which held an uncanny power. We locked eyes and at that instant the man broke into a smile, showing perfect, pearly white teeth.

The man was easily eighty if not older; it was hard to discern. While I looked my best, even Lilly agreed, I was easily outdone by the bespoke charcoal-gray evening suit, the white shirt open at the throat with an anachronistic red cravat. On one hand was a gold ring, shaped like a snake circling the ring finger.

The hostess pulled out my chair, but she only had eyes for the man, who nodded in thanks but mostly ignored her. There had to be fifty years between them, but if he asked, I am sure she would have accompanied him home. He didn't seem to notice.

"Ah, Hatteras, so glad you accepted my invitation. I would hate to dine alone," he said by way of greeting. He did not offer to shake hands so I let it alone; old men could be eccentric.

"Well, one doesn't receive mysterious invitations to dinner every day," I replied. "How could I not show up, if only to find out who invited me. And you are…"

"An old friend of your great-grandparents," he said. I felt my jaw drop open. Of course, I had never met my great-grandparents, and knew little about them, other than some wild stories told at holiday gatherings. In fact, those fantastic stories, told by grandparents as I grew up, had lingered with me. As a result, I had only recently begun researching the lives of Richard and Phyllis Hatteras for a possible book. This man was clearly too young to have ever met them.

"My name is Antonio Nikola; does that perhaps ring a bell? Please, let us sit."

Nikola. I *knew* the name. Several of those stories I knew involved my ancestors and a man with that name. The tales sounded like the stuff of dime novels, and I had started my research with that period of their lives. Could he be a namesake?

Nikola had been sipping at his water and I could tell this was a man of refined habits and character, making me feel like a country bumpkin despite wearing my Sunday best.

"You were not raised on the stories of the encounters your great-grandfather Richard had with me over the years? We crossed paths on numerous occasions and I had the pleasure of getting to know your great-grandmother, the former Phyllis Wetherell."

"Bullshit. That could not possibly be you," I blurted, feeling like a neanderthal compared to this refined gentlemen. My outburst was met with a polite chuckle, and I reddened with sudden shame.

"What have you heard?" he prompted.

Before I could dredge up the ancient tales, a waiter came to discuss the specials of the day. Nikola politely interrupted him, ordered a salad and coffee, and then ordered for me, the closest thing they had to a meat and potatoes entrée. He would only have done that if he had studied me before sending the invitation. This man was cautious, prepared, and that

333

got me concerned as to his intentions.

"Nikola kidnapped my great-grandmother," I said, carefully keeping my voice low. "My great-grandfather rescued her. They also had other encounters, the last in Venice. Nikola left quite an impression on both of them. The man was powerful and feared, said to be searching Asia for the secret of immortality. A madman seeking world domination, long before Hitler and Stalin."

"Horrible men," my host said, his eyes clouding over. "They lusted for power with no purpose. Too many needless deaths."

"But you couldn't be him," I repeated. Then the stories I had just mentioned clarified in my mind; the fantastic stories told after too much wine at holiday meals came back to me. "I was told Nikola found the formula but it didn't work."

The man calling himself Nikola was already sitting perfectly straight but seemed to gain in stature. A slight smile crossed his face. "Not as I had hoped."

"It can't be," I said. "Prove it."

"When Phyllis Wetherell married Richard Hatteras, I presented her with a collet of diamonds. I believe you gave the ring to Lilly Martindale for your engagement."

If my jaw had dropped before, now it should have hit the table. No one but my family knew about the ring and its history. I'd been handed this by my own mother when she was terminal, telling me it was to be passed on to the next generation. She'd had it and I knew it belonged to Great-Grandma and that it was a precious gift, somehow mixed up with her adventures.

"You don't believe me? Shall I describe it to you?"

I shook my head as reality was being beaten down by the surrealist nature of this conversation. While speaking with a near-immortal was newsworthy, this had become far more personal and I needed to know *everything*.

"You kidnapped her?"

"It was an expeditious act, to coerce Richard to work with me. I assure you; she was well treated."

His manner, his poise seemed completely unruffled, but there was now a faraway look in his dark eyes. Then, with a blink, he returned his intense focus on me. I could feel its penetrating, evaluating gaze. He'd make a great mesmerist at a carnival.

"What do you want?" I asked.

"I have led a long, long life," he began, and I could hear the years in his voice. "I sought immortality and paid a heavy price. It had to be done—as did the other things I worked on during your great-grandparents' lives. It's been a solitary existence, one I was born to and accepted. But when I learned of your investigations into your past..."

"How on earth could you know?" I asked. Before he could answer, my entrée arrived as did his salad and coffee. After thanking the waiter, he reached into a pocket and removed something, a packet of some sort. He sprinkled it into the steaming china cup, stirred just once and took a sip.

"Ah, Dominic—may I use your Christian name?—I could not let anyone realize I was still among you. There would be questions and intrusions, people interfering in my affairs which were mine alone. To protect my privacy, I set up tripwires, alerts to anyone prying into my past life. Since you were looking into Richard Hatteras' actions, I was informed."

"Something to hide," I asked around a forkful of the most amazing prime rib I think I had ever experienced.

"Nothing of the sort—in the conventional sense."

"Okay, the unconventional sense."

"Then, yes. What have you learned?" he prompted.

"Tibet. I guess you found your formula." A nod, then silence. "Something else—about experiments on animals and... humans?"

He nodded solemnly, sipping his coffee and ignoring the salad.

"When you are finished, unless you desire dessert, we should go. I have things to show you and your fiancée."

That caught me up short. It was one thing to involve me in old family business, but what rumors and gossip I uncovered about Nikola got me concerned. He was once the most feared man on the planet. His name, I gather, was said in whispers only, and just mentioning that name would open doors or send threats into the night. But, as I had combed through public records from Scotland Yard, INTERPOL, and even the *Direction générale de la sécurité extérieure*, there was a great deal of fear about Nikola, but never concrete actions ascribed to him. It seemed the very idea of him was enough. His handful of encounters with my family seemed to be among the few interactions of which his direct involvement is recorded.

Everything else was rumor and innuendo. He was as much a fiction as the pulp magazine villains I had heard about.

"Nothing to worry about," he assured me, breaking my concentration. "I have arranged a car service to collect Ms. Martindale and have her join us at my, heh, lair."

Lilly had said nothing to me, unless it had all happened between my leaving the apartment and coming here. I retrieved my cellphone, but there were no messages from her in any mode. I wanted to think that meant she was safe, but the more I sat here, the more anxious I began to feel.

We said little else as he impatiently waited for me to eat my meal, which I now rushed, spoiling the exquisitely prepared meat. And as tempting as dessert looked on the menu card, I recognized it was time to go. He rose, not even bothering to arrange payment, and we walked out with just a polite nod of thanks from the hostess. His mesmerizing way seemed to affect all within his presence. I recalled a comment during one of the many retellings of Great-Grandma Phyllis' experiences. She described Nikola as having this hypnotic power, similar to the way Bela Lugosi's Dracula seemed to hold sway over people in the old black and white films.

A limousine awaited us, and the uniformed chauffeur, again with no telltale marks, drove us from the restaurant. Nikola seemed weary, so I left him alone in silence as my mind raced with questions, along with a rising fear of what lay before us that required both me and Lilly. The city passed by; its vibrant nature evident even this late at night along the FDR Drive. The drive was brief, less than fifteen minutes, and we stopped at State Street, in a section I'd never been to before. Beyond us lay the East River and a spit of an island I didn't know.

A small yet elegant boat with a pilot was awaiting us, its engine purring against the street traffic. There were just two figures I could make out; one was the pilot, the other was unmistakably Lilly. I quickened my pace to reach her, but forgot my host was not a spry man and so forced myself to slow down. After all, she didn't seem to be in any danger, not that I could shake the fear from my mind.

Once we were aboard, Lilly threw her arms around me in a hug, then turned to regard our host. Nikola, for his part, smiled at her and then performed the formal introduction. I gave her a quizzical look, and she explained how an invitation matching the one I had earlier received, invited her to join us here.

"What's out there?" she asked Nikola.

As the boat got under way, he said, "That is Mill Rock. To the common man, it is uninhabited, except for the variety of bird life that have used it for their nesting grounds. The island used to be Great Mill Rock and Little Mill Rock, with the former hosting blockhouses to defend America from the British during the War of 1812. When nearby Flood Rock was destroyed to clear shipping lanes, the rubble was transported here to join the two islands and form Mill Rock."

I'd been born and raised in the city and knew none of this, and yet I knew Nikola was widely traveled and wasn't known for spending much time in any one place. Stories told of him living out of a suitcase, the most itinerant international criminal I'd ever read about.

"So, why are we here?" I asked.

"The reporter is ever anxious for his facts, eh?" Nikola asked, a touch of amusement in his voice. "Shortly, Dominic." Lilly and I shared glances and she appeared as mystified as I was, but there was also a gleam of excitement in her eye. That sure beat being terrified.

Once we docked, the pilot helped the three of us onto the shore. A little used, unlit path was all I could make out, leading to two small, low structures. The light pollution of Manhattan helped guide us, but he walked with slow, steady steps. Lilly held on to my arm, as curious as I was, but I suspected I was the more concerned of us. She'd always been the more fearless half of the couple, suggesting outings like skydiving and bungie jumping, which I reluctantly indulged her in.

He withdrew a ring of keys, which I had never heard jingle once in his pockets, and unlocked the door of the nearest structure. As we entered, he threw light switches and the place came to life. It was a tastefully furnished living space with dark oak furniture and overstuffed couches that possibly cost more than my starting salary at the *News*.

"Make yourselves comfortable, I will be right back," he said.

We took seats, letting him dictate the pace of the evening. He withdrew into a back room and as he did, out came a large black cat with a single pure white streak running along his right side. Following the cat was a tall, broad man in dark clothing. He had a severe haircut making

337

him look ex-military, borne out by his gait and mannerisms. Stiffly he inquired if either of us wanted a drink, but we both declined. He nodded and withdrew. The cat settled itself at Lilly's feet, languidly licking a paw.

"I see you've met Apollyon," Nikola said as he emerged from the rear. The suit was gone, replaced with a different sort of evening attire, formal, but less so than the previous outfit. This time he was in Navy blue, still with the scarlet cravat.

"Follow me if you will," he said and began moving to the opposite side of the small building. We followed. I was dying of curiosity, which I admit was outweighing my sense of dread.

We crossed to the second building, which the servant (butler? bodyguard?) had already unlocked and lit up. It was a laboratory. There were shelves with expensive equipment I didn't recognize: microscopes, large flat-screen displays (showing he had kept up with the times), beakers, test tubes, centrifugal force machines, and more. Everything was gleaming and well-maintained. There were swinging double doors that led to a space in the back, and beyond that I heard sounds. They were cries and babbling, but not human. No, I recognized these sounds from visits to the Central Park Zoo. He had animals back there, so I had to conclude the experiments he was performing more than a hundred years before (and I can't believe I am accepting this as fact) had continued.

"You have only begun to come across accounts of my colorful past," he began, standing near one wall. "You also have only heard snatches of my history with your ancestors. They have no doubt been altered through the telling, omitting details. Your great-grandparents never kept formal journals or diaries. That in itself will inhibit your research, I'm afraid to say. In fact, they were circumspect in what they told law enforcement about our meetings, for which I was grateful.

"The last thing your great-grandfather said to me showed he was a far more astute judge of character than I credited him. His words, which I committed to memory, were: 'The life you lead is so unlike that of any other man. You see only the worst side of human nature. Why not leave this terrible gloom? Give up these experiments in which you are always engaged, and live only in the pure air of the commonplace everyday world. Your very surroundings—this house, for instance—are not like those of other men. Believe me, there are other things worth living for besides the science which binds you in its chains'."

We listened intently, hoping he'd get to the point soon, Clearly, Great-Grandpa was a more patient man than I was.

"He never truly grasped why I did what I did. Why I sacrificed much to access the monastery and obtain the elixir of immortality. Why I risked being chased by Quong Ma, the killer. I did it to buy myself time."

"Time for what?" Lilly asked, but he held up a hand that silenced her. It was his story and he would tell it his way.

"The nineteenth century was not a pleasant time for mankind. Country after country enslaved others, imperialism ruled the world. Countless lives were lost to slavery and war. You know of just your Civil War, which was bloody enough, but the battles were worldwide. The drive to have deadlier weapons fueled industry. We had already begun polluting our air with the so-called industrial revolution, but the befouling accelerated as scientists began to harness physics, building steam engines, then railroads. Mass communication united countries in ways heretofore unimagined. But the costs were ignored, the price of doing business, as people describe self-destruction today.

"But, my dear Hatteras, I was born with a superior intellect. I trained my mind in ways unlike my contemporaries. As a result, I gave myself a far more comprehensive understanding of global politics along with global destruction. My studies led me to conclude that at the rate we were clouding the air over cities, letting the poorest dwell in squalor, and consuming resources at ever-increasing rates, we were headed for a reckoning. The chase of wealth or domination made everyone in the 'civilized' world ignore the damage being done.

"I saw it coming. I calculated the death of the Earth and was horrified at the result, because a normal lifespan would not be enough to effect changes to save humanity. I sought immortality to have the time I needed to save us all."

The speech made him weary and he paused.

I gestured around the lab and asked, "What about the experiments?"

"Mutations and a growing number of malformed humans suggested we were already affecting our development. I made a detailed examination of mankind's monstrosities. I took a keen interest in men like Joseph Merrick and the writings of Darwin and Moreau. I traveled the world in search of information and possible next steps.

"My experiments, Dominic, were to find a way to guide man toward a state that would allow him to thrive when the temperatures grew too hot, the clean water too scarce. I had to start on animals, that's what your ancestors knew about, but not the why. A good judge of character, Richard was, but not a big-picture thinker," Nikola admitted.

"Things have accelerated beyond even my projections, a rare lapse. A recent example to show this is not all in the past: *Fritillaria delavayi*, an herb grown in the Hengdun Mountains of China, has adapted, replacing its green and yellow flowers with gray and brown leaves to protect itself from being harvested into extinction. The planet is trying to protect itself from us, and I fear will lose that race."

"That's a lot to take in," Lilly said, speaking for the two of us. If I could spell that herb, I could verify the information like a good reporter should, but somehow I trusted his word. There was a sincerity mixed in with the authority in his voice.

"When you began investigating your past, and I learned of it, I was reminded of why I was doing all this. I was lost in my studies, living in my laboratories around the world, gathering evidence, watching how global warming had changed migratory patterns, made animals smaller, wiped out thousands of species. Scientists warn of a tipping point, but I conclude we're past that and the time has come to change."

"All by yourself, that's a horribly lonely life," Lilly said.

"I was destined to always be lonely. And my intellect was so unique that I could never find peers. Yes, there have been many brilliant thinkers during the decades, but their interests and mine never coincided. No, Ms. Martindale…"

"Lilly."

"Lilly. No, Lilly, it was always going to be just me. What I also realized was that the thing I warned Dominic's ancestors about was coming to pass. One of the last things I said to Richard was, 'The time is not far distant when I must leave the world! When that hour arrives, there is a lonely monastery in a range of eastern mountains upon which no Englishman has ever set his foot. Of that monastery I shall become an inmate. No one outside its walls shall ever look upon my face again.

There I shall work out my destiny, and, if I have sinned, be sure I shall receive my punishment at those hands that alone can bestow it'. When the elixir rapidly aged my body, I thought my time was over. But I endured, not an immortal, but someone with an extended life. This body has reached it limit, and it is time to permanently withdraw from human affairs, my work incomplete.

"I don't believe in fate, Lilly, but my failing body and Dominic's explorations seem to have dovetailed."

I was absorbing and processing the information, and a part of me imagined the kinds of stories this would lead to. But there was also the more immediate need to understand more about Nikola.

"I'll accept that, Nikola, but why reveal yourself to me? If your time to leave is coming, then leave your notes with someone appropriate."

"There is no one else!" he said, his voice louder than before, the closest to a true sign of emotion he had revealed.

"There are notes, right?" Lilly asked, taking a step closer, putting a comforting hand on his forearm, It rested there for a moment before the cat protectively hissed at her. Nikola bent and picked him up, petting him to calm him.

"Richard was right in that I saw the worst in humanity. It has grown worse with every passing generation. Those working along parallel lines of study are dwarfed by authoritarians and charlatans who can't think beyond power. As I travel the globe, collecting specimens, I have also looked for the right person, the right institution to bequeath my work."

"So what, you will take all this with you to the monastery and leave us twisting in the wind?"

"I would not have worked all these years just for that, Dominic. No, I have made discoveries and wanted to make a proposal. As you now understand, my knowledge is the ideal blending of the Western rationalism to the Eastern esotericism. My studies are unique as a result. The elixir was flawed, hence my current appearance. But I have managed to correct the imbalances."

"You've developed an immortality serum?" I asked. While that sounded bizarre to my ears, my mind recognized this fit the narrative and felt right. The word 'Pulitzer' began echoing in the back of my mind.

"If not immortality, certainly more than the lifespan I have endured."

"What about your genetic experiments?" Lilly asked, seemingly anxious to change the topic.

"Ah, there has been progress there, too. I believe I have gone beyond your CRISPR technology and can modify the next generation of humans to adapt faster to the changing world. My success rate with animals from rats to chimpanzees has been improving. I've even begun experimenting with the serum and the next generation of mankind, giving the future more time to save the world."

He fell silent, and I could see he was tiring. He really didn't have much time left, but we were brought here for a reason. Neither of us were scientists, so he wasn't going to give us all his research. I suppose if he did, I would take it to some organization to vet before going public. This would upend all other current events, and I could see how immortality would also bring out the worst in people. Yeah, I'd probably keep quiet about it.

"Yes, revealing this too soon would be a mistake," he said, seemingly reading my mind.

"You said something about an offer," Lilly prompted.

"When I learned of your investigations, Dominic, I was concerned but also took the effort to research you both. I was pleased with what I saw. You, a driven, dedicated reporter, respected by your peers. Lilly, a rising young lawyer with a nonprofit. You both speak to the goodness still left within mankind, and I think your great-grandparents would have approved. That is when I concluded I needed to bring you here, show you my work, and make you an offer.

"I have managed to customize the elixir to match both your DNA. I can bring extended life to you and your offspring. My models also show that I can make your children the harbingers of the next generation of humanity."

"What?" Lilly exclaimed, a hand reflexively protecting her womb.

"Why us?" I demanded.

"Richard and Phyllis were people of good character. They helped me when I needed it, and diamonds were a meager way to show appreciation. No, I wanted to honor their legacy. But more than that, you would understand."

"Understand what?"

"What your great-grandfather understood. I see the worst in mankind. He didn't and you don't. Your reporting has uncovered graft and greed, yes, but you have also written more about good than bad. You would understand my goals better than he would have. But this is a terrible secret to ask you to keep."

"It is," Lilly agreed. "There has to be someone to entrust this knowledge to."

"That is where I think the two of you, with more time than I now have, can find that person. Agree to take the elixir and use the time to help your fellow man. Search in secret, show the files to your chosen one only after Dominic has vetted them."

"In secret…" Lilly said.

"A cutout," I said. "No, a fiction."

Nikola studied me and nodded. "I am done with it, so yes, it's yours."

"Huh?" Lilly blinked in confusion.

"We resurrect Dr. Nikola, the feared international figure. It is Nikola who is seeking scientists for his schemes. It is Nikola who is traveling the world, with sightings posted here and there. I can easily seed social media with mentions, tap into my network of fellow journalists. We slowly spread the word and begin searching."

"You want us to take his elixir? Just on his say-so?" Lilly asked.

I took her hands in mine. "It's a leap of faith. A crazy one, but my instincts say he's truthful. If you want, I can have the elixir analyzed independently before we try it, make sure he's on the up and up."

"I am."

Lilly shot him a look.

"And then we drink it, live forever, and *become* Doctor Nikola as we try to save humanity."

"Til death do us part."

Loose Threads

Ben H. Rome

H.G. Wells' *War of the Worlds* originated as a serialized story in 1897, published in *Pearson's Magazine* in the UK and *Cosmopolitan* in the United States. Considered one of the foundational novels of science fiction, there is a lot Wells says within it about colonialism, natural selection and evolution, and the nature of good and evil. It's also one of the first science fiction novels I ever read, alongside Verne's *20,000 Leagues Under the Sea*. I always wondered how our world would look if both Wells' and Verne's stories were nonfictional accounts taking place on the same Earth, and if science became our all-consuming *raison d'être*.

Ben H. Rome has, over the span of three decades as a multi-genre writer, won multiple awards in the communications, marketing, and tabletop wargame industries. He has been a member of IAMTW since 2007, serving annually as a Scribe Awards judge and enjoying the many talents of the association's members. When not serving as a full-time communications leader in the association space, he is a voracious gamer, LEGO addict, and toy photographer. He currently resides in the DC area with his wife of more than twenty-five years and remains a committed cat dad. Visit his website at benhrome.com or follow him on Twitter at @bhrome.

Loose Threads

THE ANTICIPATED LETTER ARRIVES. IT IS THE GLIMPSE OF THE SILVER embossed seal of the Institute that sets my heart racing.

> *We, the esteemed Board of Scientists and Trustees of the Institute, invite you to take the entrance exams for the Earth Defense Against Mars initiative.*

Included is travel information and other useful details, of course. But those can wait.

My hand shakes, and I sit on the floor of the entry hall. Deep sobs heave from my chest. A sense of profound relief washes over me as the truth dawns: the past twenty years of my educational pursuits have me at the cusp of a lifelong quest. To join the esteemed rank of the Institute is all I ever wanted since my father received his invitation two decades prior.

At long last, I was about to see him again, joining in the ultimate endeavor: preparing Earth against the looming Martian threat.

I heave myself to my feet. There is much to do and, as I scan the remaining materials for details, only a few days to accomplish it all. My small house and belongings need sold. My life as a citizen is effectively over; all that remains are goodbyes.

Turning the Tied

Acceptance into the Institute—assuming I passed the qualifying exams—means starting a new life. None of this around me matters anymore; the Institute will care for all my needs.

The global accord—the aforementioned Earth Defense Against Mars initiative—says as much. It was established shortly after the Martian invasion in 1894, as world leaders gathered to find a way to reach Mars and bend the offending alien civilization to humanity's will. The invasion was an egregious act that humanity wished to punish our solar neighbors for.

And I'm about to join their ranks.

I put on the coffee pot and settle at my desk to read the materials in full. I take a notepad and pen and begin crafting a list of actions necessary to end my current life and ready for a fresh start.

~

Preparation takes exactly thirty-seven hours, plus an additional six for a relatively light nap. The cab arrives precisely five minutes early. We encounter modest traffic on the way to the airship dock. I therefore have time for a short goodbye with Alexa and James, my only two acquaintances, who await me at the departure gate.

"So excited for you," exclaims Alexa, pressing her lips lightly across my cheeks. "If you can write, please do."

"I do not know if that is permissible," I respond. "Our focus is to be on advancing mankind; distractions only serve to reduce our speed in achieving our greatest goal."

"How very unemotional and droll of you, chum," says James. "I can see why they selected you."

"Jealous, James?" chides Alexa. "I think it is wonderful to know someone selected for such an honor." She grasps my shoulders and looks me steadily in the eye. "In another life, another path, my dear." Her voice is low, full of possibilities.

I am uncomfortable with her confession. Once, a long time ago, I considered pursuing my childhood friend for a life of comfort and idyllic family. But the siren call of science was too powerful to ignore. "Once, yes, but now…I must do my part for humanity to survive."

"Dear God, they've brainwashed you already," scoffs James. He punches me lightly on the shoulder. "Do go, my friend. Your banality is sucking the life from this beautiful day."

"Alexa's right, James. You're just jealous that I'm smarter than you, and therefore worthy of attention," I snap. "Not some athlete who seeks fleeting glory from whatever game it is you play."

James frowns and turns his back to me. He stomps away, a large child in adult clothing. I pity him for only a moment, wondering why I am about to do all of this for the likes of the uncouth such as he.

"Never mind him," says Alexa. Her eyes dart upwards, and she smiles. "I've always loved that bowler on you."

My fingers reach up and tug at the brim of my hat. "A wonderful gift from you, Alexa. It fits perfectly."

Alexa nods, her lower lip quivering. She bites it, looking once more like the ten-year-old freckled girl I remember meeting so long ago. I check my watch; I only have a few minutes to spare.

She sees my glance, knows it is time. Alexa steps forward, hugs me tightly, her head against my shoulder. A moment passes before we disengage. Her hand reaches up and picks at a loose thread on the brim of my hat.

"Can't have you going like that," she says, rummaging through her purse. A small pair of scissors appears, and she snips the offending thread from the brim. "Do try to remember, my dear, to watch for loose threads. They will unravel and ruin everything if gone ignored." She cups my cheek and leans in to kiss me lightly on the lips.

I pause. The sensation flits across my thoughts as a scattered butterfly. My head gives a quick shake, and I step back from her. "I must reach the gate, Alexa. Thank you for coming to see me off."

"I guess this is goodbye, then." She dabs a tissue against the corners of her eyes. "Have a nice life, dearest. Do us all proud."

I nod, pick up my bags. I enter the terminal without looking back.

~

The airship flight takes twenty-six hours, including a few stops at other metropolitan stations. Obviously, the passengers are others accepted to the Institute; it is the primary topic of conversation. I share a cabin with three; fortunately, none of us talk beyond cordial greetings and pardons for any societal infractions. Our meals are also silent affairs. We spend time to ourselves; mine is occupied with mathematical formulas and resolving theoretical physics problems regarding Mars. I make up questions based on the limited research and information we have discovered about Mars and its inhabitants since the invasion. Then I attempt to solve them.

The questions only serve to frustrate me. It is obvious we still do not know enough. I look forward to delving into the secrets contained inside the walls of the Institute.

The information sent indicated the final stop at Tabor Island, on the Antarctic Sea's edge. The Institute is located on the continent of Antarctica, the last great unexplored land of Earth. The unwashed masses can't understand why the Accords put this most crucial facility in the most desolate place on the planet. Logically it makes sense: it is territory unclaimed by any nation—and remains as such due to the EDAM initiative; it is frigid, which approximates the best hypothesis about Martian conditions; and it is removed from all other governments, empires, and civilizations, which protects it from undue influence and the innate greed of powerbrokers who might turn the Institute's science against others when the genuine threat remains on Mars.

Tabor Island is the debarkation point, the last chance for those who harbored doubts to exit the journey.

It is a marvel of human engineering. Only a quarter of the island is natural; the remnants of a place shattered near the end of the nineteenth century by the eruptive explosion of nearby Lincoln Island. As the airship commences its landing approach, most passengers join me in the observation lounge on the lower level. Below us is sprawling concrete and steel; we can see the steamship at dock awaiting our arrival.

I overhear snippets of conversation around me. They are inconsequential; most are frivolous statements or hypothetical guesses regarding mass, materials, or construction methods.

I choose to observe and see what I need to see: the gateway to my new life steeped in science and discovery.

I feel alive.

Debarkation is smooth, primarily because I am near the front of the line. I turn in my passport and other certificates of passage, as well as the last remaining monetary script in my pockets. I hear the guards tell others who object that they must comply; the Institute supplies all needs, so money is worthless past the checkpoint.

Clear of these distractions, I stride to the gangway and onto the steamship. The voyage will be roughly half a day, and I secure a seat in the stern. I take this opportunity to close my eyes and rest.

My rest is short. When I awaken to an announcement from the captain, we are under way. I stretch and notice I am the only passenger here. A member of the ship's crew is nearby, smoking a cigarette.

"This time of year, the sun doesn't quite set." He gestures towards the sea that stretches to the horizon. The sun is a glowing orb of red, barely skimming the waves.

"Of course. Due to the tilt of the planet and..." I trail off. The crewman is disinterested, realizing I'm not an uninformed civilian. We say nothing further.

I stare out at the unending waves. In time, the crewman snuffs out his cigarette and retires elsewhere.

I am alone.

My mind occupies itself by calculating the Earth's track against the sun's position. I am deep into working out an orbital equation when I become aware of an anomaly on the ocean spread before me.

It is midway between the ship's stern and the horizon; a large fin and subsequent humps can be seen as I squint. A large whale shark, perhaps? A blue whale? Species not uncommon in these waters, but this silhouette seems oversized from my recollections of these animals.

Also curious is the appearance of an orange dot of light, near the front and along the waterline. It briefly seems as an eye...and then it is gone, slipping beneath the waves. The remains of its wake prove it is not an imaginative thought.

I ponder this new mystery for many minutes. An experimental vessel from the Institute? How exciting would that be to see another technological innovation birthed before my eyes! Much as when the first airships and oil-powered locomotives debuted, technology developed by the Institute that revolutionized society.

Imagine what space travel, when we finally unlock that secret, will do for humanity!

The strange vessel, as I deduce it to be, does not reappear. I decide I am hungry and make my way to the ship's main deck, where food stations provide quick meals for those passengers in need.

I quickly devour my small bowl of soup and an accompanying wedge of bread. I barely notice the taste; my attention is reserved for those around me. I observe and listen to nearby conversations, assessing my fellows' intelligence, and silently crafting hypotheses of their chances. Based on the topics swirling around me, I am confident few stand to challenge my inevitable success.

Soon enough, I am bored. I dispose of my trash and make my way back to the stern deck; no one else has claimed a space. I am once again alone. I recline and doze off.

~

I awaken to the ship's horn cleaving the air. I can see a few hours have passed; the sun shifting upwards in trajectory, a dim coastline now visible to the east. With bags in hand, I move to the gangplank.

Debarking is effortless. The air is crisp and cold; I pull the zipper up on the coat provided me by the ship's crew. Hunching my shoulders, I look about and spot a steward holding a placard with my name on it. He recognizes me instantly and takes my bags. I follow; no words need to be exchanged. I do not wish to waste breath; the cold wind takes away unnecessary exhalation.

The steward leads me into a sprawling building that transforms into a labyrinth. I quickly lose track of where I am. Each hallway is long, with thick black doors spaced evenly on both sides. "Testing rooms," says the steward. Nothing more is forthcoming.

Presently, he stops at an unremarkable door and unlocks it. A light clicks on as I enter. The steward places my bags in the entryway, then hands me a sheet of paper. His gaze is vacant as our eyes meet; with a slight nod, the door is closed.

I note the general layout of my temporary quarters: bathroom, bedroom, study area with a small kitchenette. Basic linens and toiletries on the shelves, a folded change of clothes on the bed in my approximate size. Outside of necessary furniture, no other amenities. I place my bags on the table.

The paper is two-sided; the front lists several rules. All provided test supplies will be collected at the end of each day. Failure to return them will impact scoring. The same penalty applies to other infractions: vandalism, disobedience towards Institute staff, no trespassing in designated areas, no deliberate contact with other invited guests, and so on. Rather strict, but they make sense. This is about keeping the tests as pure as possible to elevate the best and brightest towards humanity's scientific achievements, not power-brokering or catering to selfish motives.

On the back is the schedule of tests to occur over the coming weeks. I know that the number of tests passed, combined with the scores, determine the discipline of research to which one is assigned. A scant few will fail. These unfortunate souls will be pointed home at their own expense, often leading to poverty, destitution, or, in many cases, suicide.

I am confident this will not be my fate.

The slate of tests selected for me covers a wide range of scientific disciplines, beginning with mathematics and basic earth sciences. The more challenging exams, covering more theoretical sciences and mathematics, are a few weeks away.

To achieve my goal, I know I must succeed in each with high marks. There is no option for failure, not if I wish to talk to my father again.

But I also know this is mostly conjecture, because life at the Institute post-testing is entirely unknown. I do not know what is needed to reach the same level as my father. We never knew what position he secured; I only assumed it was the most elite because that is the only success worth my father's intellect.

Upon his acceptance, we received a letter announcing his success and the watch that now adorns my wrist, accompanied by a small note: *It is beyond understanding. Question everything, from every angle. Even time. Love, Father.*

I end my first day lying on the bed, still fully clothed, sheer exhaustion dragging me into the dark.

~

On my first testing day, it becomes apparent why my guide refers to these as 'testing rooms,' as all of the exams are conducted in the space where I eat, sleep, and pace.

The testing regimen is severe, perhaps to facilitate the minimizing of distractions. At precisely 8:00 a.m., the steward arrives with a modest breakfast tray and clears away dirty linens and trash. An hour later, he takes the tray—regardless of whether you've finished the meal—and leaves a packet. This envelope contains the day's test, plus whatever tools will be needed, from scratch paper to writing implements to a calculator. I discover at the end of the day that none of these items may remain when the steward returns at 6:00 p.m. with dinner; all implements, paper, and the test is removed at that time.

Discussions with the man prove short and unfulfilling. The brevity of the servant's intrusion into my day is breathtaking. In the past few days, he has spoken no more than ten words, many of them of the 'yes' or 'no' variety.

>Have some participants already failed? *Yes.*
>Am I permitted outside to facilitate exercise? *No.*
>Is the weather hospitable here? *No.*
>Do you like working here? *Yes.*
>Are you the only one working? *No.*
>Am I being tested right now? *Yes.*

My primary focus, however, remains on the tests. These exams start relatively simple. I complete my first, on algebra, within two hours. I spend the rest of the day alternating between compulsive pacing and studying for later topics. This comes through rote memorization and creating practice problems that I work out on the provided materials, as we were not allowed to bring reference books. I cannot exit to explore. The door remains secure during the day. I discover this fact shortly after completing my first exam.

Each day the tests are more complicated. My days end as they start, empty and alone, with nothing to occupy me except my voracious mind.

Midway through the second week, at the end of a complicated advanced chemistry exam, the steward comes as usual to clear the evening meal. Before departing, he turns to me, places a key on the table, and says, "Curfew is midnight. You are reminded of the rules." As I process this new bit of information, he exits.

This intrigues me. I move to seize advantage of this new variable. Because of each corridor's sameness, I play it safe and use a simple pattern of travel; all right turns, at ninety-degree angles, and quickly find myself back at my door, which I marked using a bit of dental floss from my provided toiletries.

Though brief, the sense of freedom is incalculable. It takes me a long time to fall asleep.

Each night, I expand my wanderings by altering my pattern. Within a week, I believe I have mentally mapped the entire building's network of hallways and can wander for a few hours without becoming lost. During this time, I discover I do not need to wait for the evening visit by the steward to begin; a simple question posed provides a positive answer.

My curiosity drives me to complete my examinations quickly, which wars with my desire to get the highest marks. This constant push-and-pull in my mind takes a toll on my mental wellbeing.

~

It isn't until my eighth excursion that I see another person. She is far ahead down the corridor and doesn't respond when I call out. She turns the corner. By the time I reach the bend, she is gone.

The second person I encounter is another steward. This gentleman wears the same livery as my own, along with the same blank look and monotone delivery. He also provides directions towards the entrance, which is closed and locked when I arrive.

The excitement of my freedom fades within a week. Every corridor, every door, every wavelength of light is the same. The same striations on the wall, the same spacing of ceiling vents, the same pattern of the tile. I meet no one else, though I do hear occasional noises behind various doors.

It is more than a week later, after a particularly grueling exam in physics that lasts up until the steward arrives at dinner, when I resolve to begin trying doors.

I am sure a lesser-willed man would not have waited so long. However, I still have scoring considerations. Though the rules did not expressly forbid entering other rooms, I do not want to toy in the "gray area" just in case. However, the questions burning at the fore of my mind are becoming maddening. I need some type of action to settle the disagreement in my brain.

I grip the first door handle, the one across from my room, and push downward. I meet resistance; the door is locked, just as mine is. I feel a nervous laugh escape, which I squelch, looking around guiltily.

Nothing happens.

I move on to the next, with the same result. For the next two hours, I pursue this singular purpose, convinced that the next handle will open, that some wondrous location will be revealed. That I will find something—anything—to sate the voracious beast of curiosity growing in my head.

Just as I am about to collapse to the ground as a sobbing mess, giving in to my perceived failure, I hear a noise, a steady, soft rhythm of clicks. It is coming from the intersection several yards away.

I glance up just in time to see what appears to be a metal leg disappear around the corner.

In haste, I run to the intersection and peek. A small four-legged carriage is clicking its way down the corridor. Sitting in the central hub of the device is a woman wearing a similar uniform to the stewards. I cannot get a clear glimpse of the whole of the conveyance since I can only truly see its back end, but it appears to move with supple grace. It is reminiscent of a large cat or other animal and has little hint of its mechanical nature.

I remain at the corner, hesitant to pursue this wondrous sight. My decision is prudent, as the legged carriage stops halfway down the corridor. The woman steps from the torso to the floor and approaches a door. A key appears, and she passes into a room.

I nearly jump from my skin when the contraption moves, turning to face the door previously entered by the woman. I can now see the carriage in full profile; four legs hold the torso up. Another set of arms (or legs?) extends forward, holding what appears to be a shallow platform functioning as a cargo lift. It is similar in look and nature to one of the new forklifts I saw at the airship terminal. As I watch, the platform lowers to the ground. The woman returns to the hallway and helps another person to stretch out upon it.

She straightens the person on it, actions that remind me of a time spent at the emergency room when I was a child. Someone had staggered in and collapsed; the nurses helped move the man onto a wheeled gurney and then maneuvered him out of sight.

The woman mounts the central hub and the platform elevates as the carriage turns, moving down the hall.

As it turns the corner, I dart down to the room. The door stands ajar. Before I can think, I am in the space of another person.

The overwhelming chaos of the space hits me in the face. It is dirty, disordered. The smell is pungent. There are indecipherable markings all over the walls. The feel of the room is damp, thick. I look around wildly, trying to take it all in so I can dissect it at length before bed.

I notice a small stack of paper on the cluttered desk. I take several sheets, stuffing them into my jacket, along with a pencil. I do this without thought. My brain is on overload. I quickly stumble back into the cold order of the hallway, lest I faint away in the room, be discovered, and suffer a catastrophic loss in scoring.

I don't remember getting back to my room, nor my nightly ablutions. It is hours before I can sort out the torrent of thoughts and images impressed on my mind. It is another few days before I realize something about the six-legged contraption.

It bears a striking resemblance in form and design to the Martian machines of the initial invasion.

~

I begin the last week of my exams with flagging strength and mental fortitude. Due to my nightly wanderings, my sleep has been minimal, often returning to my room with minutes to spare. It takes a few hours to catalog my observations, my mind continuing to chew through probabilities and theories.

My discovery keeps my mind churning, working out a problem that has come to be my defining bane of existence.

The chance encounter with the carriage is only the beginning; the tip of an iceberg, if considering metaphor. I do not venture out for several days, pouring myself into the exams.

My next encounter occurs shortly after I resume wandering; my curiosity has overtaken irrational fear. I turn a corner and run into another guest. She looks familiar; I remember her from the ferry vessel. She was in the food line, bragging to her companion about her two collegiate degrees before her sixteenth birthday.

She backs away without looking at me, mumbles an apology, and continues on her way. "Hello?" I call after her. That only prompts her to walk faster and turn another corner. I do not see where she went.

But she had dropped something. Resting on the tiled floor is a crumpled ball of paper. I pocket it and return to my room.

Smoothing out the paper, I sit and stare at my find. A list of notes written in a neat, even script fill most of one side, though several words are smudged out; the other reveals a partial sketch with rough lines and shading as if done in a hurry.

I am astounded; the sketch is of a vessel possessing the mysterious silhouette I had noted from the ferry's stern rail. Furthermore, I now recognize the shape and form of the ship. It bears a striking resemblance to the sketches that Jules Verne had done of his *Nautilus* submarine. There were some differences, to be sure. Still, the prow, the sleek fin-like sail, the large observatory window resembling an eye—it is a very close approximation.

But how? The submarine had been reported scuttled around the Lincoln Island eruption in the 1870s, decades ago. Had it been found? By whom? And with what means?

I flip the paper over again to the list of notes.

- *Few participants remain {smudge}*
- *Richard heard {smudges}...contextual problems concerning high-output heat projection...*
- *Where are the other outbuildings? Only main dormitory observed. Are facilities underground?*
- *6 craft identified; facility seems {smudge} ... additional observations*

- *Verified from other participants area appears crater-like {smudges}*
- *Power source? No generator {smudges}*

And so on. It is a jumbled list of observations and conjecture, each seemingly weak on its own. But the picture they paint appears to cast a different light. And what of the sketch? Is that something she observed here at the Institute?

That night, I pull from my coat the sheets of paper taken from the madman's room. My steward never inquired about them; indeed, I had forgotten their existence. I begin jotting down my thoughts, theories. Before turning in, I fold them, along with the mysterious woman's notes, and return them to my jacket's inner pocket.

Lurking in the background of my mind is a budding hypothesis so unreal, I cannot readily face it. I spend my downtime singularly focused on preparing for exams, keeping my mind fixed upon questions and hypotheses that make sense within the realm of science and avoiding the lurking intruder demanding attention.

I do not wish to ponder the dark thoughts that lie beneath.

~

Two days later, I discover another open door.

During my wandering, I return to the portal through which the carriage had disappeared. Previous occasions yielded fruitless attempts. This night, however, proves different.

The short hallway from the door ends in a large room. It is chilled. I feel pinpricks upon my skin from the cold. Four metal tables line up alongside one wall, two occupied with what could only be human bodies under white sheets. Bluish-gray feet marked with a toe tag poke from under one end.

The other side of the room sports an array of vials, tubes, and strange-looking machines. One has several vials secured inside; all contain varying amounts of a red liquid that I assume is blood. This is a morgue. More importantly, it also appears to function as a laboratory. I recognize several pieces of equipment suited to biological experimentation.

On the counter is a row of neatly sorted pipettes, long thin glass rods of varying sizes and lengths. I suspect the drawers beneath contain other blood-related tools such as rubber tubing, swabs, inhibitors, and the like.

I turn back to the corpses and notice something strange: a thin tube snakes from under one corpse's sheet and down, connecting to a larger vial on a low-slung stand. The stand's four-legged metal design seems familiar; it is similar to the loading carriage I previously encountered, but smaller. The legs appear articulated. Arranged in the central tray, along with the vial, is a short array of pipettes, a rubber tube, a small bellows, a spool of suture wire, and various types of needles.

I have a sudden urge to see who is under the sheet. I pull the cover back and recognize the madman from earlier. Whoever works in this lab is draining this man's blood for experimentation. Or harvesting it. I suddenly recall an account from Dr. Well's printed recollection of the invasion.

But why?

Suddenly I do not want to be here.

Without thinking, I pocket one of the needles and withdraw. I spend the rest of the night writing as much down as I can on my purloined papers.

A technological construct, blood testing, a hermetically sealed submarine. The implications are staggering: is the Institute close to a breakthrough regarding the Martian threat?

I must see to the end to make sense of it all.

~

Several days after the incident in the morgue, there is a knock at the door after breakfast on the last scheduled day of testing. I open the door. My steward is there. "Follow."

"I'm sorry, what?" I am still a bit dumbstruck. This is a definite break in routine. Generally, at this time, the exam is being delivered for the day's test. I just assumed the final test would follow the pattern.

I nod, grab my jacket and bowler, and follow. I suspect I won't be returning.

After a couple of turns, he stops in front of a door and unlocks it. He steps aside and gestures for me to enter.

I nod my thanks and oblige.

The door closes behind me.

I make my way down a short flight of stairs and into a large room. Opposite me is a wall dominated by a glass mirror; it has the look of a one-way observation window, so I assume it as such. Two long tables occupy most of the floor. The other walls are covered in diagrams, schematics, and chalkboards. An open door to my right leads to a small water closet. A row of cabinets suggest supplies, which I quickly confirm.

With the array of materials and the observation window, it is apparent this is my final test location. I am equal parts terrified and giddy.

An intercom clicks on. "There is no time limit. You may not leave until you have completed the exam. Be sure of your answers before indicating you are done." The voice is raspy and flat. "Congratulations on making it this far."

The voice ends with a short click. I inhale deeply, close my eyes, attempt to quell the nagging questions that have built up over the past weeks. Pushing them aside, I dive into the test.

After several hours, I pause to nibble on some food. I am already feeling more relaxed. The questions plaguing me before seem to be confirmed through the information I discover in the exam room.

There are detailed topographical maps of several areas on Mars, including soil metrics, temperature logs, and more. I am stunned at how in-depth the Institute's research is on the red planet.

There are schematics for automated, self-powered cargo platforms that resemble the one I witnessed in the hall. These can carry a tremendous load and traverse rough terrain; they are perfect for handling what would be a prolonged mission to the surface of Mars. Some of the models have designated slots for various weapon types, including a modified heat ray device. It appears the Institute is addressing the need for aggressive actions in a Martian landing.

With some excitement, I find several pages of notes with familiar handwriting. This engineering project is one my father contributed to! Renewed with energy from this knowledge, I move to the next set of research.

I find comprehensive blood analysis and testing, both for long space journeys and extraterrestrial expeditions. There are extensive notes regarding contagions and unknown pathogens. It appears this research is hugely comprehensive. Some research goes back several decades, before the Martian invasion. How is this possible?

The special surprise is discovering several models and detailed engineering plans for the Earth capsules that will carry humans to Mars. These rocket vessels bear a striking resemblance to the *Nautilus*, with some slight modifications. Of particular note are the details regarding its engine. I am eager to meet the scientist who deciphered Captain Nemo's source of power for the *Nautilus*.

I arch my back, stretching. It appears my budding hypothesis, formed over the past several weeks, is proving true. The Institute is close to bringing humans to Mars. To putting a stop to the shadowy threat of a Martian takeover.

But one critical question remains. And I realize that is what my final test is about.

Covered are the questions of transportation, supply, and survival. What remains is the most important of all: how to *get* to Mars. Astrophysics is mostly theoretical. I know I can answer it. My life has been dedicated to science. This is my grand purpose.

I will not fail humanity.

Clearing a section of space in the room, I begin.

~

I do not know how many hours—or days—I spend. The steward brings hot meals at intervals, though I only discover them after they are long cold.

I nap only when exhaustion threatens to overwhelm me. I push my life and needs aside, singularly pursuing this one goal, the only one that matters.

With vigor and determination, theorems and calculations flow from my fingers to the chalkboard. Possible solutions surface, new data points evolve, outcomes become hypothetical.

Finally, I step back. I can go no farther. Calculations, graphs, sketches cover the chalkboard and hundreds of pages. I rub my face, surprised at the roughness of stubble covering my chin. I become aware of my own smell.

But I am done. I solve my question and dozens of others besides. Based on my answers, humanity can reach Mars in a year, possibly two, using just the research present in the exam room. We can finally hit the Martians back and preempt whatever follow-up they were planning.

I turn to the mirror. "My exam is complete."

A moment later, the steward appears. "Follow me, please."

He leads me to a changing room, where I shower and refresh.

The steward leads me to another door. I enter a plush anteroom, reminiscent of my grandparents' Edwardian salon. I notice the steward's presence; instead of departing, as usual, he takes a position in front of the only door.

I spend a moment gathering myself; indeed, I will be meeting the Institute's head and discovering my new station in the pursuit of science. Perhaps I will be made team leader of the Martian launch project, considering my overwhelming success a few scant hours prior.

Opposite me is a richly appointed wall, dominated by a massive painting of a scene from *20,000 Leagues Under the Sea*, where a giant squid grapples the *Nautilus*. I admire the rendering of Ned and his spear atop the vessel's sail tower. I then notice the squid appears all wrong; the eyes are too close together, the tentacles are all wrong, the body disproportionate. It appears more like…

The wall panel slides open. I expect every conceivable variable and personage to greet me. What enters the room instead is a shock.

Dragging its way into the salon, a massively elongated lobe of reddish, wrinkled flesh reveals itself. Its large, lidless black eyes stare at me. A hardened beak the color of bone snaps crosswise at the lobe's base; eight tentacles alternately writhe in the air and maneuver the monstrosity into view.

The thing entering the room is a striking resemblance to the monster in the painting.

||**Welcome**||

I gasp, mouth gaping as a hooked fish. My mind reels, still grappling with reality. I remember a vivid description from Dr. Wells' account of the invasion.

A live Martian. In front of me.

Its voice echoing inside my brain.

||To answer your obvious question, yes. I am what you call a 'Martian.' My designation is Krrt. I am speaking inside your mind.||

I stare. I think several other questions. The silence between us stretches.

||Speak. You have more questions. I cannot read your mind, just speak to it. Decades of observation of your primitive species have given us exceptional ability to predict your behaviors.||

I am sweating. "Um, fine, yes. So, how are you even here? There have been no sightings of launches from—"

A few of Krrt's tentacles wave in approximation to the human gesture of 'not important.' ||I will be forward with you—many of your questions will go unfulfilled. Due to your brilliant success just now, you deserve to know your fate firsthand. We respect superior minds and owe you that. But I will not waste time answering frivolities.||

I pause. Mentally I sort through the plethora of queries jumping to mind. "I passed." It is a statement of fact. "What does this all mean? A façade simply to return your kind to Mars?"

The Martian's beak snaps a few times. Was it laughing? ||Hardly. The Institute is a construct we created to safeguard our planet, our growing empire.||

Another moment to reflect. A sudden, horrible thought. "You…use this process…to identify those of us capable of…advancing human thought and knowledge."

I pause again, working out the implications.

Krrt sits patiently, resting on some of its tentacles. Its stare is unnerving.

Truth dawns upon me. "This is how you determine how close we are to cracking the secrets to reach Mars. To defeat you. To subjugate you."

||Correct, mostly.||

The creature's casual admission causes my stomach to sink. "So what happens then to those who pass? I assume you allow the failures to return home, to perpetuate the lie."

||There are three outcomes to this procedure. First are the weakest who fail; these are sent home intact to further the lie. Second are those who show some scientific aptitude to a certain point. Their minds are altered. We have perfected, over the years, a process similar to what you know as lobotomization. After the

process, they are given a choice: serve us or not. Those who choose not to serve are harvested, as they cannot function in your society without questions being raised.||

I feel ill. "And...the third? Those like me who pass?"

||Yessss.|| Krrt drags out the word, sounding like a child anticipating an iced cream dessert. ||Those who pass the final tests are selected to further our experiments.||

I blink. My head pounds. I struggle to remain calm. "They are killed." No status as a leading scientist, no further research pursuits, no science elevation for all humankind.

||After a period of intense examination, yes. But be assured, through these experiments you are furthering our scientific exploration into intelligence, longevity, and evolution.||

I sigh. My fate appears sealed. But maybe there is a way... "Since I will soon be contributing to your latest research, grant me a couple of boons, if you may."

The thing stares at me a moment, tentacles twitching. ||As one of our prized discoveries, you may ask.||

"How did you survive Earth's bacteria after the invasion?"

Several tentacles writhe in apparent agitation. ||Our colony on the polar cap was here long before the rebel insurrection. We discovered the bacterial problem early but were unable to warn our brethren, as our capacity for extrasolar communication was damaged in our initial landing.||

A pair of tentacles gesture towards the painting on the wall. ||We discovered this vessel nearby, on the ocean floor. It serves as a perfect example of atmospheric compartmentalization. We were able to replicate that engineering, then capture and suborn those humans who wandered too close to the colony. These vessels ensure we and our progeny survive until our experiments with human blood and pathogens render us curative medicines. With that now achieved, we can focus on more permanent immunities.||

I focus on a word Krrt mentioned previously. "Insurrection?"

Krrt gnashes its beak. ||**After not hearing from this colony, a small, aggressive faction launched an invasion. When they landed, we chose to not pass along our discovery of the bacteria problem.**||

I remain silent, working through the implications. Before I can articulate, it shuffles closer.

||**We chose to use the problem to our advantage. Built upon humanity's bonding over the perceived threat. Maneuvering our human puppets to provide advice, eventually bringing about the EDAM and this Institute.**||

I nod. It makes sense. "Now you sabotage human achievement simply to protect your planet."

||**A waiting game only. We will eventually return to this bountiful world armed with better knowledge. And then we will continue our dominance as before.**||

"Why?"

Krrt stares at me. ||**That should be obvious even for your primitive brain stem. Survival. Our planet is dying; we wish for a new home.**||

The Martian shifts in irritation, slapping an appendage on the floor. ||**Enough questions. I sense there is one last request. Ask, for it is almost time.**||

I exhale. "I wish some time to prepare my soul for its release."

The alien rears back. ||**I am surprised. There has been no indication of your interest in such things.**||

I smile sadly. "Often, when humans face the inevitable, they turn to spiritual comfort to help ease their fears. I only wish the same."

I feel Krrt's gaze burning into my brow.

After a long moment, the beast stirs. ||**Very well. Thirty of your minutes should suffice. The steward will collect you when it is time.**||

I watch as the Martian drags itself from the room. Idly, I notice only minor difficulty in moving. It has acclimated to Earth's gravity rather well.

I look at the steward. "If you don't mind, I'd like privacy." He nods and steps from the room.

I am alone.

I take my notes from my jacket's inner pocket. For the next several minutes, I furiously write on the last blank spots available and erase what I now know to be false assumptions. It is a scribbled mess, though I take care to not smudge the marks. I proceed to hide the papers and fervently pray my final gambit will work.

I am adjusting the bowler on my head when the steward re-enters, a four-legged stand walking alongside him. There is a black bag resting on the tray.

I hear the panel whisper open behind me.

||**Made your peace with your soul?**||

"I have. One last request, if I may be so bold." I turn to face Krrt.

The tentacles writhe, erratically slapping the wall and floor. ||**You may. But this is it. I am eager to begin experimentation. You are by far the best subject we have had since your father.**||

Though I suspect as much, the admission turns my guts to ice. I ignore the feeling and focus.

"As you did for him, then, allow me to send a token and a note to someone." I watch Krrt's beak gnash. Hastily, I continue. "To further the façade, as you say. No one will question my absence if they are reassured of my success and happiness. It is, after all, what spurred me to follow my father's footsteps."

||**Excellent points. Very well.**|| Krrt turns toward the steward, who nods and steps from the room. He is back within moments, Institute stationery in hand.

I take the letter and scrawl a quick note, then jot a name and address on the envelope. I hand both the letter and the bowler to the steward.

||**Your coat appears to have given out before you.**|| A tentacle tip points to the tattered sleeve.

I look down at it with a wry grin. "Seems there was a loose thread, and it unraveled. That's how it goes, I suppose. Can't keep anything pristine these days."

||**Indeed. Humans are messy creatures.**|| Krrt stares again at me, then clicks its beak. Turning, it moves back towards the wall panel. ||**Follow. It is time to give yourself wholly to science.**||

"Let it be said at least that I gave my heart to humanity," I murmur.

I pass through the threshold.

~

A messenger hands a brown box to the woman, who offers a small tip and retreats into the warmth of her home. She glances at the attached letter. Her face lights up. Eagerly, she opens the envelope and reads the short message within.

Slightly bewildered, she sits and unfastens the twine from the package. She lifts out a black bowler hat. Her eyes glisten; she recognizes it. Her hands turn the hat over as she examines it closely. Her fingers pick at a spot on the inside brim, which quickly unravels the inner lining. Several handwritten pages fall from the hat into her lap.

She glances through the pages then clutches the hat to her chest, tears sliding down her cheeks. The letter falls from her lap to the floor.

My dearest Alexa:

Our paths remain separate but remembered. Take this, a token of past affection and future hope. Please check for loose threads, for as you are fond of saying, they do have a tendency to unravel and ruin everything if ignored.

I do not wish to be ignored.

I loved you.

Cyrano De Bergerac and Baron Munchausen Go to Mars

Steven Paul Leiva

Cyrano de Bergerac (1619-1655) and Hieronymus Karl Friedrich, Freiherr von Munchhausen (1720-1797) were both real individuals and fictional characters. Cyrano de Bergerac actually was a famous swordsman and author of one of the first works of science fiction, *The Other World: Comical History of the States and Empires of the Moon,* sometimes known as *A Voyage to the Moon.* Hieronymus Karl Friedrich, Freiherr von Münchhausen, or Baron Munchausen, was infamous as a teller of outrageously tall tales at dinners he hosted. Cyrano was fictionalized by French playwright Edmond Rostand in 1897. The Baron never wrote down any of his tales, but tales attributed to him were published by a series of writers. They were not licensed to do so, and the Baron was not happy about this. Nevertheless, is it possible that these scribes were the very first tie-in writers? It is to wonder.

Steven Paul Leiva is a Scribe Award winner and the author of nine novels in a mix of genres, and a book of essays on his colleague and friend, the late Ray Bradbury.

For more, see emotionalrationalist.blogspot.com

Cyrano De Bergerac and Baron Munchausen Go to Mars

1
France 1641

SAVINIEN CYRANO DE BERGERAC, A YOUNG MEMBER OF THE KING'S Guards, sat in his cups after several cups of a not-very-distinguished wine in a little tavern in a not-wholly-decadent section of Paris, but certainly not a dignified one. It was close to the theater where Cyrano and two of his fellow Guardsmen, the twins François Jacques and Jacques François, had spent the better part of their evening. François and Jacques tried their best to lighten Cyrano's mood, for besides being in his cups, Cyrano, his head buried in his folded arms on the table, was in a morbid melancholy.

"Cyrano," said Jacques (unless it was François), "you are the most irritating guardsman of my acquaintance."

"Mine too!" François said (unless it was Jacques).

"You had a great triumph tonight. You bested and mortally wounded a great swordsman in a duel of honor at the theater. And this while still suffering some pain from the neck wound you received in the Siege of Arras. It was *spectaculaire!* (Which, of course, means spectacular!) *Magnifique!* (Which, of course, means Magnificent!) *Affreux!* (Which means Awful! But in this case, "full of awe" and not "objectionable," for obviously François—or Jacques—was not objecting.) "It will only enhance your repute, your fame, your legend!"

Cyrano moaned and slowly raised his head, bringing into the low gaslight illumination of the tavern his *spectaculaire*, less than *magnifique*, but certainly *affreux* nose. He looked at the twins, his fellow men-at-arms, and said in a slurred voice, "I would rather be known for my rapier wit than for my rapier." Then he dropped his head back onto his folded arms.

"You see," said one of the twins (we will dispense with trying to figure out which), "that is your problem, my friend. You care more for your books, your poetry, and mooning after your cousin than defending France and your honor with your incredible talent with the sword."

"Some talent," Cyrano said, raising his head again, his face mapped with disgust. "Sticking pigs! And what a pig he was! Not just of the body, but of the mind. How did he insult me? Was it at all clever? Was there some felicity to his words? An apt way to offend me? No, just your mundane, *'Mon Dieu, mais tu as un gros nez!'*" (Which means, "My God, but you've got a large nose!" But it sounds better in French). "Oh, if only I had answered back with some wit, some poetry, possibly with how he could have cleverly insulted me if he had not been so witless. No, I just answered with the inarticulate *clang, clang, clang, clang* of metal! Oh, why do I always think of the witty things to say, the beautiful bon mot, *after* the duel?"

The twins looked at each other and shook their heads. They had heard all this before; they understood Cyrano's anguish no more than they ever had, and it was boring. Time to pick up their friend, plop his white-plumed cavalier's hat onto his head, and escort him home.

But Cyrano did not want to go home. He bid farewell to his friends, despite their objections, and took himself off to a bit of countryside nearby where there was a lone spike-like Italian cypress tree along a lonely road that he felt to be his friend, for it stood as oddly in this landscape as Cyrano did in the Guards. He loved to sit under it at night and look up at the sky, especially on a night like this, a night of a full moon.

The moon, the moon, Cyrano thought as he stared directly into the moon's man-like face. *Earth's companion in the sky. No, not just a companion, but a brother. What are you like, brother? Who resides there, brother? What are your secr—*

Suddenly a wispy cloud appeared before the moon. No, not a cloud, a supplanting face, transparent at first, moonshine flowing through it. Slowly it came into solid integrity, and Cyrano realized that standing before him was a man, strangely dressed, wearing an odd triangular hat and sporting a broad, cheerful grin, and...and...and...

"Mon Dieu, mais tu as un gros nez!" Cyrano said as he looked up at the man.

2
The Man in Front of the Moon

"Yes," said the elegantly if strangely dressed man before him. "It is a magnificent nose, is it not? A real Hanover hooter! It flows freely from out of my face and curves down quite beautifully, the whole forming an aspect like the side of a gently rolling mountain. I am quite proud of my nose. Although I suppose the pride actually belongs to my progenitors. But be that as it may, allow me to present myself, I am Hieronymus Karl Friedrich, Freiherr von Münchhausen, but you may call me Baron Munchausen!"

At any other time, being presented with such an aristocratic fellow, Cyrano would have jumped up and shown due respect with a flourish of a bow. But as he was perfectly comfortable sitting against his cypress, and not entirely convinced he was not dreaming, it seemed the better course to stay as he was. Still, apparition or not, Cyrano needed to address the stranger. "Am I correct, sir, in assuming you are a citizen of the Holy Roman Empire?"

"Ha! As your fellow countryman Voltaire will someday say, it is neither holy, nor Roman, nor an empire."

"Will *someday* say?"

"Yes, he has yet to be born," the man in the triangular hat said offhandedly. "I prefer to say that I am from Bodenwerder in the Electorate of Hanover. But that is just Geography, my friend. More to the point, I am from the future! 1790, to be specific."

"I must," Cyrano said as he dropped his head and shook it to reorder the confusion within, "I really *must* stop drinking cheap wine."

"Oh, stop whining about your wine, and stand up, man, and embrace me, for we are fellow authors!" Baron Munchausen scooped Cyrano up as if he were but a child, a small child, possibly, even a rag doll, and brought him into the fellowship of his arms.

"But...but...I am not an author," Cyrano said once the Baron had released him.

"You will be, my son, you will be."

"No, no, I am a King's Guardsman, a swordsman, a man of duty and honor."

"Poshtiddle!"

"Poshtiddle?"

"You will quit the guards this year and begin studies with Pierre Gassendi."

"Gassendi? The philosopher?"

"Yes, yes! He will tickle your mind as he opens it, and then you will write poetry, plays, and prose. And you will write about going to the moon!"

"Going to the moon? I was just thinking about the moon."

"Who doesn't think about the moon? So obvious, so mundane, even I have written about going to the moon. But now, I could truly go there."

"What?"

"And I could take you."

"What?"

"But, I will not!"

"For pity's sake, why not?"

"Because I have come here to take you to Mars!

3

Baron Munchausen Explains Himself

"In my time and world, I am known as *Lügenbaron*, The Baron of Lies!"

Cyrano's eyes flashed with righteous anger as his long and promontory-like nose twitched in agitation, for he could always sniff out an insult. "What an affront! I would kill any man who so disparaged me."

"No, no, Cyrano! It is not an insult. It is a perfectly precise appellation, indeed a fine honorific! For I have told the most outrageous, ridiculous, absurd, unbelievably tall tales of any man living or dead. And yet people hang on my every word, often with the most beatific grins on their faces, enraptured by my lies, it would not be a lie to say. It has been a most pleasant occupation for me."

"But, Baron, to what purpose?"

"Why, to amuse, Cyrano, purpose enough."

Cyrano looked down upon the ground and saw there—*there* being within himself—a truth. "Not for me."

"Yes, I know. You will put philosophy in your writing, the true nature of things, promoting ideas that will not, I must say, please your Church. But that is the nature of your essence. But I am here to inspire you to do it with some panache, some flare, some outrageous and glorious lies!"

"Here?" Cyrano questioned. "You have still not explained how you happen to be here, in Paris, in 1641, instead of Hanover in 1790."

"Ah! Yes, a strange and wondrous thing that. I was walking one day in the mountains with a group of friends hanging on my every word, as I told them of how one day when I was standing on the edge of the White Cliffs of Dover in the island kingdom across the channel, a lightning bolt shot down from the heavens and streaked through my legs—I was standing akimbo at the time—and snatched me up into the sky. I told them how I rode that bolt like I would ride a fine steed, all the way to the Antipodes, specifically New Zealand, another island country, where I found myself in the company of a tribe of well-spoken koala bears. Just as I was beginning to elucidate on the koalas' customs and taboos, I was—truthfully, in actuality, very, very, realistically, and with great veracity—struck by lightning. It burnt my clothes and frizzed my hair and singed my nose, and I fell into a deep stupor. My companions transported me back to my hunting lodge—for that is where we were staying—and tended to me with great tenderness for the next forty days as I emitted an intermittent glow and, quite unconsciously, recited many of the works of Lucian of Samosata. Upon waking after forty days I felt perfectly fine and saw no reason we should not carry on with our holiday. That night, my friends and I—there were five of them, aristocrats all—played a card game of English Whist. I was telling them of my great adventure in mid-Africa, where I battled an enormous crocodile, besting him by reaching down his throat and grabbing the inside of his tail and pulling him inside out. They were, of course, mesmerized by my tale, glued to their seats, as it were. Then all of a sudden, an enormous crocodile burst through the wall and gobbled up three of my five aristocratic friends."

"Stunning!" said Cyrano, who was sitting on no seat to be glued to, but was mesmerized still. "Amazing! And so tragic."

"Well, the three ingested ones were lesser aristocrats, whereas the surviving two were higher born."

"Are you saying their deaths were less tragic because of the position in society their births gave them?"

"My dear Cyrano, there is a reason why the low-born are called the low-born."

"But my dear Baron, are we not all *low*-born? Wasn't it only Athena who was born high?"

After a short period of perplexity, the Baron suddenly got Cryano's allusion to the ancient myth and shook with laughter both Teutonically and tectonically. "Ah, you are so clever with the words, so ready with the wit, my fellow possessor of the proboscis colossal!"

By reflex, Cyrano shaded his nose from the moonlight as he lamented, "Oh, were that so, Baron, were it so. But forget my wit or lack of it. Are you saying you conjured up a real, living, enormous crocodile by your lie?"

"Yes, my friend, that is exactly what I am saying. I have become such a consummate liar, such a fabulous fabricator, that my lies can now become part and parcel of the fabric of the universe. I have but to tell them to make them real."

"That is—that is unbelievable!"

"So is virgin birth, my friend, but…"

"But…but…"

"But how do you think I got here in an instant from Hanover—not to mention 1790? I just told myself the story of me being here—and I was here! I will prove it to you. On this lonely country road, I will lie up our conveyance to Mars."

"Would not the moon be closer?"

"Poshtiddle!"

"Poshtiddle?"

"The moon is but a low-born satellite, a servant of Earth, colorless, barren, and uninteresting."

"A servant? How does it serve?"

"By moving our ocean tides in and out, of course."

"Not according to Master Galileo."

"Master Galileo was right about many things but wrong about this. But that, my dear Savinien Cyrano de Bergerac, is not the point. Do you not realize that the Earth and all the planets are the children of mother Sun? That the planets were born one after another from her fiery womb and sent out into space? As Mars is farther from the Sun than we, then it must be older. It must have a civilization of peoples more advanced and mature than we. Think of the wonders we will find there, the knowledge we can gain."

"But what if it is like an older sibling happy to torture the younger?" Cyrano asked by way of warning. "It was, after all, named after the God of War."

"A mistake of antiquity, my friend! No, no, look at Mars! Not all white and pale like the weak moon, but red, sanguine, a good fellow, optimistic, I'm sure. But we can talk about all this on the way. For now, let me lie up our conveyance. I think I will use the chariot of Queen Mab that I featured in my tales of African adventures! Give me but a moment."

The Baron began to mutter, chuckle, and finally exclaimed, "The chariot of Queen Mab be here!"

And there on that lonely country road appeared the most strange of all conveyances ever imagined by man. It was huge, a prodigious, globular coach that looked like a giant hazelnut, mainly because it was a giant hazelnut. There was a hole in the shell as large as a normal coach-door, and the interior, which the Baron invited Cyrano to look in and examine, featured a luminous representation of all the stars of heaven. It goes without saying that Cyrano was amazed! But I just said it, so it's too late now.

Suddenly breathless, Cyrano backed his head out of the coach and stumbled backward to fall against his cypress tree, sliding slowly down the trunk to sit, composure having abandoned him. But it did afford him a full view of this wondrous mode of transportation. Nine bulls were hitched to the chariot of Queen Mab to provide forward motion. The lead bull was enormous, with horns that may have reached into the next district. Behind him were eight normal-sized bulls, but positively not minuscule in bulk and strength. The bulls were shod with the skulls of men, which the Baron explained gave them extraordinary abilities to transgress any landscape, indeed, any seascape, and—the Baron said it would soon be proven—space itself. On the back of the nine bulls sat nine postilions, nine riders to direct the nine bulls, for there was no coachman to drive the chariot of Queen Mab. Just one postilion seated on a lead animal is normal, but having nine of them is not what was strange here. All nine postilions were crickets the size of monkeys! Their chirping was loudly incessant, as you would expect of *Grylloidea* (in a story like this, it is always good to throw in a little Latin) of such inflated size.

"And now, Cyrano, get up and join me in the coach."

Cyrano rose in apprehension. "But will we be warm? I have heard that the higher up you climb the great Alps, the colder it gets."

"We will be perfectly warm, I assure you."

"And will we be able to breathe? I have also heard the higher you go in the Alps, the thinner the air becomes."

"Yes, yes, we will be warm, and we will breathe because I will lie us up some heat and air. If I have not convinced you yet, Savinien Cyrano de Bergerac, what more can I say?"

What more, indeed, Cyrano thought. He was not a young man of faith, except the faith he put in his swordsmanship, so how could he put his faith in this apparition from the future? Or this conjuring demon from the present? But the Baron was so imbued with confidence, and his offer of the most unique of adventures was so compelling, that Cyrano did raise himself and, with no hesitation, joined Baron Munchausen in the giant hazelnut, closing the coach door behind him.

"How long will it take us to get to Mars?"

"Who knows? No one has ever gone there before."

"Do we have provisions?"

"When I think 'breakfast,' we will have breakfast. When I think 'lunch,' we will have lunch. When I think supper, dinner, dessert, and wine, we will have those as well. And the best part is—there will be no clean-up! Now, let us go on to Mars!"

Each monkey-sized cricket on the back of each bull chirped louder and louder until the sound was almost deafening; the chariot of Queen Mab shook violently, tossing Cyrano and the Baron side to side, until the shaking became an intense vibration. Then forward ballistic movement threw the men against their seatbacks as the hazelnut coach sped faster and faster along the lonely country road until the huge first bull in the lead leaped up in a great bound into the sky. They ascended at such an incredible rate that the Baron and Cyrano flattened like *Homo crêpes*.

4
The Trip to Mars

They knew they had escaped the Earth's massive pull of gravity when they unflattened and recovered their fully dimensional selves.

"That was an odd experience," Cyrano said as his face took on a chartreuse hue, and rumblings in his stomach made an unpleasant prognostication. But the Baron simply lied about Cyrano's condition, picturing him as a fellow in a fine fettle, and the future was bright again.

"Well, Cyrano, how should we pass the time? Shall we play cards?"

"I am not that fond of games, Baron."

"How about I regale you with some of my fabulous adventures."

"Meaning no offense, Baron Munchausen, but I think the fabulous adventure we are currently on commands our attention more, don't you?"

"How so?"

"Well, for example, I've just noticed that this coach has no windows. There is nothing for me to look out of, to see where we are, where we are going, or, for that matter, where we have been."

"What do you need to see, my dear Cyrano? We are in space somewhere between Mars, which is where we are going, and our mother Earth, which is where we came from."

"But wouldn't you love to see our mother Earth from out here? To see that it is a globe spinning in space?"

"You don't believe it is? You need evidence?"

"Well, of course, *I* believe it. But just think what it would mean for all those less educated among our fellows if they could see it and be disabused of atavistic notions."

"Such as?"

"Such as that the Earth is flat."

"For most people, my friend, for all intents and purposes, the Earth is flat. Why try to unbalance them with details?"

"But, Baron, don't you think it would be fabulous for people to see the Earth in space? I'm pretty sure they would not be able to see our arbitrary and often disputed borders. If all people in the past had been able to see that we are all one people on one planet, I'm sure then I would not have suffered this neck wound while being a loyal French subject fighting just as loyal Spanish subjects at the Siege of Arras."

The Baron smiled a gentle, yet somewhat patronizing smile, as he said, "Ah, my dear friend, just because you cannot see the trees for the forest does not mean the bears are not shitting in the woods."

"What?"

"I would much rather muse on what we are going to find on Mars. The possibilities are endless."

"*Oui! Oui!*"

"You need to urinate, Cyrano? Don't worry; I can just lie your bladder empty."

"No, I meant, in your language, *Ja! Ja!*"

"Just a little joke, my friend. In the future, *badezimmer* or, if you will, *salle de bains* humor will be quite the thing."

"I didn't know they had humor in Hanover."

"Ah, *Touché*, as you like to say!"

"But, to muse on Mars, yes I think that is a fine idea. I am intrigued by this idea of yours that the inhabitants may have a civilization more advanced and mature than ours."

"It is the only rational assumption, do you not think? Have we not advanced, become more cultured, since the days of darkness following the Fall of Rome?" the Baron asked.

"Certainly, Baron. Outside of slaughtering each other over religious differences."

"Ah, well, you see, you prove my point. In my time, we no longer make war over religious differences—we make war over trade! An obvious improvement! But now, I propose we consider what Mars and its inhabitants are like in three categories: The inhabitants themselves. Their architecture. And inventions, machines, and such. You go first!"

"Ahhhh," Cyrano said and stretched to bide time while he thought slowly in virgin territory. "I wonder, um, whether they walk upright, like us."

"Why wouldn't they?"

"We are the only animals to walk upright on Earth, an obvious minority. Perhaps they walk on all fours?"

"Are we not the finest of all animals on Earth?"

"Certainly."

"Then walking upright is obviously the superior mode of ambulation. Why would the mature Martians be in retrograde? But, at the same time, why would they be stuck ambulating like their younger brothers, we? I suggest that they float!"

"Float?"

"Gently from place to place as they contemplate the great questions. Or speedily if time is of the essence. I think they do this in a seated position, their legs crossed and their arms resting on small clouds they manufacture for this purpose."

"So you see the Martians as having at least the same appendages we have? Legs and arms?"

"Certainly. What could be more practical and utilitarian than our four major appendages? Five for males, of course, but we need not go into that."

"I disagree, Baron. I will be quite interested to see how the Martians procreate. And whether love is involved?"

Hieronymus Karl Friedrich, Freiherr von Münchhausen, looked quite aghast. "You are so *French*, my friend. I believe Martians have left all messy interpersonal relations behind. Possibly they do not have sex differences at all. Think of the time that would save! I believe Martians are divided biologically only into classes."

"Like we are?"

"No, no, not like we are. Classes of kind, not of position. I believe there will be the Thinkers, the Doers, the Adventurers, and the Know-nothings, the Do-nothings, and the Unadventurous."

"Oh. Like we are?" Cyrano asked rhetorically as his smile indicated that he was silently saying, *Touché!*

"Humph!" heaved out of the Baron. "Architecture! What do you think Martian buildings will be like?"

"Wondrous structures, I suppose."

"Exactly!" the Baron said, excited that he and Cyrano might be sharing a vision here. "Made out of luminous organic materials and in colors never seen by the eye of man."

"But, red—"

"Ah, yes, you are right! Colors in variations of red, then, never seen by the eye of man!"

"And tall?"

"Of course tall, very tall buildings. Intelligent beings always reach higher and higher. And as they can float, there is no limit to how high they can go."

"And the buildings connected by, oh, let us call them sky bridges when the Martians would prefer to saunter instead of float."

"Marvelous! Yes! Now you are wondering well!" the Baron said, not understanding the slight satire of Cyrano's suggestion.

"And what of their inventions and machines, Baron?"

"Sailing ships that provide their own wind. Machines that create artificial heat in the winter and sweet, soft cool breezes in the summer. Clothes that repel all dirt and stains so as never to need washing. A small, tiny, minuscule machine that surreptitiously picks your nose for you—that will be handy for both you and I, eh, Cyrano? Beds that recreate the conditions inside your mother's womb so you can get a decent night's sleep. A machine that swats insects with a sound irritating to them but pleasant to people. Clothes that protect you against the elements, but weigh next to nothing, look fabulous, and never—never bunch up in dark secret places."

"Wonders!" Cyrano exclaimed, genuinely impressed and awestruck over the heights of the Baron's imagination. "Absolute wonders! What people! What architecture! What inventions! What wonders await us on Mars! But, Baron, what about Mars itself? The landscape."

"The landscape, yes, yes, we must consider the landscape. Surely as our Earth is dominated by blue, green, and brown, then reds, pinks, and rust dominate the Martian landscape. The Martian trees, for example. I see red, translucent trunks with translucent pink leaves."

"Why translucent, Baron?"

"It is obvious, my dear Cyrano. Mars is farther from the Sun than Earth. Sunshine then is weaker. The trees are translucent to allow—after the trees have gathered what benefits they need from the Sun—to allow the residue sunshine to pass to the ground to benefit other creatures. Also, as our leaves turn yellow and red with colder weather, I believe Martian leaves will turn first a light green then darken to an intense deep blue, like lapis lazuli."

"That should be stunning to see."

"Absolutely!"

"Do you think there will be great oceans on Mars?" Cyrano asked, thinking perhaps about childhood days at the seashore.

"Without a doubt."

"How can you be so sure?"

"Where else can they sail their great auto-wind ships?"

"Ah. And great rivers like the Seine?"

"Yes! Flowing down from all the magnificent mountains, every one of them pink snow-capped, because remember, being farther from the sun, Mars in the winter gets much colder."

"And what about deserts, Baron? Will there be vast stretches of near-lifeless deserts on Mars?"

"Cyrano, my friend, try to take our musing seriously. Of course, there will be no deserts on Mars. The Martians are so advanced they would never allow even one hectare of their home to be anything but verdant—or possibly I should say, *rougeant*."

"Yes, I suppose that follows," Cyrano acknowledged. "But something is bothering me, my dear Baron."

"Pray, tell?"

"You have been waxing quite enthusiastically about the details of Mars, but with your power to lie things into existence, are you not possibly bringing them about?"

"No, no, my dear sir! Not at all. You see, to lie effectively, you must first know the truth. Since we do not yet know the truth, but only speculate, there is no danger of my altering reality with my superior imagination and perceptive abilities."

Cyrano simply nodded at the Baron's declaration, and the Great Munchausen began to consider all the various non-intelligent Martian creatures that might populate the red and pink landscape.

The Baron talked and talked for a duration that may have been long or may have been short or may have been somewhere in between. There was no way to tell as the chariot of Queen Mab contained no timepieces, and they certainly could not tell by the daily track of sun and moon. The only punctuation in the flow of time and talk was when the Baron suddenly became hungry and would lie up German delicacies for him and French ones for Cyrano. The limits to the Baron's abilities became clear to Cyrano when he discovered to his dismay that the Baron's imagination of French cuisine never quite got the sauces right. But Cyrano, being a gentleman, would never have said a word about it to the Baron, assuming he could have gotten a word in edgewise to have done so.

5
Cyrano de Bergerac and Baron Munchausen on Mars

"We are here!" Baron Munchausen exclaimed with excitement and a non-Teutonic giddiness.

"How do you know?" Cyrano rightly asked.

"We have landed. We have stopped. There is no movement."

"I have felt no movement since leaving Earth."

"I am not used to being doubted, Cyrano!" the Baron said with very Teutonic umbrage.

"My apologies, my dear Baron, I do not mean to offend."

"Already forgotten, my friend. Please open the coach door and let us introduce ourselves to Mars!"

"Ah, Baron, one moment before I do that."

"Yes, yes?" The Baron anxiously wanted to get on with it.

"Since it may be colder on Mars than we are used to, and since we have no idea if the Martians breathe the same air we breathe, would it not be prudent for you to lie up a surrounding bubble of our native atmosphere?"

The Baron was impressed. "A fine idea, Savinien Cyrano de Bergerac. And to think you have not even begun your philosophical studies yet. So, I extend this bubble out, oh, say, one-quarter of a kilometer. Now lets us see Mars!"

Cyrano opened the coach door, and the gentlemen exited the chariot of Queen Mab and looked around.

In complete synchronization, each man's mouth slowly opened until their jaws allowed no more mobility. As if connected in a dance, each man's eyes widened beyond believing. When it came to voice, only the Baron managed to speak.

"Well—*this* is a disappointment."

Stretching out before them was a reddish expanse of a desert under a light pink sky. Cyrano and the Baron saw no life anywhere. No life at all, animal, vegetable, or even mineral. There were no structures, no buildings, not even anthills. Nothing intelligent floated in the air, nor did anything dumb. All they saw was the rusty earth of Mars laid out before them with various tracks along the ground as if giants had scratched them, and with barren mountains off in the distance, and rocks, rocks, and rocks scattered in no discernible logical manner all along the ground.

"Is it possible that this is but one geographic feature of Mars?" Cyrano asked. "That Mars does indeed have deserts, and we just happened to have landed in one? And that the civilized portion of the planet with fabulous architecture and wonderful floating people are elsewhere?"

"Yes, yes, my friend. Back into the chariot of Queen Mab!"

The Baron then lied them to a multitude of longitudes and latitudes. But, upon opening the coach door at each location, they could see only slight variations of the original landscape in which they had landed.

The Baron was inconsolable.

"Time to go home, I think," Cyrano said to Hieronymus Karl Friedrich, Freiherr von Münchhausen.

"Yes, I agree. But it is hard to lie when you have faced the truth."

"What, surely not for you! You said—"

"Knowing the truth is not the same as facing the truth."

"But you are *Lügenbaron!* You were *Lügenbaron* before we came to Mars, and you will be *Lügenbaron* for a long time after."

The Baron looked upon the young cavalier before him. A handsome young man, despite his nose. The Baron smiled and waved his right hand in a circular motion. Suddenly the nine postilion monkey-sized crickets goaded the nine bulls forward faster and faster until the lead bull made his incredible leap, and they were off, streaking away from the disappointing red planet.

6
The Return to Earth

After experiencing the flattening of escaping Mars' gravity—a diminished experience compared to breaking away from Earth's gravity, but uncomfortable nevertheless—Cyrano and the Baron settled themselves for the journey home.

Cyrano sat upright and quietly focused his internal attention on all he had seen on Mars, trying his best to memorize all the views of all the landscapes they had experienced. They were all quite similar, but with enough differences to give each one a hint of uniqueness. It was mentally cataloging this uniqueness that occupied Cyrano. Oddly, these slight variations in barrenness thrilled Cyrano.

The Baron, though, seemed to have given up his Baron-ness, slumping into his seat, taking on a woeful continence to rival the great Quixote, as he rested his head on the palm of one hand.

Cyrano was concerned. Where was the confident, prideful, gloriously inflated Baron he had come to know in this deflated man before him? "My dear Baron, please, do not become *découragé*. We have gone somewhere and seen something no other humans on Earth in your time or mine have ever gone to or seen. We are the greatest of explorers, the exclusive holders of truth! We must now return to Earth and report what we have seen to the world. We will travel the globe, speaking before every society of natural philosophers in each nation that has one. They will be amazed! They will be thrilled! They will bestow so many honors on us we will have to build a warehouse to hold them!"

Despite Cyrano's enthusiasm, the Baron was unmoved. He looked up at Cyrano from his slumped position and hand-hammocked head. Then, while sighing, he slowly raised his head as upright as he could tolerate it. "*Au contraire*, as you French like to say along the Seine, we will be bestowed with curses and condemnations and cries of 'Off with their heads!'"

"Baron Munchausen! You do not mean that!"

"I do, my dear Cyrano, I certainly do. Someday, Man will want to know, indeed, need to know the facts about Mars that we have discovered. I predict that. But how will they ever get to that position without first having the wonder of speculation? The inspiration for imagining? The lies that lead to truth? Do we not tell children lies first to prepare them for realities? No, no, my dear Cyrano, we must continue to lie to the children of Earth to fill them with that questing spirit, that forward motion to get there themselves, to see for themselves. If we tell them that Mars is nothing but a big, empty, and quite dirty rock, they will just say, 'Oh, okay, what's for supper?' No, better, we should fill their heads with the amazement they desire until they can handle the facts they require. So, as for me, I will continue to conjure, to spin tales, to lie. I suggest you do the same."

It is not accurate to say that Cyrano was shocked by what the Baron said. He wanted to be and tried to be, but just could not be. The wisdom of the Baron's statement seemed much too clear to him.

"And Savinien Cyrano de Bergerac…"

"Yes, Baron."

"Study your philosophy and write. And do compose your *Voyage to the Moon*. It will be good. Oh, just a small step, of course, but certainly foreshadowing giant leaps. But, if I may make one small suggestion, hopefully without altering the future."

"I would be honored, Baron Munchausen."

"You will come up with several clever ways to fly to the moon using bottled captured dew that ascends in the early morning sun, and magnets, and such. They are not as imaginative as this great chariot of Queen Mab, of course, but clever. However, one of them, this idea of attaching rockets to a machine to go off in stages and then drop back to Earth one after the other—that's a much too absurd idea even for me! I would not embarrass yourself with that one."

When they returned to Earth, the Baron lied them back in time to a moment just after they had left. They exited the chariot of Queen Mab to stand on the lonely country road by Cyrano's cypress tree. As the hazelnut coach faded from existence, Cyrano, suddenly feeling exhausted, staggered to his tree and sat with his back against it. He was ashamed of himself; he wanted to bid a gracious farewell with a deep flourished bow to Baron Munchausen, but he just couldn't stand. As his eyes drooped, demanding to shut, Cyrano managed to keep them open long enough to see the Baron's magnificent head slowly fade, allowing the moon to reappear and dominate. Cyrano's eyes finally fully closed as he muttered, "Rockets?"

Turning the Tied

By early morning, when the sun was just rising, Cyrano was still under his cypress tree in a deep sleep and snoring. It was a subtle, musical snore, almost flute-like in sound given his long, luxurious nose. It rose up into the air and joined the many lilting, lovely songs of early birds out looking for worms.

What Men Ruin, We Shall Raise

Kelli Fitzpatrick

I have long been captivated by the wondrous worlds of Jules Verne, especially *20,000 Leagues Under the Sea*, but have always wanted to see women in the leading roles. I explore that angle here in a story that is imagined as a sequel to both *20,000 Leagues Under the Sea* (1870) and *The Mysterious Island* (1875).

Kelli Fitzpatrick is a science fiction and fantasy author, English educator, and contributing writer to the *Star Trek Adventures* role-playing game from Modiphius. Her *Star Trek* story "The Sunwalkers" won the Strange New Worlds 2016 contest, and her essays on pop culture media appear online at StarTrek.com and Women at Warp, and in print from Sequart and ATB Publishing. She is a strong advocate of the arts, public education, and gender rights and representation. Kelli can be found at KelliFitzpatrick.com and on Twitter @KelliFitzWrites

What Men Ruin, We Shall Raise

*T*HIS IS THE RECORDED LOG OF LILY MORAIN, ADOPTED DAUGHTER TO *Prince Dakkar of Lincoln Island, better known as Captain Nemo of the* Nautilus. *I have returned to that island where Captain Nemo raised me, to witness its destruction for myself, having heard that a volcanic eruption recently rendered it nothing but submerged rubble. In our years together, my father taught me to dive, not only with a diving suit but with my naked lungs. And despite the risks, I decided to descend and enter the* Nautilus, *the ship that lies scuttled on the seafloor. The ship that once was my father's home. The ship that is now his tomb. I knew what I would find inside, both an end and a beginning. Death, and yet, perhaps, a chance at a different kind of life. A legacy of hope. In the event that legacy eventually outlives me, I would like someone to know: it began here.*

Captain Jetta Kalreth of the Nautiloid fleet sat in the empty library of the *Jaunt* submarine, a thousand feet below surface level, playing the recorded logs of the Progenitor through the comm system. Her youthful eyes were creased as she listened intently, running a hand through long frizzy hair. What a wondrous sight the original *Nautilus* must have been when Lily found it, some hundred and fifty years ago, Kalreth thought. What courage it must have taken to return to that place of sorrow. How could she have known her legacy would last this long? That on this day so many generations later, the seventh iteration of the *Nautilus* would meet her new captain.

Kalreth took a deep breath. That legacy would soon be *her* responsibility.

She waved a hand over a slit in her desk and a screen of fine mist sprayed upward. A second later it lit up with the outline of a topside news anchor: "—around the globe celebrating this Equinox, marking new beginnings at the halfway mark through the twenty-first century. But some experts are concerned about the failing infrastructure of the Bay Area Sea Wall, especially in light of recent seismic activity." An enormous white hexagonal tower loomed over the Bay Area skyline. "Wealthy American elites continue to flock to resort towers to escape rising heat, water shortages, and flood threats, but they are receiving heavy criticism from humanitarian groups for leaving the rest of the population at the mercy of the conditions some say they created through decades of climate denial." Frustration boiled in Kalreth's chest. Where was the responsibility in this picture?

The report continued. "In Shanghai, another four million people were displaced as levees failed and rising oceans reclaimed low-lying districts."

Images flickered—scenes of chaos and flooding, screaming children and floating belongings. She remembered those screams. Some of them had been hers. She fingered the small folding multi-tool in her trouser pocket. The only piece of that life she had carried with her here, to this world beneath the waves.

Kalreth's executive officer, Vic Alanje, strode into the room, tall and lanky, looking middle-aged despite being the same late-twenties as Kalreth. He carried a garment bag. "I know you've been concerned about this, so I am pleased to report all your books and materials are safely installed in the *Nautilus VII* library."

"Thanks, XO. But my concerns were actually with topside."

Vic extracted a crisp blue dress jacket. "Some unpleasant tragedies occurring up there." He motioned her to stand.

"You're an expert at understatement, you know."

He held out the jacket for her to slide into. Kalreth could never get collars to lay flat, and she fussed at it until Vic stepped around to help. "Why do you think I was offered this role, Vic?"

"I should think because you are highly qualified. You've served in the Nautiloid fleet for over a decade, with five years in command, if my count is correct."

"Six if you count the yards."

"No one counts the yards, you know that. But your record doesn't need it." He began tying her neckerchief. "You are a capable leader."

They started closing the seemingly thousand sea-glass buttons. "Are you sure you want to follow me into this new post, XO? I'm confident Elana can handle the *Jaunt* when we depart, but this isn't some whirlwind tour. The *Nautilus VII* will sail for thirty years, and if I die before my term is complete, you will be charged with carrying out my aims."

Vic looked stricken. "I thought this was a five-month pleasure cruise. My mistake." His face melted to a dry smile. "I know what I'm here to do, Captain. And if you don't mind, I'm quite good at it." He brushed the shoulders of the dress jacket.

A comm note chimed above. "Elana to Kalreth." The young woman's voice was steady, Kalreth noticed. Good for her. This was a big day for them both. "The *Nautilus* pod is docking, Captain. Standing by to assume command of the *Jaunt*."

"Very good." Kalreth watched Vic's long fingers pin the medals on her chest, little stars of coral, one for securing the shipyards during a hurricane, and one for engineering applications for bio-synthetic compound 23, which revolutionized new construction in the Submerged City. She was just doing her job both times and didn't see what all the fuss was about, but Vic said being inducted as the next Nemo was a customary time to wear them. Vic was usually right about such things. And it did make her feel more...official.

"There," Vic said triumphantly, pushing Kalreth in front of the vapor mirror. "Never mind my expertise in psychology and logistics, this is why you really keep me around, isn't it?"

She looked at her reflection and saw a title staring back. Only the sitting Nemo wore blue in the Nautiloid fleet—everyone else wore pale green or white. She ran fingertips over the smooth seagrass fiber, dyed the gray-blue of tempered squid ink. She had been captaining the *Jaunt* for five years, usually with jacket tossed in a corner and hair spraying loose, bio-synth smeared up to her elbows as she helped a crewmember fix something, but Vic had been right—the title deserved this decorum. "Not bad, XO. Shall we go accept a ship?"

"You'll be accepting a ship, Captain. I'll be accepting the other twenty thousand things that will crowd your to-do list after this morning."

Kalreth laughed. Vic's dry humor always lightened her mood. They had worked side by side since the shipyards.

A slight tremor shook them. The first rumblings of that projected seismic activity. She glanced out the porthole into the green water beyond, a vast frontier of forces that would go on shaking the world for eternity.

Ready or not, she would soon be one of those forces.

When I dove down to the scuttled ship, the Nautilus *rose up before me like a specter. The pressure accosted my eardrums, but I had dived these cliffs so many times with father, I knew I could prevail. I found the secret hatch, a wet-dry airlock in the stern, and cycled the pump. Luckily, it did not require power to function. My father always thought ahead.*

The passageways of the ship were preserved precisely as I remembered them—dry, echoey, frozen in time. It was a stately place, even in that eerie stillness.

I knew exactly where I would find him. There was only one room that defined Captain Nemo, his repository of knowledge, his hall of treasures.

The library.

Indeed, upon entering the room, lit only by the pale green light from the water outside, the artifacts of a hundred seas and lagoons all gathered, choir-like, on shelves around my father's body, which lay peacefully on his couch, books strewn about, his last set of notes resting on his chest. It had been some weeks since the island's destruction, and I feared he would be in an unmentionable state. But his form was preserved, no doubt the result of his chemacology prowess. I knelt at his side, overcome by tears for this man who had saved me from shipwreck, who had loved me—Lily Morain—as his own, when I had nothing left in the whole of the world. I clutched his cold hand, and there, in his palm, was a folded piece of parchment with a symbol sketched upon it.

It was, unmistakably, a lily.

Kalreth's mind reeled with color and light. She strode through the passageways of the *Nautilus VII*, freshly minted, with all of the previous

Nemo's upgrades installed. The ship was bullet-shaped, and all its lines were smooth and arcing, nearly every surface shimmering with rainbow reflectiveness. There were mist screens everywhere, a quiet, more efficient condenser engine that combined hydrodynamics with magnetism, and the indispensable stealth tech that let the Nautiloid fleet remain incognito from topsiders.

It was achingly beautiful. And it would, after the ceremony, be hers.

Captain Nemo Fahari approached. "So? What do you think?" She grinned.

"I'm speechless. Are you sure you want to entrust me with this marvel?"

"The Circle of Captains is never wrong. Unless you want to turn down the nomination."

"Like hell." She ran her hand along the bulkhead, and a schematic of the ship appeared embedded in the metal. So much to explore. So much to learn.

"In here," Fahari motioned, and they stepped into the large library, where a dais and podium were set up. Several dozen people milled about. She noted with satisfaction that her book collection now indeed adorned the shelves. Scanning, she found Vic's face in the crowd and breathed a sigh of relief.

"Got your speech?"

Kalreth checked her jacket pocket and nodded, then followed Fahari up onto the dais. Her heart was pounding, in nervousness or excitement, or more likely both.

"Welcome retired Nemos and representatives of every vessel in our fine fleet," Fahari boomed. "Welcome crew of the *Nautilus VII,* and welcome to our Namesake nominee. There are no rulers in our domain, no monarchs, no empires, and no classes. There is just this Circle of Captains, passing the mantle down through time."

Neera Fahari had served as sitting Nemo for thirty years and was a powerful speaker and formidable captain, both in presence and accomplishments. She stood tall with strong shoulders, with reddish-brown skin and hair. During her term, she had devoted herself to curbing ocean pollution, using the collective force of the fleet's engines to whirlpool the great oceanic garbage patches into a central compactor that produced nuggets of fuel—plasticoal, she called them. Kalreth had seen the images of the process. They burned clean in the drives of the *Nautilus V* and later, and all later ship engines might make use of this fuel source. She had worked with a network of bike messengers in New York City to strategically place plasticoal on the doorsteps of eco-tech startup execs, along with instructions on how to replicate the results. "We all know who was really responsible for the energy boom last year," she quipped. The room laughed.

Kalreth listened as Fahari then recounted the other side of her legacy of Disruption: the EM pulses that deadened countless plastics plants, critically disrupting the single-use plastic industry. Thanks to her friends the janitors, those plant managers found cultures of algae in their offices, algae that could be heated and hardened for single use, and would break down with exposure to sunlight. The endgame for that particular disruption was still in play.

"Our course is our own," Fahari intoned. The Second Principle of Nautiloid society. The crowd echoed it back. "The Circle will now form to honor the history that brought us here, and populate the *Nautilus VII* library with artifacts of Nautiloid heritage." Fahari motioned Kalreth to stand at her side.

The crowd moved fluidly into a circle beneath the dais and turned to face the wall of purpose, the centerpiece of the library. It was fashioned from a massive fan of dried coral, blinding white, with six words carved across its chalky face, one aim for each Nemo who had served. The Changeover Ceremony happened only once every thirty years or so and was invitation-only—this was the first time Kalreth had witnessed one. She noted there was room at the bottom of the wall for her to carve her own word eventually. The wall was flanked by two built-in display cases.

"We begin at the beginning. Representatives of Captain Nemo, Prince Dakkar, first citizen of the sea: what have you brought to symbolize his term?"

A pair of young men stepped forward, carrying a box between them. "We bring a page of Prince Dakkar's notes, the specifications for the original *Nautilus* propulsion system, which heralded the way for the later condenser drive, and allowed our truly independent society to thrive." They lifted the lid in unison, revealing a yellowed page with precise hand-drawn diagrams, encased in archival glass. They secured it in a display compartment and rejoined the circle.

"Thank you. Representatives of Captain Nemo, Lily Morain, Progenitor of our society: what have you brought to symbolize her term?"

A little girl not older than eight stepped forward and thrust out a chunk of hardened volcanic rock. A beat went by, then a woman whispered something in her ear. "Oh! I bring lava from Lincoln Island. In the mist...middest...midst of destruction, the Progenitor chose action." She placed the rock in its designated spot. Kalreth smiled.

The parade of legacies continued: a vial of stealth ink representing innovation, a knob of bio-synth compound representing fortification, dried cultivated kelp symbolizing ocean conservation. Fahari added the first nuggets of plasticoal ever produced to represent her own term. When all the items were archived, Fahari retook the podium.

"There are many trials and threats to the sea in this era. You face a steep charge, Captain Nemo, Jetta Kalreth: keep us hidden. Keep us safe. And sow something in this world worth remembering."

There was applause. Kalreth read her prepared remarks, vowing to uphold the mantle as best she could. But reports of imminent flooding topside continued running on the news mist at the back of the room, and Kalreth kept finding her eyes drawn to it. Massive seaquakes were forecasted. Kalreth swore she could feel more faint shakings through her feet, though she was not yet accustomed to this new boat's hum. It all still felt so surreal. She ended by welcoming her new crew, and the many voyages they would trek together.

The ceremony concluded with a drop of distilled water from the *Nautilus VII*'s condenser drive being placed on Kalreth's tongue. They were bonded forever, now, Fahari decreed, this captain and this vessel. It had taken Kalreth more than a year to feel in sync with the *Jaunt,* but the *Nautilus VII* felt more like a being than a boat, and she looked forward to getting to know it better in the coming years.

Fahari invited everyone to stay and enjoy the view of the ocean and refreshments. A musician ascended the podium and began singing softly. Before Kalreth could circle back to the line of retired Nemos, a professionally dressed woman in plaid cornered her against the dais. Great.

"Professor Reiana, how nice to bump into you. Again. Our last chat was so...intense."

"You're the seventh female Nemo in the line of succession," Reiana said. "Only one man has held the title. What of those who say men ought to be considered for the Namesake?"

Seriously, she wanted to debate gender equity, here? "Men are free to lead in almost any capacity. Govern in the City, certainly. Serve in the fleet, sure. Take the chair? Not yet."

"Don't you think that's a bit sexist?"

"I think men had a few thousand years to run things, and mostly ran them into the ground. Women raised the *Nautilus* legacy from rubble, reformed it for a new era, and we shall continue to safeguard it for the time being. At least until our trust is earned." Kalreth scanned the room. Where was Fahari? The older woman was excellent at handling these kinds of situations. Kalreth had probably said a half dozen 'undiplomatic' things already.

A slight tremor shook the ship, rattling the glasses on the side tables. The singer did not miss a beat.

"The Seafloor Directorate predicts strong seismic activity today," Reiana said. "The Earth is very angry, and rightly so. Humanity has betrayed *her* trust, you see, poisoned her oceans and skies, and now she strikes back at those who stoked her fever. I think the Earth is wise in this regard. Perhaps you will consider using your term to restore the *Nautilus* to her original purpose."

Kalreth cocked her head. "Isolation?"

"Vengeance."

"Ah." Kalreth sighed. Fricking Nihilists, a fringe faction who wanted to watch all of topside burn at any cost. She hadn't pegged the professor as the type to be taken with acidic rhetoric. "Or perhaps I will restore the ship to a watery grave beneath a collapsed volcano. That's as original as it gets, no?" Reiana drew back sharply, apparently disgusted by the irreverence. Good. Kalreth had no ill will toward Prince Dakkar, the original Captain Nemo who had scuttled the first *Nautilus*—his flight from topside civilization spawned a magnificent submarine. But she loathed the assertion that only *his* ideals were relevant to Nautiloid society a full seven generations later. There were too many hard-working female bodies and minds standing in that gap. Kalreth leaned forward, and the medals on her jacket clicked. "More likely, Professor, I shall chart my own course, as is the sacred charge of every Nemo Namesake."

"And what course will that be, Captain?" Reiana nearly spit the last word. She wasn't backing down. "Really, I must know. Your remarks during the ceremony were hazy at best. Tell me, into what bold future do you plan to lead our great enclave of independent souls?"

Kalreth's blood chilled. She honestly had no idea. After months of diligent preparation for the assumption of this time-honored role, after all the research and reading and picking the brains of the fleet's old guard, she still had no viable plans of her own. At least, none in which she held enough confidence to ask others to follow her down into them. She was freediving in unknown depths, to be sure, but she had no intention of letting Reiana see that in this moment—Kalreth held her gaze. "As you well know, Professor, explorers cannot name the wonders they have yet to discover. But I promise you it will be a future worth remembering."

"How very...underwhelming. This ship could level a topside city in one stroke. You hold lightning in your hand, and you contemplate using it to pick through shells." Reiana sneered a polite smile and sauntered off, brushing roughly against Fahari as she stepped up.

Fahari frowned. "What's jammed under that one's scales?"

"It seems the good professor has joined the Nihilist movement. She is now staunchly on team *Warship Nautilus*."

"Heh. Some folks haven't cultivated enough discernment to lead, and that gets to them like sand in your eye. So to feel important, they stir up trouble just to watch the Maelstrom churn. Their way of feeling engaged without putting any real skin in the game, or offering any real solutions the world can actually live with." Fahari grabbed a drink off a platter, a bright pink liquid with a frilly stalk of sea kale sticking out of it. "One captain to another: don't let yourself get sucked down. It's only muck at the bottom."

"Indeed." The vocal music in the background swelled easily through the room. "Fahari, I've been meaning to ask you—"

"Call me Neera."

"All right. Neera, how did you settle on Disruption as the aim of your term?"

"Ha! Settle. You make it sound like a turtle digging a nest. You don't settle on an aim, Nemo. You grab it by the tentacles and wrestle it as far as you can."

Kalreth opened her mouth to answer, then closed it again. Tentacles? "But how did you know what—"

"It's already inside you. The thing that burns you up like lava. The thing that angers you and excites you precisely because you know your own skills fit the shape of the space that needs stepping into. For Dakkar, it was the sea itself, its wonders and refuge and biodiversity all waiting to be witnessed and documented. For the Progenitor, it was the future ghosts of women yet to lead, who needed a chair hewn from the wreckage she inherited. The Circle wouldn't have nominated you if we thought you'd be anchorless. Your aim will make itself known when you need it to. Usually in a way you can't ignore. That garbage patch story I told during the ceremony? Happened on my very first tour. I left out the part where it almost sank my damn ship. Whatever you tackle, it will inevitably be too big and too hard and too dangerous. Tackle it anyway. You are Nemo. You are no one. You are all of us."

"Captain Nemo!"

Both women turned as an aide strode up to them. "The crew is assembled to greet you in the passageways on your way to the bridge, and the chair is ready when you are."

Fahari smiled. "She's talking to you, Namesake."

"Right." Kalreth smoothed her hair back into its clasp, and breathed deeply.

"It's your adventure to chart." Fahari winked. "Don't let anyone convince you otherwise."

Kalreth nodded once, then filed through the maze of people, shaking hands along the way.

It was a map, this note my father left me. A map to a cache of raw materials on another deserted island. And a series of schematics for other ship designs like the Nautilus.

My father left me the means to raise a submarine fleet.

You will surely understand that I forthwith cursed his genius and his pride, right there in his sacred sepulcher, with every foul and tender word I could conjure. I cursed him for leaving me this wretched, glorious responsibility. I cursed him for trusting me alone.

Kalreth sat in the captain's chair on the bridge of the *Nautilus VII* and found herself tightly clutching the armrests. *Relax. This is your adventure.* She surveyed her bridge crew—she had studied their bios and even spoken with them via mist message, but had not met them in person. They sounded off around the room, ending with the helm officer, Helena Prajit. "Where to, Captain?"

"The Submerged City. We have a reception to attend."

The crew cheered.

It was not far. Kalreth always loved the approach to the City, because it felt like coming home, but it was especially meaningful now, in the *Nautilus*. It was the kind of underwater metropolis that Prince Dakkar would have loved, a fully self-sufficient city with sustainable cruelty-free agriculture, bio-glass buildings that were both break-resistant and renewable, and syphon-powered air filters that required no outside power.

It was a true sanctuary city, a place of safety for the refugees of the world whose homes were no longer livable, and whose nations and neighbors refused their obligations to assist. As ocean levels rose and superstorms increased, that population was rapidly rising. The Nautiloid fleet showed up off these coasts, sent their rescue pods in, and offered people a choice. Stay and take your chances. Or bring your family to the sea floor.

Many chose to come. She had. The rest were asked to keep silent, though there were several wild rumors circulating about the return of Atlantis.

As they reached the perimeter and were allowed inside the city's magnetic shield bubble, Kalreth ordered a view of the City below on the main viewer. Several divers were out swimming in the streets, for exercise or transport or fun. All of them waved.

"Helm, let's wave back."

Prajit smiled. "Aye, Captain." The grappling arm of the ship unlatched and waved to those below.

∼

The reception at Submerged City was held in the central domes, whose giant bubble-like bio-glass windows dominated the iconic cityscape where Kalreth had spent most of her late childhood. They were some of the oldest structures in the City, built long before Kalreth's time, but their standard reinforced glass was upgraded to bio-glass when the technology became available. Kalreth had helped install one set herself, and therefore held a fondness for this place.

In contrast to the futuristic smooth curves of the *Nautilus VII* interior, the reception ballroom was styled after a 1920s jazz hall, with some obvious marine flair.

Parties weren't really Kalreth's jive—she preferred quiet conversations—but Vic loved them. She spied her friend playing the synthesizer in the corner, a peppy metropolitan beat. He somehow looked both perfectly poised, and perfectly fluid. It made her happy to see him happy.

More people congratulated her than she knew even lived here, it seemed, but she enjoyed walking the room and listening to Olga Norencranz, the oldest living retired Nemo, tell her tales of trying to stop climate change when the first indications surfaced. She tipped off journalists to coral bleaching, helped young advocates secure platforms, "but the corporations would not listen, and the governments would not enforce," she said. "We must do the conserving ourselves."

Kalreth paused beside helm officer Prajit, who was struggling to open a reusable drink bottle. "I got it." She pulled out her multi-tool and popped the top.

"Thanks, Captain. May I ask where you got that?"

"Carried it in from topside when I arrived. I was nine when my village flooded. Last piece of my parents I have, so I like to carry it with me. Plus...it's occasionally useful." She smiled.

Prajit nodded. "I was twelve. Thankfully my aunt survived and immigrated with me. The flooding happened so much faster than we were led to believe."

They shared a thick beat of silence.

"So why join the fleet?" Prajit said. "After surviving that chaos, why not stay in the City where it's safe?"

"I might ask you the same," Kalreth said. "In truth? Because I think we can make things better. Not just as Nautiloids, but as humans. And because I think we owe it to the rest of our species, and the larger ecosystem, to try."

"Owe?" Helena raised her eyebrows. "Captain, with all due respect, the First Principle clearly states as citizens of the sea, we owe nothing to anyone."

"I take that to mean we owe our dignity to no one. That is ours, always. But would you not say we owe some part of our privileges, our ability to build on them, to the dedication of the women who came before us? To the Progenitor? To the line of captains who chose to keep that legacy alive, keep reforging it and expanding it each and every generation, despite the fact that it is always easier to simply guard what you already have?"

"I think it's reasonable to say our privilege rests on a bed of their labor. But all those women were Nautiloids, not topsiders."

"They all became Nautiloids, but Prince Dakkar was born a topsider. So was the Progenitor. So were you. So was I. Go back far enough, and all our blood has dirt in it." She swirled the ice in her glass, then smiled curiously. "What would you do with the chair, Prajit, if you were nominated?"

"Captain?"

"What word would you carve on that wall?"

She considered for a long moment. "Compassion, I think."

"Compassion for whom?"

"I don't know...The sea has no borders. Why must my word?"

Suddenly, something exploded near the window, followed by shrieks and people ducking onto the deck.

But no water rushed in, and no one seemed injured. Kalreth and Vic hurried toward the affected area, directing people toward the back exit as they went. Kalreth knelt and examined a small glob of purple goo stuck to the thick bio-glass, surrounded by a blast scorch. "What do you think? Tri-calcite composite?"

Vic nodded. "That color is fairly distinctive." He scanned the window unit with his ring. He pulled out a tiny mister and spritzed the air, then shone a light from his ring into the cloud. The data materialized. "No fractures or damage of any kind."

"City procedure is still to go into lockdown until the situation is fully resolved. The bombers would have to know tri-calcite explosives don't stand a chance of breaching this bio-synth reinforced installation. Perhaps the attack wasn't meant as an attack—"

"But as a distraction." Vic's face assumed an expression of strong disapproval.

"So where is the real vulnerability? Are all our outposts reporting secure, all vessels accounted for?"

Vic pulled up the comm alerts. "All clear. I shall tell them to stay on alert. What about the timing, Captain? Why today, do you suppose?"

"Well, today is the Changeover Ceremony, obviously, and the Vernal Equinox. It's also...pull up those seismic readings again."

Kalreth looked over them. "The anticipated seaquakes will rumble us but won't pose a threat, not this deep. The only thing the quakes will threaten is—" she went silent. "The surface. The shallows. The coasts."

"I don't understand. That is regrettable, but how is that connected to a potential bombing?"

"XO, if you believed all topsiders should be eradicated, that they fundamentally deserved to die horrible deaths via natural disasters because of the damage their institutions have done, but they kept coming up with shoddy defenses to stave off the disasters...what would you do?"

"I would weaken those defenses so that when the next disaster struck...Oh. The sea wall. The Nihilists are going after the Bay Area sea wall."

"The wall that is already crumbling and that will take a beating from the coming quakes. Add some tri-calcite to the mix—"

"And you get disaster."

"You get millions dead. And millions more refugees. Recall all hands and prepare the *Nautilus* to depart immediately."

"Aye, Captain."

She crossed her arms and peered out at the green abyss. Somehow, the forces had intensified.

~

Sometimes Kalreth hated being right.

They found the tri-calcite explosives lodged deep in the existing hairline cracks in the sea wall. There wasn't time to dig them out manually. They would have to neutralize them with an ionized spray. Luckily, one of Captain Fahari's additions to the *Nautilus VII* design was a set of high powered water jets ensconced in the nose cone of the vessel.

"Well, Captain, what are your orders?" Vic waited.

What *were* her orders? This was it, the first real decision she had to make as Nemo. She had found the problem, but what was the correct solution? The seconds spread out like wet sand.

"I...Get me an open comm line to Fahari. I need insight, now."

The XO looked at her, then nodded and danced fingers over controls. "Calling it up."

A voice rang through the bridge, but it was not Fahari's. *"With the map to the shipyard and materials cache now in my possession, I must determine my course of action. I sat for hours this evening on the sole promontory of rock that remains of Lincoln Island, watching the sun set."*

Prajit turned toward Kalreth. "That's the Progenitor. We had to memorize her logs in school. I recognize this part, it's when she decides to become, well, herself."

"Apologies for the mixup, Captain," the XO said calmly. "Let me just correct—"

"No, wait." Kalreth stood, stared out the viewport at the towering wall and drank in the words as they played.

"Beneath me is a tomb and a dying mountain. Is that to be our legacy? Flooded wreckage and dashed potential? Endless violence and greed? My father's ego could span the Pacific, but I do not think he wished such a fate on humanity, not even those who walk the land. But I suppose it does not matter anymore what he wished. The legacy is mine now to direct."

No one moved on the bridge.

"I hold the map to a new beginning in my hands, resources and knowledge far beyond what most of the world could ever dream. I know the sea. I know oppression still chokes the planet and its organisms. How can I not press forward? I shall find my own allies. What men ruined, we shall raise, renewed, in steel and spirit and name."

The recording clicked off, signaling the end of the entry.

Kalreth cleared her throat and pulled up topside aerial footage of streams of humanity rushing out of the flood zone. She knew they would never make it to safety in time. She had been following the climate crisis briefs for years. Their government and corporate classes knew the walls would fail eventually, had known the scope of the problem for decades as Olga had pointed out. But the people in power did not reside in those sunken suburbs, were never in any real danger, and so had no motivation to trade profit for progress. Kalreth choosing to stand by while a city drowned would not teach the leaders of these nations anything. It would only make the vulnerable suffer.

On the other hand, tipping the Nautiloids' hand to topside, after a century of successful clandestine existence, might jeopardize the lives of everyone who called the sea home.

What kind of legacy did she want to leave?

Every officer on the bridge had eyes on her, waiting for orders. For action? For a decision. "The course I'm about to take flies in the face of seven generations of Nautiloid tradition. But I believe it is in keeping with the Progenitor's legacy of doing what must be done to protect the innocent. As sitting Nemo, I need no one's permission to take such action."

Silence.

"Our data is clear: that sea wall is going to crumble, imminently, unless we intervene. Three forces have conspired to weaken it: the negligence of topside government, the zealotry of our Nihilists, and the fury of nature. We cannot stop an earthquake, but we can nullify that explosive and deploy bio-synth compound sheeting to reinforce the sea wall structure long enough for evacuations to take place. Even if we are successful on all fronts, there may be leaks. I intend to deploy the rescue pods for those caught in flooding, and ferry them to safety."

"We...we will be seen, Captain," the science officer said. "The pods for sure, and possibly the *Nautilus* herself. The stealth technology was not designed for close range, and they will undoubtedly recover samples of the bio-synth later. They will possess that technology."

"I am aware. As I said, I am breaking our tradition of remaining hidden, but I am going to give the privileged among them an ultimatum, a course of action much more in keeping with Prince Dakkar's mission than the Progenitor's. I intend to use the magnetic confinement beams on the *Nautilus* to topple the tower of their elite, the refuge they built for themselves to rise above the threat of swelling seas, to escape the climate change they caused through unchecked industry. We will lay the tower down, gently, on its side, placing its population of corporate officials and rich citizens—"

"In the same path of the deluge as everyone else." The XO's eyes flicked about, calculating the logistics. "They will hate you, Captain. But they will be willing to bargain."

"Let them hate me. The ultimatum I will issue is this: change your policies to help your people and I will intervene to reinforce the wall. The negotiation could get ugly. The task of saving this region will not be easy."

"What if they refuse to negotiate?" Prajit said.

"Then we will nullify the explosives and use the pods as the fleet always has—to rescue as many people as we can. I will not surrender our bio-tech without assurance of policy change." That was hard to say. But she knew it was her only chance at creating lasting change. "As officers of the *Nautilus VII*, you have sworn an oath to me and this vessel. But I also recognize there is no higher right than the right to walk away. I ask for your courage now to risk our ship, our lives, and potentially our entire society's cover. There are four million topsider lives in the balance, and the potential to leverage real reform for the world's most vulnerable populations. That is a risk I am willing to take. If you disagree with my plan or do not wish to engage with topside in this manner, I ask that you please exit the bridge now. You will not be—"

"Course laid in, Captain, awaiting your mark," Prajit said. "I'll get us as close to the tower as I can."

"Defensive targeting module active," the sec officer said. "If the Nihilists show back up, they will have to get through me."

"Stealth system engaged—"

"Scanning for seismic intervals—"

"Pods prepped and ready for launch—"

"Notifying cargo bay to unpack some bio-sheets and spool up the grappling arm—"

"Comm line on standby, Captain," the XO said. "In case you want to notify the rest of the fleet of our plans."

Our plans. At the end of her term, what had the Progenitor really

407

built? Not just a fleet. A community. A vision. Kalreth blinked that realization from her eyes. "Alright then. Prajit, take us in."

∼

In the height of conflict, time often refracts. Kalreth had experienced this in diving encounters with sharks. Time slowed, and for the seconds that her mind was buoyed by adrenaline, she saw over the top of the present moment and peeked into the future. As the *Nautilus* sent its powerful magnetic beams into the cliffside to sever the foundations of the mammoth tower, she saw her future self recount the moment to a crowd, describing the slow toppling of the tower like an iceberg lying down on a deserted beach. It bent, more than fell—she had no wish to take life.

She saw herself being interviewed about the tense audio negotiations with a representative of the tower elites, of explaining their shared plight with the rest of the region and the danger of the imminent flood, of her offer to reinforce the wall in exchange for radical policy shifts. Biotechnology in exchange for reparations, relocation assistance, basic needs allocation, immediate climate action. Of course they feigned having no ownership. Of course she still held them to account. As she caught the crack of earnestness in that leader's voice, she suddenly saw herself at nine, standing waist deep in filthy floodwater, knowing, somehow, that her family was gone. And then she saw herself in all moments, in all eras, with every voice of every Captain Nemo, saying firmly: "Never again."

∼

"XO?"

"Captain."

Nemo and Vic sat drinking tea in the lounge with a single pair of guards on duty at the doors. Most of the crew rested from the excitement of the sea wall encounter, which was fast becoming known as the Battle of the Ivory Tower (even though no shots were fired). The existence and location of the Submerged City and the rest of the fleet remained safe for now. While the American elites scrambled with the government to implement the requisite policies that would unlock the gift of more Nautiloid bio-tech, the *Nautilus* was crossing the Pacific to meet with Asian leaders who were also interested in negotiating climate progress. No tower toppling required this time.

"How long have you and I sailed together?"

"Nine years, Captain. Counting my turn as ambassador from the *Narwhal*."

"In all that time, I have never seen you mistake a recorded file for an open comm line. In fact, I've never seen you make a mistake of any kind at your station. Quite the mix-up with that log entry, yes?" She eyed Vic over the rim of her cup. "Are the *Nautilus's* controls glitching, perhaps? Do I need to harangue the construction crew at the yards—"

"The *Nautilus* is shipshape, Captain." The XO raised an eyebrow. "And so am I. It is my job as your second to provide you with all relevant information required to make sound decisions. You *did* ask me for insight." He sipped his tea. "I will always trust you to make the right call. As I believe you did on this occasion."

"Hmm. Her choices and motivations are still relevant all these generations later, aren't they?"

"The Progenitor?" Vic Alanje nodded. "There is a reason legends last."

Nemo mused on that for a moment. "What do you think will last from this encounter with topside? What will future generations bring to the Circle to symbolize this? This, well, whatever this is we just started."

"I should think they might bring themselves, Captain. You just started a future where they are much more likely to exist."

Kalreth's throat drew tight. That was a legacy she could live with. "The *Nautilus* isn't quite shipshape yet, XO. Take this watch. I have a task I need to see to before we arrive."

Vic searched her face, then half-smiled. "My pleasure, as always."

In the library bathed by moonlight from a night sea, Captain Nemo knelt before the wall of purpose. Jacket draped over a chair, hair tumbling in her eyes, she leveraged the chisel tip of her multi-tool to carve her aim into the ancient glowing coral. And when the word was complete, she blew the dust from its letters, which sparkled in the darkness, rained onto her trousers like Antarctic snow. She traced the rough angles of each letter, all the hard turns that lay ahead.

JUSTICE.

Let Nothing You Dismay

Jean Rabe

The Ghost of Christmas Past appeared in Charles Dickens' *A Christmas Carol*, a novella published in 1843. The ghost's first film portrayal was in 1901 by an unnamed actor wearing a sheet. I always thought the ghost deserved more screen time and a little backstory.

Jean Rabe, a *USA Today* Bestselling author, has written more than forty novels and one hundred short stories. Many of her works have been tie-ins. A longtime member of the IAMTW, Jean was named a Grand Master in 2020, presented the Faust Award online because conventions closed down that summer. The pandemic afforded her more time to write and edit and ruminate about what ghost story to put in this anthology. She shares her office with a cantankerous parrot named Trouble and three rescue dogs—a Labrador, a one-eyed elderly Boston, and a one-eyed Pug. When Jean isn't writing, she tosses tennis balls in the backyard, enjoys boardgames and RPGs, and tries to put a dent in her to-be-read stack of books. Visit her website at: jeanrabe.com.

Let Nothing You Dismay

"What do you remember about that night?" The psychiatrist asked the question in a soft monotone.

"I remember it was cold, so very cold, behind the garage. And dark. The moon was out. I think it was close to full, but there was a stripe of clouds across it. There was just enough light for me to see Penny. My father made me touch her. He said I should pet her, say goodbye. I didn't want to touch her. All broken and still, I was afraid to touch her."

The ghost stood behind the therapist and watched the woman sink further into the high-backed leather chair. He imagined that it was comfortable, and toasty because it was near the register in the shrink's office, but his own comfort and warmth were distant memories to him. Too warm, perhaps, as the woman took her purse off her lap and *thumped* it onto the floor, revealing a red and green Christmas sweater, the glittery kind that could win an ugly contest. The purse was one of those over-the-shoulder things that reminded the ghost of a horse's saddlebag, and it bulged. He wondered what she'd stuffed inside it. She was toting enough emotional baggage that she shouldn't be weighed down physically as well.

"Let's talk about that a bit more, Ellen," the shrink said. "Behind the garage."

She puffed out a great breath that fluttered the thin bangs hanging over her forehead. "I think about it every December. I'm thinking about it every day, now. I just want to forget about it. Can't you make me forget? Hypnotize me? Give me a prescription, or something—"

"You're on enough medications, Ellen, according to this record. So, let's talk about the garage."

His target seemed to fold in on herself, hunching her shoulders and dropping her chin to her chest. The ghost saw a solid inch of gray roots intruding in her auburn curls. Ellen was overdue for a dye-job.

"I was wearing a plaid dress my mom had made. It had these little pearly snap buttons. It was mostly red, and it had short poofy sleeves. She said I always looked good in red, and it had blue and green stripes, to make it plaid, you know. I had a red plastic barrette in my hair. My hair was short and was blond when I was a kid. I was five years old." She rounded her shoulders even further. "I had on these black patent leather shoes. They call them Mary Janes now. I don't know what they were called then, but I had a real wide foot when I was a kid. My mom said I'd inherited my dad's triple-Es. So they had to take me to a specialty shoe store to get stuff that fit right. They had to spend extra money on my shoes. My socks had lace on the cuffs. Dressed up, you know. I was dressed up that night."

The ghost noticed that the woman, indeed, had short, wide feet, maybe a size six at best, probably ordered from a hard-to-fit online store. The woman was short, too, and her hands—fingers worrying at a thread in her ugly sweater—were small and thin and displayed only one ring, a plain gold band.

"About the garage—" the shrink prompted.

"This isn't about the garage," Ellen cut back. "This is about Penny."

"Go on."

"It was Christmas Eve and Momma took me to my grandparents. We'd brought presents to put under their little tree. They had one on a table in the living room, frosted white with those little fairy lights that twinkled in odd patterns. Tiny glass balls. Tinsel. I remember it had tinsel that twisted when the furnace came on. Anyway, I was having a good time. I was five years old. Five-and-a-half."

Ellen's fingers fidgeted faster.

"What does the garage have to do with—"

"*Behind* the garage," she corrected. "It was dark when we left my grandparents. Always gets dark early in the winter. I was five. Five-and-a-half." Another puffing breath. "We pulled into our driveway and saw that the dog was out in the yard. I asked Momma to slow down, but she turned to me and said, 'Don't tell me how to drive.' She said the dog knew to stay away from the car. The dog always stayed away from the car when it was outside." A pause. "Except that Christmas Eve. I felt the car rise up a little, heard a thump, and I knew what happened. I was five, but I knew. Momma started crying and she turned to me and said it was my fault for distracting her. My fault that she ran over the dog. Dad came out and carried Penny behind the garage. A few minutes later, he fetched me. He said it was nobody's fault, that the dog must've been blinded by the headlights."

"I'm sorry, Ellen," the shrink said. The ghost thought the man's voice flat. The shrink looked at a notepad. "That was more than fifty years ago."

"Fifty-eight," she said. "I'm sixty-three now. Sixty-three-and-a-half. And I can't get it out of my head. It's crystal in my memory. It won't go away. The dress, the shoes, the red barrette. The car rising. The thump. It was so damn cold behind the garage. I sat next to Penny, and my dad made me touch her and say goodbye. I couldn't stop crying. Before I went to sleep, Momma came to tuck me in, kissed me, and told me again it was my fault. She said if I hadn't wanted to stay so long at my grandparents' house Penny wouldn't have been outside to do her business. Penny wouldn't have been out and she wouldn't have been run over. My fault. My fault."

The ghost watched the woman knit her fingers together, the knuckles snow-white. Her face was still tipped down. He couldn't see if she was crying, but her voice sounded shattered.

"That was fifty-eight years ago, Ellen, and you weren't driving the car. You didn't run over the dog. You tried to get your mother to slow down."

"My husband is retiring the end of the month and he wants to get a spaniel. He likes to hunt and hike and he says he'll have lots of time to do both and that a field spaniel would be perfect. He's been searching rescue sites, the whole 'adopt, don't shop' thing. I told him I don't want a dog in the house. Can't have a dog. I can't. I just can't. Something awful will happen to it. My fault."

415

The ghost sighed. Ellen was seriously messed up.

"Penny's fur was so soft," she said. "It was cold behind the garage."

The ghost glided forward, nesting himself inside the hunched woman, taking her back fifty-eight years, to the car, which had no seatbelts because they weren't required then, which had big round headlights that had blinded the dog. He saw how red her dress was, peeking out from the bottom of her winter coat, how shiny her patent leather slippers—all dressed up to visit her grandparents on Christmas Eve. He felt the car rise up, heard the thump, and he swallowed those memories and drank down Momma's "It's your fault." All of them.

It's what the ghost did, and he was good at it, stealing the memories of Christmas past. Select memories.

Just the bad ones.

"I can't make you forget, Ellen," the shrink said. "But several more sessions should—"

"Forget what? What should I forget?" Ellen had brightened, her shoulders square, chin tipped up. She stood and slung the bulging purse over her shoulder and grinned.

"Your dog," the shrink started. "When you were five—"

"I had a nice little dog when I was a kid. She was called Penny. A good dog. Now my husband wants one. He's retiring. We're going to get a field spaniel from a rescue. It'll be great."

"Listen, Ellen—"

"Can't recall what I wanted to come in here for. Must be one of those senior moments. Thanks for helping me work through whatever it was. I feel good." Her blue eyes sparkled. "I have to finish my Christmas shopping."

The ghost floated through the floor and down eighteen floors to the street level. He was followed by a second spirit. They emerged onto Michigan Avenue. Big lacy flakes were falling.

"You took her memory?" the second spirit asked.

The ghost watched a portly man waddle by, arms loaded with packages.

"It's what I do," the ghost said. "It's what I've been doing for more than two thousand years. I'm very good at it, Charlie."

"Everyone calls me Charles now."

"You will always be Charlie to me."

Charlie floated behind the ghost as they passed through shoppers and ambled to Millennium Park, where a massive lighted spruce stretched up nearly fifty feet.

"It will be much prettier when it's dark, that tree," the ghost said. "I'll take you through the Morton Arboretum and the Brookfield Zoo. The decorations are spectacular. The Magnificent Mile is a must-see, too. Never been to Chicago before, Charlie?"

"Never at Christmastime."

"My eighth December here," the ghost said. "And my last for a while, I think. Next year I'm going back to Paris. It is certainly the City of Light at the holidays. Hundreds of thousands of lights from the Arc de Triomphe to the Place de la Concorde, and the Champs-Élysées. The city's Marché de Noel Christmas market is wonderfully colorful. Medellen, Colombia is good for lights, too. Singapore and Madrid are also nice. Ever been to Paris, Charlie?"

"A long time ago." The ghost hesitated. "And not at Christmas."

"I only come out around Christmas, Charlie. You know that."

The ghosts stopped in front of the massive tree covered in ice-blue lights.

"I never thought I'd see you again," Charlie said. "I've looked on and off since my death, but—"

"It was 1843 the last we met. You were still breathing."

Charlie nodded, ephemeral wisps of hair drifting around his head like a halo. "The year my novella came out."

"*A Christmas Carol*. You gave me a starring role, but not the lead. Always thought I should have had center stage."

Charlie circled the tree, passing through onlookers and stopping when he came back to the ghost. "Ebenezer was the star."

"Played by Patrick Stewart in 1999. Marvelous adaptation, I think. I was played by Joel Grey in that one. David Johansen portrayed me in *Scrooged*, a rather insipid production I found only mildly amusing. Andy Serkis in the BBC rendition. Old, young, male, female, cartoon characters. In 1901 I've no idea who had the role... some unnamed actor wearing a sheet. The movies never got me right."

"But I did," Charlie said.

"Long white hair and a face with no wrinkles, you wrote. Never assigned me a gender pronoun, just referred to me as it."

"With a white tunic and holding a branch of fresh green holly in your hand," Charlie finished. "On top of your head a bright flame."

"Because that's how you saw me."

They studied the tree in silence for a while. Christmas carols played from a speaker on a building. Kenny Chesney's "All I Want for Christmas is a Real Good Tan".

"That's how you remembered me," the ghost said.

"I was twelve, I think, the first time I saw you."

"That was in 1824," the ghost replied. "The year your father was thrown into debtors' prison."

"My father never went to prison," Charlie cut in. "We were poor, certainly. Sometimes we were poor. I had seven brothers and sisters."

"You don't remember your father in prison because I took that Christmas memory from you. I feared you would run away from home, devastated, frightened, too much put on your young head. Shame and responsibility, you were drowning in it. You'd cried for that memory to go away."

Charlie spun from the tree and stared at the ghost. It had an unlined face and long white hair, held a branch of holy between slender fingers.

"But the memory of me stayed and inspired your greatest work… what some say is your greatest work."

"*A Christmas Carol.* I came to Chicago this year because of the Dickens Festival," Charlie said. "The exhibit at the Field Museum and the library, and the Music Box Theatre showing Christmas movie classics, a day of all the versions of *A Christmas Carol.* Surprisingly popular. *David Copperfield* was always my personal favorite. I felt drawn here, I guess. Hadn't expected to see you. Never thought I'd see you again."

"Terry Pratchett, a fine author, wrote: 'Million-to-one chances… crop up nine times out of ten.' Maybe I'll see you in Paris next year. Maybe the year after in Vienna." The ghost floated away from the tree, Charlie following.

"Where are we going?"

The ghost turned and floated backward. "There's a tavern on the corner where a twenty-five-year-old bartender drinks too much the week of Christmas. I overheard her tell a reveler yesterday that her father died on her couch in her first apartment on Christmas Eve. Three years past. Heart attack. The Christmas tree all blinking pretty a few feet away. She'd bought him a bottle of Crown Royal and a nice thick sweater, and he never got to open the packages. They're still wrapped on the floor in her closet. She's messed up enough about it that I'm going to take the memory, let her get on with her life. Stop drinking so much in December."

"That's not how I wrote you."

"No," the ghost said. "You wrote me showing your Ebenezer Scrooge the good bits of the holiday, the happy remembrances of Christmas past. I can see happy memories, Charlie, always have been able to. I just can't do anything about them. I was made to take the bad recollections, to swallow them down and choke myself with anger and anguish and grief as thick as warm and sticky figgy pudding. It is what I do."

"Are you ever happy?"

The ghost paused in front of the tavern window, a shimmering outline stared back. "The firehouse is also a good place to take memories, Charlie, and police stations. Policemen, firemen, see horrible things, especially at the holidays. The Salvation Army, that's a magnet for the miserable. We'll go to those places next, after the bartender. She's held onto her bad memory too long."

"Are you ever happy?" Charlie repeated.

"Briefly I was today, when I took Ellen's fifty-eight-year-old torment and felt her spirit uplifted. I sensed her joy and I held onto that as long as I could."

"You *stole* her memory."

"Just that bad one."

"Don't you think it is wrong to—"

"What? Wrong to ease someone's pain? Ellen still remembers Penny, how soft her coat felt, that she liked to play with the dog. She just doesn't remember the dog's death and her mother's torturous words. Or how cold it was behind the garage that night."

The tavern door opened and music spilled out: "God Rest Ye Merry Gentlemen".

"That's Missy tending bar. See her inside serving customers? She'll still remember her father, who took her fishing over the state line onto Lake Geneva in the summers, who read Westerns to her when she was a child. And I will uplift her when I steal the image of him white-faced and rigid on her couch, the Christmas tree blinking a few feet away."

The ghost glided into the tavern, Charlie following.

"I am not the only soul so tasked, Charlie," the ghost said as he dove into Missy and took her back to that apartment, the dingy brown couch where her father died, swallowing her pain.

Around them glasses clinked and conversations rose and fell.

"God Rest Ye Merry Gentlemen."

"Brothers," Charlie said, as the ghost emerged and started back toward the street.

"Yes, in your time, your novella, you wrote that I had more than eighteen hundred brothers, one for each year since the first Christmas Day. There are more than two thousand now. Next year, in Paris, join me, Charlie. Be the next Ghost of Christmas Past. Be the 2,021st."

Catfather

Nancy Holder

Mary Wollstonecraft Shelley was challenged one dark and stormy night to write a ghost story. Instead, she wrote what was considered both the first science fiction novel and the first horror novel. Her *Frankenstein, or: The Modern Prometheus* proved influential upon its 1818 publication. The revised text was published in 1831 and is the version we now read. Victor Frankenstein and his creation have been endlessly adapted in every imaginable form of storytelling, including Nancy Holder's and Melanie Tem's re-imagining, *Making Love*.

Nancy Holder is the *New York Times* bestselling author of the *Wicked* series (with coauthor Debbie Viguié) and many others. She has written many novels and short stories set in the *Teen Wolf, Buffy the Vampire Slayer,* and other universes, and novelized the films *Wonder Woman* and *Crimson Peak*, among others. A five-time winner of the Bram Stoker Award from the Horror Writers Association, she received the Grandmaster Award in 2019 from the International Association of Media Tie-In Writers. She lives in Washington State.

Catfather

He had seen death before. Death had birthed him. Death had brought rage and fury. But this death, this…his hour of triumph—

This singular moment was a grief that cracked his bones and drank his blood, and filled his boiling heart with shame. He wailed like a child, keened at the sight of the pallid face of Victor Frankenstein. Seconds too late. Too late. Frankenstein was dead. He had done this, he.

But it was done to me first.

No matter.

The smile of a loving father: never. The dreams and hopes for his future: none. Nothing but loathing for "the demon." *He did not love me. He could not.* But he loved him now, loved Victor Frankenstein, the prideful, fragile man who had pursued him across ice and snow for the sole purpose of dealing him death. The madman who had pieced him together from limbs of rotting flesh, galvanized them, and, horrified, abandoned him.

Frankenstein had expired inside the captain's cabin of a sailing ship trapped in the ice. Explorers seeking the Northwest Passage. Now aboard, the Being could smell the bodies of other frozen, starved men, although the crew were not all dead, not yet. No one had noticed when he'd brazenly approached. There was no watch. What would they be watching for?

Deathwatch. Death, when it came again, would creep upon these men slowly, on little cat's paws. He knew what it was to die by inches.

The clomp of heavy boots, and then the captain of the vessel came into the cabin—the tomb—and halted. The Being was not surprised when, looking up, he saw that the captain had averted his eyes. Yes, yes, hideous to look upon. A monster, an abomination. Only a blind man had ever loved him.

The Being's mourning wails hardened into sobs, and still the captain said nothing. The sobs became words, and the bitterness and remorse and shame torrented out of him. Yes, he had murdered Frankenstein's innocent friends and family. Yes, Frankenstein had died a failure in his own eyes, not for making the monster but for not ending the monster. And so the Being swore he would do what Frankenstein had failed to do: he would take his own life.

The captain never spoke.

Tears froze on the Being's dead-white skin as he hefted Frankenstein's sled with all its contents to his ice-raft. It had conveyed him to the ship too late to lay eyes on the living Frankenstein after hundreds and thousands of miles in pursuit. He was of grim purpose now: he would leave no trace behind of his Creator, nor of himself. He gathered wood from the emptied barrels and crates around the imprisoned vessel and added those to the raft. A prodigious weight. His intention was to burn himself on a funeral pyre; but it seemed likely that before that happened, the raft would sink from its additional burdens and he would drown. By ice or by fire, he would die.

He pushed off, and the ship in its prison of ice receded. Farewell, Creator, forever farewell.

The polar sea was known to him. As the waves tossed his raft, he thought many times of falling in. How simple it would be. But he wanted obliteration, to leave no trace, and it was possible that his frozen corpse would wash up on a shore. If that happened, men would examine him, dissect him, and another ambitious scientist would use the knowledge gleaned thereby to create another monster.

Yet the sea beckoned. The waves splashed over his numb feet and soaked the heavy coat he wore more to obscure his appearance that to protect him from the elements. A human would have frozen to death by now. It was a testament to Frankenstein's compulsion to destroy him that the man lived through journeys like this as long as he had.

I held him in my arms. I wept over him. Would he have wept; would he have mourned—

And then he heard a sound between the thrash and crash of the waves: a tiny mewing. He blinked, listening. There it was again, feeble and weak.

Un chat, he thought, French of course being his first language. A cat.

In the pocket of his ragged, useless coat.

The Being dipped his hand inside and felt the soft fur, the warmth. He drew it out. It was a tiny tiger-striped kitten, all ears and eyes, very new to the world. How had it gotten into his pocket? Ships often kept cats aboard to kill the rats; perhaps theirs had had a litter?

The kitten gazed up at him and this time only moved its mouth. It must be starving. He put it back in his pocket and rooted through Frankenstein's belongings. Furs and some of the newly developed tinned foods—meat and pea soup. Perhaps the kitten was old enough for solid food; he had no milk to give it.

Forcing open a can of meat, he cleared a section of Frankenstein's sled and set the kitten down. It fell upon the tin and began to devour the contents. The Being watched; then, as a wave lifted the raft up and up, he steadied the sled with a hand even though it was well-lashed to the raft. The cat stumbled from the force of the movement but kept eating.

The day stretched out, long and stormy. Now he fought the sea. He must reach land and give this little creature its life. He could not die until he had saved it. So he would die by fire then. On land.

Just not quite yet.

~

The Being had led Frankenstein on a wild hunt for years, remaining just out of reach across deserts and snowy glaciers, gentle valleys and poisonous forests, drawing him along. Thus the Being knew the world well, and made land by following the stars—if land it could be called, as it was covered with ice and snow. By then, the cat had devoured a second tin of meat and spent hours in its fur bed purring and grooming itself.

425

When they washed up on shore, the Being carried the sled to solid earth and deposited it in a small cave. The kitten slept. After he had transferred everything from his raft, he pulled that up onto land, too. He started a fire with the driest bits of wood in his cache, and ate some tinned meat as well. Exhausted, he drifted into a languorous slumber. At some point the kitten curled beneath his chin and padded its paws against his gray, wrinkled skin, and purred.

Over time, he caught fish and birds. The kitten hunted too. He named it Ange. Angel. After some weeks of sustenance and safety, he told himself that Ange could live without him now. He could build his funeral pyre. But the cat looked small, and it followed him everywhere. At night it curled up and padded his neck and chest. So he told himself *one more night* and then *one more*, and he had no idea how long they lived in the cave.

Then one morning, ship's sails rose on the horizon. The vessel was making for land, their land. He packed everything that was left onto Frankenstein's sled in a whirlwind of worry and beckoned Ange to take its place among the furs. Snow began to fall, covering their tracks as he pushed the sled away from the soot-blackened walls of their home.

He didn't know if or when the ship landed; he and the kitten were leagues away by then, safe again.

"Perhaps it would have been better for you if I had left you to them," he said. But who could know what kind of men were aboard that ship?

~

The trek over the snowfields dragged on, long, arduous. The Being was used to it; he had led Frankenstein a grueling chase over a dozen snowfields; he had caught rabbits for the man and cut kindling for him and performed a dozen other tasks to keep Frankenstein alive so that he could hunt him down. Why had he done it, taunted the Creator so, urged him on when he could have stepped from the shadows at any moment and snapped his fragile human neck? Could he now admit the profound exhilaration of being the sole focus of Frankenstein's entire life? To be *seen* by the author of his being? Even if hated, to be *seen*?

One look at his child in the seconds after his revivification, and Victor

Frankenstein had denied him and fled from him. To know that the sight of him in the distance, a flickering presence in the fogs, his footprint on a sandy beach, were what had kept Frankenstein alive all this time…even if driven by hate, it was for hatred of *him*.

Now he was the focus of someone else. Ange lounged on its furs and ate dried fish, sipped water, purred and grew as the Being conveyed it across the snowfields, across the steppes. It stretched up from the sled and licked the Being's desiccated fingertips.

"You would do that to a log if it had rescued you," he said aloud.

He lost track of time, but the kitten matured into a cat. Scattered, occasional dots on the landscape revealed the presence of human beings. He thought he had avoided them all until one night, as he maneuvered by moonlight into a ravine, he came across a trio of youths dressed in heavy furs who hurled spears at him, shouting in a language he didn't understand. However, their meaning was clear: he was a beast, a monster, and they should kill him.

This was nothing new, but so much time had passed that it was a fresh shock. Well clear of their attacks, he pushed on into a copse of trees, watching as they scrambled out of sight, yelling at the tops of their lungs. They would alert their tribesmen, then.

Ange yowled, as if it knew something was wrong. It paced back and forth it its little den among the furs in the sled, cries rising with the wind.

"Ssh, ssh, *petit* Ange," the Being said. "It's all right."

The cat would not be comforted, and the rising tide of distress pushed the Being to hurry, though he had no idea where he was going or if he would ever stop. He thought longingly of their cave and thought of it as *home*, and realized that it was the first time he had ever thought of anywhere as home.

When the rains came, hard, Ange protested and then grew silent. The Being feared for it, pulling back layers of soaked furs to find its tiger-fur drenched in frost. The sharpest fear he had ever known stabbed through him; he picked up the limp body and gathered it against his chest, perhaps slightly warmer—he hoped so—and draped his body forward so that he created a shield from the elements. He ran through the rain, crooking his neck up as he forced the sled over rocks and newly sprung scrub. The cat did not move.

Night, day, night of rain; in the dawn, a stone hut perched like a pebble beside a swollen stream. He had no thought or hesitation except that Ange needed warmth and shelter; he guided the sled to an overhanging section of a thatched roof that had mostly tumbled in on itself and hurried to the door. He started to knock but thought better of it; one look at him and the inhabitants would never notice the little bundle in his arms.

He went to a window and peered in. There were no lights, but a flash of lightning revealed a small table and chair coated with dust and cobwebs. Deserted, then?

Emboldened, he pushed open the door, which gave way easily, and went inside. Rain poured in from several sections of the roof, but other sections of the room were dry. He made out the table he had seen through the window and laid Ange on it. He was rewarded with a tiny mew, such as Ange had made when it was a kitten.

He ran back out to the sled and hesitated but a moment before he carried everything it had contained—soaked furs, dried fish and bird flesh—then tore it apart and carried the pieces inside, laying them out like the cat to dry. Though the rain and wind washed in, he kept the front door open for the light. Another flash of lightning revealed a hearth, and in it, some half-burned logs.

He had learned to start fires by rubbing sticks together. He reached for the chair to break it apart into manageable pieces. As he did so, the rain stopped.

"*Merci*," he said aloud, although to whom or what he did not know.

Eventually he discovered three pieces of flint and a pile of dusty tinder moss on the hearth, and after no small effort he set the half-burned wood alight. Once he trusted it to continue, he carefully gathered Ange up and brought it to the warmth. He studied the closed eyes, its chest, and wondered if Frankenstein had gazed at him this way, willing life into him. The man had to have looked upon him a thousand times; Frankenstein had to have seen the Being's face and body as he put together pieces of corpses and passed current through all the fissures and stitches, welts, scars. When had wonder turned to disgust? The answer did not lie in the scientist's journal. The pages were filled with zeal and focus—the legs, the arms, the eyeballs and teeth. Charnel houses. Graves.

Had he never stopped to *feel* what he was doing?

"Ange, Ange," he whispered, as if his words could conjure the breath of life. He grimaced as the smoke snaked up the chimney and wondered if it would bring investigators. Were other huts nearby? Were people?

He sank down on his knees and in a posture of supplication held the cat toward the fire. He himself was just as wet and cold and so his embrace would offer no comfort. He made sure he was not too close to the flames. The warmth penetrated his knuckles, the skin on his forehead and cheeks; he bowed his head and studied the little face, the closed eyes. What a thing was a cat. What a treasure.

When Ange open its eyes and licked his palm, tears rolled down his cheeks.

~

The stone hut lay in close proximity to a village.

When the Being discovered that, he regretted tearing the sled apart and burning it for warmth. He had already taken large sections of the thatched roof and spread them across the floor to dry out; and torn branches off the trees as well. He could burn those to keep the cat warm. It would be difficult to rebuild the sled. He decided to fashion a simple travois and heap the furs and their good stores on it and leave as soon as possible. The plan wearied him. Though he was supposed to be immortal and endowed with superior strength, he was exhausted. Where would their meanderings take them next? Would they ever find peace?

His plan was further complicated when Ange went missing. Three days passed without sight of it. Anxiety weighed down the Being. *Cats hunt*, he reminded himself. *It is in their nature to roam.*

But he was in terror of what the villagers might do to a stray animal. During Frankenstein's pursuit of him, he had witnessed incidents of barbarity toward animals that he had attempted to forget—along with their violence toward himself. Everywhere, Frankenstein had been hailed as a savior, a knight-errant sent off with their blessings to kill the beast— the Being. So, yes, a kind widow or little child might put out a dish of cream for Ange, but there were others who would gleefully torment it.

They would do as bad or worse to him. But he could not—would not leave without his cat.

By night, he walked in ever-expanding circles, carrying dried fish to entice Ange back to his side. When it didn't appear, he chanced going out in daylight, moving closer and closer to the village until he entered the village itself. At night, he crept between the buildings, smelling their stews and breads, listening to their music, their conversations. They spoke a form of French and he could pick out words here and there. None of them were the word for cat.

He learned that there was another group of humans as well. They lived in round homes made of ice. He had heard their language before but had not learned any words. He had no expectation that they would treat him any better than the first group he had encountered, and so he moved in shadow as he searched for Ange.

Snows fell, and sleet; he kept his appointed rounds as he searched. Garbage and leavings littered the ground near the structures. The abundance of food might have enticed Ange. Someone might have taken Ange in. What if they turned on the cat, as Frankenstein had turned on him? He saw no other cats. These people did not seem to have pets. What if Ange was hurt?

He searched. One snowy night, he sensed a gaze upon himself and whirled. A figure many yards away had been following the imprints of his enormous, half-shod feet in the snow, bent over with a torch in its right hand. Now it looked up and a beat too slowly, the Being hid behind the corner of a rickety wooden building. The figure turned, ran; there was a shout.

The Being fled the village and snow covered his tracks. But he was afraid to enter the hut in case he had been followed. He hid in the darkness behind an enormous rock. No one came.

He waited some time before resuming his search. The snows were less frequent; the air was warming. He didn't know how much time had passed. He thought about leaving, about his vow to kill himself. He wanted to approach, ask, Do you have my cat? Is it safe with you? Will you give it a long life?

But he couldn't, even if he could piece the questions together. They would never hear his cogent use of language. They would only see a demon.

Now and then, he was spotted. He heard cries. Were they weaving stories about him by their firesides? Were they making plans to hunt him? One night, a rock was hurled at him.

The next night, a bear skulked between the houses. Large, brown, predatory. A small cat would be but one meal: the Being ran it down, seized it, killed it. He left the carcass where it lay: *I can be a friend to you.* But he feared the message would more likely be *I can do this to you.*

The days stretched out longer, though the nights were still cold; there were fewer dark hours to conduct his search. He grew more anxious as a group of men patrolled: they had to be looking for him. His days were numbered if he stayed.

He thought of his vow.

He fished in his river, caught fish, dried them. He trailed bits of dried fish from the village to his hut, praying Ange would track him. They were untouched. He tried again.

Untouched. He knew he had to make a decision.

That night, he took the last of his fish and returned to the village. As he crept among the familiar structures, a scream pierced the blackness.

I've been spotted, he thought. He turned to run, but caught a flash of brown as it sped past. He whirled on it: a large brown bear was joining its mate as it pursued a young woman in furs and a black woolen hood.

The Being yelled and waved his arms. The bears rose on their hind legs as the woman fell backwards, shrieking. He approached without hesitation; he shouted and picked up rocks and the bears turned from her to him.

The battle was ferocious, but only one bear fought. The other fled. The attacker slashed and bit. The Being did the same. He could feel pain and did, but in the end he prevailed. Though the bear was not yet dead, it would die. The muddy, icy earth was wet with blood from both assailants—bear and Being.

The woman's screams had brought others, who had watched and shouted. They were not cheering his victory. They were terrified, horrified.

He raced for the hut. He could move much faster than a mob. Once he crossed the threshold, he realized that he had no need of anything inside. He had thought of this place as his, and Ange's, as shelter, sanctuary. But that was a lie; he wasn't meant to live anywhere.

He was about to wheel back around and leave when he heard a yowl. Another. Ange! He thudded on his large feet toward the sound.

And there she was—for she was a she; and not only that: she was becoming a mother. Two tiny bundles lay in piles of fluids, mewing with their eyes closed as Ange strained to give birth to another.

"Ange, Ange," he said, and the cat's eyes rolled as he looked up at him. "We must go, Ange."

But when he reached for her, she shrank away, straining, yowling. So he bent down beside her, looming over her like a great mountain as he whispered encouragement: "You're doing well, *petite*. What a beautiful mother you are."

The third was born! She licked off the blood and birth sac. But she was not done. And he heard them. The cries of villagers. Harsh, angry, fearful. He had heard cries like that for years. Murderous.

"*Vite.*" Quickly, he pleaded. If only she would finish, he could gather them all up, run—

But Ange was not done.

They were outside his door now, slamming into it. *Thud, thud, thud*—something on the roof. Ange stared up at him and he smiled at her in reassurance.

"It's all right," he said softly in French. "I will protect you."

Smoke seeped in; the thatch above him smoldered, then caught fire. There was more wood in the hut's structure than he had realized; it started to catch. Flames sprouted and grew like vines.

On his knees, he bent forward, offering his back to the falling embers as Ange labored. Chunks of burning wood slammed against his coat, then burned through. That pain added to the injuries he had sustained in the bear fight; he grunted in agony, but did not move from his position. He felt the soft pressure of the newborn kittens as they bobbled against his forearms.

His coat was on fire. He did not move. His skin blistered. He did not move.

God is answering my prayers, he thought. *God sees me. I am fulfilling my vow in the best way. I am going to die protecting my cat.*

The door burst open.

But he did not know it.

~

He awoke.

He was lying in a bed in a small room. Something was pressing down on his chest. It was Ange. She mewed at him and licked his cheek.

"Ah," he whispered.

A rustling sound answered, and the young woman he had saved from the bear drew near. She held a cloth in her right hand and a kitten in the other. Its eyes were open. She approached timidly and pressed the cloth on his forehead. The kitten wriggled from her grasp and she leaned over to deposit it beside its mother on the Being's chest. Ange began to knead and pad. Her movements brought pain, but they also brought such joy that the Being smiled.

The young woman petted Ange, then smiled at him. She picked up a clay drinking vessel and raised her eyebrows: *Would you like to drink?* His hands were bandaged. She brought the vessel to his lips.

She pointed to herself and asked a question. When he made no reply, she said, "Anne." She pointed back at him. Perhaps she said, "*Vous?*" which meant "You?"

He had never had a name. He was quiet for a long time, what was to him a lifetime. *I want to tell you*, he thought, *that I have done terrible things. I took innocent lives. I killed my Creator as surely as if I had wrung his neck like a chicken.*

She put her arm around his massive shoulders and urged him to sit up. Then she pointed downward and he peered over the bed. On the floor in a basket lined with furs, Ange's kittens tumbled and played.

She pointed at him: *You did this.* She said again, "Anne."

Tears flowed: a baptism.

And he said, "I am Père *des Chats.*"

Father of Cats.

Catfather.

A Word from the President

Media Tie-in Writing is something everyone knows about, but also needs to have explained to them. It is quirky like that.

Most people have seen tie-in books, comics, and short fiction here and there. A novelization for a hot new movie. A novel set in the world of a popular TV series. A run of comics that serve as a prequel or sequel to a hit movie. These things have been around for a very long time. What surprises folks is that this is an actual genre of writing.

My introduction to Tie-in writing was back in 1967 when I discovered a novel based on one of my favorite TV shows, Irwin Allen's *The Time Tunnel*, written by Murray Leinster. I devoured it and went looking for more. What I found was that Leinster had also written a book based on *Land of the Giants*, another favorite. The books were written with the speed and excitement of the pulps. Then I found *Voyage to the Bottom of the Sea*, written by a real giant in the world of science fiction—Theodore Sturgeon, though this was based on the movie and not the TV series.

Over the years I discovered many, many tie-in books—some published before I became aware of the genre, and some well after. They allowed my inner fanboy to have more fun with beloved TV series and movies than what was available on the screen. The volumes of classic *Star Trek* novels by James Blish; the novelization of *Fantastic Voyage* by none other than Isaac Asimov (and its more scientifically astute sequel); *Battle for the Planet of the Apes* by TV scriptwriter—and creator of *Star Trek's* tribbles—David Gerrold; and many others.

There were tie-ins that were direct adaptations of movie or TV scripts, and—to my delight—others that expanded upon the original shows. The vast library of *Doctor Who* novels published by Target, for example, as well as the expanded universes of *Star Trek, Star Wars, Buffy the Vampire Slayer,* and others. And there were novels in an ever-expanding universe based on games like *Warhammer 40,000, Gundam, Dungeons & Dragons, Assassin's Creed, Resident Evil,* and lots more.

Anthologies (like this one) have become a mainstay of tie-in fiction. These include those based on active licenses—*True Blood*/Sookie Stackhouse, *Hellboy, Planet of the Apes, Aliens, Predator,* etc—to licenses no longer covered by copyright, such as *Sherlock Holmes, Plan 9 From Outer Space, Cthulhu,* and others. And some in which the license covers some, but not all, of the published works, thereby opening up the possibility for tie-in writers to have some creative fun with the characters from the first three Oz novels, the early Tarzan and John Carter of Mars novels, and others.

And there are some anthologies that revive characters who are not being actively produced but still have a dedicated fanbase. *The Green Hornet* is a particular favorite of mine, and there have been many excellent stories featuring the Hornet and his loyal bone-breaking assistant, Kato.

Media tie-in is all around us. It's a growing industry, and the sales of tie-in books contribute to the income stream for the shows, movies, and games they are based on. It's been called "fan fiction with a paycheck," and to a small degree that's true. But there's a lot more to it than that. When doing most tie-in fiction, the writer has to work with a publisher and, either directly or indirectly, with the entity that holds the license. You can't, for example, do an *Aliens vs. Predator* anthology without the consent, oversight, and involvement of Fox, who owns the license, and Disney, who owns Fox.

Writing tie-in fiction often comes with pretty solid limitations on what can and cannot be done with characters, situations, and more. Otherwise some mad fool might write a *Star Trek* novel in which Bones McCoy was a serial-murderer cannibal. As interesting as it would be to read, that would run contrary to the integrity of the license. So, while tie-in writers are granted a great deal of creative freedom, there are limits. Fan fiction, on the other hand, has no limits because those works are not legally allowed to be sold.

In 2010 I shifted from fanboy (well…fan-*man*) who occasionally penned some fanfic (I wrote a *Blake's 7/Doctor Who* crossover once upon a time) to someone doing tie-in writing professionally. My first piece of tie-in was the novelization of the remake of *The Wolfman* (starring Benecio Del Toro, Emily Blunt, and Anthony Hopkins). It was an eye-opener for me, because I'd always assumed tie-in writers got to watch the completed movie before attempting the adaptation. Not so. I got David Self's wonderful script and saw a few production drawings, and that was it. The rest was up to me. And if you think that this kind of novel was merely wrapping a paragraph around each line in the script, boy are you wrong. Because we don't get to see the film, which is likely going through last edits anyway, we have to imagine how the actors interpreted and inflected their lines; how the sets and costumes might look; how the atmosphere of the story needed to be presented. And we had to fill in all of the gaps left by jump cuts and the natural brevity of, say, a ninety-minute movie.

In order to create a novel that would be acceptable to the publisher and license holder, and which I'd be proud to have my name on, I did a mountain of research and wrote what amounts to a Gothic horror novel. It included all of the elements of Self's script, but also a lot more. New characters, new plot elements, more detail about the culture of the era (the story was set in late-19th-century England), and even down to how the police operated, train schedules, and more. The result? It was a book I was proud to put my name to, and it went on to be my first *New York Times* bestseller; and it won me a Scribe Award. That, by the way, is the award given by the International Association of Media Tie-in Writers (IAMTW). It was my first introduction to that organization, which had been founded by Max Allan Collins and Lee Goldberg—two highly successful tie-in writers who also have substantial careers with original fiction.

Since then I've had the good fortune and great fun to write stories set in many wonderful license worlds. And, somehow along the way, I became the president of the IAMTW. And I even have my own licenses in which other professional writers can tell stories, including *V-WARS*, which became a Netflix series.

That's why it delights me so to have this book come to fruition. A collection of all kinds of tie-in stories. Writers of every stripe whose one defining and unifying quality is that they all bring serious game. Superb storytellers clearly having fun telling tales in other people's worlds.

If you're familiar with tie-in fiction already, you'll find new gems here to expand your interests. And if you're brand new to media tie-in fiction, then wow…you're in for a real treat. Like me finding that old *Time Tunnel* novel.

Turn the pages here and you'll step into so many different worlds. You'll even find worlds you've never heard of before. And each of these tales is a piece of pop culture gold.

So, we hope you had as much fun reading as we've had fun writing these stories.

Enjoy!

Jonathan Maberry
President of the International Association of Media Tie-in Writers

For A Good Cause

Like so many others, we at the IAMTW watched—horrified, heartbroken, and furious—as the tumultuous events transpired in the Spring and Summer of 2020. The IAMTW added its voice of support to those fighting for better conditions, for justice, and for more equal opportunities for everyone. We didn't want to just speak up, however. We wanted to actually *do* something, no matter how small, to contribute to a solution. To that end...writers write. What could be more perfect than doing what we love to do, to help others *and* give readers something they'll enjoy? While the social upheaval in the U.S. provided the impetus for this anthology, we realize that marginalization and prejudice are a worldwide problem. One of the best means of combating the disparities is education. Therefore, all the proceeds from this book will go to the World Literacy Foundation (www.worldliteracyfoundation.org) which promotes literacy worldwide with a focus on helping those who are underprivileged. Thank you, and happy reading!

D. J. Stevenson
Executive Vice President, IAMTW

Founding the IAMTW

SEE THE MOVIE! WATCH THE SHOW! READ THE BOOKS!

Novels based on TV and movies—and novels on which TV and movies were based—were among my first literary enthusiasms, starting with the Whitman Young Adult hardcovers – the likes of *Zorro*, *Maverick*, and *Gunsmoke*. But it continued for me through junior high and high school with novelizations of *Oceans 11* (by George Clayton Johnson, one of the screenwriters) and *77 Sunset Strip* (by Roy Huggins, creator of the TV series), demonstrating that material that hadn't made it into the film or TV show could turn up in a book. This was exciting to me, even as it illuminated the stories I loved on film and on TV. As late as college, I used the James Blish *Star Trek* collections of episode-based stories to catch up during the show's last season, when I had belatedly boarded the Starship Enterprise before syndication for the greatest of all cult TV series had reared its head.

For many of us—reader and writer alike—the joys of movies and TV converge with our love of storytelling in prose form. We want more of our favorite characters, and relish a novel's ability to invite us to climb inside a story and not just passively watch it.

I got involved with tie-in writing when, as the then-scripter of the *Dick Tracy* comic strip, I was enlisted to write the novel of the Warren Beatty film. That was, happily, a successful book that led to my writing novels for *In the Line of Fire*, *Air Force One*, *Saving Private Ryan*, and many others, including *Maverick*, that favorite of my childhood. Eventually I wrote TV tie-ins as well, in particular *CSI* and its spin-offs. Finally I got the opportunity to work with the Mickey Spillane estate to write Mike Hammer novels—a dream job, since Spillane had been my favorite writer growing up and Hammer my favorite character.

The founding of the IAMTW came out of a series of panels about tie-ins at San Diego Comic Con. Lee Goldberg, a rare example of a TV writer/producer who also wrote tie-in novels, was an especially knowledgeable and entertaining participant on those panels. He and I shared a frustration that the best work in the tie-in field was ignored by the various writing organizations that gave awards in assorted genres, including mystery, horror, and science-fiction.

Individually, we began poking around, talking to our peers, wondering if maybe an organization for media tie-in writers wouldn't be a way to give annual awards and to grow this disparate group of creative folk into a community. I don't remember whether Lee called me or I called Lee, but we decided to combine our efforts. What came out of that was the International Association of Media and Tie-in Writers and our annual Scribe Awards, as well as the Faust, our Life Achievement Award.

For more than a decade, Lee and I headed up the organization before finally turning the reins over to a new generation. I have no doubt that tie-in writing will continue as long as gifted writers have an interest in (as we sometimes say) "playing in other people's sandboxes."

All this began—before home video made collecting movies and whole seasons of TV shows possible—as a way for fans to relive a film or have extra "episodes" of a favorite TV show. We've evolved into something more elaborate and demanding for ourselves and readers, perhaps because people like Lee and myself (if I may be so immodest) brought a love of film and TV to the table. He and I fought to get recognition for tie-in writers, so often dismissed as "hacks" and overlooked by reviewers and awards committees.

This volume is evidence of why that attitude was—and is—so short-sighted. It reflects some of our best tie-in writers tackling favorites of theirs in short story form.

The International Association of Media Tie-In Writers

And perhaps that is what separates the IAMTW members from those came before in the tie-in field—we are not professionals taking an assignment merely because that's what professionals do; but professionals who began as fans and continue to work out of a love for the films, TV and books that made us become professional writers in the first place.

Max Allan Collins

Also from the International Association of Media Tie-In Writers

Tied In: The Business, History and Craft of Media Tie-In Writing

A unique, ground-breaking collection of 18 lively, informative, and provocative essays & interviews from some of the most acclaimed and bestselling authors of tie-in books & novelizations about what they do and how they do it.

"*If this is the Golden Age of anything in the popular fiction field, it may be the tie-in novel...fans and scholars will enjoy the inside-the-business stuff.*"
--*Mystery Scene Magazine*

I say this without a whit of exaggeration TIED-IN is the most fascinating, entertaining and honest book about the writing life I've ever read..
--Ed Gorman

Tied In Is a fascinating exploration of the media tie-in business
--*Television Obscurities*

The IAMTW is dedicated to enhancing the professional and public image of tie-in writers...to working with the media to review tie-in novels and publicize their authors...to educating people about who we are and what we do....and to providing a forum for tie-in writers to share information, support one another, and discuss issues relating to our field.

We host the annual Scribe Awards, recognizing the best in the field, while honoring Grandmasters who have made a career out of tie-ins.

The name itself is a declaration of pride in what we do: I AM a Tie-in Writer. We say it with pride because we are very proud of what we do and the books we write.

www.iamtw.org

Made in the USA
Columbia, SC
15 May 2021